Dedicated to Jennifer, the Ideal Reader dedicated enough to suffer through a forest of rewrites.

THE GUILTY
MUST PAY

Max Cherry

Foundations Book Publishing
Brandon, MS 39047
www.FoundationsBooks.net

The Guilty Must Pay
By Max Cherry

ISBN: 978-1-64583-035-1
Cover by Dawné Dominique Copyright © 2020

Edited and formatted by: Steve Soderquist

Published in the United States of America
Worldwide Electronic & Digital Rights
Worldwide English Language Print Rights

TABLE OF CONTENTS

Sometimes, crimes remain unsolved due to failures in the justice system, but often, the most heinous crimes are unsolved because justice demands more than the justice system can provide.

When mankind's laws fail or when the system cannot provide just punishment, *Handlers* rise to the cause of the innocent and the tormented.

These sword-wielding crusaders and their partners, the *Warrior* angels, live by a simple code:

The guilty must pay.

Chapter One

The barn was red with white shutters, and Sherman and Ursa were crouched behind an empty water trough watching its front door. Ursa planted her left hand against her chin and gave it a shove. The ratcheting sound of her vertebrae grinding each other to powder, drove grunts from Sherman.

She either didn't hear him or didn't care she was driving him crazy. Ursa shoved her head the opposite direction, ratcheting it back the other way. Sherman marveled she didn't break her neck and half wished she would. After completing her suicidal neck-popping routine, Ursa cracked her knuckles, all ten, one at a time. Sherman wondered if her toes were next.

"Are you done?" Sherman asked.

"Yes. Are you ready?" She looked around the barnyard for signs of life but saw none. "The coast is clear."

"Woman, I've been ready. Just waiting on you to finish breaking your neck and giving yourself arthritis."

"Let's roll," Ursa whispered. The *Warrior* extended her wings and flew toward the barn.

Sherman coughed and fanned away the dust thrown by Ursa's beating wings. He drew his sword, *DeeDee*, from the scabbard his father made. *One more time girl, me and you. Let's do this.*

DeeDee was ready.

Inside the barn, Barclay Slane dragged Maryanne towards his Army cot for another love session, rapist style. She was only half-conscious and couldn't remember how many love sessions there'd been. Over the last two days, Barclay and his brother Kip had treated Maryanne to countless sessions.

She'd fought like a tigress the first day—both Barclay and Kip had wounds to prove it—but now she was too exhausted to resist, too sore to move, and too broken to give a damn what came next. *Death*, she prayed. It couldn't come soon enough.

Her bare feet cut wavy furrows through the dusty floor as Barclay dragged her to the cot. The furrows ran parallel to all the others she'd made. To Maryanne's fragile mind, the wavy lines looked like slither marks from a nest of a hundred snakes who had up and decided to get the hell out of the barn while the getting was good.

How many more trips would she have to make from the cot back to the wall, with its chain and shit-bucket toilet, back to the cot? How many more times would her heels snake across the dusty floor?

Again, Maryanne prayed for death.

Standing at the front door, Barclay's older brother Kip peered into the darkness. A smoldering cigarette hung from his lips. He squinted a watery eye against the rising white smoke. Kip reeked of sweat, sex, and a deeper, noxious rot bespeaking inherent evil. He called to his brother.

Barclay didn't hear his brother's first shout, because he was lost in a fantasy land where Maryanne wanted him, wanted all the things he was doing to her, *doing for her*. He pulled her hands above her head and tied them to the cot's forward legs. Viscid drool dripped onto her forehead, but she was too far gone to notice. Barclay gave Maryanne's right breast a hard squeeze, truly believing this turned her on.

"Bar, dammit! Get your ass up here! There's something out there!" Kip shouted louder.

Barclay grabbed Maryanne's chin, turning her head to his. "I'll be right back, honey. Don't go anywhere."

"What the fuck, man? I was about to lay that bitch again," Barclay said to his brother.

Kip ignored this and pointed into the dark. "What do you see out there?"

Barclay looked through the crack between the two heavy wooden doors. "Man, I don't see a thing. Stop being a little bitch. She ain't got no family. Nobody's looking for her. Come get another taste. Hell, brah, I'll let you go first."

"Do you hear that flapping noise?"

Barclay turned to leave, but Kip grabbed his head and forced his brother's ear to the cat's eye slit between the doors. "Don't you hear that? Wings, man. Giant fucking wings." Kip imagined a dinosaur-bird, black or gray with blood-soaked talons, saw-blade teeth and only one thing on its bird-brain—eating Kip Slane.

"It's too damn dark out there. I can't hear a thing," Barclay grumbled, and walked away.

Idiot, thought Kip and would've said so, but his attention was focused on the darkness outside.

Suddenly, the darkness was chased away by a blinding brilliance of unearthly white light. Something came at him, and the only two things Kip knew were that it was white, and dammit, it had wings, *giant fucking wings*.

Ursa hit the doors, feet first, wings flapping and with a flaming sword in her right hand. The doors flew open, flinging Kip backward. Tumbling head-over-ass, he skittered across the hay-strewn floor. "Knock, knock," Ursa boomed, hovering over the splintered barn doors. Her voice shook the rafters and spiders rained down like eight-legged yo-yos throughout the barn.

Kip slid across the barn floor picking up splinters in his back and legs. He tried using his hands for brakes but was moving too fast to stop. He stopped when he hit the opposite wall. He glanced at his hands, which were covered with so many splinters it looked like he was holding two porcupines. It felt that way, too.

Barclay was an all-for-one and one-for-all kinda guy, right up until the angel kicked in the front door. That changed everything. After that, he was an every-man-for-himself dude of the highest order.

The barn's back door was a simple four-by-eight wooden construct held up by three brass hinges and latched with a shiny nail and a rusty chain. It was twenty-five feet from the front doors to the cot and another seventy-five feet from the cot to the back door. Barclay saw Ursa's wings and he was all asshole and elbows toward the back door.

See ya' Kipper, wouldn't wanna be ya.

Barclay and Kip's parents weren't proud of them, but they weren't proud of any of their other children, either. Mama and Daddy Slane were criminals of the lowest sort and didn't have much to teach their destined-to-fail offspring. The only wisdom they preached was, 'Never leave witnesses.'

It was a lesson they'd learned the hard way when two witnesses ID'd them in an armed robbery. Barclay was the dumbest of their brood, but even he saw the genius behind his parents' mantra.

There were only two ways in and out of the barn, and he sure as hell wasn't going to try going through an angel. That meant the front door was out, so the decision to use the back door wasn't a decision at all. His path took him back by Maryanne.

Maryanne saw him coming. "Let me up, please!" she screamed, glimpsing a ray of hope. Might she survive the night? She hadn't dared think it, but now hope glimmered in her face and she wasn't even mad at Barclay. She just wanted to live.

Barclay never checked his pace, but as he approached Maryanne, he slipped a hand in his pocket and withdrew an eight-inch switchblade. Before reaching her, he pressed the chrome button and the spring-assisted blade flashed out. With the devil's speed and a practiced hand, Barclay sliced smoothly across Maryanne's throat without stopping. Nearly decapitated, Maryanne gargled, blood gushed up and splashed down onto her face like a water fountain.

"Thank you, Number Seven," Barclay whispered. He wiped the blade on his jeans as he ran and returned the knife to his pocket. There were six notches on his murder belt. Maryanne bled out before Barclay reached the back door and would've been his next notch of many, instead she was his last.

At the back door, Barclay's hands were shaking worse than when he'd almost OD'd on crystal meth. He struggled but couldn't pull the chain off the nail. Each time he pulled it down a tremor hit him, and he dropped the blasted thing back into place.

Calm down, he told himself and looked over his shoulder at his brother who was being dragged to the center of the barn by the angel. *It's got Kipper. There's no rush because you never have to outrun the bear. You only have to outrun your buddy.*

Barclay slowed his pulse, steadied his hands, and carefully lifted the chain over the upwards-bent nail. He jerked the door open and sprinted into the darkness.

Sherman was outside, waiting.

Barclay hit reverse, his boots slipped on the dew-heavy grass and he landed flat on his ass. He immediately crawfished but couldn't get any traction. The angel was bad, but the man standing in the barnyard was worse. Something in the man's face told Barclay to get the hell away from him, but that same something told Barclay it was too late.

Sherman said nothing. He held his sword in one hand, walked up to Barclay, and grabbed the bastard's collar. Barclay was kicking and screaming as Sherman dragged him into the barn.

In the barn, under the blinking and sputtering fluorescents, Sherman and Ursa stood side-by-side. Barclay and Kip knelt before them.

"Please..."

The lonely word hung there while Kip picked his next words carefully. "We don't know what you are. I mean we don't know what you want. We didn't do nothing." Then, realizing his lies would buy him nothing, Kip Slane hung his head and cried.

Ursa swished her flaming sword in Kip's face. The flames vanished, and with the tip of the sword pushing under his chin, she pushed his head up with the broadside of the double-edged blade. Their eyes met, and she said, "We know exactly what you did, and you know exactly what I am, and you know exactly what I want."

Kip sobbed louder. Never a church-goer, he still knew the truth. Angels are easy to deny until you meet one.

Barclay didn't cry or beg. He scanned the faces standing over him and saw many things, but mercy wasn't among them. "Do what you will, *Handler*. I'm not afraid of you," Barclay said.

The demon inside Barclay worked his mouth like a ventriloquist's dummy. The man, the real Barclay Slane, was buried somewhere beneath his own skin. He longed voicelessly for mercy, but the lost soul had no chance. On the man's left hand was a prison tattoo he inked while serving time in the state penitentiary at Parchman. It was a black pitchfork fashioned out of a long *six*, flanked by a shorter *six* on either side; Satan's mark. Barclay Slane was branded *666*—his soul claimed.

"You both have his mark. For Maryanne and the others you've treated..." the *Handler's* voice betrayed him and cracked.

Barclay laughed and mocked Sherman. "Will you weep now, *Handler*? Will you cry for me?"

"Not for you. My tears are for Maryanne," Sherman said. "For you, I have this." Sherman kicked Barclay in the chin.

Barclay's head snapped back violently, much too far back, and his neck broke cleanly at the base of his skull. Barclay did three backwards somersaults before landing lifelessly face down in a pile of cow manure.

"Oops," Sherman said. "It suits him though, doesn't it?"

"This one is mine," Ursa said with a nod toward Kip. Flames engulfed her sword again, and the *Warrior* angel leaned down until her face was only inches from Kip's. Kip was mesmerized and couldn't turn away.

Sherman watched from the side as Kip's teeth chattered violently and shattered into jagged pieces of ruined dentin. Kip's ebony hair turned white; not all at once like *presto magico,* but slowly whitening from the roots and spreading to the split ends like a cancer, a white virus. "You seeing this?" Sherman asked Ursa.

Ursa was too close to see the hair trick, but she didn't miss the smell of Kip's shame. Kip's jeans darkened in the crotch as his bladder let go and bulged in back when his bowels did the same. Kip spoke gibberish no one could understand, a whisper whose gist was, *I'm sorry*.

But it was too late for that.

Sunday night, in the Slane's barn, the *Handler* and the *Warrior* repeated the line they'd spoken together for more than a hundred years. Ursa thrust her sword through his chest, and Kip went to his just reward with the words ringing in his ears.

"The guilty must pay."

Sherman and Ursa left the barn before the police showed up, leaving another unsolvable crime in their wake. Ursa disappeared into the night sky and went wherever she went when she wasn't working, and Sherman flew home.

It was two o'clock Monday morning, and for the first time in fifty or sixty years, butterflies flew loopy-de-loos in Sherman's stomach. In a few hours, Piper and Sebastian would arrive, and Sherman would play great-grandpa again.

It was different this time, though. He wasn't dreading it. In fact, he looked forward to it with great anticipation.

This was the last time.

Sherman crawled into bed, took the picture from his nightstand, kissed Abby's two-dimensional face, put the frame back, and fell into a deep sleep. For perhaps the first time ever, Sherman Lancaster was tired.

Chapter Two

Sherman's alarm clock sounded over and over until his gnarled, arthritic fingers fumbled to its dismiss button. Overcome by timeless grief, he wanted to cry. He missed hearing his Abigail say, "I hate all that *cockadoodling*. I wish you would change that darn thing." But Sherman hadn't changed it, and Abby complained about it until the day she died. Now Sherman hated the damn rooster alarm as much as his late wife had. He kept using it because it didn't seem right to switch to the standard buzzer now, when he wouldn't do it when Abby was still alive.

Much louder than before, the alarm sounded again to let Sherman know he'd hit snooze instead of the dismiss button. He sat up, turned on his bedside lamp, put on his glasses, and read the buttons this time. Sure he'd hit the right button, he swung his veiny, blue legs outward and started his day.

Sherman Lancaster was 119 years old, and sleep was his only refuge. Last night, the refuge was closed. The precious little sleep he got was fitful. In bed, he tossed from his side to Abby's and back to his own. His nightmares had nightmares.

The memory of Maryanne's body was too fresh, and he couldn't chase it from his dreams. She looked at him with glassy, dull eyes, with dead eyes. "Why didn't you save me?" she asked through the slit in her throat instead of her mouth.

Worse still, the smell of her blood was too strong, too appealing, and hung in his nostrils like the scent of a beautiful woman. The *change* was coming, and as always, there was nothing he could do about it.

His great-grandsons, Piper and Sebastian, were out of school for two weeks to celebrate Christmas. Rather than search for a sitter— and scrounge for money to pay a sitter if one could be found—his granddaughter, Susan, asked if he'd watch the boys until their vacation reprieve ended. Susan expected Sherman to say yes. He rarely denied her anything, but his eagerness surprised her.

Sherman heard car doors slam and in a flash of lucidity, wondered why in the hell he'd agreed to babysit both boys at the same time. He knew the answer; one of them would soon be his *Apprentice*. It was past time for someone to take the sword from his hands. He waited for them, wondering whether it would be Piper or Sebastian.

Piper was the oldest and was freakishly large for his age, and he was also smarter than his brother. That didn't say a lot since neither boy was all that bright, but despite all he had going for him, Piper had a great shortcoming.

Piper was a pussy. He tended to cry first and fight second, if at all. Being a *Handler* didn't just require a great deal of fighting. Being a *Handler* was *being* a fighter. Period.

Where Piper was big for his age, Sebastian was a runt, even shorter and thinner than many girls his age. Though neither brother rocked the IQ charts, Sebastian simply wasn't bright. He was known to stare out windows for ten to fifteen minutes, or longer, looking at nothing and saying just as little. He was a square peg in a round hole sort of boy who couldn't figure his way out of an open room, but Piper's greatest weakness was Sebastian's greatest attribute.

Sebastian was young, wild, and yes, off the charts stupid, but he possessed a warrior's nature. He was willing to fight at the drop of a hat, and it didn't matter if he was fighting one guy or five. He enjoyed what he called *a good knocking*, and even though he lost every fight, he never considered losing inevitable.

As he thought about their strengths and weaknesses, Sherman was glad he didn't have to select his *Apprentice*. He liked Piper's hulking presence and impressive physical strength, but Sherman knew a big, strong, smart pussy cowering in a corner wasn't much help when demons were attacking from all sides.

Maybe Sebastian's strength would make him the ideal *Apprentice*. Time would reveal the truth.

"Come in out of the cold," Sherman said. He held the screen door for Susan who in turn held it for each of her sons. They oozed inside, letting in as much winter chill as possible.

"Good morning, grandpa." Susan kissed his cheek. "Thank you so much for doing this. You're a lifesaver."

The boys passed without saying anything to the old man...didn't even throw a quick glance his way. They dropped their bags in the middle of his kitchen floor and took a seat at the table. They each held a cellphone and were hypnotized by the flashing lights. Their fingers blazed across the screens in fleshy blurs, and they perfectly ignored Sherman.

You gotta be kidding me. They haven't been here a minute, and I already want to kill them both, Sherman thought grimly.

"Boys get over here and hug your great-grandpa," Susan said.

The boys' fingers tap, tap, tapped their phones and Susan's call went unheeded.

"Don't worry about it, Susan. I'll take care of them later."

Their behavior was the necessary and expected result of her systematic failure to teach them manners. Sherman wanted to tell Susan that she couldn't hope to correct their behavior simply by making them give out hugs. She couldn't fix their behavior—this was obvious to Sherman from the fact that she hadn't done so—but he could. He would.

He thought he had two weeks with them, and two weeks was more time than he needed to cure their attitude. One week was all he got, and their attitudes turned out to be the least of Sherman's problems.

"If you're sure. Don't let them run over you, grandpa. They will if you don't watch them," she said.

Sherman changed the topic. "Would you care for a cup of coffee, Susie?"

Susie was the name of a long dead but prized dairy cow Sherman had owned years ago, and Susan hated being called *Susie*. She prayed he didn't catch her rolling her eyes. Her grandpa could get testy in a hurry. Her daddy once warned her that Sherman Lancaster could go from zero to bitch faster than any woman he'd ever met. Susan knew it was true from bitter experience with her grandfather. She needed the old man's help and could tolerate being called a cow if it bought her daycare for two weeks.

"Yes, please," she said to the coffee.

"Would you care for a piece of sock-it-to-me cake to go with it?"

"Yes, I'd love a slice." The cinnamony, sweet pound cake dripping with a sugary, glaze icing was a diabetic coma waiting to happen.

They sat, grandpa and granddaughter, at the kitchen table. Both ate cake and drank coffee and neither talked. The room's only sounds were from the boys' fingers quickly tapping their phones. The tap, tap, tap of their fingers against the glass irritated Sherman to no end. The sound reminded him of the machine gun 'rat-a-tat-tat' of Ursa's neck-popping outside the red barn. He couldn't wait for Susan to leave. He'd break their bony fingers if he had to, but they would stop staring, lost-eyed and empty-souled into their handheld technological abysses.

"How have you been feeling? I'm sorry we haven't visited in so long. Time just flies," Susan said. She hadn't thought about visiting since she didn't know when but had to say something. The silence between them was suffocating her, weighing her chest like double pneumonia.

"I've never felt better. I don't feel a day over a hundred. I've got nothing to complain about and everything to be thankful for."

Susan made a show of glancing at her watch. Her eyes widened in fake surprise. "Oh goodness. I think I could sit here all day, but I've got to get my tail in gear." She wasn't late for anything but had to escape the awkward company.

Susan kissed her sons on the mouth. "You boys be good and mind your Great-Grandpa Sherman."

"Yuck," Piper said, and wiped his lips on his hoodie's sleeve. "That's just gross, mama."

Sebastian, not bothered at all by the intimate PDA, kissed his mama back and continued tapping his game.

Susan hugged Sherman. She leaned forward on her toes and kissed his cheek again. "Thank you again so much. This is such a huge help for me and Clark. You just don't know."

He waved her off with an "it's nothing" flick of his wrist. "Go on before you're late and get in trouble."

What he meant was *go on before I change my mind.* He waved again as Susan's car pulled away. The old man closed his door and faced Piper and Sebastian.

Sherman put his hands on his hips and dropped his voice to drill sergeant tone. "Boys, front and center!"

Piper and Sebastian stared at him but didn't move. They'd never heard the command and didn't know what they were supposed to do. Sherman was pleased because he'd frightened their eyes and minds away from the cellphones.

"That means for you to come here." Sherman motioned his finger from where they were to an invisible X in front of him. "Drop those phones and move it!" Piper and Sebastian dropped their phones on the table and raced to the invisible X, which suddenly became visible.

Sherman placed a hand on each boy's head. "It is rude to come into someone's home and not speak to them." The *change* roared in his veins, and he squeezed.

"It is even ruder when that someone is your elder." Another roar and he squeezed harder.

"And, it's rudest of all when that elder is your great-grandpa." Sherman almost lost himself to the *change* and squeezed hard enough to make Piper and Sebastian yelp.

Emotions raged through Sherman's veins and the beast was just below the surface now. Shimmering under Sherman's skin, two creatures shared the same space, and both wanted to rule the day. Sherman fought the *change*, and it was no surprise he was losing. He always lost.

Sherman's grip tightened, and the boys grabbed his hands. They tried lifting his fingers but couldn't pry them at all. They were caught in a shop vise's steel grip. The pressure was tremendous, and to the boys' horror, the vise kept getting tighter.

From somewhere deep in himself—the mythical *cockles* maybe, or the fantastical *heart-of-hearts*—peace emanated outward and washed the boys in golden light. It was love. When they'd first come in and plopped their lazy butts down and so utterly and perfectly ignored him, he fumed and his nerves raced into the red zone. They'd unknowingly crossed an extremely dangerous man.

Now, with his hands clamped on the boys' heads and a beast growling in his guts, Sherman was overcome by empathy. He read their souls, saw what the boys didn't dare confess, and the inner-beast relented. The boys' pain burned him, stung the corner of his eyes, and dried the back of his throat. It was impossible to swallow back his tears. The little boys had troubles of their own, terrible troubles, and they were about to get much worse.

Sherman's anger faded as quickly as it had flared, and his nerves dropped to the green zone. For the first ever, the *change* retreated. Totally surprised by this, Sherman released his grip and patted the boys on the head, saying, "Now, now."

Once again filled with happiness, Sherman asked, "Well turds, what do you want to do today?" Nothing else was said about their rude behavior. Piper and Sebastian looked at each other and grinned. *Turds* was a nickname they knew well. Their playful great-grandpa was back.

"Grandpa, grandpa," the young boys shouted and tackled his legs. "Tell us a story. Please. Please." Their combined weight was nearly enough to topple the old man.

"How many times do I have to tell you turds that I'm not your grandpa? Get it through your shaggy, girly hairdos that I'm your great-grandpa. From now on, if you're going to leave part of that off, leave off the grandpa business and just call me *Great*."

This satisfied the boys, and Piper said, "*Great*, tell us a story. Make it a good one, too. Make it a scary one."

Sherman said, "Yes, I'll tell you a story, a story of swords and of destinies. My father's destiny, my own, and what will be one of yours. Which of you I don't know, so don't ask. Yes, I believe I'll tell you a story of secrets and show you fantasy is real. If either of you needs a drink or to use the bathroom, now's the time. I don't want you interrupting me."

Piper and Sebastian raced to the kitchen to get their brand-new, matching, stainless steel canteens they'd received for Christmas. Matching because Susan knew what one boy had the other was sure to want.

While the boys got their canteens, Sherman retrieved a box of pictures from the top of his bedroom closet. He climbed into the center of the mattress, opened the box, and thumbed through the pictures of his family.

"We're ready," Piper said, as he and Sebastian burst through the bedroom door setting it on a collision course with the wall behind it.

"At least there's already a hole there," Sherman fussed. The doorknob fit perfectly inside the hole it created years ago when the little boogers first learned to run and slam doors.

The boys leaped from the floor to the mattress like two frogs hopping from lily pad to lily pad.. The bed was a comfy, reasonable height for a senior citizen incapable of either laying down too low or climbing up too high. Senior citizen appropriate height was also the perfect height for the boys' landing pad.

The boys jumped up and down on the worn-out mattress, launching the lightweight old man six inches in the air. "Stop bouncing on my damn bed, you little apes!" Sherman yelled when he wasn't laughing. He handed each boy a piece of hard caramel candy and asked, "My throat's dry and I need to wet my gullet with something. Either of you turds have a bottle of whiskey on you?"

Neither boy had any liquor hidden on their person, but they offered him water from their canteens and seemed ready to duke it out over whose he should use. Sherman stopped the fight before it started by settling for a sip of cold coffee from a cup that had been sitting on his nightstand for at least a day. The taste hinted it might have been there longer than that.

Both boys sat on Sherman's left side. He tried, but couldn't get his arm around both, so he tapped Piper on the head and said, "You, over here," and pointed to his right side. The boys sat eager-eared and sucking on candy their mother would've never let them have.

From the tattered and faded King Edward cigar box, Sherman pulled out a picture of himself as a baby and handed it to Piper. Sherman reached back into the box, shifted through a few photos, and pulled out a picture of his daddy from 1972 and handed that one to Sebastian.

Sherman talked.

Chapter Three

It was March 6, 1972, and Sherman Lancaster was about to be born in the pissant town of Vardaman, Mississippi. Exactly thirty-nine years earlier, on March 6, 1933, Robert Earl Lancaster was born to a woman known simply as Ma. Ma was born on March 6, 1915.

So, in 1972, the 6 of March was set to be a special day for the Lancaster family. After six previous attempts, Robert and Barbara's sexual timing had paid off and their seventh child would be a March sixth baby.

Robert wanted his child to be born on March 6 to continue the tradition, for tradition's sake. It meant nothing to him personally, but it meant a great deal to Ma and that meant a great deal to Robert. This child was Robert's last chance because at thirty-nine years old and having birthed six kids already, Doctor Wester told Barbara another pregnancy would likely kill her.

Robert wasn't risking Barbara for any tradition, not even for his sainted Ma's feelings. As soon as Doc Wester said it was time, Barbara was going on the pill.

The Lancasters weren't the only ones eagerly awaiting Sherman's arrival. In his fiery lair, Lucifer watched with great anticipation. Sherman Lancaster would be The Third Six. The completion of the Unholy Trinity. Lucifer had waited eons for this opportunity and finally, his wait was over. The boychild would usher in the promised age of darkness.

The minutes tick-tocked off the wall-clock above Barbara's bed. Her labor pains were intense, but she was a trained trooper, a six-time vet. The hardest part was ignoring her husband. Robert paced faster and faster as the midnight hour approached. When time offered no constraints he was an impatient man, but with Father Time breathing down his neck, Robert's impatience soared.

He couldn't understand the holdup. Barbara already had six kids. This wasn't her first trip to the delivery room, and she was already sweating pretty good. Her forehead was soaked, and her brown hair looked like an otter after an afternoon swim. Robert didn't see why she couldn't just push the baby down the chute and out the hole, *Wham, bam, thank you ma'am*. At the worst, he thought the doc or his small-handed nurse should be able to reach up there and drag the thing out. What could that hurt?

Barbara's legs were spread, and Dr. Wester's hands were going to town. He felt this, poked that, and announced with sardonic certainty, "Looks like you're gonna miss it again, Robert."

"Looks like you need to shut your trap and do your job."

"Come on mama, push!" Robert said, sounding more like a drill sergeant than a loving husband as the midnight hour loomed ever closer.

"You wanna do this?" she asked through her groans. When he didn't answer, she said, "I didn't think so. Just hold your horses, I'm pushing. He don't want to come out yet."

After carrying seven babies around inside her for a combined total of sixty-three months, she didn't need an ultrasound to tell her the sex of the child that was tearing her apart.

"I know, but honey look at the time. It's almost midnight, dammit!"

"Don't use that dirty language around him. Not now and not when he's out in the world, neither." Barbara had put on her mama voice and Robert knew she was fixing to start preaching. He crawfished the way he always did when she got on him about his drinking, cussing, or not going to church with her.

"I'm sorry, Mama. I know better," Robert said.

Over Barbara's bed, the wall-clock struck and chimed twelve times. Officially, it was March seventh, and Robert threw up his hands. His last chance was shot. He was pissed off at Barbara because she'd been in labor for seventeen hours and failed to produce his child on time. Now, it was too late. The deal was done. She could get up, get dressed, and forget the whole thing for all he cared. He would never have a March sixth baby. It was just one more thing that life denied him.

God wouldn't be mocked. This child wouldn't be claimed by the Old Serpent. God had His own plans for the boy. The *Unholy Trinity* wouldn't be completed by the arrival of Sherman Lancaster. The mark of the Lord was upon him, and in a few short years, God would lay His claim.

In Hell, the Serpent fumed and stomped his cloven feet, but was powerless to do anything else. He was beaten but not defeated, and he would do *something* soon. He'd have his revenge. Three years he'd wait, and the years would pass fast. When those three years were up, he'd mark the child and claim Sherman for his own.

Robert left Barbara in the tiny room without excusing himself. She was still in labor, but he had to go. He walked through the reception area which was no more than a foyer and a scant one of those. He accidentally kicked a goat on the way out. The *accident* was due to his ill-temper and wasn't accidental at all.

After he kicked the goat, Robert immediately felt guilty and apologized to the lady holding its leash. She was obviously pregnant, and the goat was payment for her delivery. He patted the goat's head and continued outside without causing additional trouble, but that was what he needed.

Robert had to get into some trouble to release the pent up and ever-increasing frustration threatening to erupt at any minute. It was midnight and his options were limited to a field of one, so he drove to his drinking buddy's house. Robert found Isaiah Barnett just as he expected to, sitting on the porch listening to the transistor and sipping from a jug of whiskey.

"Well, did she get it out on time?" Isaiah asked

"Hell no. I can't have nothing I want. You know that. I thought we'd go spotlighting and get us some meat. Bring that jug with you." The request was wasted. Isaiah would've brought the jug, requested or not.

Isaiah put the cork back in the jug, grabbed the rifle from behind his rocking chair, and spiritedly skipped to the four-wheel drive.

"How's Barbara doing?" Isaiah asked.

"She's in good hands there with the doc. He ain't never let us down." Robert said.

"Reckon you ought to be up there with her?"

"There's nothing I can do to help her and hanging around I'll just be in the way," Robert said. He snatched the jug from his friend's hands and downed two large swallows. Robert knew the drill. Barbara would be at the clinic all morning and most of the day recuperating, provided of course that the sluggish child ever let go of her guts and fell out.

Robert drove to the Chickasaw Wildlife Management Area, a wooded area he and Isaiah dubbed their stomping-ground. Usually they parked on the road but since it was out of season and in the middle of the night, Robert jumped his four-wheel drive through a ditch and parked in a thick, unforgiving stand of blackberry briars. The green and white Ford was so well hidden they would have trouble finding it on their way out.

The two friends grabbed their guns, flashlights, and the whiskey. In five minutes, they were deep in the thicket and deeper in the jug. They didn't poach a deer that morning, but Robert found something that changed his life forever.

While Sherman talked, Piper and Sebastian flipped the cigar box and busily sifted through the photos. "Who's this?" Piper held up a picture and asked. Sherman answered.

"Who's this?" Sebastian flipped a photo toward Sherman. Sherman answered.

After ten minutes, the boys tired of the name game. Sherman sifted through their mess until he found the two photos he wanted.

He showed the first one to Piper, then to Sebastian. "Boys, this is my mother."

"Pretty," they said.

He showed them the second picture. The boys' eyes widened, mouths dropped, and devious grins ripped both their faces.

"She's *really* pretty," Piper said.

"Uh-huh," Sebastian wordlessly affirmed and nodded his head for emphasis.

Her blonde hair waved on top and curled slightly at the bottom, and her dress was so red they could taste it; her lips so red they wanted to. Her smile invited thoughts of impossible possibilities and her eyes swore nothing was out of the question.

Sherman said, "Boys, this is Marilyn Monroe."

Chapter Four

obert came back to the clinic at four o'clock that afternoon and carted his aching and exhausted wife home. She held the *little disappointment* in her lap, and the only good thing Robert had to say about him was, "At least he ain't crying."

Robert was overly attentive. He opened doors, carried Barbara's belongings, and even carried the baby, but he was distracted. His mind was elsewhere, and Barbara wasn't fooled by all the attention.

What are you up to? she thought.

At home, Robert offered to carry Barbara inside. "It'll be like when we first got married. Remember that?"

She remembered it, better than he did apparently because on their wedding day he dropped her on her ass. She had enough aches and pains already, so she told him thanks but no thanks.

Barbara carried Sherman to hers and Robert's bedroom where an ancient evil awaited in the new-to-them crib. Barbara examined it closely, distrusting it at first sight and not at all sure she wanted to place her new baby in the far from brand-new crib.

"That old thing is junk," the preacher told him when Robert unearthed the crib from the church's storage room like an archaeologist digging up an Egyptian antique, blowing away dust, cobwebs, and spider skeletons so thin they were but ghostly dreams.

"Junk?" Robert had laughed. It was a turd in need of a shine, so he brought it home and polished it, and awoke the slumbering spirit living within the crib.

Barbara grabbed the rail and rocked the crib side-to-side, then front-to-back and it swayed but only slightly. She decided it would do until they could afford better. Carefully, she laid the tiniest Lancaster inside the rickety crib on a mattress smelling of Downy and baby powder. Sherman was calm, so Barbara decided it was time for her nap.

She turned toward her bed and like a beacon, there *It* was, sticking up from behind Robert's side of their headboard. "Where did you get that *sssss-WARD*?" she asked.

"Damn," Robert mumbled. He'd forgotten about Barbara's keen eyes and that she had a double-shot of female intuition. He gave himself a swift, mental kick in the ass. He swore he'd never forget those two things after the preaching and lecturing he suffered when she found his glossy Marilyn Monroe poster lovingly folded and interred deep in his sock drawer.

Robert blamed the Marilyn-discovery on that mystical—and probably fictional—female intuition because he didn't want to accept responsibility for her finding his hidden Hollywood crush. The truth was that his sock drawer wasn't the best place to hide something from the woman who did his laundry several times a week.

The *Marilyn Incident* was ten years ago, and he'd forgotten about Barbara's keen eyes and the feminine sixth sense. He'd forgotten her preaching, the dirty looks both night and day, and the long sexual drought to which she gleefully subjected him. After *The Great Sword Issue of 1972*, Robert never forgot any of those things again.

After finding the sword, Robert carried Isaiah home and then went home to hide it before returning to the clinic to claim his wife and baby, if the slug had made it out yet.

Robert hid the sword in a pair of coveralls when he brought it in the house so his older kids wouldn't see it and pester him about it. His tiptoeing and furtively moves were more suspicious than the sword would've been. The kids wanted to ask why he was sneaking around but knew the cost of the question would've been higher than the answer was worth.

Was it his fault Barbara saw the sword, the way it was his fault she'd exhumed Marilyn from the sock drawer? Indirectly, at least, yes, it was.

When he hid the sword, Robert was wearing his whiskey goggles, so it was his fault he drank the whiskey. But it was the whiskey's fault Robert didn't pay attention to the hiding place's insufficiency.

The sword's long ivory handle stuck up above the headboard like a unicorn had taken up residence back there. Why Robert thought it was hidden only a drunk could tell you. Barbara saw the handle immediately and even though she'd never seen a sword, she knew exactly what it was.

"Where'd you get it?" she asked again.

"It's mine. Me and Isaiah found it this morning. I figured God gave it to me for a belated birthday gift."

"God? More like Satan himself gave it to you. Did you find it in somebody's house?" Barbara asked, accusing him of stealing it without saying the words.

"No." He was indignant. He was a proud man and had never stolen anything.

"Did you get it from somebody's shed?" It had to have been stolen. She didn't get close to it, certainly didn't touch it, but it appeared to have jewels on its handle.

"No, dammit," he said, using a rare curse word. He was mad enough to not care about her preaching. He was no thief, and she knew it.

"Well, what do you intend to do with it?"

"I don't intend anything. I found it, and I brought it home. That's the end of the story."

"Well put it up so the kids don't get hurt messing with it."

"They know better than to mess with my stuff," he said, but he still moved the sword from its hiding place behind the bed to his closet where he should've hidden it to begin with.

Sebastian tugged on Sherman's sleeve. "There wasn't really a sword was there, great-grandpa?" He wanted it to be true, though.

"Oh, you don't think so? I told you magic was real. Sebastian my boy, this one time you can open my closet but never go in there unless I tell you to." There were dangers, real and imagined—and some of the imagined ones were real too—lurking in Sherman's closets.

Sebastian bounded off the bed and ran to the closet with his arms flailing above his head. His lunatic run tickled the old man to hysterics, and suddenly, a wall of urine threatened to explode from Sherman's bladder. Sherman grabbed his privates and held tightly until the pressure abated.

Sebastian turned the knob and opened the closet door a few inches. He peered through the crack. He expected bodies to fall out and crush him, or a family of drooling monsters to pull him in and devour him with their oversized and crooked teeth. When neither happened, he opened the door all the way.

"Reach to the right and feel for a stick. When you get it, bring it out," Sherman told him.

The boy felt. His arm disappeared into the darkness. The look on his face was a combination of fear and anticipation. "Ow! It hurts! Ow! It hurts! Let go, let go!" He struggled against the imaginary attack. He laughed and looked over his shoulder at his brother and great-grandfather. "Just kidding."

Sebastian stopped giggling. His mouth formed an O and he nearly wet himself when his fingers played over the scabbard. "I got it!"

It took both hands, but Sebastian pulled the sword and its worn leather scabbard from the closet. The sword was longer than the boy was tall, and its scabbard was thicker than Sebastian's arm. Even with two hands, Sebastian could barely pick it up, so he rested the tip on the floor and exhaled a sigh of relief.

The room's sixty-watt bulbs glistened off the sword's jeweled handle, twinkling like a million tiny stars. Sherman was delighted to see *her* again; he was every time.

"Now, do you believe in magic?"

Sebastian nodded, still mesmerized by the thing in his hand.

"That's the sword my daddy found on the day I was born. Now, put it back where you found it and never open that closet again," Sherman said.

"Come on, great-grandpa, let me see the blade. Come on. Please, please," Sebastian begged, and moved to unsheathe it.

"Come on. Let us see it," Piper joined in.

"Silence!" the old man shouted. "I said put it back in the closet and do not go back in there. This house is not safe for kids. I saw y'all brought your lunch boxes, so go get them and get back up here and let's get on with our story. But just remember...your great-grandpa ain't no liar."

The next time Sebastian touched the sword, he was stabbing Sherman in the back with it.

Sebastian went to the kitchen and came back with two lunch boxes. He passed one to Piper, climbed up next to Sherman, and asked, "He really found it in the woods?" Sebastian found it even harder to believe now that he'd seen the sword. "That's crazy."

"Yes, he found it in the woods," Sherman said. "*She* was there, just waiting on him."

Chapter Five

Robert and Isaiah were stumbling through a thicket, drunk as two skunks both carrying rifles and neither paying the slightest attention to where the hell they were going. They drained the whiskey jug an hour ago and Robert had cast it to the side of the beaver path they were insanely calling a trail. Robert called it, *making habitat*. Isaiah agreed but had no idea what his friend meant. To Isaiah, it looked like littering.

"Robert, do you know where we're at?"

"Hell yeah," Robert lied. He didn't have a clue and was already praying for a way out. Blackberry thorns ripped his jeans and shirt to shreds, and like *Big Jim Walker* from Jim Croce's famous song of the same year, Robert was cut in about a hundred places. About to admit he was lost, Robert tripped over a cypress knot and as he was falling, his flashlight's beam reflected off something a hundred yards ahead.

"I think I see something up there. Probably the Bronco." Robert prayed the flashlight was bouncing light off one of the Ford's headlights. "And watch that damn cypress knot. It jumped right out in front of me."

The reflection wasn't a headlight, and Robert soon knew it. Whatever was throwing back the light was too near the ground to be the jacked-up Bronco. Robert fought his way through the bramble of last year's blackberry crop, picking up what felt like another hundred cuts along the way, and stumbled onto his destiny.

The sword's handle was embossed with angelic emblems formed from clusters of diamonds, emeralds, and blood-red rubies. The jewels glistened in the harsh white light of Robert's six-volt flashlight. The diamonds, clear and perfect, reflected the light back into his eyes, and he squinted away in pain. He pointed the beam at the ground to let his eyes recover. Again, he raised the light toward the sword, but this time kept it low enough to save his eyesight.

The emeralds' greens and rubies' reds were like the flashing lights of a disco ball and Robert and Isaiah were mesmerized by their flashing brilliance. Neither man moved nor said a word. Robert held the flashlight steady, but the sword's lights strobed to an unheard rhythm.

The sparkling handle was an insult to the dull pine needles, oak leaves, mud, and moss. The sword was out-of-the-box, brand-spanking new, and dammit, Robert knew he'd been drinking, but the blessed thing looked like it was alive. He would've taken his oath that it was breathing. The handle swelled and shrank, rose and fell, breathed in and let it out.

I gotta give up the bottle, thought Robert.

The sword was lying at the edge of a swamped-out creek, buried in dead leaves and stuck up to its pommel in tacky mud. Robert pulled it free from the gumbo like King Arthur freeing Excalibur from stone, and when the sword was freed from mud, it was as clean as the day it was divinely forged.

The double-edged blade was razor-sharp and emitted its own inner light. Although the two drunks attributed the light to their flashlights, Robert and Isaiah knew the sword illuminated them in an eldritch glow no flashlight could imitate.

Piper, who shared his great-grandpa's love of reading, asked, "King Arthur's sword was named Excalibur. Does your sword have a name, great-grandpa?"

"Funny you should ask. I was just going to tell you that her name is *DeeDee*."

"DD? I think Excalibur sounds better," Sebastian said.

"Well, *DeeDee* is more than just her name. It's what this story is all about. It's the whole reason I'm telling you, and it will be incredibly important to one of you as you get older. In fact, one of you will get to know *DeeDee* as well as I know her."

The sword *drew* Robert, not Isaiah, so even though Isaiah was the co-finder of the sword, he never voiced an interest in it. Robert saw it, Robert pulled it from the ground, and Robert assumed ownership of it.

Robert looked the sword over carefully, bounced it in his right hand, then let it rest in his palm. It was heavy but perfectly balanced, never teetered and never offered to fall. Robert grabbed the handle and grinned at how good it felt in his hand, better than any of his guns. He hacked wildly at the bramble and blazed a trail wide enough to avoid collecting additional cuts on his way out of the thicket.

"You best be careful with that thing. It looks mighty sharp," Isaiah said when Robert hacked a little too close to Isaiah's knee.

If a drunk can be careful, Robert was, and he and Isaiah made it back to the Bronco safely. They rode to Isaiah's house in silence. Neither was brave enough to say what they were thinking. Each man considered the unlikelihood of finding the sword because that particular thicket was *thick*, but they balked at even considering the way it breathed and cast the humming life-light on them. That they tried to forget. While neither man was particularly religious, they believed the *Hand of God* was involved somehow.

They didn't know how right they were.

After their brief argument, Barbara and Robert made up easily the way long-time couples do. With nothing but love between them, they eased into bed. He kissed her cheek, and she was fast asleep before he finished saying, "Goodnight."

Robert tossed and turned, flipped and flopped, but thoughtfully so he wouldn't disturb Barbara's rest. The day's events played and replayed in his mind like the slide shows the missionaries sometimes put on at the Methodist church. Instead of images of starving kids and new churches going up in the Congo or the Amazon or wherever in the hell they'd been, Robert saw images of his memories clicking by one-after-another, frame-after-frame.

He saw the wall-clock above Barbara's delivery bed. In the first picture, it was eleven-fifty-eight. *Click.* Eleven-fifty-nine. *Click.* Midnight.

More clicks showed him kicking a goat and, in another click, he was patting the goat's head. The images clicked and clicked and there *It* was. His sword. Then the slide show ended, and he lay in bed looking toward the ceiling but seeing nothing but darkness.

Who left the sword there?

Robert had found cannonballs, antique pistols, and even a rusted knife or two in those woods. They were leftovers from the *War of Northern Aggression*, and he knew exactly who they'd belonged to *The Glorious Southern Dead*. But he knew nothing about the sword and its previous owner.

Why hadn't he found it before?

He'd walked that same thicket a hundred times.

Did someone just lose it?

If that was the case, he had no intention of returning it. The schoolyard rule was governing his discovery.

Finders are keepers and losers are weepers.

Robert was the first one out of bed, and he was out of the house before anyone else stirred. Quietly, he took the sword from the closet and stashed it behind the seat of the flatbed Jimmy. He rolled the truck away from the back door before he hit the starter, so he wouldn't wake the whole house. He floored it when he turned onto the county road, and with an impenetrable dust cloud behind him, Robert drove to a secluded place to test the sword.

The secluded place was twenty miles away in a blink of a community named Atlanta. He drove past the kennels where fighting dogs and roosters were raised, fought, and died honorably. Across from the community dump that graced the left-hand side of the road, Robert hit his right-turn signal, downshifted, and let a couple backfires fly that sounded like grenades going off in a tin building. Two miles in, he pulled off the road, killed the engine, and got out of the truck.

With the sword in hand, Robert walked a well-worn path up the side of a hill to the clearing where he and his friends gathered to drink and tell lies. Since it wasn't hunting season and most of his friends were getting their farms ready, Robert guessed the clearing would be empty. He looked around, saw no one, and thought he was right.

There in the clearing, guarded by thick, tall pines, Robert Earl Lancaster began his swordsmanship training, and training went better than he believed possible. He whacked, sliced, stabbed, and even threw the sword a couple of times with amazing accuracy. He quickly realized the sword was doing most of the work, maybe all of it. Because he was alone, Robert tried some of the kung-fu moves he'd seen on the television and even landed one or two.

But he wasn't alone. High atop a pine, Ursa, the *Warrior* angel sat crossed-legged and watched as Robert mastered the basic strokes and lunges. His progress was impressive, and she had high hopes for him. If he passed both parts of his test, she would introduce herself to him and begin his *Handler* training.

For now, he was getting a feel for the sword, but more importantly, the sword was getting a feel for him.

Chapter Six

t was mid-afternoon when Sherman's front door squealed and startled the boys. Sherman said, "What's the matter with you two girls? It's just your mama."

The wind was right, and Sherman smelled Susan the second she opened her car door. People were as distinguishable to him by their scents as they were to the FBI by their fingerprints or DNA. And when the *change* was near, they weren't just scents to Sherman. They were aromatic, savory fragrances, and Sherman closed his eyes, breathed Susan's aroma deep in his lungs, and unaware, he licked his lips.

"Boys, kiss grandpa goodbye and let's go," Susan yelled from the kitchen. She said the boys had a two o'clock doctor's appointment, but there was something about the way she said it, a look that was three degrees off right, that said it was more than the sniffles.

"Ooohhh, Mama is in trouble," Piper said. "Great-grandpa, mama called you grandpa." Piper said *grandpa* like it was a dirty word.

"Well at least you're trying and that counts for something," Sherman said.

Piper and Sebastian kissed the old man's cheeks. "I'll see you in the morning," Sherman said. He watched Susan and the boys pack into the car, and they all waved to him. He waved back and wondered where they were really going.

Sherman took off his great-grandpa hat and transformed into the *Handler*. The transformation wasn't something that happened. The changes didn't appear over a course of time. He was an old man, and then, he wasn't.

His wrinkles vanished like someone grabbed the saggy skin at the back of his head and pulled with all their might and tied a knot in it. His bowed spine straightened, and his thin, bag-of-bones frame filled out with liquid steel. Muscles bulged in all the right places, and his weight tripled in a second. His oversized ears and nose shrunk. The Chia Pets living in them abandoned their homes, and the hair sprouted on his head where it belonged.

Sherman sat in his recliner and waited. Ursa was coming, but he had hours to kill. He contemplated housework, but that contemplation turned out like it usually did. He napped until the sun went down.

Thankfully, Maryanne let him rest.

Ursa showed up as the sun winked out over the horizon. She looked the same as she did the last time he'd seen her, the same as the first time he'd seen her. Her hair was platinum, her skin was golden and bright. You could say she looked twenty, but her cherub face was ageless. Ursa had always looked that way, always would. Sherman had been born and aged, but Ursa just *was*.

He was awake when she walked into the room. "Where are we going tonight?" he asked, already headed for the back door.

"It's close. Three will pay, and there's a demon with them," Ursa said.

Killing Kip and Barclay had been too easy, and Sherman wanted a fight. The coming *change* made the desire even worse. Sending a demon back to its master was exactly what he needed.

Outside, Sherman lifted *DeeDee* above his head and shot into the sky. Ursa flapped her wings and quickly overtook him. Sherman followed her to their destination.

They landed outside a double-wide mobile home, and Sherman focused his mind on the interior. The vinyl siding evaporated, the two-by-four studs vanished, and the Pink Panther insulation and drywall turned to a foggy mist and floated away. Using his Mind's Eye, he saw inside with perfect clarity and told Ursa where the targets were and what they were doing. There were two live victims and three dead ones.

A mother and her young daughter were alive. Both were gagged and bound and not long for this world. The rest of the family had been murdered right in front of their eyes, and only the ladies' sex had spared their lives. Neither mother nor daughter was thankful for their gender.

"Any sign of the demon?" Ursa asked.

"Not yet, but I feel it. It's there, just below my vision."

The demon reduced its earthly presence to a shadow, undetectable to the human eye and to the *Handler's* Mind's Eye. In its low state, it couldn't actively participate in battles but could influence human behavior. It was a handy ability, but the demon rarely used it because he was prideful and craved recognition. He wanted to be seen.

Not tonight though. The demon felt the *Handler* and the *Warrior's* presence and had no desire to fight either and certainly not both. It stayed below Sherman's vision. It pulled and pushed the three attackers, driving them as surely as a puppeteer drives his puppets. The humans' darkened souls offered no resistance to the demon's suggestions. They went along raping and murdering, happily calling down God's wrath.

Ursa ripped the front door off its hinges and sailed it across the yard like a rectangular Frisbee. She entered the trailer with her sword drawn and killing on her mind.

Sherman kicked in the back door at the same time, *DeeDee* drawn, her blade in flames.

"The guilty must pay," they recited.

Justice was swift.

Chapter Seven

The *change* always started in his spine, but Sherman's brain knew it was coming. After they left the double-wide, Ursa went her way and Sherman his. As soon as he got home, he keyed the front door, locked it behind him, and raced to the bathroom. Inside, behind the thin interior door with only a hook and eye lock, he bellowed as his naturally curved spine straightened. The *change* was godawfully slow and unmercifully painful.

His spine straightened and lengthened a foot. His head enlarged like a water balloon filled to the point of bursting just before his lower jaw jutted outward. The top of his head grew into a powerful snout and covered his bottom jaw, and his new mouth sprouted jagged teeth. His hands and feet grew three times larger than normal, and thick black hair covered everything but his eyes. He was called Werewolf by some, but he and Ursa simply called it *Wolf*.

The *change* didn't happen exclusively on full moons, but it only happened at night, and it always cleared up before sunrise. If it had a predictable cycle, Sherman hadn't found it, but once the cycle started, *Wolf* usually showed up every night for two or three nights. Then it was over until the next cycle. Sherman had suffered the cycle once or twice a year for more than a hundred years, and he'd noticed two things.

One, the *change* couldn't be controlled. It came when it wanted, and he was powerless to stop it.

Two, *Wolf* was staying around longer and longer. The last time he'd changed he watched the sunrise wearing his fur coat. This time he wasn't sure he'd ever be human again.

Sherman's back door burst open, and *Wolf* ran into the night.

His hairy nostrils widened and his lungs expanded, tiny sacs filled with the smell of...of food.

Wolf hunted. *Wolf* fed.

Sherman was lost in a hazy dream. Everything was unclear, but blood, pain, and screams were its most prominent qualities. A million miles away, three car doors slammed and woke Sherman from his sleep.

It's morning already, thought Sherman.

Susan, Piper, and Sebastian walked to the front door. *Wolf* smelled them, wanted them, pawed at the bathroom door to get them, but the *change* was in reverse. At least half human now, Sherman was able to pull his Lycan-self away from the door. Susan was earlier than yesterday, and of course, Sherman was running behind.

Susan pressed the lighted button, and the doorbell clanged in Sherman's hypersensitive ears like an air-raid siren. Sherman couldn't answer, not in his condition. He heard the doorknob jiggle and jangle as Susan checked the knob.

When Sherman didn't answer the door, Susan knocked. She must've thought knocking would catch his attention where the screaming doorbell had failed.

The knock was no more effective, so she asked Piper to help. Susan pounded on the door while her son rang the bell. The combo attack was sure to get his attention.

There was no answer from her grandfather and she was in a hurry. If she wanted to beat *Handsy* to the office, she couldn't wait any longer. She had to drop the boys off, no time for coffee and cake. Sherman wouldn't answer the door, so she had to let herself in. A no-no under most circumstances, under all circumstances really, but she had to beat *Handsy*.

Susan retrieved the spare key Sherman kept hidden in his outdoor laundry room. She unlocked the door, and Susan and the boys walked inside. They were thirty minutes early, but right on time to be a pain in Sherman's ass.

They sat their bags down and searched for the old man. He didn't answer the door, so they assumed he was probably asleep in one of his two usual napping places.

The recliner where they'd caught him napping many times in the past was empty. Next, they checked his bedroom. The door was open, the knob still resided in the drywall where the boys put it the day before, but Sherman wasn't in the bedroom. Instead of looking carefully throughout the house—and finding Sherman in the bathroom—they opened the back door and called his name.

It was below freezing, snowing, and the wind gusted and threatened to rip the flimsy aluminum door from Susan's hands. Susan and both boys yelled for Sherman.

"Grandpa." He could hear Susan's tinny voice above the boys. It pierced Sherman's eardrums the way only a woman's voice could do.

Shut the hell up will you, Sherman wanted to scream.

He was hiding from them, waiting to come back from the *change*. It was slower and taking much longer than ever before. He didn't know if he was losing all control. Maybe it was a fluke. Maybe next time things would be back to normal. He didn't know how it would play out but being stuck as *Wolf* forever wasn't a pleasant proposition.

The boys called and called, but at least Susan was down to sporadic yells. He'd call out to them if he could. *Could they not leave an old man to his bathroom business?* He'd tell them to shut the hell up, but they wouldn't understand him. His words wouldn't be words but low, throaty growls. They would flee for their lives and only God knew what would happen after that. Forced to guess, Sherman feared he'd chase them down, break their legs, and take his time eating them.

I'd drink them first, he thought with a widening grin showcasing his enormous teeth. He remembered a line from a story his mother used to read him. *The better to eat you with.* If Barbara only knew.

"Great-grandpa, where are you?" Piper asked repeatedly as he made his way through the few rooms of the small house. After each pass, he opened the back door again and called into the frigid, morning.

Are you kidding me? Sherman couldn't hide his aggravation. Even in his hairy condition, he couldn't believe his own blood relatives would go to every room except the bathroom, the one room with the closed and locked door. It was the obvious place. It was the only place. *And why the hell would they call outside? It's below freezing*!

Sherman shook his shaggy head and released a low, growl. It was more of a rumble, a purr gone wrong. He wanted more than anything to tear them all limb from limb. That wouldn't do. It was all he could do not to attack. So, he waited and prayed it would happen fast.

Finally, the last of the hair receded. It was always the last to go. He'd changed back fully. The transformation hadn't been permanent. Sherman was himself again, one more time. Hand to the doorknob and almost twisted, he thought not. *Better check the mirror just to be sure.* He was greeted by his haggard face. Haggard but familiar. Everything else was fine. Well, almost everything. He had one small problem.

Sherman was as naked as the day he was born.

Sherman wrapped a towel around his waist, shook his head at his predicament, and walked out to face his accusers. "Oh my goodness, grandpa. What are you doing?" Susan asked when she saw the old man wearing only a towel around his waist. His saggy tits were bigger than hers and wrinkled down his chest like melting butter. She choked back laughter and managed to hold in all but a small giggle.

"Yuk it up, little girl. Let's see what your tits look like when you're 120." He grabbed his breasts and squeezed them. "Nice, ain't they? My milkshake brings all the boys to the yard," he sang, and danced a few steps.

"Why are you naked? There's no shower or tub in there. Are you feeling okay, Grandpa?"

"I'm feeling fine, darling. I just didn't expect y'all so soon. That's all," Sherman said, as if that answered her question.

"Why were you looking for me outside? It's below freezing. Hell, it's even snowing out there. Did you really think I was building a snowman or making snow angels by myself? And first thing in the morning, no less?" He wasn't yelling, but he wasn't missing it by much.

"No, I just thought you might've got confused."

Susan was right. He was confused. *I'm confused as to why I tolerate you?* What could he have been confused about that would've led him out in the dark, freezing morning? *Stupid bitch.* Physically he was changed back but mentally and emotionally the predator lingered and wanted to strike.

He wanted to slap the snot out of her and everyone else who automatically thought that he was senile just because he did something that was out of his routine or unusual in some way. If he were twenty or thirty and did the same things, folks would just laugh about it. Now, everything he did had to fit their ideas of what an old person should do. If he colored outside the lines, he was losing his mind.

He ignored their laughs and got dressed. Susan was quick to leave for work. The boys' faces couldn't hide that something was on their minds. Sherman didn't question them. He knew they'd blurt out something sooner or later. It was as inevitable as death and taxes, and it turned out to be sooner.

"We missed you yesterday afternoon," Piper said. His eyes brimmed with tears. He wanted to say more but something held him back.

"I missed you little turds too. Your mama said y'all had to see the doctor. What's wrong with you? Y'all got the cooties?"

"We're not supposed to tell you or talk about it around you. Mama said so," Piper said, and revealed the reason he hadn't said more. He wasn't happy with his mama's command and expected the old man to rescind it, but Sherman didn't have time.

Sebastian started crying, but before his sobs grew uncontrollable in a spray of snot and spittle, he blurted out, "He wanted to be sure you wasn't meelestering us."

"Meelestering? What in the tomcat hair is meeles...oh. Molesting." He laughed at the new word he'd just added to his vocabulary and hoped he didn't lose a real word making room for it. "The doc was afraid your old great-grandpa took a hankering for tiny tots, huh? Did y'all tell him to kiss your asses? Did you tell him to kiss my ass while he was puckered?"

"Great-grandpa, that's exactly what I told him," Piper said. He ran and put his arms around the old man's neck. "That's exactly what I said to him. Just like that. I said, 'Kiss my ass! My great-grandpa ain't never hurt me.' I tried to walk out, but Mama stopped me. She said we had to stay until he let us go."

Piper fell silent. He sucked in tears and wiped snot on his sleeve and spoke again. "But he didn't say anything to me. He just wrote something in his notebook. Mama said he probably blamed it on you, my saying that to him I mean. Mama said he called you a bad influence. Are you a bad influence, great-grandpa?"

"Hell yes I'm a bad influence, and damn proud of it. At least to their way of thinking. You did good boy. I'm proud of you. You're full of surprises." *Maybe you ain't the pussy I pegged you to be*, thought Sherman.

"Will you get in trouble?" Sebastian asked. "I don't want anything to happen to you."

"Let 'em come for this old man. I've got more fight in me than they think."

Carrying a tray with three cups of hot cocoa and an assortment of chocolates including homemade fudge, Hershey's Kisses, and everybody's favorite, the real crowd-pleasers, Reese's Peanut Butter Cups, Sherman sat down in his reading chair. The boys flanked him and attacked the tray. "Settle down trolls. You won't starve I promise. And Piper git your mitts off that one. That's my cup." Sherman's hot cocoa was spirited with a nip of whiskey, and besides, it was Abigail's cup. Nobody touched Abby's cup.

His reading chair sat at the end of his bed by the antique *Singer* his mother used to sew flower-patterned, flour sacks into dresses for his sisters and to stitch patches on the knees of the boys' worn-out jeans. Piper camped out on the foot of the old man's bed, lying on his stomach with his chin resting on both palms. Sebastian sat cross-legged at Sherman's feet. A frayed, tan rug saved him from catching his death off the cold, tile floor.

Sherman sat the tray down, took a long sip from Abby's cup, and smiled when he remembered how good her lips looked when she puckered to sip from it. He could see those soft pink curves, knew just how they felt and tasted. He'd give anything to kiss those lips again, but he'd have to wait a little longer for that. He pushed the distractive thoughts aside.

The boys said they were ready to hear more about the sword. Piper dared to ask if he could get it out of the closet. It chapped his buns that Sebastian had touched it, but he hadn't. Sherman cut his eyes at Piper, and the boy quickly said he was just joking around.

Sherman started, "My daddy got real good with the sword, real fast. The trouble was that he also got real broke."

Chapter Eight

t was March 1972 and the Lancasters had a new baby, so things weren't exactly normal around the house. Barbara and Karen took turns babysitting while Robert and the other kids managed the farm as well as they could without mature, female oversight. Robert did his part and didn't shirk his responsibilities in favor of spending time with the sword. The opposite was true.

His free-time was severely limited, and the sword rarely came out of his closet during the spring and early summer. Robert was running at full-speed because his crops were growing like weeds. Unfortunately, the weeds were also growing like weeds.

When he finished spraying herbicide on one field, another field was already overgrown. Moving his tractors from field-to-field was a time-consuming, logistical nightmare on the county's two-lane roads. While Robert and Theodore played musical tractors, the other kids hoed giant weeds that refused to succumb to heavy doses of chemicals they had grown immune to years ago. As soon as they finished spraying, the men grabbed their hoes and joined the others in the march against the weeds.

So, no, the Lancasters' financial ruin wasn't caused by Robert's sword obsession.

A horrendous series of storms bombarded the state in August, and the relentless pounding continued off and on—mostly on—until late September. North Mississippi's most destructive and longest-lasting storm ever advanced across the Mississippi River in late August. Those in its path named it Jezebel because it was the *mother of all bitches*.

Jezebel rolled in from Arkansas on the twenty-sixth and was in full force on the twenty-eighth. Her winds climbed to near a hundred-mph and stayed there for three days. Because all the weather recording equipment blew away, no one really knew how strong the storms were.

Old folks shook their heads when they talked about it. No one could remember downpours of such magnitude. Every creek flooded the first day, and it didn't start raining hard until the second day. The creeks didn't crest for another week, and by then, they weren't creeks at all. Everything was one big lake. There were countless deaths, and everyone claimed to know at least one victim. With the shoddy reporting of the era, the death toll remains a mystery.

The twenty-eighth of August 1972 was known as the day that half of Mississippi was blown into Alabama, but Sherman remembered the day for a more personal reason. It was his wife's birthday. As Abigail made her appearance on the world's stage, the storm's fury was fully unleashed. When they were courting, Sherman joked with her, blaming the storm on her. "Wild woman, you caused it. You, bout *kilt* my whole family."

"Just call me, Storm," Abby said and bowed. Her curly hair flipped over her head, and Sherman knew he was looking at his future bride.

Jezebel's rains flooded fields, and with all the storms following her, they stayed flooded for a month. The fields that didn't flood weren't saved. The storm blew in on a strong west wind and leveled all crops.

What didn't flood simply blew away. When the storms finally blew out, only flooded and stripped fields lay in their wake. Crops in the fields were destroyed, and it was too late in the year and too wet to plant again until spring.

The damage to area infrastructure was tremendous, but where there was electricity to power their machines, factories churned out products. Farmers weren't as lucky, and the governor declared the entire northern portion of the state a disaster area. Jackson helped as much as they could, but the damage was widespread. It was impossible for the state boys to be everywhere at once. Federal assistance was requested but help from D.C. was neither expected nor received. Too much of the nation had been affected by the storms for rural Mississippi to be at the top of the list, or even on the list at all.

For the most part, people were left to fend for their own. Fortunately, fending for their own was something country people were exceptionally adept at. As crazy as it sounded, many preferred doing so.

After the floodwater receded, Robert and Theodore cleared downed trees and limbs from fields and roads. Thankfully, the storm spared their house and sheds. If they'd lost those structures, it would've been the end of the farm, and Robert would've had to sell out and find a job in town. They'd lost the year's crops and things were bleak, and that was calling an A-bomb a firecracker. But, in the Christian spirit, they were thankful for all they had and vowed to push through.

"We're gonna have to tighten our belt," became Robert's favorite expression. He spent more money than anyone else, and he said it to remind himself to hold onto his cash.

There was canned food in the pantry and meats and vegetables in the freezer. The freezer food was used first since all the electrical lines were down, and the TVA man had no idea when they'd be up again. It took a mountain of food to fill all the Lancasters' stomachs, so none of the frozen food spoiled.

Robert and Theodore brought in fresh deer, squirrel, rabbit, turkey, and quail, and fish were plentiful in the floodwaters. None of the Lancasters went hungry, and they had enough to share with others. Robert enjoyed giving to the Methodists' charity bin a sight better than taking from it. It was good for his soul to be on the giving side of things for a change.

Nine Lancasters lived in their small FHA house, and that made for a certain level of familiarity under normal circumstances. The fall of 1972 and winter of 1973 weren't normal circumstances because there was no farming and few chores to be done. With nothing to do, the family was pushed even closer together than ever before. Fights were frequent but shockingly brief.

Barbara always prayed for her family, but during that lean time, she prayed more than usual. She prayed especially hard for Robert because he was increasingly absent. She didn't know where he was but suspected he and Isaiah were hard into the bottle and up to no good. She decided praying was better than prying, and she was probably right about that.

Prayers never hurt, but Robert wasn't out whoring or drinking and was usually alone. Isaiah knew about the sword and occasionally accompanied Robert to the clearing. Sometimes Isaiah would throw Robert's targets and *ooh* and *aah* when Robert's strikes fell perfectly. Sometimes Isaiah would sit in the shade, jug in hand, and watch, but usually, Robert went to the clearing by himself.

Robert preferred practicing his swings, stabs, slices, and chops without his friend's well-meant but frustrating interruptions. Practice was paying off in a big way, and by January of 1973, Robert was as good with the sword as he was with his guns, and that was saying something for Robert had earned the reputation as a *deadeye*.

The sword quickly lost its lengthy awkwardness, and since he couldn't farm, Robert concentrated on training. He didn't know why training was so important, but he knew it was.

At the house, there was a mixed bag of feelings.

Karen was an adult and understood the dire circumstances facing the family, and Theodore was old enough to know that things were bleaker than bleak. Lean was one thing, and they'd seen lean before. Lean was normal, but after the storms of 1972, lean didn't describe their condition.

Times were hard, a localized *Great Depression*, and Karen and Theodore knew it. The rest of the kids were young enough to celebrate the lack of work. They were happy they didn't have to miss months of school to dig sweet potatoes. That was one of the few things they agreed upon.

Going to school was a chore, but missing weeks of school was a pain in the ass. Each fall, just after the school year kicked off, the sweet potato harvest revved up. The kids had enough time to make an in-class appearance to pick up their books, and after that, they vanished for weeks at a time. Gone from the classrooms and forgotten by their classmates until stormy weather brought them to class for a day.

Farming worked the way it had worked since the days of the one-room schoolhouse filled with bare feet and tough, calloused kids. Very little changed in the country and ditto to the way country folks did things. Schools were bigger with more students—most without calluses and shoes were mandatory—but the ways and means of farming were the same. Farming was first. Schooling was a distant second if numbered at all.

Barbara coaxed the teachers into giving her the kids' assignments, and she made sure they were done on time. Karen or Barbara, whichever made the weekly grocery run into town, carried the completed schoolwork to the teachers. If there wasn't money for groceries, the assignments were delivered by a friend from church who worked in town.

Usually, there wasn't much time for anything in the way of fun during the sweet potato harvest. Farming was hard, physically demanding labor that lasted day after day, sunup to sundown, six days a week. By itself, it was a daunting job, but that was only part of it. Every evening after the day's supper was gobbled down, dishes washed and put away, and showers taken, the kids had their schoolwork waiting on them. It was an annual, three-month stint into the hottest, *stinkiest*, innermost ring of hell.

The normal harvest lasted until the last potato row was either dug up or was frozen by an unexpected frost. Usually, this was some time in November or early December, so the younger kids' excitement about missing a harvest was understandable. They had food in their bellies and a warm place to sleep. They were broke, but they never had money anyway. They had time to play, to be kids for a change. In their eyes, they were getting a much needed and greatly desired vacation.

The family was suffering, but the kids, like pigs in shit, wallowed in their stinking situation and loved it.

The screen door slammed, and screaming kids ran through the house. "How was your day?" Barbara asked her four school-aged children. She was stirring something on the stove and holding Sherman over her shoulder like a squirming sack of flour. Albert, the second youngest child, was wrapped around her leg like a Burmese python.

"Fine," from Jill.

"Horrible," from Rosalyn.

"Great," from Melanie.

"Just glad to be home," from Theodore.

They were all glad to be home. Another day was in their rearview. They had after-school chores to do, but that was nothing compared to their usual routine. Usually, they had chores on top of a fulltime job with schoolwork thrown in as somebody's sick idea of a joke. Barbara wasn't running a prison camp, so before the kids started their chores, they sat down for their afternoon snacks.

The staple snacks were vanilla pudding or tuna sandwiches or both. Theodore hit the sandwiches. His growing body craved the protein in the fish and the carbohydrates in the bread. He was already as big as his daddy and would be bigger in a year. He gobbled down four pieces of white bread and a whole can of chunk-light tuna without feeling the need to share.

Jill and Rosalyn ate pudding and fussed over who got the bigger bowl. The bowls were identical, white ceramic with an embossed green design that was somehow floral but not at all flowery. The girls argued because they were girls, and Barbara did her best to ignore them.

Melanie broke from her pudding routine and requested a special snack. She craved grape-jelly rolls, and Barbara's timing was perfect. As Mel sat in her unassigned but usual seat at the kitchen table, Barbara took the rolls out of the oven. They were steaming hot, and the Bama grape jelly burned Melanie's tongue when she took her first bite. To have so many people in it, the kitchen was exceptionally quiet thanks to food's quietening power.

In the boys' bedroom, Tom T. Hall sang *Sneaky Snake* through scratchy speakers. The record player was in the corner, and Barbara laid Sherman on a pallet right in front of a worn-out speaker. The *Snake* was winding down, and *The Barn Dance* was up after the irritating goat song Sherman would've skipped if he'd known how.

Sherman was never as happy as he was when he was listening to Mr. Hall sing about the beer-stealing snake or the animals getting down in the barn. The songs irritated the hell out of everyone else but not as badly as Sherman's *gagas* and *goo-goos*, so no one complained when Barbara cranked the volume.

When Tom sang Sherman *cooed* and *ahh'ed* but made no other noises. It was the only time the baby approached anything resembling relaxation. It wasn't his nature to sleep, but even worse, it wasn't his nature to sit still. He squirmed, wiggled, jumped, bounced, and twitched almost all day and all night long.

On his pallet, with Tom in his ears, Sherman was still. It was his nap time, but it wasn't for him to nap. Barbara knew he wouldn't sleep. Sherman's naptime was not a break *for* him but a break *from* him.

Barbara backed out of Sherman's room and joined her other children in the kitchen. She sat down, relieved to be off her feet for even a moment, and watched the older kids finish their snacks. She listened as they talked about their days. She didn't care what they said. She was just glad to hear English words. Albert could talk and did frequently, but his words were nonsense most of the time.

"Mama, I want the *ludley*," he'd say. He resorted to screaming when she couldn't produce the *ludley*. It took a while to learn a *ludley* meant *lid* in Albert-speak. Barbara didn't cuss, but after a few minutes of Albert's screaming, she'd come close. "Al, what the hel..heck is a *ludley*?" She thanked God when she solved the mystery, and she always made sure to have a ludley in her apron pocket .

Sherman couldn't talk but tried, and that was worse than silence. Barbara couldn't remember any of her other kids making the sounds that baby made. At times, she thought he had a special—*retarded* was the word she wanted to use but didn't dare—set of vocal cords. She looked to his future with great uncertainty. "Father, be with that one," she prayed often.

And the Father was listening. He would be with Sherman in ways Barbara never imagined.

Sherman stopped speaking, and Piper and Sebastian waited for him to pick up where he'd left off. Sherman rubbed his chin whiskers and lost time in reflection. *Damn, that was a long time ago*, he thought. More than one-hundred years in the *gone* part of time, and there wasn't much *yet-to-come* part of time left for him.

Sherman knew he couldn't walk the boys through each year of his life, and even though one of the most important events happened when he was three, he decided to skip ahead and come back to it as it became relevant. He didn't know it would be relevant so soon..

The boys wanted to know more about the sword, so Sherman told them, "I was six-years-old the year death came *back* to our house."

Chapter Nine

Susan beat *Handsy* to the office and sat at her desk flipping through last week's time-cards. Her primary job was tallying hours to make sure everyone was paid correctly. Her job was as easy as getting into hell since most of it was done by the computerized time clock. The only snag in the automated system was some employees worked extra hours on the weekends. These hours were written in a notebook, and the notebook had to be signed off on by the foreman. This was Susan's misfortune because *Handsy* was the foreman.

Worse still, *Handsy* was the owner's only son. As Sherman, Piper, and Sebastian ate their lunch, Susan reluctantly hit the talk button on the factory's intercom and mentally prepared to be harassed.

"Chris Wilcott come to the office, please. Chris Wilcott come to the office." Susan returned the intercom's mic to its stand, and the office door flung open.

"I'm here darling. I knew you couldn't resist me forever," Chris said. He was dressed in lazy brown slacks with *mama's creases* down the front and back of both legs and a midnight-blue Oxford shirt with one sleeve rolled up. A *Nine Inch Nails* tattoo was clearly visible on his forearm, an inside joke Susan never asked about. Chris's hands went straight for Susan's shoulders. She saw the incoming attack and spun away.

"Mr. Wilcott, I need you to sign off on the overtime hours," Susan said, and pushed the notebook between them as a talisman to ward off his evil advance. Susan handed him a pen because the incompetent bastard never had one. Chris was the foreman only because his daddy owned the place.

Chris took the pen, leaned in close, "Come here. I won't bite."

Susan let him move closer to her ear. A mistake she made because she was tired from arguing with her husband last night.

"I've got a secret," Chris said. He moved closer to her ear, so close she could not only smell his breath but could actually feel it waving the tiny hairs in her ear.

"You need to loosen up some. I'm being friendly with you. I can be a *gooooood* friend if you let me," he breathed in her ear, administering a mouth-to-ear version of *CPR*.

Then, Chris crossed the line.

His yeast-coated tongue went in her ear and tickled her brain.

Then, Susan decimated the line.

In the fifth grade, a burly girl named Becky Church pushed Susan down on the playground. The only way Susan would've weighed seventy pounds was if she was fully dressed and soaking wet and carrying a sack of rocks. Becky tilted the scales north of a hundred, fat-ass pounds. Susan hit the dirt and didn't bother to think her next move through.

Susan, a small girl with a pink dress and dirty, white panties—thanks to Ms. Church shoving her down in the mud—balled her tiny hand into a fist not much bigger than a steel bearing. Susan slammed that ball-bearing into Becky's jaw. The results were, one, Becky Church spent two days in the hospital and the rest of the school year with her shattered jaw wired shut, and two, Susan Vance was suspended and spent that afternoon in the hospital, then spent three months with her hand in a splint. And finally three, the reason for the history lesson, Sherman taught his granddaughter how to punch without breaking her hand. Susan used what she learned to ensure *Handsy* never touched her again.

Handsy's tongue entered Susan's ear, and like her grandpa showed her all those years ago, she curled her fingers half-over, tucked them backwards, and rammed her palm into *Handsy's* stud-perfect nose.

He hollered like a girl and bled like one on a heavy-flow day. Chris's knees unhinged and he fell to the floor screaming and thrashing and kicked Susan's desk hard enough to sail her monitor across the office. It crashed into the wall and exploded into a twinkling, diamond rain. Susan laughed. It was her monitor, but his inheritance was paying for its replacement.

Chris jumped to his feet, no longer thinking straight and thanks to the tears in his eyes, no longer seeing straight either. Blood gushed from his crooked and flattened nose and ran off his chin in thick, red streams. He was seconds away from hitting her back when his father came out of his office to see what was causing the commotion. Susan was wild, feral. She screamed at Chris and shoved him away and stormed inside Mr. Wilcott's office.

"Chris has been harassing me for months, Mr. Wilcott, but it's out of hand now." She told of the groping. "His hands are working on me more than they're building furniture." She told of the suggestive, lurid comments. "He said he wanted to lick all of my...*moist* places to see if I taste as good as I look." Susan was embarrassed beyond belief but continued. "He just stuck his tongue in my ear."

Mr. Wilcott managed to calm Susan and stop her alternating bouts of hyperventilation and frantic yelling. She cried and fidgeted with her purse straps. Her short fingers nervously worked the clasp open, closed, open, closed. Mr. Wilcott was afraid she would pass out or bust a vessel in her brain; neither would be good for Wilcott Furniture.

"The important thing, Mrs. Vance, is that you calm down. It's over now." He gave her the rest of the day off with pay and walked her to her car.

"Mrs. Vance, I apologize for Chris's behavior. You have my word that I will get to the bottom of this, and it'll never happen again." She unlocked her car, and he held the door open for her. "Are you sure you're okay to drive?" A wreck certainly wasn't in Wilcott Furniture's best interest.

"I'm fine, Mr. Wilcott." She wasn't, but she wasn't admitting it to him because she was leaving, and nobody was stopping her. "Please make Chris leave me alone. I'm a married woman."

Mr. Wilcott's grandfatherly voice assured her that he'd handle the situation. All was in his capable hands, and she'd not have to worry about *Handsy* again. She needed only to go home and calm down, and for heaven's sake, drive safely.

Susan pulled out of the parking lot a nervous wreck. She couldn't imagine dealing with her deadbeat husband in her condition. If she came home early, Clark would demand an explanation. That was a fight she could do without. She thought about going to her grandpa's house, but she'd have to answer questions there, too.

Quietness. That's all Susan wanted.

She drove down Jackson Street searching for a quiet spot to park. She saw a sign for the city's park and remembered taking her boys there last summer to watch the city league baseball teams. It was thunderous then with laughter and kids screaming hoorays to their teammates, but that was in July. It was winter now, and the park was deserted.

Quietness. *I'll hang out in the park without the boys,* she thought.

Thoughts like that wouldn't win her the coveted *Nobel's Mother of the Year* award, but it would give her time to settle her nerves. City Park it was, so she turned on her signal and eased into the turn lane. Susan pulled close to the park's small pond, killed the engine, closed her eyes, and rested.

Quietness at last.

Six hours later, Susan's neck was numb but hurt like hell despite the tingling deadness. A string of drool, viscous and foul-smelling, ran from the side of her mouth and formed a gelatinous pool on her right breast. It soaked through her blouse and was almost through her bra. She smeared it with a leftover napkin from their last family outing at Houston's Sonic Drive-In.

Susan said, "Thank you, Lord," for the napkin and for the peppermint the carhop gave them with that meal. Her mouth was dry and pasty and the peppermint helped generate enough saliva to swallow. What she needed was a drink but didn't have any liquid in the car. Pond water seemed like an acceptable source until she looked at the pond's murky surface and decided against a trip to the emergency room.

Six hours ago, a nervous, panicky Susan killed her engine at City Park. Remarkably, she settled into something like relaxation, but more akin to pure exhaustion, and fell asleep in the front seat of her car. If she'd dreamed, she didn't remember it, and that was fine with her. Ever since she'd married Clark, her dreams weren't the kind she wanted to remember anyway.

The clock on her dashboard read 5:13, in electric-blue numbers. Susan left work not wanting to go home early and fight with Clark.

Now, she'd be lucky to make it home on time, and being late was worse than being early. The Green-Eyed monster would be on Clark's back, whispering no telling what in his ear. At least she'd turned the engine off. If she'd ran out of gas and had to call Clark to pick her up at the park, he would've talked to her about that. He would've *talked hard.*

The day was a disaster, but it was time to put it behind her. Susan pulled the shifter to drive and went to get the boys. Being a Christian and a firm believer in looking for the best in even the worst situations, Susan said aloud, "At least I won't have to deal with *Handsy* anymore."

Susan didn't know how right she was, but unfortunately, she soon would.

Chapter Ten

hile Susan got closer to *Handsy* Wilcott than she'd ever wanted to or even thought possible, Sherman and the boys finished their lunch. Piper and Sebastian wanted to go outside and play. They nagged Sherman to give in but gave up when he wouldn't so much as acknowledge them. Listening to the old man talk beat watching him nap, so Sebastian said, "Finish the story, great-grandpa."

"Very well. Put the dishes up," Sherman said, acting as if it was a problem but continuing the story was his intention all along. Seated comfortably in his recliner, Sherman *sensed* trouble brewing. Was it trouble for him? Maybe for the boys? Perhaps for everyone.

Sherman remembered when the *sixth* part of his brain came to life, and he felt trouble for the first time. How could he forget? It happened in 1978, and he'd never forget how wrong he'd been. It almost cost him everything, and it was the perfect place to resume his storytelling.

Nineteen-seventy-eight was the year Robert's cousin came to live with the Lancasters. His name was Kelvin Smith, and he was thirty-one-years old. Kelvin's farm had gone under the year before and he showed up at Robert's front door, begging for a place to stay until he could get back on his feet. Robert remembered the tough years he'd had after the 1972 floods and was happy to help a fellow farmer through a hard time.

"Robert, I sure appreciate you letting me crash here," Kelvin said, and dragged deeply on an unfiltered Camel. "I promise I won't be any trouble. You'll hardly know I'm here." Kelvin exhaled a thick cloud of blue and white smoke that burned Robert's nose and stung his eyes and already, Robert detested his cousin.

Robert fanned the smoke from his face. "Keep them coffin nails away from the house. I don't want to smell them and don't want 'em around the kids. If Barbara sees you smoking around the kids you'll be out on your ass, cousin or not."

Walking towards the house, Kelvin asked, "Which room is mine?"

"You won't be sleeping in the house. There ain't enough room for Barbara and me and the kids. I put a mattress in the tool shed for ya'. There's power out there, and it's dry and clean. There's a small TV and little radio but keep the volume down so's you don't wake us."

"I ain't got much stuff, Robert. A couch will do for me." Kelvin's plans didn't include sleeping solo in a tool shed.

By 1978, three of their kids had moved out, but Robert and Barbara still had four kids living at home. The brick FHA house was much bigger than the wooden shack they lived in before it, but no house was big enough for two families.

He didn't wish to upset his host before he even settled in, so Kelvin said, "It'll be fine, Robert. I figured I'd stay in the house with y'all, but beggars can't be choosers."

"There's room at the table, and Barbara says for you to use the bathroom anytime you need it," Robert said. "There just ain't no extra sleeping room."

"Thank you. I appreciate a place to put my head." Kelvin's resentment threatened to burn out of control. He crushed out his cigarette, slipped his right hand in his pocket and balled it into a fist. His filthy fingernails sliced four half-moons in his palm. The blood and pain brought his runaway anger to heel and Kelvin smiled again.

Make me sleep outside like a dog. I'll show you.

It was spring when Kelvin moved into the tool shed and the sweet potatoes were already in the beds. Their bushy tops had grown tall enough to been seen from the back door, a congregation of green hands waving in the steady spring breeze. It was an unusually warm spring, and the farm was a month ahead of schedule. If the weather held out another week, Robert would plant early, and if it held out long enough, he'd harvest early, too.

Kelvin was a sweet potato and soybean farmer the same as Robert and knew all there was to know about raising both crops. When he first came to stay with the Lancasters, Kelvin kept his nose to the grindstone and worked like a slave. Needing no oversight, Robert *gave* him his head. Rosalyn, Robert's youngest daughter, hadn't noticed anything missing yet and the real trouble was still months away. Robert thought he'd happened upon the rainbow's end.

Kelvin did more work than he had to, so Robert felt obliged to do less. With unexpected spare time, Robert disappeared to the clearing where he continued training.

His last six years of training had paid off and Robert was an exceptional swordsman. He handled the sword with surgical precision, not swinging it, but operating with it. It was as if he wasn't holding it at all. Indeed, it was as if all the training had fused them seamlessly together. The sword stopped being a tool and was a razor-sharp extension of his body.

He handled the sword one-handed and two-handed equally well. Normally, his left hand had no standalone use and was relegated to supporting roles only, but when he held the sword, Robert was as good left-handed as he was right-handed. He knew this was the sword's doing, not his.

Four years ago, Robert made a leather scabbard and sling from the hide of a ten-point buck he killed in the exact spot he found the sword. He cinched the sling and positioned the sword's jeweled handle just behind his left ear. Robert's draw was lightning quick, the blade seen only as a wink of quicksilver.

He carried the sword to the dump for target training. Robert grabbed bottles from the trash heap and tossed them into the air. The sword flashed into action, just barely visible glints whistling with each stroke. It wasn't unusual for him to land two or three strikes before the pieces hit the ground.

Robert struck right-handed, left-handed, and two-handed. He struck while performing acrobatic flips and spins that would've left any Olympic gymnast jealous...and would have left Barbara wet between her legs if she'd ever watched him practice. It was amazing, almost certainly miraculous, and more than a little frightening that he could do any of those things. But above all, it was the sword itself that astonished him.

The blade sliced through almost anything. He easily cut down small trees with a single stroke like a crazed lumberjack with a sword for an ax. He couldn't cut through the thicker trees—yet—but something told him that was his fault, and not the sword's. No matter how many trees Robert sliced through, and no matter how many times he harpooned concrete blocks with it or speared it in the ground, the blade never dulled. Not even metal plates or iron rebar could dent or dull the blade, and the sword didn't sharpen itself. It didn't have to.

It simply never dulled.

It was as sharp six years later as it had been when he pulled it from the mud. It defied logic...defied belief. It defied all he knew about the world. Robert wasn't sure, but there were times he thought it glowed. And he'd never tell anyone—hell, he'd scarcely admit it to himself—but he occasionally felt heat rising from the blade. And, he was still nagged by the feeling he had when he first saw the sword.

It's alive.

The sword was perfect, period. There's no other way to say it. It did whatever was asked of it and it did so without losing its capacity to do it again and again. It was beautiful when he found it. Now, six years later, his appreciation had deepened into respectful devotion. It was love, pure and simple.

Robert didn't know where it came from, what it meant, or what he was to do with it, but he knew it had a purpose. *A thing like that must have a purpose*, he reasoned.

And if the sword had a purpose, so did he.

Rosalyn and Albert got off the school bus and trudged up the long driveway as slowly as possible. They were so focused on their afternoon chores they didn't talk. Albert had to slop the hogs, remove fallen limbs from the pecan orchard, and hoe the garden. Rosalyn had to clean the hen house, gather eggs, and feed Robert's bird dogs. After sedating their sorrows with Barbara's sugary afternoon delights, the kids changed their clothes and marched outside to earn their keep.

Rosalyn fed the dogs first because it was the easiest and cleanest of her jobs. Gathering eggs was kinda fun, in a lunatic way she'd never confess. Cleaning the hen house was a dirty, smelly job, and she hated it worse than any other job on the farm. She scraped chicken poop from the plywood floor with a paint scraper. One or two flakes of dried shit never failed to pop up her nose or flutter into her eyes, infecting her with God knows what. When her buckets were full, she dumped them in a compost pile behind the hen house.

"You want me to do that for you, darling?" Kelvin called from the tractor shed.

Rosalyn wore a pair of cut-off blue jean shorts and a small, sleeveless shirt that was tied in the front instead of buttoned. She was straining with a bucket in each hand when Kelvin spoke, but he'd been watching her the whole time. Watching Rosalyn was the highlight of his day and all he could think about at night when he filled his palm with himself.

"Thanks, but I better do it," she yelled back, blushing but not too red. Kelvin was muscular and handsome, and Rosalyn was pleased she'd caught the older man's eyes. It was a feeling she'd soon get over.

Albert hated his jobs as much as Rosalyn hated hers, maybe more. He would've gladly switched with her if switching was allowed. Picking up limbs wasn't too bad, but he hated it all the same. Hoeing was a dirty job, but he didn't complain because nobody would've listened. Of all his chores, Albert hated feeding the hogs the most.

Albert carried the bucket of slop from the back porch to the hog pen. His face pressed into a concentrated scowl as he damn near tiptoed to keep from sloshing it on him. The slop was a fetid mixture of table scraps from last night's supper and whatever was scrapped from that day's breakfast and lunch. The slop bucket vibrated with the susurrus of what seemed like a million green flies.

The flies tangoed across the slop, flew to the hogs and crawled around, and then *kamikazed* back toward Albert's face. He backed out of the pen, swatting flies and calling, "Suuu-weee!" Done for the day, Albert put the slop bucket on the porch and went inside.

Albert let the back-door slam shut and saw Rosalyn staring contemptuously toward the other end of the kitchen. Sherman and Barbara were sitting in the floor and the snot-demon was smiling and having fun without a care in the world. Sherman had his mama playing the *Which Car is It?* game. Rosalyn *hmphed* and left to take her bath, but Albert watched with disgust as his little brother cackled and toyed with their mother. Albert hated that stupid-ass game, and not just because Sherman invented it. Albert hated it because he thought their mother was oblivious to Sherman's cheating.

The game was as simple as its creator. Sherman lined up a few cars, maybe a truck or two, definitely a tractor, and then asked, "Which car is it, mama?" If he didn't get her undivided attention immediately, he'd ask again, "Which is it?" The second time was louder, sterner, and more demanding. When Barbara focused her full attention on the game, Sherman made engine noises that sounded like, "*Vroom, rattle, grrr, vroom, vroom.*"

Barbara had to pick the car responsible for the noise. Simple in theory. Only this game's malevolent creator hated losing.

Since they played the game almost every day, chance should've worked in her favor at least once. It never did. In all the games played in the seven years Sherman insisted upon playing it, Barbara never guessed the correct car. Phenomenal odds, impossible when you think about it, but Barbara never complained about losing. She only smiled.

Sherman's conscience never bothered him a whit until he watched his mama draw her final breaths. Before she faded away, he wept by her side. "You guessed which car it was way more than you missed," he confessed, and added, "I love you." Barbara smiled, not surprised by either piece of information, and died. Sherman's tears fell freely, but he smiled as he patted her cooling hand.

You knew. You always knew, he thought.

"Boys?" Susan called from the kitchen.

"Mama, mama, great-grandpa is telling us the story about Cousin Kelvin!" Piper blabbed. "Do you know that one? Huh? Do you? Come and sit down so he can finish it before we go home." Piper enjoyed Sherman's story well enough, that was true, but there was another reason the poor kid didn't want to go home. Sherman wanted to know what it was.

"No Piper, I don't know that one. I hate to break it to you, young man, but we have to get home."

"Just a little longer, please, please. Kelvin stayed with them after the Big Storm. Do you know about the Big Storm?" Piper asked, stalling.

She looked at her grandfather and asked, "Is that the one grandma caused?"

"The very one," Sherman said. He fumed inside but was outwardly calm. *I'm going to have to talk to that boy.* Piper would learn to keep his mouth shut.

Susan paid no attention. Her neck hurt, and she was worried about her job. "I wish I could stay longer grandpa, but I've got to get the boys home and get supper started." Her eyes told a story, and Sherman's *sixth sense* raised the Red Flag again.

"You just have to learn to let shit pile up and ignore the pile," Sherman said. Those were his daddy's words of wisdom, and although Sherman had trouble learning how to make the pile, it worked like a charm once he figured it out.

"Is everything okay, Susan? You look like something's on your mind, something heavy."

"It's just work. The foreman is a horny prick who refuses to accept no for an answer," Susan surprised herself by spilling anything but didn't dare tell the whole story.

"You tell Clark?" Sherman asked.

"Oh no. He'd go ballistic and probably make me quit. We need the money. And besides, I think I took care of it today. He ain't the first man I've had to shoot down."

"Let me know if there's anything I can do for you. I can be persuasive when I need to be," Sherman said as he held the front door open for her.

"I will, grandpa," Susan said. She fastened the boys in the car and drove home. That night, Mr. Wilcott kept his promise and ruined Susan's life.

Sherman stood at the door watching them leave. As Susan left, *Wolf* arrived.

Chapter Eleven

everal hours after the change, Ursa showed up at Sherman's front door. The interior door was wide open and the screen door set ajar, its hinges bent in ridiculous angles. She knew what it meant, and his stifling musk confirmed it. The tattered remains of his clothes made a breadcrumb trail from the hallway to the front door. The restraints he'd tried to put on lay unused on the floor. Ursa had to find him and stop him before he hurt someone.

From the top of Bull Mountain, Sherman had fully changed into *Wolf*, and he howled. He didn't think when he was changed; couldn't think. He felt. He sensed. He knew. *Food* was just ahead.

Two men were hunting raccoons, laughing, and going about life without knowing they'd seen their last sunrise. They weren't murderers, but they had their secrets, their sins. They were married to decent women, had respectful children, and worked hard jobs for the county. Hunting eased the stress of their back-breaking, thankless jobs. Cares that would trouble neither man much longer.

Sherman flanked them and crouched behind a sun-warped juniper. The hunters listened closely, but in vain, for their dogs. Spotty was a mongrel bulldog/Chihuahua mix that had to have been someone's idea of a joke. He died instantly from the huge bite that snapped his neck and punctured his heart at the same time. Rover was a full blood Bluetick hound and was digesting in Sherman's stomach.

Charles Sprattling was the older of the two hunters, and his deep dark secret was that he was guilty of jacking off while he touched underage boys. *Wolf* leaped from the shadows and rose on its hind legs. The beast roared and tore Charles's arms from his torso. Charles screamed himself into shock's nothingness and was fortunate to never regain consciousness.

Johnny Duncan wasn't as fortunate, and his great secret wasn't a secret at all. It was written all over his wife and kids in blue and yellow bruises. Johnny nervously fumbled the shotgun's safety off and fired two shots in *Wolf's* face and chest. The shotgun pellets didn't penetrate the supernatural hide.

A hairy, distorted hand snatched Johnny's gun and slung it into the woods. The search party found it three days later missing two shells and bearing three impossibly deep scratches in its blued finish.

"What the fuck?" Johnny asked as he retreated.

Wolf pounced, and Johnny shrieked as the beast's tremendous weight crushed his spine. Paralysis was instant. Johnny was unable to move, even screaming was impossible. Sherman dragged Johnny over by Charles, and since he was still alive, Sherman drained Johnny's blood first. Charles was next, but to Sherman's dismay, the man's blood had seeped into the ground. Disappointed but not deterred, Sherman slowly devoured his kills.

When he swallowed his last bite, Sherman howled at the moonless sky and was set to find his next victim when Ursa grabbed him from behind and slammed him into a giant oak. He growled and turned to kill the fool who'd dared touch him. *Wolf* lunged, throwing all his weight into the charge, and rammed its head into Ursa's stomach.

Chomping at her head, *Wolf* tried to end the fight with each bite, but Ursa dodged the frothy snout and caught his mouth in her hand. She dropped to one knee and dragged *Wolf's* huge body to the ground with her. Her sword was handy, but she wouldn't need it.

Her blow was fast and hard but not enough to kill him. A sonic boom echoed through the woods as her fist contacted the top of *Wolf's* head. Sherman was unconscious, and Ursa took him in her arms, a heavy shag carpet with arms and legs. She carried him home and hid him in his tractor shed because he was too bloody to go in the house. In the dim glow of the coming dawn, she sat with his shrinking head in her lap and petted his smelly coat.

"Will this ever end?" Ursa asked.

"Damn," was Sherman's waking thought. It took several minutes before he could move on. *Damn. Damn.* He was happy Ursa was gone. He would've tried his damnedest to kill her if she'd been there.

Ursa tried to kill him and disappeared before he woke up. "Just like a woman," he murmured. She left him lying naked on the cold, cracked concrete floor of his tractor shed. His chilled bones and nakedness awakened his memory to last night's activities.

One guy didn't scream, never knew what was coming. He was lucky. *Oh, but the other one knew. He was awake through most of it.*

Sherman stood on wobbling knees, an old man, his body painted in dried blood. He peeled a large jigsaw piece of blood off his arm and popped it in his mouth like a potato chip. *Yuck.* He spat it out. *Wolf* loved blood, but without the *change*, Sherman didn't care for the taste. Forgetting what he'd just done, Sherman lifted a sizeable piece off his chest and stopped it just before it went in his mouth.

That's enough of that shit, he told himself. He *pop, pop, popped* his palm against his aching head to startle his brain into working. He had to get ready for Susan and the boys.

Sherman's stomach rumbled. Last night's meal wanted out and was taking the *backdoor* to freedom. As painful as that often was—and his asshole was already dreading it—at least it meant he wouldn't have to see what he'd eaten. Yakking up undigested man-parts was unnerving as hell. You don't really know how you feel about yourself until you've puked up an eyeball, a finger, or some poor soul's ear. The good news, and he didn't hesitate to thank God for it, was that he'd changed back, fully. He hadn't lost control, wasn't lost for good.

Fuck you, Ursa! Sherman's brain shouted again. His headache would linger for days and forgiveness was hard. She did what she did to settle him, to stop him from hurting anyone else, and he knew she thought she was doing him a favor. He also knew he couldn't kill her, so there was no reason to hold a grudge. He'd just move on and deal with Ursa later.

Sherman jogged to the house, naked and holding his swinging genitals. The snow was ankle-deep and did nothing to improve his foul mood. He perked a little when the shower's hot water steamed on his freezing head and ran down his shuddering back. Sherman let the hot water loosen Charles and Johnny's dried blood from his body. While he waited for the blood to swirl down the drain, Sherman planned his day.

He decided to surprise the boys with a field trip instead of keeping them cooped up in the house again. Of course, he'd continue telling them about Kelvin. Piper and Sebastian had to know about 1978 to understand what Sherman was, what one of them would become. The story had to go on, but stories are just as good, and sometimes better, when they come with a few visual aids. Sherman knew their destination and knew the boys wouldn't object.

They were going to the *Clearing*, and Piper would keep his mouth shut about it or else.

Chapter Twelve

Susan was earlier than Sherman expected. If she kept getting earlier each day she would soon be able to spend the night and save a trip. Susan got out of the car and Sherman could tell she'd been crying. Her nose was pink and so were her cheeks, which she could've blamed on the weather, but her eyes betrayed her emotions. Sherman didn't guess why she'd been crying. He stopped playing that game decades ago. With women, tears came too easily, and they could mean everything, or nothing at all.

If a woman was happy, she'd cry.

If a woman was sad, she'd cry.

If a woman was hurt, she'd cry.

If women's tears had any meaning at all, it was impossible for a man to discern. The best bet was to wait. Hopefully, the tears would go away on their own. If they didn't, their cause, reasonable or not, would come out sooner or later.

Susan helped her boys out of their coats and shed her own by dropping her shoulders and letting it thud on the floor. "Sorry, I had to run last night," Susan said. Her voice was clear and steady even as she sniffled back tears.

"Don't worry about it, sweetie," Sherman said. He was impressed. It was almost impossible to tell she'd been crying.

"How are you feeling this morning, grandpa? Can I get you anything before I leave?" Susan asked as she headed towards the Mr. Coffee blinking on the counter.

"Piper, take your brother to the playroom so me and your mom can talk. Grown-up stuff."

Piper said nothing. He took Sebastian's hand, and they walked silently to the playroom and closed the door gently behind them. The way they shuffled their feet, the way they never looked up said things weren't good. Sherman feared the worst.

"I know you like it hot and black," Susan said as she set a steaming cup of Folgers Classic Roast in front of him. It was the only coffee he'd buy. He would drink other coffee if he were away from home and had to do so, but he'd never buy anything else for his house. Routines mattered to Sherman.

Susan knew he always drank from the same cup and that was the one she placed in front of him. Even though he appreciated Susan's kind gesture, Sherman would've preferred she keep her fingers off Abby's cup.

"Thank you, sweetheart. It's impossible to beat a fresh cup of joe," Sherman said, and didn't mention the coffee cup issue because Susan looked to have too much on her mind already. He had to know if the boys were all right, so he pried.

"How are things with you? You and Clark getting along okay now?" Sherman feared Clark was responsible for Susan's tears. Feared Clark was responsible for the Red Flag Sherman *sensed* yesterday. Feared the boys were doing the *Clark Shuffle* this morning. Sherman feared what he might have to do.

"Oh yes. We are the perfect, happy couple," Susan lied. "Grandpa, let's just say that we're working at it day-by-day. He says he's trying, and I guess maybe he is."

"If a man has to tell you he's trying to do something, he's either a liar or a failure. He ain't put his hands on you or either of the boys, has he?"

The ice in Sherman's stare chilled Susan's blood. She remembered their deal.

Years ago, Susan arrived at the annual Lancaster Family Reunion with a black eye and contrasting yellow bruises on both cheeks. Her dad and Sherman immediately dropped their fried chicken and armed themselves with their favorite go-to guns. Susan cried and begged them to not hurt Clark. They put their guns away and both promised to leave him alone, but Sherman grabbed Susan's face, squeezed it hard enough to get her attention, and pulled her close.

Sherman's breath, much hotter than 98.6 degrees, burned her face in a way that wasn't humanly possible. He made certain that Susan understood that his promise was only for the times the *wife-beating-piece-of-shit* had previously hit her. He told her that if it happened again, a bucket of tears and a year of begging wouldn't save Clark's worthless life.

Sherman knew it was an inevitability, that it wasn't a matter of *if* Clark would hit her again, but *when*. While their faces were inches apart, while he had her knock-kneed and frightened to nearly pissing on herself, Sherman warned her.

"If you're dumb enough to let him off, that's on you." Sherman's voice deepened and his hateful blue eyes pierced her soul. "If he hurts one of those boys, I'll kill you and Clark. You're responsible for those kids' safety, and you're knowingly putting them around a man who can't control his temper. That's on you, too. You have a choice, right now. Let me finish him."

She didn't relent, so Sherman made her acknowledge that she understood the conditions. Her soul was saved by Jesus, but her life was forfeit if Clark ever hurt Piper or Sebastian.

"I wouldn't want to live with the guilt of knowing I let it happen," Susan told him.

Sherman released her face and kissed her bruised cheek. He told her what would happen to her and didn't skimp on the details. He prayed it would change her mind, but it didn't work. She accepted the condition, and there was nothing more he could do. Sherman spared Clark's life, and there'd been no more bruises, no more black eyes. He prayed for them both, for the boys, and so far, things had been good.

Clark had apparently amended his wayward ways.

Maybe he had gotten good at hiding them.

"Oh, no. Absolutely not," Susan answered. "Clark doesn't put his hands on us. He knows I won't put up with that crap again. I thank God. Clark is good most days," she lied again.

Sherman wasn't fooled. He wasn't sure what she was lying about but was sure she was lying. He was so taken by her smile, by how much she looked like his wife, that he let it go for now. "You look so much like your grandmother. She is so proud of you," Sherman said.

"She is? Don't you mean she would be? She's gone to heaven, grandpa. You know that...right?" Susan fought the urge to question him. *What day is it? Do you know what day it is? Who is the president? Do you know who the president is, grandpa? Do ya, huh do ya?*

That was a screw-up. He'd have to be more careful.

"Of course, I know that, sweetie. Sometimes my old brain ain't as quick as my old mouth." Thank God for the old age card. Sherman played it often and played it well. Susan bought his act but retained the option to revisit the issue in the future if the old man had any more mushy-brain, slip-ups.

"What's this business about me molesting the boys? Sebastian is too cute. He calls it *meelestering*," Sherman asked.

"Grandpa, I don't know where they got that idea. Their principal called me at work and told me to come to the school. He said it was urgent. Of course, I raced over there. I didn't know if maybe something was wrong with one of the boys. The counselor, the nurse, and the principal along and two old biddies from Child Welfare ambushed me. They said that they'd received an anonymous tip that you were abusing the boys."

Sherman didn't say anything, but had his suspicions concerning anonymous tip's source. "Why didn't you tell me about the meeting? Did you believe that there was a chance the tip was on the up and up?" Sherman asked and watched her face for lies.

"They scared me. They said if I told you they'd take the boys into protective custody until the evaluation was complete. I didn't doubt you, but I didn't doubt them either. I knew they were just looking for any reason to take my kids, so I played by their rules. You've got to believe me, grandpa. I know you wouldn't hurt the boys."

The funny thing was, he did believe her. "I believe you." He touched her hand for reassurance. "I'd do *anything* to protect those little ones. Do you believe that?" Sherman asked pointedly.

"Yes, of course I do," Susan answered, fearing what might come next.

"Well, are they satisfied that the boys are safe with the pervert?" Sherman asked to lighten the electrified air between them.

"Yes, thank God. The evaluations are over. They recommended I use a professional childcare service in the future...to better tutor the kids they said, but they found nothing suspect about your relationship with Piper and Sebastian. That's the way they said it, nothing suspect."

It was finally too much for her. The meetings with the school officials, the trouble with the Wilcotts, and Clark, always trouble with Clark. Susan sniffled again. She was country-strong and hiding pain was her way of life, but Sherman saw through her wan smile. For her sake, but really for the boys' safety, he made her talk.

"You want to talk about it? I'm all ears," Sherman said.

Through her pain, with tears she couldn't hold back, Susan had an inner laugh. Sherman's old-man ears were comically huge against his swiveled, old-man head. In a way, he was *all ears*. She peered up at him without fully raising her head, puppy-like. Her eyes said, *Yes, I want to tell you, tell somebody, tell anybody.*

"You know I told you yesterday about the guy at work...you know, the one who wouldn't keep his hands off me?" Susan told Sherman about her fight with Chris Wilcott, leaving nothing out this time. "My boss called me last night and told me they'd cleaned out my desk and that my stuff was with the receptionist. Two days, he gave me. After that, he said I could get my stuff from the dumpster, so I've got to go by there first thing and get my stuff and then go to the Job Service to see if they have any listings." Susan wept.

Sherman held her until her tears stopped, and Susan said, "He said he was going to take care of it. He promised he'd handle it. He said..."

Chapter Thirteen

It was eight-thirty at night when the phone rang. Clark was slouched in his recliner, watching a replay of a football game. Susan sat in her matching recliner preparing a lesson for her next Sunday school class. The seven-to-ten-year olds were the rowdiest bunch in the church, and Susan Vance loved teaching them about their Lord and Savior. They, for the most part, didn't give a rip about Jesus and only wanted to play.

Nervously, Susan answered after two rings. She shot a quick glance at Clark to make sure he wasn't staring at her. She was supposed to answer on the first ring, but this time, Clark was engrossed in an instant replay and didn't seem to notice the phone at all. Softly, she said, "Hello?"

"Mrs. Vance?"

"Yes, this is Susan Vance."

It was Mr. Wilcott. "Mrs. Vance, I spoke with Chris. He told me the full story, and I'm sorry but we've got to—"

"Mr. Wilcott, I'm not sure what Chris told you..." Susan butted in.

"Please don't interrupt me, Mrs. Vance. This isn't easy; it's never easy letting someone go—"

She cut in again. "Excuse me? Letting me go? You're firing me because your son stuck his tongue in my ear?" Clark, jostled from his slouch by the disturbing news, muted the TV so he could hear better. He knew who won, anyway.

"Mrs. Vance, don't make this any more difficult than it has to be. Chris told me everything. We're going to need you to come by and pick up your belongings."

How dare he think he's going to fire me when this is all his son's fault! "You can't fire me over this!" Susan protested.

He enlightened her to the very fact that he could fire her for any reason or for no reason whatsoever and was firing her. He insisted she take his decision and just go with it. "It's just how it has to be, Mrs. Vance. I assure you, there's nothing you can do about it."

"I'm not a piece of trash that your son can tongue and have his daddy kick to the curb when I don't bend over and take it. This isn't right, and you know it."

Susan begged him to reconsider, and Mr. Wilcott expected nothing less and wouldn't change his mind. This wasn't the first time Chris went too far with a woman who failed to appreciate he was God's gift to the female population. Susan wasn't the first woman to lose her job thanks to Chris Wilcott, either. Daddy Wilcott didn't like it, but Chris was his only son.

Clark's alcohol dampened comprehension kicked in when he heard what Susan said.

Tongue.

Bend over and take it.

Clark wasn't used to hearing words like those from Susan's sweet little, Sunday-school-teaching mouth, and he certainly wasn't sending her to work to run around on him. He didn't know what was going on, but he was going to know, and know right now.

"What the hell are you talking about, Susie?" Clark asked.

She forgot Clark was in the room. When he wasn't yelling at her or one of the kids, it was easy to forget about him. Clark made his presence known, and *wham*, suddenly it was a different situation, one that could easily spiral beyond her control. Susan's body still ached in the hidden places, and she knew it was time to give up before things got worse. Susan swallowed her pride, and Chris Wilcott was off the hook again.

"I'll be by first thing in the morning for my stuff," Susan told her now ex-boss and hung up without waiting for his gloating response.

"Well that old scoundrel," Susan said as she returned the phone to its cradle. "I guess I'll go by the Job Service in the morning. I'm sure God has something better in mind for me." Susan was scared. Scared of being jobless. Scared there wouldn't be a miracle job from heaven. Mostly though, she was scared Clark was going to *talk* to her.

Clark was riled and was as likely to turn his anger onto her as one of the Wilcotts. *Talking hard* was more easily accomplished with a 98-pound woman than a 220-pound man. The men talked back, just as hard. If she was lucky, Clark would fall back into the stupor brought on by his cheap beer, old football game, and his natural stupidity.

Quietly, Susan picked up the Sunday school planner she dropped when Mr. Wilcott called. The planner's pages were bent because Susan paced when she was frustrated. Mr. Wilcott's call definitely frustrated her, and as they talked, Susan paced. She trampled the planner and laid down creases she couldn't straighten with a hot iron.

Susan slipped into her pink, fuzzball slippers and gathered her stuff as nonchalantly as her nervous hands would allow. She was doddering, head down out of the living room when Clark called.

"Hold it, Little Susie-Q. What the hell was that?" Clark sat his empty beer can down with its fallen kin. The pile beside his recliner was a recycler's wet dream. Susan was too far away for him to see clearly, and there were too many of her moving in a semicircular rotation. He couldn't focus on just one of them, so he cast his eyes in the center of them all.

Rather than her face, he was looking at Susan's knees and pointing at her with a crooked index finger. If she hadn't been terrified, it would've been funny.

"You lose your job tonight, or what?" No time for her to answer. "Was somebody messing with you?" They weren't rhetorical; he wanted answers but was too mad and too stupid to give her time to answer. "Were you messing around with somebody?" Still there was no break for her to speak. "I know that even you ain't that stupid." Final question: "Are you?" Still no break in his speech. "Get over here so I can talk to you."

She didn't want to hear those words. The thought of running for the door and screaming down the street crossed her mind, but she glanced at the pictures on the mantel. Piper and Sebastian, her boys, her reason for staying. The recliner's springs let go an ominous metallic sigh. The light cry of the metal was a somber warning as Clark came for her.

Susan didn't run, couldn't leave her boys. Clark talked to her and he *talked hard*.

Telling Sherman what happened improved Susan's mood considerably. She wasn't smiling exactly, but there was a light in her eyes that wasn't there before she vented. She neglected to mention Clark's participation, but something behind her grandpa's eyes said he knew anyway.

"I've got plenty of money if you need some till you get going again. I know how tight it can get with a couple little mouths to feed," Sherman said.

She thanked him, but it hadn't come to that yet.

"If you change your mind, just say so. Don't be too proud to let me know. It's only money. Just remember that when I die most of it is yours anyway. That can't be too far in the future. Hell, I'm a hundred and nineteen damn years old. You can get some of it now and that way I can watch you spend it. It'll be more fun for me that way."

Susan hugged him, thanked him, and silently prayed it didn't come to her taking his money. He'd already done so much to help her and Clark and the boys. She would beg, borrow, and steal from everybody else before she asked any more from her grandpa. "You'll probably bury us all, grandpa, and live forever."

God, please let her be wrong about that, he prayed fearing she might be right.

Susan hugged the boys and told them to be good little gentlemen and to mind their great-grandpa. They promised they would and they would try. In the end, they'd fail at it as little boys do when they try to be good. Susan left to collect her things from Wilcott Furniture, and the boys turned to their great-grandpa.

"Mama is sad because she got canned. That's what daddy said anyway," Sebastian blurted out as he hopped in Sherman's lap. The boy's small foot found his great-grandpa's testicles, and Sherman's groin exploded in prickly, red agony.

"Well your daddy don't have to worry about that happening to him since he's too damned lazy to get a job. You boys need to be especially good to your mama. She's having a tough time right now. Getting canned don't make you a bad person. I was canned more than once in my working years."

"What's on the agenda, pops?" an upbeat Piper asked.

"You and Sebastian want to take a field trip today instead of staying around the house? And if you call me pops again, I'm going to pop you in the mouth." Sherman put his fist against Piper's lips demonstrating his intent.

As Sherman expected the boys jumped and shouted approval for his plan. "Field trip! Yay! Gooooooo field trip!" They danced around like the boys from the *Lord of the Flies*, lost and crazy-eyed. Sherman would've worried if they'd had spears.

Sherman led Piper and Sebastian to the tractor shed. The shed was behind the house and down a snow-covered hill, so the trio held hands for support. Maybe it was a good idea, but if one fell, they were all going down. They made it to the shed still on their feet, and Sherman opened the first bay door. He threw the light on and said, "We're taking that."

Sherman pointed to his customized blue and white 1984 Ford Bronco. Its blue fiberglass top had been removed in advance, and it sat there looking like a turtle stripped of its shell. It was going to be a cold-mother of a ride, but Piper and Sebastian would love the open-air freedom.

"Climb in boys."

Sherman turned the key, and the Ford's souped-up 460 roared to life and shook the Bronco like a washing machine. Sherman clutched and shifted into first. He revved the gigantic V8 and popped the clutch. The four-wheel-drive jumped to life and sent both boys to their butts. Sherman caught second coming up the snowy hill with all four wheels throwing up blizzards. He hit third coming out onto the county road, and the all-terrains grabbed for purchase, found it, and propelled them down the road like a rocket on wheels.

They were on their way. The boys were in the rumble seat screaming at the top of their lungs, and Sherman joined in from the front. They were three outlaws, bandits on the run, and up to no good. The speakers belted out Hank Jr. singing the hell out of, A Country Boy Can Survive, and Sherman carried the boys to the clearing for their first taste of magic.

Chapter Fourteen

Sherman drove across the county line with the boys playing behind him. The turtle-top was off, but they didn't notice the freezing air. The kids were doing what kids do, and Sherman wanted to join them. They were on their way to and through Vardaman and on to the Atlanta community.

"Look right there. Years ago, and boys I mean a bunch of years ago, right over there was the clinic where your great-grandpa was born."

Sherman enjoyed the trip down memory lane, but what he was really doing was familiarizing Piper and Sebastian with the places they heard about in his stories. Seeing is believing, and if a picture is worth a thousand words, seeing something in person is worth a thousand pictures. For their part, the boys weren't as interested in his stories as they were in trying to throw one another out of the Bronco.

They left town and ventured deep into the country. Driving south on Hwy 341, Sherman marveled at how things had changed, but what he was looking for—that being the old Garbage Dump Road—was right where it had always been. He hit his blinker, slowed to a non-tipping speed, and wheeled the Bronco to the right.

"Boys, this is where my daddy brought me to shoot rats. Look right there on top of that hill." Piper and Sebastian looked at the fresh mound of red dirt that would soon be the foundation for another house. "That's where the old kennel was, where they bred and raised those fighting dogs I told you about."

"And roosters," Sebastian said to show he remembered the story.

"Correctomundo, young man." Sherman nodded at Sebastian's promising attitude.

Garbage Dump Road was *where* it had been, but it wasn't *what* it had been.

It had been a one-lane dirt road with a rock or two of county gravel sprinkled on it. Every week or so, folks swapped paint while passing on the old road, and driving it above forty miles per hour was suicide.

The new Garbage Dump Road, which almost certainly had a new name to go along with its new face, was brightly paved and wide enough for cars to pass easily without swapping paint. The white lines were freshly white and blindingly bright and looked like they were painted that same morning. The yellow lines and dashes were just as bright, and the asphalt was jet black and so shiny it looked oiled.

"Where's the dump, great-grandpa?" Piper asked as he strained his eyes to see what wasn't there.

"There's not one now. People got too lazy to make the trip and started throwing trash everywhere. Nobody wants trash all over the place, so they made landfills. Nowadays, you have to pay somebody to do what we used to do for free."

Sherman slowed to a crawl and pulled off the road. "This is where we used to dump trash." He pointed down an embankment covered with the dried remains of the previous year's kudzu crop. There was no trash, not even a beer can or candy wrapper. "They've got it cleaned up real good, don't they?"

He envisioned how the dump looked in 1978. He didn't see how his mental picture of the old dump with its mountains of garbage bags, some torn open by animals and some by time, rusted white refrigerators (always white), ovens (also always white and always rusted), and busted TV sets could be the same place he was looking at now. The old and the new were as different as night and day, and reluctantly, he admitted new was better.

He killed the engine and stepped out. "Come on boys." Instead of using the door the old man held open for them, Piper and Sebastian jumped over the sides.

"Geronimo," they yelled.

Boys will be boys, thought Sherman, and then said, "We're going to take a little walk."

"Where are we going? Piper asked.

"We're going to the clearing. *Duh*," Sebastian said mimicking the way his older brother made fun of him when the dunce hat was on the other head.

Piper did an about-face and lunged at his brother. He would teach the little puke the rules of great power politics: the biggest, strongest wins. Might makes right every time. Sherman caught Piper's collar and pulled him back.

"Now, now, boys. Calm it down a notch or two. Piper, your brother is right, though. The clearing where my daddy trained is just ahead." Piper turned around and filed Sebastian's trespass away for now. Piper desperately wanted to thrash his little brother, but seeing the clearing was presently more important. Sebastian would pay, but he would pay later.

Sherman stopped so abruptly Sebastian walked into him. The old man knelt on crackling knees. "Boys, we have to talk before we go any farther." His tone was serious and worrisome.

"I promised you two magic, didn't I? And I told you I'd tell you secret things," Sherman said, prying them with his eyes. "The clearing is a secret. Do y'all know what that means?"

"Yes sir. It means that we put on our *policeman* and take the secret to our graves," Sebastian said, having no idea what a grave was.

Immediately Piper understood that he was in for a 'talking to.' He'd opened his mouth to his mama about Kelvin. Thankfully, the talk was short, but the old man was crystal clear on one thing.

Piper would shut up or his great-grandfather would shut him up.

"So, we are clear then? Unless I tell you it's okay to tell somebody else, you don't tell it. Not even that we took a field trip. When your mama or daddy asks what we did today, you tell them I told stories. If they ask if anything was new or different, you tell them there's nothing new under the sun." He was talking to both boys but staring at Piper.

"I shouldn't have called this place the clearing. The clearing where my daddy first trained is long gone. Look around. We're standing in the middle of it."

"I don't see a clearing, great-grandpa," Sebastian said. He didn't want to say it outright like that, but unless he misunderstood the meaning of clearing. And Sebastian was as sure as an eight-year-old could be that he didn't misunderstand it. His mama made him clear the table after dinner, and he couldn't stop until the table was clear. So, Sebastian thought he had a solid grasp on the meaning of a clearing—there was no clearing in sight.

The place they stood was a forest, not a clearing. Pines and oaks and maples and sycamores grew everywhere. The trees were wall-thick, and it was impossible to see more than a few feet in any direction. Ivy hung from treetops in giant twisting ropes. Poison ivy snaked along the ground and screwed itself up tree trunks until it disappeared among the upper branches. Poison oak grew in lush winter patches so green and inviting it was almost impossible to resist playing in it. Saplings, full of hope and promise, sprouted and searched for sunlight under the thick canopy. The rotting corpses of the saplings that came before them spoke of their future among the elder trees.

"What happened to the clearing?" Sebastian asked.

"Time happened. Hunters stopped gathering here and people forgot about the place." Sherman kicked over some stones that once formed the edge of the hunters' fire pit. "Time happens to everything on this side. After the thing with Kelvin, daddy stopped training here, and started training there," Sherman pointed to an impassable briar thicket the boys couldn't see through. "Doesn't look much like a clearing, does it?"

No, it didn't. The boys agreed on that, and they agreed they weren't going in there no matter what their great-grandpa said. That impenetrable wall of green and brown two-inch thorns would debone the fellow foolish enough to attempt a pass through it.

"It's not just a clearing," Sherman said. "It's a magical *clearing*."

Chapter Fifteen

Sherman pulled the sword from his pocket. It was no bigger than the midsized, three-bladed *Case* pocketknife he carried. His sword was the size of a novelty item, something sold to bored office workers so they could *Samurai* their envelopes open instead of using their boring letter openers. The boys' mouths fell open when they saw it.

"What happened to it?" Sebastian asked.

"What did you do to it, great-grandpa?" Piper fussed.

"That's just part of her magic. Watch."

Sherman stood in front of the thicket and motioned for the boys to step away from his sides. In a magician's *now you see it, now you don't* style, he opened his palm and showed the shrunken sword to the boys one last time. He held his arm away from his body and closed his hand. Lightning flashed between his clenched fingers and blinded the boys. When Piper and Sebastian could see again, the sword was full size.

"Ooohhh! Holy Crap!" Piper yelled. "That was awesome! Do it again. Do it again."

"Man, oh man. That's wicked," Sebastian said in his usual, reserved and controlled voice. "I'm seeing it folks, but I'm not believing it."

"You ain't seen nothing yet," Sherman said and turned to face the briars, then he lifted the sword over his head. He shouted to the heavens, "*Eph-pha-tha!*" The boys understood the ancient language even though they had never heard it. *Be Opened!* Sherman had commanded.

The earth trembled, a few dead trees gave up their vertical hold and crumbled in on themselves like demolished buildings. A tiny, jagged line cracked the thicket's face. The line zigzagged from the ground to the sky, and happy, yellow light glinted from the other side. The tiny line slowly widened and widened. Warmth replaced cold, and the boys forgot it was winter.

"Th...they're...opening," Sebastian said. His voice rising and falling like he was talking through the *chopping* of a whirling fan.

The impenetrable briar wall unzipped and revealed the hidden entrance to the *Clearing*. "This is the real *Clearing*," Sherman said. He returned the sword to his pocket and threw his arms around the boys. Piper and Sebastian clung to Sherman's legs, not knowing what to expect, but anticipating the greatest of things.

They weren't disappointed.

The boys were wide-eyed and fully convinced they were dreaming. Whether it was a nightmare or a fantasy hadn't been decided. They wanted to say something, but their vocabulary failed them. Everything they knew about the world changed. Their one constant was Sherman. They turned to him for comfort but found none

Their great-grandpa was no longer the old man they knew. In the warmth of the *Clearing*, Sherman pulled off his coat and toboggan.

Wearing only boots, jeans, and a tee-shirt, Sherman resembled their great-grandpa, but it was a slight resemblance only. His bald head was gone. In its place was a brown, floppy mop that touched his ears and curled. His skin was healthy, tight, and brown, and his ugly, black and sinister-crimson age spots vanished as if erased by God's time-eraser. He was changed, new, and somehow *fresh*.

Sherman was young again, looked as young as Piper and Sebastian's mama and daddy. Muscles ran like steel cables through his chest and arms, and his leg muscles bulged and threatened to shred his jeans Hulk-style each time he stepped. He looked taller, and a ruler would have proven it a fact. He stood three inches taller and weighed a couple hundred pounds more. His ears and nose were again proportionate to his head.

This wasn't Sherman's young body. It was his spirit body, a term that would've meant nothing to Piper and Sebastian if Sherman had told them, so he didn't. He let them think he was young again.

The zigzag doorway zipped itself shut behind them, and the *Clearing* came to life.

Sebastian put his head in his hands and started crying. "I wanna go home." His thumb went instinctively to his mouth, his mind retreated to the safety of infancy.

Piper hugged his brother. "What's up, little bro? Don't be scared. This place is like...well it's heaven." There were no streets of gold or pearly gates, so Piper knew it wasn't heaven. He thought maybe it was a sample of heaven; maybe a new Eden.

Slowly, Sebastian came around. He opened his eyes for a second, then for two seconds, then for three. Eventually he was able to leave them open. His tears dried and with great effort, he audibly *popped* his thumb from his mouth.

The *Clearing* was beyond Sebastian's imagination and outside his vocabulary, and he couldn't express what he was feeling. "Gosh," was all he could say. The sights thrilled him. The sounds—when they weren't scaring the shit out of him—excited him more than he'd known possible. He achieved his first erection, and that growth was scarier than anything he saw or heard.

Unicorns pranced in the distance. Some of them were pink and they all flew on tiny, white wings. Sebastian swore one of them winked at him. Were they real or just figments of his imagination? He quickly figured it didn't matter because they were *cool beans* either way.

A monkey walked by in a black top hat. As the bearded old simian passed, he tipped his hat to Sebastian in a silent *Good day, my good man* gesture. Sebastian, taken aback and not knowing the proper response to a *good day* from a monkey, did a curtsey. The monkey was pleased enough and didn't mind the feminine gesture from the human boy.

Sebastian looked to Sherman, mouth agape, and jerked his thumb over and over toward the monkey and mouthed *a monkey.* He didn't dare speak it because he was afraid he might jinx the illusion.

Three birds walked by. They talked about the mild weather and complained about the lack of food. According to the grumpy red one with the orange beak, worms weren't as plentiful as they had been when he hatched. None of them tipped their hats to Sebastian, and they got no curtsey from him. The monkey watched from the distance and laughed. Nobody liked those damned angry birds.

The brothers held hands and strolled through the knee-high, blue and red grass that populated much of the *Clearing*. They were burning up and sweating profusely but didn't have the stability of mind to remove their coats. They were mesmerized by the *Clearing's* magic. Piper bent to pick a flower. It looked like a rose, but when he closed his grip around it, it protested.

"What do you think you're doing, young man?" Rose slapped his hand with three of her petals and made sure a thorn or two poked him. "That is no way to touch a lady." He grabbed his little brother, and they darted away from Rose, laughing and punching each other on the arms.

They walked across the pond to the far side of the *Clearing,* not even aware they didn't sink because abnormal things are normal in abnormal places. They met fish that walked and greeted them with puckered lips. There were bears and lions and tigers smoking cigars, and those ignored the boys entirely. Piper was upset and wanted to hear them speak, but Sebastian was content to be ignored by the predators.

Sometimes the best attention is no attention, thought Sebastian, and he shared his thought with his brother. Piper took a second look at the apex predators' gleaming white fangs and decided his little brother was right.

A band of mermaids sunned on the pond's rocky beach and beckoned to them to step into the water. "It's always the right temperature, boys. Join us, won't you?"

"Something's fishy," Piper said. The scent was in the air. "Get it? *Something's fishy.*" Piper giggled at his cleverness as the prettiest mermaid slipped under the pond's surface and splashed the boys with a mighty swish of her scaly tail.

Sebastian got it, all right. He got it and was ready to get away from it. The mermaids were too fishy, so he pinched his nose tightly and backed away from the water. "Let's go, Piper. I don't think we should be here."

The brothers darted from the half-human creatures. They insisted they weren't running because they were afraid. They only ran because it had to be time for them to go home.

They didn't know how long they'd been there, but they'd walked for miles and knew they'd been there a long, long time. Their mama had to be looking for them. If they were too late, their daddy would look for them, and if Clark got involved, he'd want to *talk hard* to them. If Susan got in the way, as she always did, Clark would *talk* to her, as well.

Believing it was time to go, the brothers laced fingers and skipped back to their great-grandpa.

Sherman stood in the shade of a giant oak, watching the boys gallop toward him. "It's gotta be time to go," Piper said.

"There's no hurry, boys. Time can't touch us here."

There was light but no sun. It was daylight, but that meant nothing because it was always daylight when light was needed, and always night when darkness was required. Time didn't exist, not in the land of eternity and home of forever. No matter how long they stayed in the *Clearing*, when they stepped back through the briar wall, only one minute would have passed.

Sherman jumped high in the air, crossed his legs, and light as a feather, floated to the grass. He patted the ground next to him, and the boys joined him.

"Great-grandpa, I want to come here every day!" Piper said. He pointed over his head to a dangling triangle of juicy grapes. "Can we eat those, or will they bite back?" Piper remembered Rose's lesson well.

Sherman gave them the go-ahead. "Yes, eat your fill. There are apples, oranges, and bananas here too." There were other fruits the boys had never heard of.

Sherman's favorites were *Flarmies,* which he explained tasted like a cross between cherries and pomegranates but looked like miniature cantaloupes. *Gobbles* were an especially sweet, round fruit that looked like yellow plums, but tasted like sugar-sweet watermelons. Ursa's favorite were *Sappydrops*.

Sappydrops didn't grow on trees or vines but appeared sporadically on the ground. They would stay around for an indeterminate amount of time and vanish without warning. In a world with no day and night cycle it was impossible to pinpoint when they might show up. According to Ursa, not knowing when or if they would appear made them taste even better. Sherman thought their name was fitting since they tasted like pine sap to him.

The boys stuck with the traditional fruit because sometimes familiar is best.

Sebastian polished off his third green apple and started whining about a stomachache that continued growing until it was a proper case of diarrhea. While Sebastian was taking care of his business behind a tree, Piper tapped his great-grandpa's shoulder over and over like he was tapping out Morse code.

Sebastian returned to his companions. Shame-faced but grinning, he warned them, "Don't go over there."

"Great-grandpa, tell us more about Kelvin," Piper said. He stopped tapping Sherman and kicked off his shoes then removed his socks.

"As you wish, my boy. Kelvin wanted to stay in the house and was upset he'd been pushed out to the shed. The reason he wanted to stay in the house was because he wanted to be close to my sisters."

Chapter Sixteen

Kelvin's evil manifested immediately but went unnoticed for two weeks. At first, he worked hard, kept his head down, and focused on Priority One: Getting on everyone's good side.

His insatiable appetite made it impossible to keep up the charade. It had to be fed, and each time he fed it, it grew. Like an evil black hole, it got bigger and hungrier with each feeding, and the greater the thrill he fed it, the faster it grew.

The day Kelvin arrived Robert introduced him to everyone. Barbara remembered Kelvin from a family reunion fifteen years ago, but it was a first-time meeting for the others. Kelvin shook hands and smiled like a carnival barker or Baptist minister. Everybody loved him. Rosalyn loved him more than the rest because she was a teenage hormone machine who didn't quite understand the blood ties linking them. A wild firework show erupted when their hands touched, and Kelvin knew he had to have her.

That evening, Kelvin had his first meal with his new family, and sitting next to Rosalyn at the oval table, their knees touched. They locked eyes briefly and both grinned.

Harmless.

Later that evening, Kelvin jacked off in their bathroom for the first time.

The bathroom was designed for space conservation and utility. There was a toilet on the north end, a tub and shower unit on the south end, and a sink hung off the wall between them. The laundry basket slid under the sink, easy to see and out of the way. The door swung inward and missed the tub by six inches, the sink by a foot, and the toilet by eighteen inches.

Kelvin came in, stood by the sink, and closed the door. He urinated standing in front of the toilet the way most men do and then washed his hands the way more men should.

He didn't go in looking for a thrill or intending to rub one out. He had to pee, so he went to the bathroom. Kelvin washed his hands and looked at the laundry basket. A pair of pink, cotton panties was on top. They were a lighthouse beacon his obsession could no more turn down than he could rope the moon.

I'm not touching that, he lied to himself as he bent and snatched the panties like someone was racing him to them.

Kelvin dropped his pants and pee-stained underwear, closed the toilet lid, and sat down. He examined the panties and checked their size. Whose were they?

Size...small.

Color...pink.

Pink was a girly color and was no help in identifying the owner, but the small size narrowed the field to two. Barbara's *small panties' days* were behind her. It's not that she was fat, because she wasn't, not at all. She was just too wide for small panties after pushing out seven babies, four of them busting through at nine pounds and three ripping her at ten. This pink treasure was peeled off Karen or Rosalyn's sweaty *seams*.

Kelvin wanted them to be Rosalyn's, so they were Rosalyn's, at least to him. He held the crotch to his nose and inhaled deeply. The cotton was richly feminine, musky, and wild, totally feral. Smelling wasn't enough, just a tease. Kelvin had to *know* it better. His heart pounded and his sandpapery tongue was white and dry. He raked it over the panties' cotton crotch and tasted what was there.

He didn't intend to masturbate any more than he'd intended to pick up the pink cotton to begin with. Kelvin did what he did because he was what he was. Intention had nothing to do with it.

After the first time, there were countless panty-licking episodes each day, but each one was less thrilling than its predecessor. Kelvin stopped licking the crotches and started chewing them while he handled his business. For him, they were cottonized, pussy-flavored gum!

Nine out of ten perverts can't be wrong, Chew Crotch Gum.

He was ecstatic the first time he put the whole crotch in his mouth and the flavors exploded. After a week though, his appetite, that Black Hole, expanded again and *Crotch Gum* was just dirty panties. The Black Hole was insatiable, and screamed, "*Bigger! Bigger!*"

No longer content with just one pair, each night he selected two pairs of panties and no longer gave a rip whose they were. One pair went in his mouth. The other he wrapped around his penis like a holy shroud and stroked until he came, always careful to not soil the panties. Leaving them stiff with dry come would've been a dead giveaway and Barbara would've known what it was when she washed the laundry.

His new perversion satisfied the Black Hole for a week, maybe ten days, but as always, excitement was lost in repetition. He shrouded it, chewed the *Crotch Gum*, licked, and snorted the panties all he could, but Kelvin's flaccid penis refused to cooperate. He had to have something new, something bigger. It had to be phenomenal.

Work, damn you, WORK, he mentally screamed at his limp dick. He worked it inside the panties, stroking hard like a madman priming a busted pump. Disgusted with it, he hung his head not in shame or regret, but in a blind rage. Rosalyn was his original target, but he'd tasted all their panties and made room for Barbara and Karen in his fantasies. *I know how you all taste, now I have to know what it feels like to be in you,* he mulled. He worked the panties through his hands like the Devil's *Rosary* and so deep was his concentration, he forgot they were in his hands.

He didn't think of it the way a man thinks of a solution to a complicated math problem. The idea came to him the way *ah-ha* moments always do, flying in out-of-the-blue. Kelvin stood, pulled up his pants, and without a thought, he crammed the panties in his pocket while he was zipping up. He washed his hands and reached to unlock the door. He remembered the panties.

He didn't return them.

The next day, Kelvin came in for breakfast especially upbeat. "Good morning, everybody," he greeted the sleepy-eyed Lancasters. They grunted salutations but only Rosalyn bothered with whole words.

"Good morning," she said. Kelvin's handsome smile stretched across his face. His eyes beamed life and joy and all the pleasures Rosalyn wanted to claim for herself. He'd been terribly solemn lately, inching ever closer to absolute doldrum, but this morning the old Kelvin was back.

"How are you this morning?" Rosalyn asked. She didn't know her panties were stretched over Kelvin's throbbing penis.

Wearing the panties in front of them, them clueless to his sin, was his biggest thrill yet.

Kevin changed panties three times the first day, making sure he wore each pair in front of each girl, so he'd know he was looking at the owner of the panties he was wearing. The second day he stretched all three panties on at the same time, and although the pressure on his balls was crushing, he wore them all day. By day four or five, the panties were too stretched to return. Day seven, he burned them behind the house because they no longer smelled like his women. Now, they were acrid like his sweaty balls. Night seven, he swiped three more pairs from the laundry basket.

Day eight, the shit hit the fan.

Chapter Seventeen

Rosalyn came home from school, trudged up the driveway and ate her snack in dreadful anticipation of the chores to come. The one bright spot on her horizon was Kelvin, and she would soon be outside with him. Their occasional glances, swapped while he was working on whatever he was working on and while she was feeding dogs or dumping chicken poop, were quick at first, barely more than blinks thrown in each other's direction. Three weeks in, they were up to lustful stares that were only a step away from full-fledged *eye-fucks*.

Question: Who can tell the difference between an *eye-fuck* and leer?

Answer: A teenage girl.

The back door screeched and Kelvin entered. Rosalyn gazed upward, hiding nothing in her big brown eyes. She wanted him, wanted to see him, and wanted to be seen by him, but he didn't look at her. He wiped sweat off his forehead with a filthy red handkerchief and patted Albert's head.

"Whew, that old plow is locked up. I can't get the damned blades off," Kelvin said. He looked at Albert's snack, and not liking what he saw, he moved his eyes to Rosalyn's bowl of vanilla pudding.

"Girly, that looks good," he said. "You wanna give me some?"

It wasn't anything he said, and it wasn't the way he said it. It was an internal click, Rosalyn's own *a-ha* moment. She'd never taken her eyes off Kelvin, waiting patiently the way only young girls in love can wait. Kelvin turned his eyes upward, caught her stare, and for the first time Rosalyn doubted her first love's intentions.

Kelvin read her face accurately and quickly. His face transformed as surely as the caterpillar transforms into the butterfly, but rather than taking a month, the change was instantaneous. He threw his best *eye-fuck* her way, and she did her best to return one. She couldn't give up on love because of one strong rapey vibe. That's not how love works, nor how true love dies.

True love died that afternoon when Rosalyn put away her clothes.

Barbara washed the family's clothes every morning during the farming months. She took a break during the winter, only washing every other day because without farm labor, clothes didn't dirty-up as fast. She washed the clothes and if it wasn't raining, she hung them on the line. Each afternoon, she brought the clothes in, folded them, and placed them in neat stacks at the foot of everyone's bed.

Rosalyn did her chores begrudgingly, not able to look Kelvin's way no matter how badly her little heart wanted to. When she finished, she came inside, washed up, and put away the day's clean laundry. Shirts she put in one drawer. Shorts went in another. Bra went in the with panties...but where was yesterday's panties? This was the second time she'd noticed panties missing from her stack of clothes. She checked Karen's stack, and same as before when she checked, Karen didn't have panties either.

Did I not change panties? she quizzed herself but knew the answer. She always changed panties. Barbara insisted it was healthy, and Rosalyn was deathly afraid of developing into what the boys at school called a *tuna-twat*. The first time they disappeared, she convinced herself the panties must've been too old and worn and her mother threw them away, but she couldn't fool herself twice.

"Mama, did you throw my panties away?" Rosalyn asked.

"Of course not," Barbara replied as she prepared supper dishes.

"Did you see my panties? They weren't with my stack of clothes."

"If I washed them, I put them with your other things. If you didn't put them down last night, I didn't wash them. Now, you better hurry and get cleaned up before supper." Barbara never considered her own panties. Barbara changed panties last night just like Rosalyn and Karen and just like her daughters, Barbara didn't have any panties in her stack either.

It wasn't the creepy look in Kelvin's eyes. It wasn't the missing panties. It wasn't even that rapey vibe her inexperienced *perv-dar* detected from Kelvin that told her the truth about him. It was everything combined. Any one thing by itself wouldn't have changed her mind, but together, they were too much for even her puppy-love to cover.

Rosalyn got her towel and washcloth and locked herself in the bathroom. She stood in the shower longer than she should've, using more than her share of hot water. She cried silently but truly. Her first love ended the way they often do, with her first broken heart.

When the water stopped, the tears did too. She was sickened, convicted of her lustful desires, but mostly, she was madder than a red hornet. She was also determined. *He's had his last cheap thrill*, thought Rosalyn.

"Mama, I think you're doing too much work. I want to help," Rosalyn said. "From now on, I'm going to wash the clothes."

The Lancaster's bathroom ritual wasn't handed down by God on precious stone tablets, and when emergencies came up, like the time Robert spilled diesel down his chest and had to take a shower before anyone else, they were handled without complaint. Without emergencies, the bathroom ritual was strictly adhered to out of habit.

Sherman was first because he was usually around the house doing nothing, so it was easy to get him in and out of the tub. Karen was second, Rosalyn was third, Albert rushed in fourth, and just before supper, Barbara jumped in for a quick shower that was much cooler than she liked. Supper was served while the water heater churned, gurgled, and screamed out thirty more gallons of hot water. After supper while Barbara and the kids tidied up the kitchen, Robert took his shower, and the day's last bather was Kelvin.

After Barbara finished her cooler-than-everyone-else's shower, Rosalyn slipped into the bathroom before supper was served. She replaced the laundry basket with an empty one and crammed the dirty clothes in the washer. "I'll hang those out first thing in the morning," she told her mama.

"Be sure you don't forget, or I'll have to wash them again," Barbara said, fully expecting to have to rewash them tomorrow.

Robert took his bath and retired to his recliner. Ready to replace the panties he'd torched, Kelvin went in the bathroom for his daily dose of panty sniffing and crotch chewing. Rosalyn listened. She wanted to hear him curse or moan or something, anything, but she heard nothing. The shower came on, *splish-splash*, the shower went off, and a few minutes later, Kelvin came out said goodnight to everyone and went to his room in the shed.

Score one for the good guys.

Kelvin was fiery pissed. *That little bitch. I can't wait to make her feel it.*

The next day, Theodore was running a do-all over a hundred acres of rented land when something *clanged* loud enough to get his attention over the engine's roar. A second after the *clang,* the tractor jerked violently to the right and almost threw him out of the seat. A support chain broke and *clanged* against the back of the cab. Before Theodore could press the brakes, the harrow crashed onto the ground, digging in like an anchor and jerked the John Deere to the side. He removed the harrow, put it on top of the do-all, and limped to the tractor shed. It was a simple repair, and he expected to finish the field after lunch.

Theodore unhooked from the busted do-all and parked the tractor by the fuel tanks. He killed the rumbling diesel to let it cool before refueling. He called Kelvin but didn't get an answer. It was close to lunch, so he figured he'd catch him in the house. Theodore kicked his boots off and went inside. Sherman launched a guerrilla attack on his older brother.

Of course, the ambush failed. Theodore grabbed Sherman by his ankles, flipped him upside down, and dangled him by his heels. Because he was hanging upside down, and because gravity sucks that way, the contents of Sherman's pockets spilled out into the world. The six-year-old, dirt poor, farm-boy didn't own much, and all he had in his pockets was dirt and a few small, round rocks earmarked as slingshot ammo. Thanks to sucky gravity, the dirt and rocks fell into Sherman's open mouth.

"You seen Kelvin?" Theodore asked Sherman.

"Negative," the future Parchman prison alumni answered.

Barbara came around the corner, hugged her eldest son, and confirmed Kelvin's absence. "I saw him for breakfast, but I haven't seen him since. Me and the *booger* have been in the garden all morning, so I haven't really been looking for him. Do you want us to help you find him?"

Theodore thanked his mama but told her it wasn't a big deal. Kelvin would show up eventually. With that, Barbara grabbed Sherman's shoulders and directed him back to the garden and Theodore went outside and ate his lunch under the shade of a hundred-year-old mulberry.

Theodore didn't eat slowly, but he ate slower than usual, thinking Kelvin might show. Kelvin never showed, and Theodore finished his lunch and walked to the garden to tell his mama goodbye. Theodore told Barbara that when she saw Kelvin to tell him the do-all needed repairing as soon as possible.

Theodore hugged Barbara, punched Sherman in the gut, and went back to work.

Theodore fueled the thirsty diesel, hooked-up the hippers, and quit worrying about the do-all. It was a worry, but not his. If, by chance, he finished rowing up the other fields before the *Incredible Disappearing Cousin* fixed the do-all, Theodore would come back and fix it himself.

Theodore drove the tractor out of the farm's circular drive, turned north and passed the front of the house. Half of driving a tractor is *hoot-owling* your neck to check the implement behind you. Theodore *hoot-owled* and thought for just a moment that he saw a head peeking out of the curtains in Karen and Rosalyn's room.

A barely audible brain-voice suggested, *It's Kelvin. He's in your sisters' room*. Theodore considered the suggestion but failed to come up with any reason why Kelvin would be in there. Theodore put the crazy thought out of his mind and figured it must've been Sherman peeking out, because Sherman never needed a reason to do something foolish.

Kelvin woke up that morning in a fit. He'd burned his only panties because they were stretched, and he was sure he could replace them. But he was wrong because the little bitch washed clothes before he could restock. The laundry basket had been empty. It could've meant nothing, but Kelvin was smarter than that. It meant everything. It meant Rosalyn knew.

It was a blessing. That's what he decided. If he'd been able to keep up the panty thefts, he might've postponed advancing to the next stage of his plan. Rosalyn's move was just the kick-in-the-ass he needed. The panty-play was over, and his appetite demanded bigger things. Kelvin knew his next move. It was always part of his plan. It was time to do it.

Kelvin kicked things up a notch and when Barbara and Sherman went to the garden, Kelvin snuck into the girls' bedroom.

Chapter Eighteen

*A*t breakfast that morning Barbara let everyone know it was house-cleaning day. She said this not because anybody cared what she did, she said it to put everyone on notice. Get what you want. Get out. Stay out.

Barbara didn't tolerate people tracking through the house while she cleaned. The least they could do was wait until it was clean before they dirtied it up again. Conversationally, she added that she was also going to walk to the garden and pick as many hornworms as she could find. With fifty tomato plants, it would take the rest of the morning, and half of the afternoon to find the elusive green worms camouflaged among the plants' green leaves.

Kelvin smoked and pretended to work, but only watched the back door and waited for Barbara to make her way to the garden. A pack of Camels later, Barbara and Sherman disappeared into the five-acre garden and Kelvin slipped around the opposite end of the house and entered through the front door. He quickly made it to Karen and Rosalyn's room and closed the door behind him.

In the room, he gazed from wall-to-wall like a man who'd just summited Everest. The air in there was crisper, fresher; a little closer to God. Kelvin looked at the double bed the sisters shared and imagined taking both girls there at the same time. *I'll make them touch each other.* His pulse raced and a dizzy, white film settled over his eyes. Nearly faint, he slowed his breathing. His pulse and eyesight returned to normal.

He'd jacked-off enough and licked and chewed enough crotches to last him a lifetime. He had to see what he'd been tasting, see what he'd soon feel from the inside. Kelvin the Panty Thief was dead. Now, he was Kelvin the Peeping Tom.

Kelvin tried the closet first. The doors were full-length mirrors and set on tracks. He opened one side. Disgusted with all their junk, he opened the other side. The closet was packed with cardboard boxes with fountains of old pictures spilling over their tops, along with stacks of shoes and old magazines. The racks were packed accordion-tight with shirts, skirts, and blue jeans. Peeping from there was out of the question. His only option was under the bed. *I'm the boogeyman under your bed*, he thought with a lunatic smile.

He knelt, looked under the bed, and was immediately discouraged. There were shoe boxes all around the outside rim. Frustrated at all their girl-shit, he examined the area closer and was thankful he did. The boxes were pulled to the outside for easy reach. Behind the boxes was an empty, man-sized cavity. *Girls and all their shit*, he thought again, but this time with a smile.

Working quickly, he shuffled the boxes out of his way, slid under the bed, and pulled the boxes back into place. With the wall of boxes shielding him, he was hidden from everything except the closest examination. If they checked that closely, he'd bypass his clandestine plans and take them right then and there.

He checked the angles and found his best view came from lying on his stomach and looking out from the foot of the bed. Thanks to the full-length mirrors on their closet doors, Kelvin would get the whole show, front and back anytime one of the girls undressed.

Kelvin counted his blessings. He had the perfect hiding-hole and hadn't been bothered by Barbara or her retarded baby boy. He heard them in the kitchen talking to Theodore, but none of them came in the girls' room. A little later, Theodore opened the throttle on the John Deere and Kelvin pulled the curtains back to watch the tractor pass. Kelvin's head was only visible for a few seconds, a flash Theodore was able to dismiss.

It'd been a highly productive morning, and Kelvin returned to the tractor shed. He worked on the do-all for the rest of day, but never fixed it. He'd worked like a man possessed when he first got there, but with each passing week, he did less. He was bidding his time, and his wait was almost over.

Robert came home just before dark. He'd been training all day and his clothes were soaked with sweat. He reeked of strong ammonia and kept his windows down on the way home as to not gas himself. When Barbara tried to kiss him, she turned away in disgust. "You smell like a passel of cats peed on you." She then told him to take a bath before supper.

"Well thanks, honey. That's exactly what a fellow wants to hear from his gal."

"Don't forget to shower before you sit at my table." She pinched his cheeks. "I love you even if you do smell like cat pee." She held her breath and kissed his lips.

"Mama..." That's what Robert called Barbara when kids were around. "I'm going to check on Kelvin before I hop in the shower."

"Theodore had trouble with the do-all today but couldn't find Kelvin to fix it. I don't know if it got fixed or not. Oh, it may be nothing, but Rosalyn said Kelvin's acting a little...well, a little *forward* with her and Karen. And I hate to say it, but he's getting on my nerves a bit too." Barbara then whispered, "Maybe you can put him on the right path."

"I'll talk to him," Robert said. What he would say to Kelvin was a different matter. Barbara didn't give him much to go on. *Acting forward.* That could mean anything, but it probably meant nothing. Robert brushed his lips against Barbara's and left to find his cousin.

"Kelvin, whatcha' up to?" Robert asked as he stepped behind the shed. Kelvin sat on a bottom-upwards five-gallon bucket with a burnt-down cigarette in his mouth and one in his hand waiting to get called up. Robert paid zero attention to how Kelvin was dressed but didn't miss the whiskey bottle clamped between Kelvin's legs.

Kelvin saw the object of Robert's attention and said, "Hey, Robert. You want a pull?" Kelvin held out a nearly empty whiskey bottle.

"There ain't a decent pull left in that damn jug. Kelvin, that bottle was supposed to last you the month out. What's it been, a week n' a half since I gave it to you?"

"Yeah, I worked pretty hard on that International today and probably woulda' finished it if Theo hadn't brought that do-all by for repairs. I've been polishing off this bottle, listening to the radio, and relaxing before supper. Join me," Kelvin flipped another bucket upside down for Robert. "Hell Robert, if you want to, we can go into town and get another jug."

Robert wanted a swig of Wild Turkey but didn't want it bad enough to deal with Barbara when she smelled it on his breath. "I think I'll skip."

Robert decided, without consciously deciding, to not mention Barbara's complaints to Kelvin. Instead, Robert asked, "Why did it take so long to fix the do-all? Shouldn't have taken more than half n' hour to fix." He didn't care much for the way Kelvin's shifty eyes refused to meet his own.

"Well, Robert, there was more to it than that," Kelvin said. He sealed the empty bottle and sat there like a scolded puppy.

Robert realized Kelvin was more than a little lazy, but Robert hadn't yet scratched the surface of Kelvin's character defects. "Supper'll be on soon. Let's eat so we can get to bed early. I'll stay here tomorrow and help you get caught up," Robert said, hoping his presence would curtail any trouble brewing in his absence.

Kelvin showered earlier that day and came to the house wearing his best Sunday suit. It was a high-sheen, powder-blue polyester that hurt to look at under the kitchen's harsh incandescent lights. When Kelvin walked in, Barbara said, "What's the special occasion? We don't normally put on our best clothes for supper unless royalty is coming." She did a double-take, then a triple, and couldn't help snickering. Kelvin looked ridiculous in that blue puke of a suit while everybody else was wearing shorts and white tees.

"No, ma'am. I just wanted to look nice for supper. To show my appreciation for all y'all have done for me." Her snicker flushed his cheeks. The redder he got, the madder he got. *I'll get you too, you smart-mouthed bitch.*

"Well you look very nice and you're welcome," she said. It wasn't a lie if it was said to make someone feel better, and she had to say something to make up for the snicker.

No more was said about his attire. The color left his cheeks, but his anger didn't subside. They prayed the blessing and ate in relative silence, because with that many people, all silence is relative. Kelvin felt the eyes of the family on him and had a pretty damn good idea what a goldfish felt like. He was a spectacle, and deep inside, he knew they knew he was up to something.

Fuck'em. I won't be denied.

He would have his day, and they would get what was coming to them.

"Kelvin, I guess we'll start on the do-all in the morning. That's the most pressing, ain't it?" Robert asked.

Kelvin smiled a greasy but easy smile. "I think you're right, Robert." He didn't care what they worked on tomorrow. He just wanted everybody to stop staring, stop looking at him before they saw through him.

There were plenty of other things to fix. Broken equipment was a staple on small farms. There was never enough money to fix everything, so the farmers performed rural *triage,* fixing what was most important. Currently, the do-all claimed the top spot. Next in line was the potato-setter because it would soon be needed in the field. The potato digger was on the list but was farther down because it wasn't needed until the end of the summer. Even though it wasn't needed immediately, Robert planned to fix the digger as soon as the must-haves were repaired. If Robert was exceptionally lucky, and he was counting on being exceptionally lucky, the mild weather would hold out and he would begin harvesting in August, a month ahead of schedule.

Robert hadn't mentioned to anyone other than Kelvin that he was planning a rushed trip to Alabama to buy parts to fix the digger. Kelvin didn't mention to anyone at all that while Robert was in Alabama, Kelvin planned to feed his slimy appetite the ultimate meal.

When all the plates were empty and everybody had a full belly, Kelvin pushed away from the table. "Barbara, Karen, thank y'all so much for that meal. It was a feast, for sure."

"You're very welcome. We'll see you for breakfast, Kelvin. God bless and goodnight," Barbara said.

Karen said nothing. She and Rosalyn ignored him all night and didn't even look his way when he thanked her.

Barbara, Karen, and Rosalyn put away the leftovers and cleared the table. Albert and Sherman washed, rinsed, dried, and put away the dishes. When the dishes were dried and put away, Barbara read *Goodnight Moon* and *Where the Wild Things Are* to Sherman and put him to bed early, because she and Robert had plans

The head and footboard of their bed were made of wrought iron, and the springs were older than Karen. She and all her siblings were conceived on the old mattress and box-springs. How old was the bed? Neither Barbara nor Robert could remember for sure, but they agreed to something in the neighborhood of twenty-seven years. They bought them either immediately before or immediately after they were married, but tonight it didn't matter.

The bed got the working out of a lifetime and old or not, it held up just fine.

From the shed came noises not entirely unlike those from Barbara and Robert's bedroom. These noises were the sound of a man lost in his fantasies, lost so deeply he forgot the thinness of his walls. Outside those thin walls, two ears heard names that shouldn't have accompanied those sounds.

Karen was going to do *this*. The ears didn't understand what *this* was, but the ears were sure Karen would object to doing it. Rosalyn was going to do *that*. The ears knew for a fact that Rosalyn hated Kelvin and wasn't doing *that* with him, whatever *that* was. Barbara was going to give him *head*. Kelvin already had a head so the listening ears didn't know why Kelvin wanted Barbara's head, but the ears were certain that Robert would take all of Kelvin's heads if he messed with Barbara at all.

Kelvin kept on and on. *He would have them all. It would be sooo good*. The ears had all they could stand, and their feet swiftly carried them to the safety of the house. Those ears also had a mouth, and in the morning, it told all.

Chapter Nineteen

The sun came up one minute before the *Old Farmer's Almanac* said it would and to Barbara, that was pretty good for guesswork. She'd been up since four-thirty reading her Bible, kneeling at the end of the kitchen table in reverent prayer and cooking enough breakfast to feed an army. Looking out the backdoor, she watched the Eastern Star until the rising sun blinded her, vanquishing the star for another day. The oven's timer chimed. It was time to wake the rest of the family.

Everybody gathered around the big table. The seating arrangement wasn't assigned and had never been planned, but nobody ever sat out of place. A fight would surely have erupted even if the fighters didn't know exactly why they were fighting.

Robert sat at the head of the table, which was the north end and closest to the backdoor. From his position, he could watch for any deer or turkey foolish enough to venture into the open field behind the house. Barbara sat on his right side. Kelvin, the newcomer, sat on

Robert's left in a position created just for him. It sat at an angle off the corner, a wedge rather than a genuine position.

Down from Barbara and finishing the right side was Albert's place. The next position was the foot of the table, opposite Robert's head position, and the spoiled-brat, baby boy occupied that position with pride. To Sherman's right, on the other side of the table was Karen's position. Rosalyn sat between Karen and Kelvin and was the least happy about the seating arrangement.

Rosalyn usually sat at her daddy's left hand. Now, Kelvin was wedged in there. When Kelvin first arrived, Rosalyn loved the arrangement. She and Kelvin rubbed knees and occasionally played a little innocent footsie. Not anymore. Rosalyn sat as close to her sister and as far from Kelvin as Karen's elbows would allow.

Breakfast went off without a hitch. No fights and surprisingly, there weren't any fusses. The school kids dressed and walked to the end of the driveway to wait on the school bus. Robert and Kelvin went to work outside. Sherman got his toys and tried to stay out of the way while Karen and Barbara cleaned the kitchen.

Sherman returned to help with the dishes once everything was off the table. Karen washed the dishes and silently wished her baby brother would stop helping. His help cost her time and often ended in a bigger mess than the original one. She tolerated him though because that was the sort of thing big sisters did.

Albert waited until he saw Kelvin walk to the shed before saying anything. Instead of telling his mama or daddy, he told Rosalyn. "I was outside last night after supper, and I heard Kelvin making noises. He sounded like he was *going-at-it* with himself, and he was saying your name over and over. He said he was going to give *it* to you. He said the same thing about mama and Karen. It was sick."

Albert didn't know what *going-at-it* was exactly, but he had some idea after listening to the older kids on the playground talk about it. He looked at Rosalyn, pretended to poke his finger down his throat, and made gagging sounds at the thought of what was going on in the shed.

"Yuck!" Rosalyn said. Her first impulse was to run back in the house, tell her mama, get her daddy, and have Kelvin beaten to death and buried in the back forty.

What to do? What to do? Did she go back to the house and tell, or wait?

What to do? She decided to take the day to think it over.

"Let's go to school and I'll take care of it when we get home. Don't say anything to anybody else. I mean it, Albert. Keep it to yourself." Rosalyn's eyes said she meant it. Really meant it. She *Big-Sister-Meant-It*, and Albert knew better than disobey her.

"I didn't even want to tell you. I ain't telling nobody else. I want to wash my ears out and pretend I didn't hear it."

Kelvin was definitely a creepo, a sicko, and she'd been foolish to ever think she'd loved him. *What kind of grown man plays footsie with a teenage girl*, she thought now that she didn't want him. Rosalyn was going to see Kelvin pack his bags and leave for good, and she was going to see it sooner rather than later. If things went her way, he was leaving tonight.

Things didn't go her way.

Chapter Twenty

Susan was determined not to cry. Her legs and back hurt, her kidneys felt three sizes too big. After Mr. Wilcott's phone call, Clark *talked hard* to her. She hid it from her grandpa the way she always did, but alone in the car, everything throbbed. Hiding Clark's abuse was easy because Clark only hit the *hidden places*. Susan thought her kidneys had bullseyes drawn on them because Clark's fists always found them.

This morning her urine darkened the toilet's water, and for the first time she feared Clark might actually go too far one day and really hurt her—maybe even kill her. She had to get away, but that was for later. Right now, she had two boys depending on her. Stoically, she pressed on.

Fighting back tears, not sure whether they were from anger or pain, she stopped at Wilcott Furniture for her belongings. She parked at the front door on the curb, not in a parking space and left her engine running.

The fat, unfriendly receptionist sat behind a four-foot-high counter, which thankfully hid most of her body. Her bouffant hair, the color of soap scum rose over the counter as a warning to stay away. As Susan approached, the receptionist, a hog who'd never liked Susan because the sow wanted to be sexed-up by Chris Wilcott, smirked and heaved a cardboard box over the counter.

Susan wanted to lose it right there, grab the receptionist's poofy hair, and scream at the unfairness, but didn't. Instead, Susan took the box and thanked the receptionist.

"Have a blessed day," Susan said. Her kind words were spears to the rude bitch's heart.

In the car Susan tears wouldn't wait any longer but she refused to cry. The tears fell on their own, somehow lonelier without Susan's sobs. The Job Service wouldn't open for thirty minutes, so Susan drove to the city park to wait. Susan thought she was in control, but as she slid the shifter into park, the tears came again.

Sniffling, she pushed her seat back as far as it would go and sat the box in her lap. The first thing she pulled out was the bracelet Clark gave her for their first wedding anniversary. He'd told her it was gold, real gold like their love. She was young, naïve, and enthusiastically believed him. She had to admit she wasn't surprised when it turned her arm green and stuck to a magnet when she'd finally worked up the courage to test it.

The bracelet wasn't real gold like her lying, lousy excuse of a husband wasn't real gold. Susan lowered her window and threw the bracelet into the duck pond. It splashed and quickly sank. Susan wished Clark would join it at the bottom.

Next, she removed a shiny, brass picture frame from the box. It was hinged in the middle and held two, four by six photos. Without opening it, she knew the faces inside were the two most beautiful faces she'd ever seen. She opened it and stared into her sons' eyes, first one, and then the other. "Mama is going to take care of y'all. I'll get another job. We'll be fine," she told them to reassure herself.

Everything else in the box was meaningless office garbage. There were pencils, pens, a stapler—Swingline, not Boston and red of course—pushpins, and sticky pads.

There was a small calculator with a broken LCD display that made it impossible to tell eights from sixes and a wireless mouse that only worked with the company's computer.

There was a pencil sharpener that wasn't hers, but she was keeping it as severance. It wasn't much, but a little is more than nothing.

Susan dried her eyes, sucked in the last of her snot, and removed a floral cosmetic bag from her purse. Through female-designed witchery, the cosmetic bag was bigger than the purse itself. Susan applied her makeup with her compact's tiny round mirror, not because she wanted to, but because it was her only option. She sat it on the dashboard behind the steering wheel and bobbed her head left and right to view her whole face. *This would be much easier with a bigger mirror.*

Susan glanced at the windshield where the rearview mirror once protruded. She shifted her eyes to the roof where the sun visors used to be. There was a small, jagged hole in the windshield where the mirror should've been, and nothing remained of the visors but two tiny holes in the headliner.

She couldn't remember where they were at the time, but knew she was driving. Apparently, Clark was watching her closely. "What color is the car behind you?" Clark screamed. "No," he shouted when she turned to look. "Don't you dare look in that damned mirror now!" He shoved the rearview upwards so all Susan could see was the ratty, brown headliner.

Susan didn't know what color the car was or whether there was a car back there at all. She heard a *pop* when Clark ripped the mirror from the windshield. Small pieces of safety glass sprinkled the dashboard like salt. "If you ain't gonna use it, you don't need it," Clark said.

The sun visors met a similar fate when Susan carelessly checked her makeup while they waited on a red light to turn green. Clark ripped both visors off and tossed them out his window. As she drove to church, trembling and oozing nervous tears, Clark said, "All you ever do is check your damn makeup in those fucking mirrors. You're gonna get us all killed." She would've loved to have known how checking her makeup at a stoplight would facilitate their deaths but was smart enough to not ask.

The pastor preached about self-control, on not losing it. She prayed Clark got the message but didn't think he was listening. Clark sat through the service as he always did, his hand clamped over hers like a vise. It was a reminder, a warning.

I'm here. I'm always here.

Susan arrived at the Job Service a few minutes before they opened. The parking lot was empty, and she prayed it would stay that way. Unemployment was embarrassing, and Houston's Job Service was located on Main Street. Like so many other Main Streets in so many other towns, it was the main drag. Everybody who went anywhere either started or ended their trip by going one way or the other on Main Street. Susan quickly walked in with her head down so if an acquaintance passed, they wouldn't catch a glimpse of her shame.

No need to worry about that, little girl, because everybody you know is at work. They aren't losers like you, her mind said in a voice she immediately recognized as Clark's. It let her know her proper place: *Loser.* The neon sign on the door went from *Closed* to *Open,* and Susan walked inside.

"Good morning. My name is Allison, may I help you?" the chipper receptionist asked. Allison could definitely teach Wilcott's receptionist a thing or two about general politeness and professionalism.

Susan was all smiles looking in at the receptionist through the bulletproof, ballistic glass separating them. After years of hiding Clark's abuse from the world, Susan was a professional makeup artist and could fake emotions like an Oscar winning actress. She was a ball of raw nerves and prickly pain on the inside, but on the outside, she was polite and friendly. The receptionist later described Susan as *bubbly*.

"I'm here to apply, please," Susan whispered toward the tiny perforations in the glass.

"Okay, please take a seat right there," Allison said, pointing to a rather uncomfortable looking chair. "It'll just be a moment. You're our first client of the morning and this old computer takes its sweet time starting. Would you like a cup of coffee while you wait? I just made a fresh pot."

"No thank you," Susan replied. Her bladder was full already, and she was anxious enough to claw off her own skin. Caffeine was not in her best interests. Susan laughed at being called a *client*. She was just another unemployed woman desperately needing to get her butt back to work. *A Loser*, Clark reminded her.

"There's a bubbly blonde out here to see you," Allison told her boss.

"By all means, send her in," the pot-bellied office manager said. "I don't want to keep a bubbly blonde waiting."

"Hello, my name is Peter Jacobs, but go ahead and call me Pete, everybody does. You're looking for work, I'm guessing, or else you wouldn't be here, would you?"

"Yes sir, I am, and I can start right away. Today wouldn't be too early." Out of the blue, she added, "I was fired from my old job last night." *Might as well let 'em know you're a loser from the get-go,* Clark's voice encouraged her. "I was working data entry at Wilcott

Furniture. I was very fast. I don't know if you have any openings for that kind of work, but I'm really good at it."

Peter chuckled, and his good-natured laughter put Susan at ease. "The only position I have for that type of work is the one I received this morning from Wilcott's HR department, no doubt trying to fill your old position. You don't have to tell me, but if you don't mind my asking, why were you fired?"

She decided a lie right here would beat the hell out of the truth. Besides, who was ever going to believe that a beggar, a *loser*, like her had been fired for turning down a man's advances? Women like her, *losers*, didn't turn men down. They jumped at every swinging dick that swung their way.

"I don't mind your asking, and I'd be happy to tell you if I knew. I thought everything was going great. I got a call last night and they fired me over the phone. That was the first I knew of there being a problem." Susan then said she'd showed up on time, worked hard all day, worked overtime when they needed her, and she minded her own business. She didn't know what had happened.

"Have you got anything else along those lines? If not, I'll take whatever you have available. I really need to get back to work as soon as possible. I have two young sons who've grown accustomed to eating at regular intervals."

"I'm pretty sure we can find you something, but we're getting ahead of ourselves. This was just a shake hands and say good morning meeting. So good morning," he put his hand out. She took it, pumped it a few times, and surprised him with the strength of her shake. "Allison will give you an application, and once it's filled out, we'll see what we can find for you."

Susan thanked him, for nothing other than talking to her and not throwing her out on her *loser* ass. The application was on a clipboard with a blue ballpoint pen tethered to it. It looked to be fifty pages thick. Susan thought it'd take all day just to read it.

"You can fill it out in there," Allison said, pointing to a small room off to the right of the reception area.

"Thank you." Susan traced the invisible line from Allison's finger to an empty chair in the other room.

The chair loomed large and terrifying like *Old Sparky*. Slowly, nearly down to a shuffle, Susan walked toward it. Her heart pounded. Her hands and back were clammy and anxiety threatened to shut off her oxygen supply. She wondered if this was what the condemned felt when they entered Parchman's death chamber.

It was too late to run, and besides that, there was nowhere to run. There was nothing left but to do it, so Susan took a deep breath and walked in.

Chapter Twenty-One

Entering the room, Susan was slapped by and almost fainted from the strongest perfume smell she'd ever had the misfortune of inhaling. Immediately she sneezed and sneezed and sneezed again; there were always three. Two women to her right, probably friends and possibly lovers judging by how closely they were sitting, said, "God bless you" at the same time. Their blessing was polite but did nothing to alleviate the sudden onslaught of pain flowering in Susan's brain. Apparently, the place crowded up while she was talking with Peter Jacobs, because the office was empty while she arrived

The lesbos' look told Susan she wasn't the only one who thought the room smelled like a whore's den. Susan took a seat and scanned the room. Other than the two suspected lesbians, there were seven other applicants, and at least one of them was the inconsiderate cause of the room's fetid odor. Susan couldn't hate them, though. They all looked as desperate as she felt.

You're with your kind now. All losers, her Clark-brain shouted.

Susan thought she'd be embarrassed to beg for a job, even if she was only seen by other people begging for jobs, but she wasn't embarrassed. What she felt wasn't shame. It was warm kinship, like she'd showed up late for her family reunion. Everyone was polite and seemed grateful another family member showed up. Those that didn't speak to her at least gave the friendly, traditional nod that said, "I see you. You're not invisible."

Susan was quick with a return smile and nod of her own. She even said, "Good morning," to a few. Susan took a seat and grunted in the face of the fifty-page application.

A quick flip through the pages greatly relieved her apprehension. The application was thick, fifteen pages including the last, a signature page, but there were multiple applications on the clipboard. *Whew*, she thought. Fifteen pages were bad, but much better than the fifty-page novella she feared.

Susan filled in the blanks and noticed the other applicants were fidgeting and shifting in their chairs as they tried to produce responses most likely to get them hired. After five or six minutes in her chair, Susan fidgeted and shifted, and she understood why no one else was sitting still. Her red chair was easily the most uncomfortable place she'd ever sat. It would be a welcome addition to any *inquisitor's* lair.

The scratched, red seat was hardened plastic coated with a waxy substance of unknown nature. Probably toxic. Kids, or perhaps bored adults, had carved their initials in the wax. The stiff seat was bolted to flimsy metal tubes that angled forward instead of backward and swayed side to side even when she sat perfectly still. The resulting sensation was of being ejected from the wobbly seat that shimmied left to right under its own power.

Susan fought gravity to remain seated. Her kin fought the same battle. The constant fidgeting and shifting filled the room with the squeaks, scoots, and slides of the chairs dancing together in a *u-shaped* chorus line. They weren't the only sounds. The harmony included the applicants' grunts, sighs, and muffled curses. Concentration was out of the question.

She didn't know how many jobs were available but prayed there was a bundle of them. The front door's chime was never silent for more than a few moments at a time. Often before one chime fell silent another person was chiming his or her way inside.

Person after person, the rooms filled quickly. Sometimes two and three came in at the same time. The waiting room was full, and the spillover was flowing into the application room. Susan overheard Allison tell people to come back later because the building had exceeded its fire marshal approved capacity. It was a helluva time to be unemployed, because half the town was unemployed with her.

Clark was one of the lucky ones, if lucky meant lazy. He received a monthly disability check because the poor guy injured his back at his last job. Or so he claimed.

Clark was never one to hold down a job for long stretches. He'd work when he needed a new gun, or a new boat, but would either quit or get fired after he'd bought his new toy. According to him, he was picked on and forced to work harder, longer hours because his bosses or coworkers—usually both—were too lazy to do their portion. Clark was always mistreated. Life wasn't fair. *Poor, poor pitiful Clark*, Susan thought when Clark whined about the injustices he suffered at the hands of an unfair world. Something was wrong with every job he had, and Susan had to provide the stable, dependable income.

Clark's last job was operating a forklift at the wood mill in Bruce. On the day of his *accident*, he was transporting a stack of four-by-fours from the mill to a warehouse. He hit a bump in the concrete, the forklift bounced slightly, and a portion of the load he was carrying tumbled off the forks onto the ground. According to his story, which was supported by his drinking buddies, he was busily restacking the lumber and felt a *'ting* in his back. He immediately went to the company nurse who sent him home with instructions to, "take it easy" for a few days.

Clark was paid for those few days and got a taste for free money. He deserved it for being mistreated over the years. He made an appointment with a shady *sawbones* with a reputation for dishonesty in workers' compensation cases. The doctor stated that the sensation Clark felt, the *'ting*, was a ruptured disk. The damage was permanent, and poor Clark was crippled for life. The laws of the state prevented him from filing a lawsuit against the wood mill, or he would've sought additional compensation for his pain and terrible suffering. "The damn commies down in Jackson love that big business money, so they always fuck the working man," Clark said about Mississippi's lawmakers.

Susan knew he was perfectly able to work. He hunted, fished, and played baseball and football with his good-for-nothing friends. He could find work less stressing than those things, but Clark was a lazy bum and didn't look for work. Now that she was unemployed, Clark's disability check was their only income.

Clark usually spent his monthly check on beer, cigarettes, and bullets. Susan didn't complain because it kept him from spending the money she earned. He didn't know it this morning when she left him in bed nursing another hangover, but he would know soon. They were using his check for food and bills until she found another job.

He could go along willingly if he was smart or after her grandpa's encouragement. One way or the other, he would do it, because Sherman scared the hell out of Clark. Clark would do whatever the old man told him to do, and if he didn't, Susan would love to see the old man make a believer out of Clark.

Susan gave the clipboard with her completed application to Allison. The tethered ink pen refused to hang inside the clip's mouth and swung like a pendulum. When Allison reached for the clipboard, the pen swung back and forth and inked several blue lines on Allison's hand. "Don't worry about it," Allison said, as Susan apologized and frantically searched her purse for an unused napkin. "I look like a sketch drawing every day by closing time." Allison took the application and handed the clipboard to the next person in line. Susan waited.

And she waited.

It was misery, the waiting. Susan remembered a quote by someone suggesting that *the anticipation of death is worse than death itself.* Waiting to die was allegedly worse than dying. She'd always scoffed at the quote because it was written by someone who didn't know what the hell they were talking about, mainly because the author was still alive. Sitting in the waiting room, Susan had a change of heart and started thinking that the quote might be right. Finally, after what seemed like two eternities, Allison stuck her head out of her office and said, "Mrs. Vance, Mr. Jacobs will see you now."

With his office overflowing with the unemployed masses, Peter wasn't nearly as talkative as he'd been earlier. Maybe he couldn't be loquacious, but he was still friendly, professional, and put Susan at ease. "Sit down, Mrs. Vance. I've got good news."

A company was hiring and not just any company. This was a *good* company, a *great* company. They offered higher than average salaries and tons of benefits. He mentioned insurance, lots of vacation time, and profit sharing. "There are other benefits too, too many to mention," were his exact words. That was all great and fine, but the only benefit Susan was interested in was a weekly paycheck. Then, he told her the bad news.

There's always bad news to go along with good news. Bad news often flew solo, but in Susan's experience, good news never left home without its buddy. The bad news was the company only had three positions to fill and there were hundreds of applicants throughout the state vying for the positions. The company was hosting a pre-employment workshop on the coming weekend, and Peter recommended she go if it was at all possible.

"They almost always hire at the close of the workshop," he said. "And your previous experience makes you an ideal candidate."

Susan said she'd be there or be square. He gave her a sealed packet containing directions to the workshop and a thorough itinerary for the two-day event. Susan didn't know how she'd get there or where she'd stay, but she knew she was going. Money was too tight to waste, but she thought it would be a bigger waste not to go, not to try. *Maybe grandpa will watch the boys.*

Susan walked out of the Job Service feeling much better than when she'd walked in. Still, a foreboding weight hung on her. The job sounded great, but, and there was always a but, the competition was unbelievable. Did she really have a chance when hundreds of other people were applying? The answer came in that bastard's all too familiar voice.

Loser, you don't stand a snowball's chance in hell.

Chapter Twenty-Two

Rosalyn stepped off the school bus with Albert on her heels and her speech, working title: *10 Reasons Why Kelvin Should Leave*, memorized word for word. Thanks to her friends' patience, Rosalyn's delivery was perfect. She knew exactly when she'd bring on her tears, knew when to raise her voice, and knew when to throw her arms around her daddy's neck.

"I'm telling mama as soon as we get in," Rosalyn said. She was too happy, too full of hope for things to turn out the way she wanted. Albert considered telling her as much but decided to let life teach his blissfully ignorant sister a lesson he'd learned long ago.

Hope was a fool's paradise.

"I hope you get what you want," Albert said.

Rosalyn and Albert were almost to the front door when Barbara's voice called out, "Kids, your snacks are on the stove." They turned towards their mother's voice and Albert smiled. Rosalyn didn't.

Robert and Barbara were sitting in the mulberry shade with Kelvin. They were drinking iced tea and laughing like the best of friends, and Rosalyn's plan died in their idiotic chuckles.

That was the last time those three sat together and laughed, and it was the last time Robert cracked a smile until after he'd passed his first test.

When he first arrived, Kelvin had been Robert's replacement, and Robert had ample time to train with his sword. Now that Robert was working at home and monitoring Kelvin's behavior, things were different. Robert's beloved sword stayed locked inside his Bronco, and Robert felt like a drug addict denied his fix. A day without his sword was too long. He didn't know why he was, but Robert was mean. He was mean to everybody. He even fussed with Barbara in front of the kids, a thing he'd never done before. The kids got the worst of his wrath. If one did something wrong, he whipped them all, and if nobody did anything wrong, he whipped them for prevention. He argued the sunup and down with Theodore and Kelvin over every detail of the farm and was wrong more often than right.

Sherman was only six that year, but he had no trouble remembering his daddy's frightful demeanor or how it changed one night. Robert wore the *Meanest Man in the World* shirt for weeks, and *poof*, he was his fun-loving self again. No warning. No nothing. Just *presto-changeo*.

Robert didn't tell anyone why or how he snapped out of his psychotic funk. He left the house one night and came back a new man.

The change happened after a long day of smelling Kelvin's cigarette smoke and listening to him whine about one thing after another. Finally, Robert bottomed out. All the yellow *CAUTION* lights in his head went off and came back on as bright red *DANGER* ones. "We're knocking off," he told Kelvin. "Be sure you lock up this time. I don't want these damn doors left unlocked again," he shouted in a whisper, letting his icy stare convey the volume.

Yessa, massa, Kelvin thought but didn't dare speak aloud.

Robert didn't leave his work boots outside and didn't bother swiping the bottom of them on the green, turf mat that once read *Welcome* but was now reduced to: *e...me.* Robert left a trail of mud from the doorway to his bedroom.

Barbara was cooking supper and was more than a little stressed over her own busy day. The mess called to her like a wailing siren and Barbara immediately noticed the muddy trail. Incensed by the mess, she gave chase. She rounded the corner into their bedroom ready to pounce but took one look at Robert and pardoned him.

Robert rummaged in his closet and didn't notice his wife's stare. He pulled a .30-30 rifle and a box of round-nose ammunition from the closet and laid them on the bed. Aware he wasn't alone, he looked into Barbara's eyes and said, "Mama, I'm shot." He loaded the rifle.

She saw his eyes and knew he wasn't exaggerating. Robert's deep, sapphire eyes weren't merely bloodshot. The sapphire was unnoticeable in the sea of red. The blood vessels in the white of his right eye had taken over and turned his eye into a pulsating, thumb-sized alien that threatened to explode. His left eye wasn't as bad but was racing the Devil to catch up. Whatever he needed to do to get *unshot* was precisely what Barbara wanted him to do.

"Is there anything I can do to help? I love you," she said.

"Nothing comes to mind. I'm going out. Don't wait up," he said. He grabbed his Bronco's keys from the key hook and left her hanging without a return *I love you.*

Robert tore out of the driveway in a cloud of dust. Barbara stood on the back porch watching his taillights fade from red to pink into the dusty, darkening evening. She prayed for his safety and went inside to finish supper. It was out of her hands.

The eight-track player filled the Bronco with Charlie Pride's voice. Robert was paying attention but paying it in the wrong places. He was singing along with Charlie and scanning the road for deer. The lever-action rifle was in the passenger seat with a twelve-volt Q-Beam by its side. Robert wanted to kill something and thought spotlighting a deer was a damn fine place to start. He was singing *Mississippi Cotton Picking Delta Town* when he rounded a curve on Thorn Road, over-steered and skidded, and lacked four-whole inches running over Burt Moore.

Burt's truck was half on the shoulder and half still in the traveling lane. The old man was out of his truck and standing in the middle of a hairpin curve, a terrible location for a man who couldn't have jumped out of the way if he'd wanted to and had a week to do it. Mr. Moore looked at his flat tire with his hat in one hand and his walking stick in the other. He shook his head at his bad luck and didn't notice Robert swerve around him.

Burt Moore was ninety-one years old and was stooped by arthritis and osteoporosis. He hadn't seen the world from a vertical position in ten years and was trapped, staring at his feet. He stood with the help of a homemade walking stick that was whittled to a point on both ends. For each step, Burt popped the stick in the ground and dragged himself behind it.

Robert parked in front of Burt's truck and slammed his door. "Burt, what in the *Sam-Hell* are you doing standing in the damn road? You wanna get run over or something?" Robert's anger redlined.

Burt couldn't turn his neck, so he slowly turned his whole body toward Robert. "Well, howdy, Robert. I didn't see you pull up." Burt's eyes lit with joy like he'd just met the Savior. Completely unaware he'd almost been creamed, Burt said, "I sure am glad you come along when you did. I'm in quite the fix here."

He deafened Robert. Burt was clinically deaf and tried to speak loud enough to hear himself. Every word came out as a yell, each louder than the one before it because Burt never heard a word but kept expecting to.

Robert was furious and wanted to leave, but his upbringing wouldn't let him abandon the old man. "Tell me you at least got a two-bit spare for this rattle-trap of yours."

Over Robert's left shoulder, in the cloudless East, a wolf howled and a bone shaking cold rode in on a wind from nowhere. Something strange was in that wind and Robert considered getting his rifle. The wolf howled again, and the wind from nowhere intensified. Robert's skin broke out in gooseflesh, a shiver running up his spine and rooting in his brain, and dammit, he liked it. It felt like death. Like murder.

That's no ordinary wolf, Robert thought.

"What's that ya say? You gotta speak up, Robert. I don't hear so good. Dern old hearing aid ain't hardly worth a glob of snot, neither." Burt cupped his hand around his ear to catch Robert's voice from the rising wind.

"A spare. Do you have a damn spare tire?" Robert yelled.

"Robert, there's a spare in the bed of my truck and a tire tool in the passenger floorboard. I'll get it for you." Burt *pop-dragged* himself towards the passenger side an inch at a time.

"Don't worry about it. I'll get it, Burt. You just get out of the dang road before you get creamed!" Robert hollered, and heard the wolf howl again. *Closer*, he thought.

Robert lifted the spare out of the truck and rolled it to the blowout. He opened the passenger door for the tire tool, and there were bags of clothes and other belongings on the seat and in the floor. The curved, lug-nut end of the rusty tire tool jutted from under a partially unzipped, duffel bag. Through the small opening, Robert saw stacks of twenty-dollar bills. He used the tire tool's flat hubcap end to open the zipper wider. Robert estimated Burt had well over ten-thousand dollars laying in his rusted floorboard.

Shit, there's probably three or four times that in there, Robert thought.

"Are you on the run, Burt?" Robert asked.

"Huh? You say is this fun?" Burt couldn't hear and moved closer to Robert.

Burt stepped into the road, and tires squealed, skidded, and screamed into the night.

It was all over in five seconds.

Chapter Twenty-Three

Burt was making his way to Robert when a four-door, hotrod blasted around the hairpin, hit the shoulder, and headed straight for the backend of the disabled truck. The driver, a local idiot everybody called Buster, was lighting a joint with his car's cigarette lighter and had barely bothered looking out the windshield the last two *Creedence Clearwater Revival* songs.

Buster lifted his glassy eyes upward and the first thing he saw was that his car was running off the road. The second thing he saw was the tailgate of Burt's truck. Buster sank lower in his seat and cut the wheel.

Buster's tires gripped the pavement for a second then gave up and skidded. The car went sideways, and Buster worked the wheel like a white-knuckled maniac.

He passed Robert and Burt doing seventy-five, completely sideways in the opposite lane. The rear tires were still spinning and pelting the two men with gravel from his tread like they were tin-ducks in a carnival shooting gallery. Robert ducked, but still went home with numerous whelps on his cheeks and neck. Burt, being stooped at the waist, wasn't hit once.

Buster stabbed the brakes to regain control of the car. He skidded each time he braked, and to someone unacquainted with Buster, it looked like he knew what he was doing.

Buster waved to Robert and Burt and fishtailed back and forth across the road as he fought to control the hotrod. He got straight again and hammered the accelerator to the floor. The powerful V8 unleashed all its horses and the rear tires disappeared in clouds of blue smoke. He put his smoldering joint to his lips, took a deep drag and held it until he was out of sight. In a minute, Buster was on his third *CCR* song and had forgotten the whole deal.

"Buster, you fucking bastard," Robert screamed as the gravel hit him. If he didn't hate leaving Burt, he would have given chase, but Robert shook it off and stayed on the job. Barbara told him to count to ten when he felt he was losing control.

One, two, three, four, five, six, seven, eight, nine, ten...oh hell this shit don't work! Robert went back to work on Burt's flat. He was out of his mind and completely out of control. Instead of giving in to his rage, he turned to Burt.

"It looks like you robbed a bank or something. Are the cops looking for you? If there's a reward, I might turn you in and collect," Robert said.

"Dadgum it, I thought I had that money covered up better than that. Robert, throw something over it, will you? If the wrong person caught an eyeful of it, I'd be in more trouble than this dang flat."

"What gives, Burt? Seriously. You find a money tree? I could use one myself if you have two of them." Robert used the tire tool to break the lug nuts free and positioned a bumper jack on the rear bumper. Robert raised the truck in four pumps.

"Nothing like that. I sold the home-place to that Dendy brothers' outfit from Tennessee. You know the ones I'm talking about?"

Robert knew the Dendy brothers were hounding everybody to either sell outright or sell them insane, ninety-nine-year leases. The Dendy's weren't well-liked and had been run off several properties by the business end of a shotgun because they started the first corporate farm in Mississippi.

The Dendy's bought up all the available land and made plays for small farms. There were holdouts who wouldn't sell or lease to them. Some folks held out for more money, but most people held out on principle and wouldn't sell at any price.

"Is that right. I can't believe you sold out to them damned carpetbaggers. What did you get for your place? Probably not half what it's worth," Robert said. He had the tire changed and contemplated beating Burt to death with the tire tool. The wolf howled again, and Robert's mind turned to his sword. *Much better than a tire tool*, he thought.

"I drove a pretty hard bargain. They bought the land, house, and all my equipment for fifty-five thousand. Plus, they paid off my banknotes and left me free and clear for the first time since I was a young man. The old house weren't hardly fit to live in what with the floors caved in and shingles flying like leaves every time the wind blows. I settled up with the bank and I've got just over seventy-three thousand sitting there in that floorboard. That's a lot of change for an old chump like me." It was more money than Burt Moore had ever imagined.

"You moving to Beverly Hills like Jed Clampett?" Robert asked, hoping humor would quieten his murderous, red rage.

Burt laughed and coughed up something Robert thought looked vital. "Maybe if I'd got it a few years ago, but I ain't got the time now. I'm giving it to my boy up in Tupelo. That's where I'm heading now. He can sure use it with them four kids of his. My doctors say I got the Big C and ain't long for this world. I told them they were fools if they thought they were telling me something I didn't already know. I said I don't need no bunch of schooling to see I'm out of time. Don't need no cancer, neither. Old age is killing me just fine. I'll be ninety-two next February, and I don't believe I'll see it. And that don't bother me one cotton-picking bit. I've lived too long already."

Robert lowered the jack and finished tightening the lug nuts. He stewed over Burt selling out. "Is that right?" he mumbled knowing Burt couldn't hear him.

There was no reason for Robert to be mad. It wasn't Robert's land, and Burt sold his farm out of love for his family, which is a pretty rare thing. But Robert was mad already, and sometimes when a man is mad all he really wants is to get madder. Robert slipped the tire tool under the money bag and evil squiggled its way into the darkest part of Robert's mind.

"Robert I can't thank you enough for your help. I can pay you some and be happy to do it too, if 'n you'll take it."

Robert didn't say a thing. He was at his Bronco, fetching his sword. His mind was set. It was going to be a good day after all. *Oh, you can pay all right, and pay you will, you sellout. Not with your blood-money, though. You'll pay with your blood.*

Fifty yards away, the wolf howled and stepped onto the road to watch events unfold.

As he imagined Burt's death, the cold wind hit him and caused another round of shivering gooseflesh. Robert settled his nerves and breathed in easy and deep; a predator's breath.

Burt *pop-dragged* himself to Robert's Bronco with a handful twenties. "Robert," he said. "There's a thousand dollars in here. Take it for helpin' me out of this jam and for being a good friend all these years. Buy Barbara something nice."

Robert's hand tightened around the sword's bejeweled handle. He saw the coming sword-stroke in his mind like he was remembering something that had already happened.

In one fluid motion, Robert drew the sword in an outward and downward angle. The tip cleared the Bronco's side panel, and Robert twisted right and brought it up. The razor edge struck Burt under his right arm and passed through his body. It cut through his collar bone and exited between his left shoulder and neck.

Because he was stooped with arthritis, the gleaming blade passed just beneath his chin as it sliced through muscle, organ, and bone with equal ease. As he died, the last thing Burt Moore saw was the two pieces of his walking stick falling by his sides.

Robert grinned at what was about to happen. Truly, he was a predator.

Standing ahead of the two men, the wolf howled, and Burt heard it this time. Robert Lancaster didn't. Robert heard something different.

No one is here. Do it. Finish it. The money is yours. The voice was from nowhere but seemed to be everywhere.

"Leave me alone," Robert said to no one. His body shook with crazy rage and he squeezed the sword tighter.

Another howl broke the silence between the two men.

He is a traitor. A SELLOUT! Kill him. He deserves to die, and you deserve the money. No one will ever know.

Robert glared hungrily at Burt's reflection in the Bronco's window. The nowhere voice was right. The old bastard was a sellout and deserved to die, *deserved worse*.

"No. I refuse!" Robert shouted to himself.

The wolf didn't like how things looked. It stood on its hind legs and Satan transformed from the wolf to his man-form. He stood in the darkness and forced his thoughts to Robert's mind.

Robert's first test was in full-bloom, and Satan couldn't back off. Robert was deciding whether he'd be a *Handler* or another of Satan's playthings. Satan opened his mouth, and Burt heard another howl. Robert didn't.

Satan changed tactics. *He hasn't got long anyway. He is dying. Do him a favor. End his suffering. Put him out of his misery.*

"I refuse *YOU*!" Robert shouted. He released the sword, and Satan vanished in a cloud of sulfuric dioxide.

Robert passed his first test. He'd spared the innocent and proved his heart was strong enough to resist Satan's bloodlust. Robert would face the second test before the next full moon. He'd spared the innocent. Now, Robert had to prove he was strong enough to claim the guilty.

"Burt, put that money away and see that your boy gets it. Me, Barbara, and the kids are doing just fine. We're better than fine. The Lord has blessed us with more than we need." Robert put his arm around Burt's shoulder and helped him to his truck.

Burt tried again to get Robert to take some money, but Robert wouldn't budge. "Be careful getting to Tupelo. You can't see worth nothing in the daytime, and it's black as death out tonight. Why don't you follow me back to the house? You can spend the night with us and start off to Tupelo in the morning with a good night's sleep under your belt and a fresh breakfast in your stomach."

Burt thanked him but declined. "I may not have but a few more hours, Robert. Death's breathing down my neck right now. I want to be sure to see my boy one more time if I'm lucky enough to make it there. Thank you for being a friend and for helpin' an old man out."

Burt drove away and arrived at his son's house ninety-minutes later. At dawn, surrounded by his family, Burt Moore died. He was smiling.

Barbara and the kids cringed when the Bronco pulled into the drive, but when he came through the backdoor, Robert was wearing a grin from left ear to right. He hugged them all, and for the first time ever, he apologized for being mean and fussy. He scooped Barbara in his arms and planted a big kiss on her lips.

The bedsprings were exceptionally noisy for an exceptionally long time.

Robert woke up happier than he'd been since childhood. After breakfast, he played with Sherman while Barbara and Karen did the dishes. Then, Robert walked to the shed.

"How's it going this morning?" Robert asked. He'd made no noise approaching the shed and Kelvin didn't realize Robert was there.

Kelvin's mind was on Rosalyn, Karen, and Barbara and the wonderful pleasures they'd share. The crescent wrench he had in his hand slipped off the nut he was tightening and *voilà,* two bloody knuckles. He thanked Robert for scaring the ever-loving shit out of him, and said, "Fine, till you showed up." Kelvin flicked his wrist and slung blood on the shed's concrete floor.

"Hey look, it's old Hank," Robert said, and pointed to the end of Kelvin's blood trail.

Some of Kelvin's blood dripped in a four-foot long, straight line, but most of it splattered at the end of the line. There, the droplets came together like a dot-matrix image of Hank Williams.

"What are you talking about? That ain't nothing but a bloody mess," Kelvin said. As an afterthought, he added, "And you're cleaning it up."

"Sure it is. Looky there. That's his narrow face right there, and here's that Hank Williams' chin. And right there, on either side, thems his ears." Robert pointed it out carefully to Kelvin who was becoming a reluctant believer.

"Okay, maybe you're not crazy. It does look like him. A little," Kelvin admitted.

"Well at least I know you're not completely blind. Gimme that wrench before you hurt yourself again," Robert said.

Kelvin walked outside to the water hydrant and washed his wounds. The water was cold and there was no soap, but he managed to get most of the oil and dirt out of his busted knuckles. He heard

Robert singing a Hank Williams' song, and that infuriated him to no end.

Go ahead and sing Bobby, my boy. The trials of Job are coming your way. Kelvin went back to work and waited for the right moment to strike.

Chapter Twenty-Four

"What's that noise? It sounds like a giant bird," Sebastian said, interrupting Sherman's storytelling.

A giant bird. Sherman knew the sound well. "Boys I would like you to meet a friend of mine." Ursa landed hard in front of them, stowed her wings, and glowered down at them.

With a swipe of her hands, she put the boys into a trance. Piper's head conked right. Sebastian's conked left. They made a hairy tepee. "What are they doing here?" Ursa asked.

Sherman said, "*pfffftt,*" dismissing Ursa with a flick of his wrist. "There's no rulebook, Ursa. Calm it down and wake them up so y'all can meet."

"Your behavior is unacceptable." I know you're ready to *finish*, but you'll wait until the decision is made.

"Which one of us is in charge? It's me, right?" Sherman asked.

"That can change," Ursa said, wishing it were true but knowing it wasn't. He was in charge. The *Handler* was always in charge. Her lot was to assist.

"The boys being here mean nothing. One of them is to be my apprentice. We can wipe the other one's memory when it's time. Now wake...them...up!" Sherman's stern voice worked to no effect on the angel.

"Get them home, Sherman Lancaster. They don't need to be here." Ursa passed her hand over the boys, and they shook their heads as her spell lifted. Grogginess hung over Piper and Sebastian's eyes in opaque shades. Ursa jetted into the clouds as they regained their vision.

The sky's peaceful, marshmallowy clouds disappeared in the face of dark stormy ones that rolled in like spilled ink. Thunder clapped forcefully enough to shake fruit from the trees. The falling fruit struck the boys and hastened them from their grogginess. Purple-blue lightning struck the ground leaving fulgurites in smoking patches of bombed earth.

Piper tugged on his little brother's sleeve and asked, "Who was that?"

Sebastian shrugged, shook his head, and whispered, "I have no idea." He grabbed Piper's hand and squeezed hard enough to hurt them both.

"Great-grandpa, was that God?" Sebastian asked.

"That wasn't God, but we better get out of here all the same." Sherman stood as the first drop of freezing rain hit the grass. "Looks like the weather is turning nasty." The low-hanging, black clouds opened, and torrents of rain and hail beat down on them.

They stepped through the briar wall into cold forest. With the magic of the clearing behind them, Sherman transformed into an old man before the boys' disbelieving eyes. They quickly walked to the Bronco, and soaking wet, Piper and Sebastian embraced for warmth until they made it back to Sherman's.

Sherman backed the Bronco into the shed and Piper led the charge up to the backdoor with Sebastian on his heels. Sherman unlocked the door and followed the boys in the house. They changed into dry clothes and folded themselves in blankets like tightly wrapped fajitas. Sherman suggested they all take a nap.

Piper and Sebastian thought that was just about the finest idea they'd ever heard, because they felt like they'd lived a month in the last four hours.

Before they fell asleep, Sherman said, "Remember, not a word about our little trip today. And Piper, not another word about the story I'm telling, either."

Sebastian nodded because he understood secrecy from the beginning, but Piper said, "Yes, great-grandpa. I remember."

"Where's my little men?" Susan called as she walked in the house. Piper and Sebastian frantically scrambled toward her and Sherman didn't know whether they were going to hug her or tackle her.

Sherman was in his recliner reading a book when Susan walked into the room with Piper and Sebastian hanging off her like two little parasites. So far, neither boy had mentioned the *Clearing*. Sherman closed his book and knew something was on her mind by the way her eyes pleaded for understanding.

"Grandpa, I hate to ask. God knows I do. You've done so much, but I don't know who else to ask. Can you keep the boys this weekend? I know it's short notice, but the company I'm trying to get on with is hosting a workshop this weekend in Jackson. I need to go to be competitive and—"

Sherman held his hand up in a policeman's stop gesture. "Susan, don't go on and on. I've told you a thousand times, I'm here to help. I'm happy for them to stay, anytime."

"Boys, we get to spend the whole weekend together. Can I get a *whoa—weekend*?" He put his hand out low so the boys could reach it.

Piper and Sebastian put a hand on top of Sherman's, and all three shouted, "*Whoaaaaa....weekend!*" as they brought their hands up.

Turning back to Susan, Sherman asked, "Do you have enough money to go down there? I know hotels and meals ain't cheap. Let me help you if you need it. It'd do an old man's heart good to be able to help out."

"Believe me, you're already helping more than you can imagine. I'll go down there and get back as quickly as possible. I'll be fine."

When Susan returned from Jackson, she was anything but fine.

Chapter Twenty-Five

An hour after Susan took the boys home, Ursa walked in and found Sherman as Susan had left him. Still occupying his recliner and napping with an open book on his lap. He sensed Ursa's presence and felt the coming attack. The angel silently drew her sword and moved to strike. Out of Ursa's line-of-sight, Sherman opened his left hand, and *DeeDee* unsheathed herself and streaked from the closet to her *Handler*. As Ursa's stroke fell, *DeeDee* landed in Sherman's hand. The blades clashed in a brilliant explosion that erupted into millions of twinkling sparks.

"I almost got you, old man," Ursa said.

"You weren't close. Woman, you will never get fast enough to take me...no matter how old I get." From his seated position, he leapt into a double forward flip and brought *DeeDee* to rest against Ursa's neck. "I'm the *Handler*, not you."

Ursa's divine radiance flashed as she threw out her wings and knocked Sherman to his knees. He was faster than her and, in most ways, a superior fighter, but he could never prevail against her, not permanently anyway. If he cut off her head, an act Sherman had considered on more than one occasion, God would put it right back.

"No more games, we have work tonight," Ursa said.

"Speaking of work, I have something I need you to do for me this weekend," he said.

"Do I get to kill somebody?"

"You may very well get to do that, darling. I'll tell you all about it," Sherman said.

Sherman transformed into the *Handler*, and Ursa checked his eyes the way Barbara did when he was a teenager to see if he'd been drinking. Ursa wasn't looking for signs of alcohol consumption. She checked for the telltale wildness signifying *Wolf's* presence.

Sherman's pupils contracted and dilated over and over when the *change* was coming, but tonight, his gaze was steady. "Please tell me I do not have to worry about you," Ursa said.

"I feel right as rain. I don't think you have anything to worry about. I believe the cycle has passed." Usually, he felt his *changes* coming before they happened, but all he felt now was the weight of Ursa's condemnation. He didn't care for it. In fact, he realized he didn't care much for her at all. Did he hate her?

Thinking the h-word meant only one thing. The other *monster* was near. It was the truly dangerous one because it hated everybody. Should he warn her? He decided he could control the *change*—for a while, anyway.

"Are you sure?" she asked. "We can't have you freaking out while we're working."

"You act as if it's my fault. I'm innocent in it, you know. I didn't ask for any of this and I'd give it all back if I could."

"I know you're innocent," Ursa said, gently placing her hand against his cheek. "I love you, Sherman."

He loved her too, had since he was a child. Sherman the *man* loved her. Sherman the *Handler* loved her, but he still hated her because there were other things living inside his skin. He was man, *Handler*, and monsters, and the monsters were as much a part of him as the *Handler* was.

Sherman was the best at his job because, unlike the other *Handlers*, he'd paid his debt, but that wasn't the only reason he was the best. The monsters—Satan's curses—allowed him to regenerate faster and more completely than the other *Handlers*, and even after 120 years, his body refused deterioration.

"That's what I wanted to hear," he said. Sherman grabbed her chin and turned her head toward his like he was going to plant a sloppy kiss on her lips. "You and me, against the world. You got that? By the way, I love you, too...bitch."

Ursa didn't laugh.

They stepped off his porch and flew into the night. Her on wings, and him with *DeeDee* held in front of him like a *Masters of the Universe* character. Through the darkness they streaked, faster than sound and untraceable by radar.

Ursa half tucked her wings and pinwheeled to the ground. She touched down as softly as a feather. Sherman shook the world when he landed. Dust rose around him like smoke at a NASA launch. "Smooth. Very clandestine of you," Ursa said.

He grinned. "I love to make an entrance. Let's kick some ass."

The house they entered was far different than the trailer they recently destroyed. It was a four-story, eighty-room mansion. Using *DeeDee*, Sherman cut a hole in the glass patio door. He let go of *DeeDee*, and she hovered in place, waiting. Sherman caught the falling glass before it crashed to the floor and slung it over his shoulder. It landed somewhere out of earshot. They walked inside and saw how the other half lived. The other half smelled of mahogany and pipe tobacco. To Sherman, the trailer smelled better.

Ursa put the servants in a trance and followed Sherman toward the muffled sounds of pain. The smell of blood was in the air and the *monster* tore at Sherman's soul. His fingernails yellowed, but he fought off the *change*, barely. The cries grew louder, and a young girl whimpered...*stop, oh daddy please stop*, but Sir Blake Barksdale didn't stop.

Sherman flew up the final two flights of stairs instead of wasting time walking. He lunged *DeeDee* into a solid wood door. The blade penetrated easily, and the door exploded into a funnel cloud of mahogany sawdust.

Sherman entered the bedroom. "Am I interrupting something?"

In his right hand, *DeeDee* flamed and raised the temperature in the room five degrees a minute. The flickering sword drew their shadows on the wall in a frenzied dance choreographed in hell.

On the biggest bed Sherman had ever seen, Sir Blake Barksdale, the richest man in Yorkshire, was too scared to speak and pissed himself when he saw Sherman. Barksdale's daughter wiggled free from under her father's weight and ran toward Sherman. Ursa caught her and covered the child's nakedness with her wings.

"You don't need to see this, dear-heart." Ursa carried the girl downstairs.

Margaret Barksdale was on the bed. She threw the cover back and tried to roll off. "You stay where you are, whore," Sherman said. Eager to comply, she froze with one leg in the air and her back a few inches off the mattress.

"I didn't do it," she protested. *He doesn't care*, her internal legal advisor said. She'd known and done nothing, and now, it was too late.

"No, you didn't. You didn't do anything, did you? This man raped your daughter night after night, and you did nothing. When he did it in her room, you did nothing. When he brought her to this room, to *your* room, you did nothing. You didn't even leave the room. You are guilty of what he is guilty of. Together, you make one flesh."

Ursa put the twelve-year-old girl to sleep and heard Sherman's, *"The guilty must pay."*

After two flashes of blinding light and two soul-crushing screams, there was nothing left of Blake and Margaret Barksdale except the shadows seared into the room's carpeted walls. Sherman walked downstairs with *DeeDee* in her scabbard. The girl was still asleep.

When she woke in the morning, the girl remembered nothing of the two figures that entered her parents' bedroom. She remembered all the abuse but had no recollection of what happened to her parents. The authorities looked for the Barksdale's. It wasn't every day society learned one of its billionaires was a wife-beating, incestuous pedophile. It was even rarer for the billionaire and his wife to vanish, leaving their fortune behind.

The mystery of the Barksdale's disappearance would remain unsolved forever.

On their way home, Sherman landed in a soybean field and Ursa landed at his side. "What are we doing here?" she asked.

Sherman pointed to a small white house in the distance and told Ursa what he needed her to do. "Don't kill him unless you have to," Sherman said. "That pleasure is mine."

Chapter Twenty-Six

Clark was waiting when Susan came home. He was in the kitchen with a beer in one hand and a lit cigarette in the other. Tired of Clark's crap and overwhelmed by how out-of-her-control her life was, Susan forgot her place and swatted away the toxic smoke. "Stop smoking around the kids, Clark. You're killing them."

Getting hit wasn't on her mind. The prospect of a good job which carried the prospect of a good life, meaning a life without Clark, was on Susan's mind. Clark's fist landed directly above her left ear. She was out and on the floor before her last word escaped her mouth.

No woman was going to tell him when and where he could smoke, certainly not in his own damn house. When Susan hit the floor, Clark sent the boys to their room.

"Don't come out less'n I tell you to. Y'all got that?" he growled. Piper objected and started towards his father, but changed his mind when Clark came forward to meet him. "Don't come out, or it'll be you on the floor," Clark said, and slammed their bedroom door. "And clean that damned pigsty!" he yelled over his shoulder.

Clark returned to the kitchen, but Susan was gone. He found her in the living room. She was on her knees with her elbows propped on the coffee table and appeared to be praying to the television. Susan's eyes were half-open, and the visible half was only dimly lucid. She watched Clark like a wounded mouse would watch a cat closing in for the kill.

"Did you find another job?" Clark asked as if up was up, down was down, and he hadn't just clobbered his wife.

Susan didn't answer, but she wasn't giving him the silent treatment intentionally. If she'd had any control over her thinking and speaking faculties, she would've answered. For the first time in a long time, Susan had hope. It was dangerous to hope, actually forbidden in a life with a wife-beating bastard like Clark Vance. But hope crept in, nonetheless, and she wouldn't have jeopardized it on purpose. She didn't answer because she couldn't.

Clark's right foot—thank God he was wearing socks and not his cowboy boots—connected with her ribcage just below her left breast, actually pinching her nipple between his foot and the coffee table. The breaks didn't happen in a cascading sequence of three separates snaps. They broke all at once, and without an X-ray, Susan knew what had happened.

"*Congratulations, you have three broken ribs,*" she imagined a gameshow host announcing.

For a second Susan wanted to scream, but the pain was unbearable, and she slipped into black, blessed nothingness.

Clark wasn't sure if she was still conscious, so to check his abusive handiwork, he pulled his leg back like a placekicker and let her hip have it. The kick wasn't hard enough to break the bone, but it was enough to disjoint it. He jammed two of his toes in the process and blamed her for the injury.

She came to three hours later, still on her knees at the altar of the TV. Clark was in his recliner, still drinking. He heard her grunt and knew she was coming around. Without looking away from the WTVA newscaster, he asked, "Well, did you get another job or what?"

Where do women find the strength to go on? Maybe God infuses their DNA with some divine *mojo*. Susan answered, "I got an interview." It was all she could say, and thankfully, it satisfied Clark.

Susan's chest was a field of thorny pain. She thought she would die with every breath. She vaguely remembered being kicked in the ribs, but she remembered the excruciating *wham* perfectly. She thought standing might relieve her chest pain, but when she tried to stand, she learned something was terribly wrong with her hip. Each agonizing step brought waves of nausea. Her left leg would only make one step for every two made by the right one. The obvious result was her left foot dragging behind. She crawled into bed and let the blessed nothingness have her again.

The next morning, Clark asked about her job interview. Susan told him about the Jackson trip and made it sound mandatory. "Grandpa Sherman is going to keep the boys, so they won't be in your hair all weekend." Susan rattled off the job's benefits. There was no doubt this job was the answer to all their prayers.

Clark didn't believe a word out of her mouth. *How do you know when a woman is lying? Her lips are moving*, was one of his favorite jokes. "I don't know why you let that old pervert keep them boys all the time. You know I reported his sick old ass to the Child Welfare Department."

You're the finger-pointing chickenshit that sicced the government on grandpa. If he ever found out, he'd kill you twice, thought Susan.

The news wouldn't have been news to Sherman. Sherman suspected Clark was the anonymous tipster.

Clark wasn't enthusiastic about her going to *Sin City* for two days, but what the hell. He told her to call with her hotel information as soon as she checked in. "You can't trust cellphones," he told her, and he wanted to be able to get in touch with her if something happened to one of the boys. Clark's statement: "You never know. Accidents happen all the time," sounded ominous.

Susan promised to phone with the information as soon as she had it. "What do you want for breakfast?" she asked, steering to a nonvolatile topic.

"Don't you need to take the boys to your grandpa?" Clark asked.

Susan planned to spend time with Piper and Sebastian while she was out of work, but when she told Clark this, he said, "I don't think so. The weather's shit and I'm stuck inside. I don't want them damn babies running around. Drop their asses off with the old *perv*. I've got plenty for us to do." She nearly cried when he squeezed the breast he kicked last night. Summoning the *mojo* again, she smiled and kissed his eager mouth.

It was Thursday morning, and Old Man Winter showed off. Ice clung to treetops and gave off arthritic creaks each time the wind blew. There were mountainous snowdrifts that would've been at home around the Great Lakes but had no business anywhere in Mississippi. Sherman accepted the weather as a sure sign God wanted him to spend the day in his recliner, sipping coffee, and reading. Until the phone rang, he was equally sure he'd do those things alone.

"Hello," he answered.

"Good morning, grandpa," Susan said.

Oh shit, he thought. It was five o'clock a.m., and there couldn't be any good behind this call. "Hey sweetie. What's up, doc?"

Susan asked if it was okay for her to drop Piper and Sebastian off. She wanted to check before she brought them over. It was common knowledge she was a jobless *Loser* and should be at home with her children. She apologized repeatedly for asking, for even considering such a thing, but Clark was adamant they spend some alone time while they were both out of work, not that he was considering rejoining the workforce.

"I understand," Sherman said. "It's good for a man and his wife to be alone every once in a while. Besides, I love the little rascals being here."

Sherman didn't need to call the Psychic Friends Network to know Susan's voice was off, and was confident Clark caused the offness. Sherman was happy to have the boys over. That wasn't the issue. It was the perfect opportunity to finish Kelvin's story. The issue was whether the boys, and Susan for that matter, were safe around Clark at all. *At least they'll be safe while they're here*, Sherman comforted himself.

"Thank you so much. We'll be over in a few minutes," she said, and hung up.

Sherman thought she must've called from the end of his driveway because she came through the door not fifteen minutes later. Piper and Sebastian were carrying their own bags this morning, and Susan left the car running. "Looks like you're not staying," Sherman said.

"No, grandpa. I've got to get home. Clark has a busy day planned for us. It'll be great to lay around the house with him, not that I won't miss you two pumpkin pies," she said as she hugged her sons.

"Well, you're welcome to stay, or if you get bored being there, come on over. We'll be sitting around the heater trying to stay warm. Tell Clark I'd love for him to come over, too. I'd love to talk to him."

Susan would love it, too. Why didn't she speak up? This was the perfect opportunity. She was safe. Piper and Sebastian were safe. She could start by saying Clark made the anonymous tip that Sherman was *meelestering* his great-grandsons. If that wasn't enough to get Clark killed, she could show off her impressive collection of bruises. Why didn't she say any of those things?

Why does water run downhill? It just does, and she just didn't. It was her chance, maybe her last chance, and it passed.

"I'll tell him, grandpa. Now, I better go. Come give your mama a kiss," Susan said. After the kisses were out of the way, she turned to leave, dragging her left leg behind.

"What's wrong with your leg?" Sherman asked, as if he didn't know.

"Just a little crampy this morning. Probably the weather." Susan eased into her car and drove home.

"Well boys, come on in and get comfortable," Sherman said.

Piper and Sebastian shuffled into the living room. They were worried about their mama, but she'd made them promise to keep Clark's behavior a secret. Coming so soon after Sherman preached the virtue of keeping secrets, neither boy would tell. Sherman knew something was on their minds, and he guessed that something started with a *D* and ended with an *addy*. He decided against prying and settled in between the boys on the sofa.

"I guess we can't go back to the *Clearing*, huh?" Piper asked.

"Not today," Sherman said. "Maybe once the weather clears up."

"Shoot," Piper said. "Will you at least tell us what Kelvin did after your daddy made him hurt his hand."

"That's easy, Kelvin went batshit crazy."

Chapter Twenty-Seven

Rosalyn lay on her bed in disgusted silence. Her whole family was blind to the creepazoid living amongst them. Everyone except Albert, and he was too detached to care what happened. Kelvin smiled at breakfast. He smiled at dinner, and he smiled at supper. He laughed at jokes, worked hard, and was always available whenever anyone needed his help. Not that she'd ask him for it. If Rosalyn was dying and Kelvin was the only doctor...*hello darkness my old friend, here I come.*

If she could prove Kelvin was as creepy as she knew in her heart he was, her daddy would chase him from the homestead with a shotgun. But what could she prove? Not a damn thing, not a single damn thing. Kelvin rarely even looked at her anymore and talked to her even less. He just wore that ear-to-ear monstrosity that was more wolf's grin than smile, but his smile didn't mean he wasn't up to something.

It didn't mean that at all.

Rosalyn wanted out. Out and away from her pain-in-the-ass little brothers. Out and off the farm and away from the stinking chickens. Out and far, far away from Kelvin and his creepiness. Jill and Melanie made it out. As soon as they graduated high school, they got factory jobs and left the farm. The ink on their diplomas was still wet when they left.

"Is it as great as you thought it'd be," Rosalyn asked Melanie at last Sunday's family dinner.

"Oh Roz, you can't imagine. I don't want to rub it in, but yeah, it's great," Melanie said. "Each Friday, I get a paycheck, and the money is all mine. Sure, I have a few bills, but after them, whatever is left I get to spend however I see fit."

Melanie failed to stress the monotony of the assembly line because it was too depressing to talk about. For eighteen years she'd lived on a farm and was only indoors when it rained or snowed. At the factory, she spent nine hours a day, five and sometimes six days a week in a noisy, windowless tomb. Some days Melanie wondered if she could survive another shift, but the assembly line never stopped, so neither did she.

If she could've faced the truth, she would've admitted her mistake and begged to come home. Instead of warning her sister, Melanie told Rosalyn, "Soon as you graduate, I can get you hired on." Melanie wasn't cruel, but misery loves company.

"Are you ever going to move out on your own?" Rosalyn asked Karen as soon as her older sister walked into their shared bedroom.

"Why? Are you trying to get the room to yourself?"

"No way. I love that you're here. I've never had a room to myself and don't know if I could sleep alone. I know if I were you I'd be out in a flash," Rosalyn said, forgetting she just admitted not knowing if she could sleep alone.

"I'll move out when the time is right. I have no idea when that might be. Probably after I get you kids raised," Karen said. Outwardly she was the loving older sister, sometimes more mama than sister, but inside she wondered if she'd ever make a break.

Rosalyn lay on the bed and rolled to her side. She stared dreamily at the guys hanging on her wall. John Schneider was there three times. Tom Wopat showed up twice, but skanky Catherine Bach was nowhere in sight. Rosalyn gave Bach's pictures to Albert.

Albert was more than happy to take them off his sister's jealous hands. Sherman didn't know why Albert wanted the pictures of that girl and flat refused Albert's repeated requests to pin Daisy Duke on their bedroom wall.

The Duke Boys weren't alone on Rosalyn's walls. Greg Evigan was there, as was Parker Stevenson and Rosalyn's favorite singer of the day, Shaun Cassidy. When she was depressed about the dirt under her nails or not being allowed to date, Rosalyn lay on her bed and imagined being swept away by one of the *wall-guys*.

To hell with the star-gazing, philosophical academics. If the big-brained scientists of the world wanted to study dreams, fantasies, imaginations, and the other pondering powers of the human mind, they needed go no farther than the confines of a teenage girl's bedroom. Where oppression rules reality, imagination runs wild.

Rosalyn's dreams were surprisingly abstract and generalized in many facets but were also intricate, down to the smallest details in others. She dreamed of the life she shared with John. Their house was in Beverly Hills, of course, and they lived in a generic mansion that lacked a front, roof, and sides. It smelled like cinnamon and holiday spices all year long.

Of its many rooms, Rosalyn's favorite was the bedroom. It had double glass doors that opened into an expansive backyard and the happy couple's Olympic-sized pool. Unlike real life, where she couldn't swim a stroke, Rosalyn was an excellent swimmer in her dreams, and she and John spent hours frolicking in the pool.

The concrete pool had a Confederate flag painted on the bottom, and its sides were orange. It was a cement General Lee. What else would John have painted in his pool? The poolside had twenty sunning chairs, fully reclined with thick, fluffy towels draped over the backs. Ten towels were pink with embroidered carnations—Rosalyn's favorite flower—along their frilly edges. The other towels were blue with white stars forming triangles in each of the four gold-tasseled corners.

There were four glass tables with tropical-themed, thatched umbrellas where John and Rosalyn gathered with celebrity friends for frosty, refreshing drinks. The blazing Californian sun was always out and always hot but never caused sunburns no matter how long they were in it. They lived the life she wanted them to live and each day was better than the one before. Wonderful as they were, the days were merely preludes to the real pleasure. The white-hot Californian days couldn't hold a candle to the couple's steamy Californian nights.

Sherman didn't tell the boys, but naturally, Rosalyn touched herself, down there, while she fantasized. She waited until she heard Karen's sleep-breathing, and the real fantasy started. Sex wasn't the reason for the fantasy, it was a by-product. The fantasy was to escape the farm, her family, and the grinning creepo living with them. The byproduct, the orgasm, was her release, and without it Rosalyn would've clawed someone's eyes out. Besides, it was Bo Duke, and dammit, they were married. What could she do? Bo had needs, and he married the perfect gal to take care of his needs.

When it was over and her breathing and heart rate returned to normal, depression quickly swamped Rosalyn's euphoria. Leaving Beverly Hills for rural Mississippi was enough to depress any teenage girl. Rosalyn opened her eyes and was back in bed with her sister instead of stretched out on a lounger with Bo Duke playing the *Big Spoon*.

Rosalyn wasn't a fool and knew she couldn't have the wall-guys. But she was a good-looking girl, and it didn't feel wrong to think so. Guys asked her out all the time and that had to mean something. When she graduated, she'd have her pick from a sizable bachelor pool.

There were no John Schneiders or Tom Wopats in her pool but there were some good-looking guys. One of them would be hers, however, that was for later. Now, her mind turned to her pressing problem. *How to get rid of Kelvin?* She fell asleep looking for the answer, completely unaware Kelvin was watching her sleep.

Chapter Twenty-Eight

Sherman told the boys Kelvin went batshit crazy, and it was the truth. Kelvin couldn't get to his hiding spot under the girls' bed, and it drove him insane. He tried sneaking in several times, but Rosalyn was a relentless bitch who watched him constantly. He couldn't get their panties and jerk-off with the taste of their pussies in his mouth. Kelvin had no way to satisfy his crazy, so he lost all control.

And the waiting. The damn waiting made him feel like there were death-beetles under his skin gnawing him with their terrible pincers. If Robert didn't hurry his ass to Alabama, Kelvin was wigging-out and shooting his cousin in the head and taking the girls.

While Rosalyn fantasized about John, Kelvin peeped through her window and saw her lick the forefinger and middle-finger of her left hand. *Lefty*, with its moistened fingers, disappeared beneath the flowery sheet. Rosalyn's face distorted as soon as her fingers hit their mark. Her body rocked gently, and from her hips, the motion spread up and down like waves. The waves reached her face, her chin rose slightly then lowered and waited for the next wave. When the waves reached her feet, Kelvin watched her toes curl beneath the thin sheet and then straighten in anticipation of the wave that would take them all the way.

Kelvin's hand dropped to his zipper, and he took *It* out. He didn't even have to think about it. It just happened. Kelvin stared into Rosalyn's face, stroked *It*, and imagined what it was going to be like to be with her, in her. Betty Jo would feel so...*wait...no Rosalyn, not Betty Jo...*

Kelvin didn't just forget where he was. He forgot *when* he was.

Kelvin could hardly remember her face, but her pigtails were clear. Betty Jo was a year ago. She was his first, and at twelve, was a little younger than Rosalyn. His motto was, *If they're old enough to bleed, they're old enough to breed.*

Betty Jo's father was dead and her mother was a fat bitch of a woman who pretended to take Kelvin in out of Christian charity. Turned out she wanted something for herself. She fed him food that was exactly one notch above garbage and demanded he work around the house. At night, she tried to seduce him and acted like she was doing him a favor. The thought of having sex with the woman was nearly disgusting enough to make him forget Betty Jo.

Betty Jo's father died a hero in Vietnam. She wished she could say she remembered the man, but she couldn't. Leaving a wife and daughter alone to fend for themselves didn't seem heroic to her, but what did she know about such things. There'd been a younger brother, but he took ill and died.

Times were tough but the Baptists' charity and state-assistance kept her and her mama in bread and cheese and kept the power on and the water running. Betty Jo and her mom did housekeeping for the wealthier families in town, and when Kelvin showed up needing their help and offering his in return, it was a perfect match.

It seemed less so when he slit her mama's throat with a straight razor and walked into Betty Jo's bedroom. Kelvin twirled the razor between his knuckles like he did quarters and fifty-cent pieces to show off. The moon's glint made a flickering metallic smile as the stainless steel passed over Kelvin's knuckles. Using the seagrass string from the hay baler, he tied her hands and feet to the bed.

Betty Jo cried.

Three nights later, Kelvin brought a sledgehammer into her bedroom. He climbed onto her bed and straddled her. Kelvin raised the hammer and for the first time in three days, Betty Jo stopped crying. Kelvin brought the hammer down on her face, and while he wasn't sure, he thought the crazy bitch met the ten-pound hammer with a smile.

The first blow killed her, but he hit her again in the chest and once in her tiny, white abdomen. It was his first time, and he had to see what would happen. The snapping bones, splattering blood, and intestinal odors turned him on more than he could stand. He raped her mutilated corpse. His only regret was he couldn't kiss her. Betty Jo was faceless.

Lesson learned.

He would start with Rosalyn's gut and hammer his way up, saving her face for last.

From outside her window, Kelvin watched as Rosalyn's hips rocked faster and faster. She licked and parted her lips. Lost in fantasy, she kissed empty space as her breathing accelerated. Kelvin's motions increased to keep pace, and they climaxed together. His milky jizz drew a runny ghost on the red-brick wall beneath the girls' window. He zipped his pants and used his shirt to clean the come off the wall.

He knew he had to stop this. He was taking too many chances, risking too much. Kelvin had to have the real thing.

He kissed his index finger and pressed it to window. "Soon," he whispered. Kelvin walked to the next window and peeked inside Albert and Sherman's room.

Sherman didn't see Kelvin's eyes, but he didn't have to. Ever since he was three, Sherman knew things he couldn't know, saw things he couldn't see, and heard things he couldn't hear. He knew something was out there and knew it wasn't the imaginary *ghoulie monster* he pretended to fear.

Whatever was out there was real, and it was dangerous, a real monster—not a mulberry tree with rough branches casting shadows on the wall that he and Albert imagined were bony arms trying to snatch them out of their beds, break them to bits, and eat them with its tree-trunk-teeth. Whatever was out there wasn't like the *ghoulie monster* at all.

Sherman stirred and knew the eyes were on him. He sensed danger but felt the danger was distant; something far off and could be worried about later. He didn't doubt the feeling and think it was his boyish imagination playing tricks on him. His error was in his interpretation, but he was only six. Sherman thought he'd have to face the danger in some unknown where and some unknown when on life's highway.

He was wrong.

From the *Otherworld*, Ursa watched over young Sherman and saw Kelvin peeping in the window. She wanted to shake the young boy and beat some sense into him, but now wasn't the time. She knew Sherman's thoughts and wanted to tell him the distance he felt from the danger wasn't temporal. It wasn't about time but about objects.

Sherman wasn't the object of the monster's interest, so he felt removed from it. With time, Sherman would master the nuances of his abilities. Would he do so in time to save his sister? Ursa thought not.

Sherman stirred a bit longer, uneasy under the weight of Kelvin's stare, but eventually fell asleep. Kelvin returned to his room. Ursa, as always, watched.

Back in his shed, Kelvin was livid. He spent five minutes tearing everything off the walls and breaking everything that wasn't made from steel. Then he spent four hours cleaning and hiding what he'd done to the place. When Barbara called him for breakfast, Kelvin was sitting cross-legged on his floor with his thumb in this mouth. He muttered something about Betty Jo tasting oh-so-good and dreaming of how much better Rosalyn would taste.

Kelvin sat at the breakfast table and said, "Good morning." He picked up his fork and looked at Rosalyn. She turned away.

Kelvin smiled.

Chapter Twenty-Nine

On the drive home, Susan thought about her interview and her potential new life as a single woman. She often had the Single Woman fantasy, but with the Good Job prospect the fantasy was markedly sweeter. As sweet as it was, it wasn't enough to keep her mind off what was coming.

Last night's pain was a searing, red agony in her hip and chest, but she was happy to focus on it rather than think about what was waiting on her when she got home. If she'd thought about the coming pain, she'd have turned the car around and ran back to her grandpa.

She was only five miles from home when she pulled to the side of the road and spent three minutes bawling into a napkin. It wasn't just the coming torture. Susan cried because she feared she'd never get a Good Job, never leave Clark, never live the Single Woman fantasy for real.

Susan was a *Loser* and cried a loser's tears.

It took seven minutes to get over three minutes of crying. Susan made herself presentable because Clark would be upset if he thought she'd been crying. He would think she'd cried while spilling her guts to Sherman, and spilling her guts was strictly prohibited.

Our business is our business, Clark said too many times to be forgotten.

She parked and eased out of the car because getting out was the worst. Straightening her gimp leg, her body's weight falling to her hip and her muscles pulling on that swollen joint made death seem like a reward rather than a payment. Walking was no picnic, but once in motion, she gimped along well enough.

At the front door a wave of nausea washed over her. It started with her knees wobbling the tiniest bit, rose to a bubble in her stomach, and settled as a fine, white fog behind her dizzy eyes. Thinking about going in was too much, actually going in and facing what awaited was impossible. Susan held onto the doorknob to stay upright. She gripped it two-handed like a lifeline and steadied herself and finally, she turned it. No doubt, Clark was watching. She couldn't linger, mustn't do anything to upset him or arouse his suspicions. He must believe his *beatfreak* was still in the subservient place he'd put her.

Only two more days, she told herself and went inside.

"What took you so damn long?" Clark asked. He was at the kitchen table having his sixth beer for breakfast. "You have to cry to your grandpa about your ole' *meanie* husband? Get over here and kiss me."

Susan smiled. This was her best opportunity to turn the tide of the day in her favor. It was going to be unpleasant, but there was no use in making it worse. Her interview was two days away, her chance at freedom, maybe her only chance at freedom. She would go to the workshop beaten black and blue if she had to, but like *Bartleby*, she'd prefer not to.

Keep him happy.

"You know I didn't tell grandpa anything. Those roads are slick, so I had to drive crazy-slow to stay out of the ditch." Susan laced her fingers behind Clark's neck and passionately kissed him the way he liked. Her tongue almost tickled his tonsils. When they pried apart, Susan asked, "Would you like some breakfast? I believe we have another pork chop."

"Maybe later. The only thing I want is between your legs. Come on." Clark drained his beer, left the empty can on the table and stumbled down the hallway towards their bedroom, bouncing from wall-to-wall like a drunken pinball.

Susan threw the can in the trash, wiped her eyes, and followed him. She promised herself she wouldn't cry.

She lied.

Clark called it *Round One.* It was thirty-two minutes of hell.

What worried Susan wasn't what he did. He'd done all those things before. What worried her was his plans to do it again. After all, nobody names something *Round One* unless they anticipate a *Round Two, Round Three*, and so forth. How many rounds could she take? She didn't know and had no desire to find out.

Susan stood at the stove cooking Clark's fried eggs and pork chop. She had whelps on her back, buttocks, and legs, and there were trickles of blood from her ass-crack, down her inner thighs and fading away just above her ankles. It's crazy what the human psyche takes pleasure in and Susan took a grain of lunatic pleasure in the fact that her blood congealed on her ankles before dripping onto the floor. Cleaning her own ass-blood off the cheap, cracked linoleum would've been truly pathetic.

Round One, Susan thought...*Round One.*

Clark sat at the kitchen table, Susan's back facing him, and he admired his handiwork. He'd given it to her hard, just the way he liked it, just the way she deserved. All that crying was her way of letting him know he was hitting all the right spots. He knew her mind better than she did because it was a simple thing, a woman's mind.

Eat, fuck, and sleep.

That's all a woman thinks about. Everything else is just killing time until she can eat, fuck, or sleep again. And lie. That's the main one, and Susan was a blue-ribbon winner when it came to lying.

Her big job interview, a trip out of town, and boy, oh boy, it was going to be good for the family. "It's just the break we need," she had told him. Like he believed that shit. It was just the break *she* needed. She was planning to break up his home, take his kids, and leave him for some other guy. Well, he had a thing or two to teach her. *Round Two* was already on his mind.

Susan heard rushing air as Clark opened his ninth beer of the morning. *Hope*, that wriggly, squiggly maggot of a feeling, wormed itself in again. He was drinking one after another, and the odds of him passing out improved with each beer he downed. *Round Two* might never happen. Susan turned the stove eye's control knob down from Notch Four to Notch One. Notch One was labeled *Simmer*, and simmer was just what Susan wanted Clark to do.

Simmer.

Clark finished his tenth beer as Susan sat his breakfast in front of him. "Would you rather eat in the living room?" she asked. She looked at the cushionless, wooden chair next to Clark as a modern *Judas Chair*. Her recliner was, considering her current physical condition, a far more appealing target for her backside.

"No, this is fine. What are you eating?" Clark asked, and of course, the bastard wanted to eat in the kitchen when her sit-down equipment was out-of-order.

"I'm not hungry. If you'll excuse me, I'm going to the bathroom. I need to clean up a little. Can I get you anything else before I go?"

Clark said he was fine and turned his full attention to his meal. In the bathroom, Susan stepped into a cool shower and cried. She'd been here before and regained her composure faster than a first-timer. The important thing was letting Clark have enough time to finish his breakfast and get another beer without—this was paramount—upsetting him. That meant she couldn't linger in the bathroom too long because Clark hated waiting on her.

She patted dry because toweling off was out of the question. She put some ointment on her bleeding holes and dabbed some aloe on the worst of her whelps. Susan turned down her plushy, terrycloth robe for a pair of loose-fitting pants and an oversized top. She didn't want to entice Clark any more than necessary.

Clark finished his breakfast and left the dirty dishes on the table. He wobbled to the refrigerator and took out beer number eleven and cracked it open. The shower stopped in the bathroom and he prepared for the next round. *You've got it coming this time, babe.* Susan opened the bathroom door and Clark was already in the bedroom.

"In here," he called.

No, no, no, she thought, but Susan went to her husband.

Forty-five minutes later her grandpa and her sons were finishing their lunch, her husband was passed out beside her, and Susan was out of breath, gaped-mouth, and had no clue what the hell had just happened.

It started the way their love-making sessions always did. Clark staggering and stripping while she peeled out of her clothes. Their days of passionately undressing each other while groping all the feel-good places were so far behind them neither could remember the last time it occurred.

Susan braced herself, fully expecting Clark to inflict pain in a new or old way, but it didn't happen. Clark surprised her by lovingly and, oh-so-very slowly, lowering her to the bed. There she was, sitting on the bed, her legs hanging over the mattress, and her feet dangling above the floor. Then her husband, her bastard of a kidney-punching husband, did what he'd never done, not even when they were dating and first exploring each other's bodies. He dropped to his knees, pulled her thighs to his ears, and let his tongue do the talking.

Teasing at first, he brought her to the pleasure threshold then laid off only to resume when her breathing slowed, and her rocking hips stilled. He was all tongue, and Susan didn't know how long he was down there. She only knew she stopped counting orgasms when she rocked out number five, an all-time high, but Clark's tongue piled on a few more before he rose from his knees. He entered her slowly, teasing a bit there, too.

For the next twenty minutes, he was Conway Twitty, *Slowhand* himself.

When the last orgasm hit, Susan's body contorted into some crazy, bass-ackwards letter *C*, the twenty-seventh letter of the alphabet. It was as much pain as it was pleasure, and she knew if he didn't stop, Clark would finally kill her. Not with kidney punches, but with pleasure. A helluva note for a death certificate.

Cause of Death: Multiple Orgasms.

As if sensing she'd reached her breaking point, Clark rolled off her without finishing and passed smooth out. He didn't even drunk-snore the way he usually did. For the first time since they were newlyweds, she couldn't find anything he did wrong.

Round Two was as different from *Round One* as night was from day, and Susan wasn't sure she feared *Round Three* because she thought it would be like *Round One,* or because she was afraid it might be like *Round Two*. Either way, she thought, would be the death of her.

She needn't have worried because *Round Three* never came. Clark slept most of the afternoon, waking only once for a bathroom break and when he finally emerged from the bedroom, Susan was cleaning the living room. She had a can of furniture polish in one hand and a dusting cloth in the other. She heard him say, "Hey, good looking, whatcha' got cooking?" Susan dropped her can of Pledge and went to him. His hair was up on the side in an enormous cow-lick that was so damned endearing she temporarily forgot she hated him.

"Thank you for that, Casanova. You were perfect...and I mean that," she told him and kissed his nose.

"You deserve better," he said. "Let me help you finish before you have to get the boys."

Together, they cleaned the rest of the living room. Susan dusted, and Clark cleaned windows and straightened their magazine rack. They talked about the boys and how each was doing in school, and they talked about Susan's trip to Jackson. Clark offered advice: "Best stay on the interstate as long as you can. It's easy to get turned around and lost down there." Susan said she would and even found herself appreciative of his input.

At a quarter till six, the house was clean, and Susan said it was time to get the boys. She asked Clark to join her but he declined, preferring rather to hop in the shower and wash the sex off. They locked lips again and felt each other's tongue for two minutes. As she backed out of the driveway, he watched from the window with his phone in his hand. When she was gone, Clark dialed his best friend Dewayne and bowed out of their weekend hunting/camping trip.

Bitch thinks she can fool me...well, I'll show her who's the fool. He packed his travel bag.

Clark Vance was going to Jackson.

Chapter Thirty

Susan walked toward the house with only a slight limp, and Sherman admired her smooth gait from the kitchen window. She caught him watching and threw out an exaggerated parade-wave and smiled a toothy, foolish smile. The up-turned frown was so out-of-place it was creepy.

This wasn't the same woman who'd dropped off two sullen, little boys just that morning. This woman was happy—giddily so. It had been years since he had any experience in such matters, but if Sherman remembered that look correctly, Susan had been fucked silly. Somehow being fucked silly had, at least temporarily, cured her limp. If news of this miracle cure got out, the physical therapy industry was certainly in for a rush.

Piper held the door open for his mama. She kissed his forehead and said, "How's mama's big man?

"Fine. Are you okay?" Piper's worry wasn't ambiguous.

"Mama's perfect. Where's your little brother?" she asked without looking into her son's eyes.

Without speaking, Piper thumbed towards the bathroom, letting that suffice as his answer.

"Looks like you had a good day," Sherman said, and winked.

Susan searched his eyes, old eyes that knew more than they should, and the smile returned. First, little breaks of white popped out on her face, then her lips parted into a full-face smile again. The smile made her look ten years younger, more vivacious, simply beautiful, but it frightened Sherman more than her tears ever had.

"I sure did, grandpa. It was a great day." She winked back and hugged him.

Sherman wanted to ask, *"Why are you so happy?"* But that's sort of a lunatic question, wasn't it?

He should be happy for her, but his thoughts ran in a different vein. A woman who goes from weeping and limping in the morning to smiling like a shit-eating opossum and bounding like one of the *Ten Leaping Lords* in the afternoon is a woman who's aces at hiding her true mentality. That, or she's infected with a serious case of *hope*. If it was the latter, and Sherman guessed it was, he feared Susan's case was worse than serious. It was likely terminal because hopeful wives don't leave abusive husbands.

Susan loaded the boys and waved goodbye to Sherman. She wasn't only smiling as she drove away, she was singing, too.

Hope.

Susan pulled into her drive and Clark met them at the car. He opened her door and carried all the boys' bags inside. At the front door, Clark opened the door and stepped aside, letting them go in before him, before the *man-of-the-house*—Clark's favorite moniker. Piper and Sebastian went to their bedroom and closed the door behind them with every intention of not opening it again until morning. A knock at the door changed their plans.

Thinking it was his mother, Piper started toward the door. Before he got there the door opened and Clark poked his head in and Piper tried to hide his disappointment.

"You boys want to get pizza and watch movies tonight?"

It's neither fair nor entirely accurate to say Piper hated his daddy, but it was fair and entirely truthful to say he didn't care much for the man. Spending the night with his daddy was one notch above spending the night trapped on his bed with *Boogie Woogie Wu* skulking beneath, waiting to chew his little-boy toes off. But there was pizza to be considered, and forget Henry Clay. Pizza was the *Great Compromiser,* so Piper was in.

Sebastian was a harder sell. He played his cards close to the vest and didn't like his daddy, pizza or not. He loved his mama, though, and she was happier than he'd seen her in a long time, maybe his whole life. Wasn't his daddy part of the reason she was happy? It was for his mother's happiness that Sebastian smiled and gave pizza-night an enthusiastic two-thumbs-up.

There was no debate over the movie. They watched some Disney shit Clark hated and the boys and Susan laughed all the way through it.

The pizza was another no-debate issue. They always bought a large pan, half supreme and half pepperoni with extra cheese plastered over the whole pie. They bought a two-liter Coke to wash it down and for the first night since he couldn't remember when, Clark didn't drink a single beer.

After the first Disney feature, Susan popped in another and the laughter continued. Clark laughed when the others did, and after they'd taken an intermission to put the leftover pizza in the fridge, he held her hand until the boys dozed off. When they'd tucked Piper and Sebastian in for the night, mama and daddy returned to the living room and snuggled on the sofa.

"Are you ready for *Round Three*?" Clark whispered in her ear.

"My goodness, Clark, you're a beast today," Susan said and kissed his neck. "I don't think my poor va-jay-jay can handle any more rounds tonight."

He'd never been more relieved to be denied sex. Instead of making love, they crawled in bed and talked about home renovations they'd like to make as soon as they had the money. Susan fell asleep, and Clark lay awake watching the rhythmic rise and fall of her chest. He wanted to choke the life out of her, but now, wasn't the time.

He watched her sleep...

...and waited.

Chapter Thirty-One

Sherman watched Susan drive away and he tried to worry about them. Even though he knew they were in danger, he couldn't. He had a rather large problem himself and he knew his problem was only getting worse.

Twice today he'd had to pause his story-telling and excuse himself to the bathroom. He'd sat in the dark and fought back the yellowing skin, but it'd had been a close call both times. The *change* was coming, slowly right now, but if it came at him hard he'd never prevail against it.

Ursa walked through the backdoor as the orange sky faded to black. She didn't know what to expect, didn't know whether Sherman would be the *Handler* or something else. Relief washed over her when she saw him strapping *DeeDee* to his back.

"It's good to see you," she said.

"It's good to be seen." He didn't tell her about the two close-calls. She already suspected the *change* was close, or she soon would.

Either way, she had work to do tonight and the information wouldn't help her.

He reminded her that this was their last mission for a few days. "I'm going to have the boys this weekend and you have something to take care of."

Ursa grinned. Deviously, even seductively, she said, "Yes, and I hope he's a bad, bad boy. I know what to do with bad boys."

"Speaking of bad boys, let's find some," Sherman said.

Their supersonic flight ended abruptly over a made-to-order subdivision outside Lexington, Kentucky. The houses were yellow-brick, with black asphalt shingles and each looked exactly like the one on either side of it. Looking at them as a whole picture, without street names and house numbers, Ursa wondered how any of the humans found their way home. *Like looking for a needle in a stack of needles*, she thought.

She landed silently outside a shrub row and Sherman eased down at her side. "Is this the right place?" he asked.

"Yes, it's the right place. I feel the presence of evil here."

Crawling behind the shrubs they worked their way to the corner of the front yard. From there they raced to the wall and squatted behind a high, double-window. Sherman checked for the prying eyes of neighborhood looky-loos and seeing none, he rose to his feet and peeked through the window.

It was a kitchen with an island sink below a hanging rack of pots, pans, and skillets of every size, shape, and material. There were no hangers or visible means of support, and if not by witch's magic, Sherman didn't know what held them in place.

He saw down a short hallway and into the living room but couldn't see anyone. He turned his *Mind's Eye* inward and searched the two-story house top to bottom and saw nothing.

"You see anything?" Ursa mouthed.

"No. Wait." Sherman's mind dropped through the ground floor to the basement, but there was nothing there. He went even lower to a secret cellar, its doorway and staircase hidden beneath a table in the basement. Sherman's *Mind's Eye* revealed a man's swollen face. The guy's body was distorted, blurry like a half-erased pencil mark and his sallow skin was the bluish-gray of asphyxiation. The man faced the corner with his attention focused downward.

Suddenly, the bloated face turned to Sherman. *A Handler*, the man said and raced toward the corner.

Why are you running? Sherman asked himself.

Sherman turned his inner sight to the cellar's darkest corner. A bony white face stared back at him from the dark. The girl's dark hair had turned sickly gray and fallen out from lack of nutrition. Some of it she'd eaten to buy another minute of life and the rest she'd used to wipe herself after doing her business on the ground.

"Elizabeth," Sherman whispered.

"I'm coming!" his whisper was now a shout, looky-loos be damned.

Elizabeth's father ran to the corner and kicked his six-year-old daughter in the face. She was too exhausted to fear him and too dehydrated to cry. Her daddy brought his heel down on her throat.

Elizabeth Crane died with Sherman less than a minute away.

Sherman growled, "Stay out here and let no one in and no one out. I'll kill this bastard. He starved her to please Satan—starved his own daughter. I felt him when he killed her. He was upset he had to do it so quickly. He'll pay." Ursa would've protested, but Sherman didn't give her enough time.

Sherman struck the wall with *DeeDee's* flaming blade and the solid, yellow bricks burst into a dusty yellow cloud, reminding him of springtime pollen. Sherman descended into the basement, slung the table against the wall and flung open the cellar's hidden door. Instead of climbing down, he stepped into the hole and landed next to Ted Crane.

"*Handler*, are you ready for your reward?" Ted asked, and slashed Sherman's abdomen with filthy fingernails filed to strong points.

Sherman staggered back, saw Ted Crane's red eyes and death-bloated body and knew ole' Teddy was possessed by a *Feeder*, an incorporeal spirit, evil without physical form. Ted had Lucifer's mark on his forehead and the demon was in full control, ready to fight.

With speed Sherman forgot they possessed the demon landed an uppercut that lifted Sherman from the earthen floor and slammed his head on the basement's floor-joists above him. "I guess this means we're through talking, huh?" Sherman said as he picked himself off the ground.

The rabid man bit and chomped at Sherman, snapping like a reanimated corpse hungry for brains. Sherman dodged the chattering teeth, and the *change* hit. Instead of fighting it, Sherman dropped *DeeDee* and let the *change* come. The confused *Feeder* stepped back, as Sherman's body contorted and was thrown to the floor in writhing fits.

Wearing cracked, yellow skin and seeing through gray-stained eyes, Sherman levitated to his feet and floated within an inch of Ted's face. Sherman's rotten, putrid breath turned the demon's head in disgust. Sherman bared his fresh fangs.

"My turn."

With crazy-slick speed, Sherman jerked forward and sank his fangs into Ted's neck.

Ted howled from the bottom of his forfeited soul and fought his way upward through the *Feeder's* mind control. The *Feeder* fled Ted's dying body and Ted shouted, "Save me!"

The half-*changed* Sherman replied coldly, "You can't be saved, for you took *The Mark*. Theodore Crane, your fate is sealed."

When he'd spoken those words, the *change* reversed, and Sherman was the *Handler* again. *DeeDee* flew to his hand and Sherman brought her to rest against Ted's jugular.

"Thank you. Thank you. I owe you my life," Ted said, thinking Sherman meant to spare his life.

"Do you think I'd kill you so quickly after what you did to Elizabeth? Not a chance. You will suffer as she suffered." In one liquid movement, Sherman sliced off Ted's right arm. *DeeDee's* heated blade cauterized the wound and Ted screamed for Heaven.

The doors of mercy were shut to him.

Ursa heard Ted's banshee scream and apparently, so did everybody else, because lights popped on throughout the subdivision. Ursa imagined terrified fingers dialing 9-1-1 and went to get Sherman. She quietly entered the cellar and saw Ted Crane prostrate on the ground. His arms were missing, as was one of his legs, and he was kicking away from Sherman with that remaining leg. Ted's left arm and right leg were on the ground, flinching as spastic muscles died. Sherman stood over Ted, beating the crying man with his own right arm.

"Stop this blasphemy!" Ursa yelled.

"He deserves no less," Sherman said, and struck Ted in the face with the severed arm.

"*The guilty must pay*," Ursa said and decapitated Ted Crane.

"What is wrong with you?" Ursa took the arm from Sherman. "This is not how a *Handler* behaves. You're better than this."

"He let her starve. She was only six and he let her starve."

"Let's go." Ursa led the way up the stairs.

"Stop or we'll shoot," two cops shouted. "Get on your knees and put your hands on your head." Their twin Glocks trained on Ursa's chest. As per their orders, she raised her hands and the two cops fell asleep.

There were more cop's upstairs and an army of blue uniforms on the front lawn. Outside, the cops were joined by a crowd of concerned neighbors. Sherman and Ursa entranced them all and flew home.

Twenty minutes later, the crowd awakened with no memory of why they were gathered at the Crane's house, but Elizabeth's body gave them a clue.

After their return flight, Ursa asked, "What was that back there?"

Sherman eased into his recliner and ignored her.

"Answer me, *Handler*. I've never seen you like that before." Torture was evil, always evil, and Ursa's nature couldn't abide it.

"*It's* coming again." Sherman pushed up his sleeve and revealed a yellow patch of crispy skin above his elbow. "*It* took me in the cellar." Ursa touched the skin and knew exactly what *It* was.

"No, Sherman. Not now. What are you going to do? Piper and Sebastian are coming to stay with you. You can't turn into that...that...*thing* around them. You know what it will do to them."

Sherman looked at his old friend through tired, bloodshot eyes. He took her hand and held it to his cheek. She put her arm around his head and pulled it to her breast, and they embraced. The silence was heavy with dread, and finally, Sherman spoke. "At least things can't get any worse."

He was wrong. They could, and they did.

Chapter Thirty-Two

Clark waited for the sun, and when its rays cracked the dark bedroom, he tiptoed to the kitchen. How long had it been since he'd cooked breakfast? He remembered taking Susan breakfast in bed while she was pregnant. Was it Piper or Sebastian? Who could remember a thing like that?

"Wakey wakey," he whispered in Susan's ear. He didn't blind her with the bright overheads. Instead, he opened the curtains and God's yellow *Hello* gently lightened the room.

"What's going on? Something wrong with one of the boys?" Her crackly voice sounded like she was talking through a mouthful of rocks.

"No, no. They're sleeping. I wanted to do something nice for you. It's been awhile since you were treated like a princess. Eat-up while I clean the kitchen." He kissed her lips and ignored her dragon-breath.

Susan saw the tray, the eggs and bacon, and her tiny heart *pitter-pattered* in her chest and dammit, despite herself, she fell in love again. She sipped orange juice and softened the rocks in her throat and thanked him for the gesture. "Clark, this means so much, thank you." She smiled and wept as he left.

Clark stewed while he scrubbed the iron skillet and returned it to the stove eye for seasoning. *All I do to keep the peace around here*, he thought. All Susan had to do was be a woman and do what he said. Was that asking too much? He waited twenty minutes before returning to Susan's side.

Susan quickly closed her Bible when Clark entered out fear that the book or the man might burst into flames, given their proximity. "Thank you again, Clark. Everything was perfect. Get over here." He leaned in and she wrapped her arms around his neck and kissed him passionately.

"If you're done with the tray, I'll get it out of your way," Clark said, and swallowed a fragment of partially chewed egg. Given the go-ahead, Clark carried the tray to the kitchen and cleaned the dishes. Once everything was wiped dry and stashed in its proper place, he crawled into bed with Susan.

"Do you want to keep the boys here today?" Susan asked. It wasn't the kind of thing Clark usually went for, but since he'd apparently turned over a new leaf, she figured she'd ask.

Clark wasn't hip to her idea. "I know you want us to spend the day together, but I'm feeling a bit selfish and want you all to myself. Plus, you saw how excited Piper and Sebastian were about going to your grandpa's. He's filling their little heads with his old war-stories, and they love him for it."

Susan gave in without a fuss. Why ruin a good thing? She threw on some old clothes and woke the boys up and made their breakfast. While the boys ate, Susan packed their day-bags and started the car so it would be warm for her little men. "I'll be right back, honey," she told Clark, and walked out with a boy clinging to each hand.

Susan helped the boys inside but turned down coffee when Sherman offered. "You sure you have to rush off?" the old man asked.

Susan was sure. She pecked his cheek but was moving so fast he didn't feel her lips brush his weathered skin. She kissed Piper and Sebastian, told them to be good boys, behave, basically be everything except little boys. Out the door she went, trotting to the car without any sign of limp. Just a woman in love.

"Boys, your mama's in rare form this morning. Y'all must've had some kinda night last night."

Piper told Sherman about family night and acted out his favorite scenes from the movies. Sebastian filled in supporting roles and usually died when the scenes ended. The pizza was delicious, the culinary architect responsible for the masterpiece actually understood that *extra cheese* meant a shit-ton of cheese, not a few bonus sprinkles. Piper had so much fun last night he had trouble leaving his mama and daddy this morning. The smell of pizza hung in the house, reminding him of what turned out to be the last good time he shared with his family.

Sherman searched the boys' eyes for any sign of trouble. There were none. Piper and Sebastian were kids and if they'd been pushed to recall, they would've remembered Clark's past abuse. But this morning the only things on their minds, the only things showing in their eyes, were last night's festivities and their gross parents being all *lovey-dovey* the whole time.

Sherman considered asking the obvious question. *How are your mama and daddy getting along?* Or maybe even more pointedly. *Is your daddy hitting your mama?* The boys were both happy, though. Sherman was a *Handler* and responsible for meting out justice, but he was also a great-grandpa. Seeing Piper and Sebastian's smiles did his old soul good. They were happy, and he was happy for them.

The boys sat in the living room and Sherman brought in three cups of hot chocolate laden with marshmallow icebergs. They sipped and enjoyed a few moments of silence.

Susan was happy, the boys were happy, and Sherman had every reason to believe things would be all right. But he didn't believe it for a minute. As he continued telling Kelvin's story, Sherman feared Susan and the boys were living in the calm before the storm.

He was right.

Chapter Thirty-Three

K elvin's eyes traveled from face to groggy-eyed face. He smiled and said, "Good morning," to each of the Lancasters, but when his eyes landed on Rosalyn, they went no farther. "Good morning, Rosalyn." The thing in his pants jumped to attention when he called her by name.

"Mama, can we skip this morning? It's revival. It ain't even real church," Albert whined. "We can watch one of the TV preachers. It'd be same thing." Wearing his tighty-whities and a t-shirt proudly proclaiming, *Dummy on Duty* across the chest, Albert waited for her to deny his request. She promptly obliged him.

Sherman saw Albert's attire and sang, "Panty butt, panty butt, Albert's got a panty butt." Albert wanted to smash Sherman's aggravating face but sulked silently.

"I hope everybody slept as good as I did," Robert said, ignoring his sons. "Mama, this smells great." He palmed her bottom as she walked by.

"Robert Earl Lancaster, *beeehave* yourself." She snickered from the appreciated attention. "The kids can see you."

He chuckled. "Y'all don't mind, do you kids?"

"Ewww," Karen mouthed, not wanting to think about what she'd seen.

"Yuck," Albert said, and slammed his head into his outstretched hands.

"Gross," Rosalyn agreed. Inside she thought it was romantic that her parents still loved each other after all their years of marriage. That's how it was between her and John, too.

"Hmm?" Sherman asked. He wasn't watching but wouldn't have cared if he had been.

"Traitoring ingrates, the lot of you," Robert said. He was unusually playful and stuck his tongue out at them. Everyone laughed, even Albert, who was still half-pouting, blew raspberries back and forth around the table until Barbara stopped their foolishness.

"Kelvin, I'm sorry you had to see this," a shame-faced Barbara said.

"Oh, they're just having fun," he said without taking his eyes off Rosalyn's lips. Oh, how he wanted to see her pink tongue slip between her lips and moisten them the way she had last night. He almost came thinking about it.

"I don't suppose either of you men care to join us for service this morning, do you?" Barbara asked and jarred Kelvin from his fantasy.

Robert and Kelvin looked at each other before turning to face her condemning glare. Kelvin claimed to have some personal affairs that couldn't wait, and Robert said, "Maybe another time, mama."

"Well, I'm glad Jesus didn't have either of your attitudes. We'd be in a fix then, wouldn't we?" Neither man replied because she was the expert on such matters.

Robert supported Barbara's Christian activities and agreed the praying, the preaching, and the church-going were good things for the kids. He couldn't help feeling bad for them because as Albert said, it was revival week. There would be a visiting preacher at the pulpit, a traveling choir would handle the hymns, and outsiders would flock to the service for their yearly dose of righteousness.

All of that spelled one thing—*strangers*. In Robert's mind, a man ought not to meet a stranger unless somebody he knows dies. That way he never gets to know too many people.

Robert was sorry his kids had to go to revival, but his remorse faded as soon as Barbara's white 1975 Fury roared to life. It had four mix-matched tires and rust holes in three of its doors, but it never failed to get her where she was going and back. The Fury charioted his wife and kids out of the driveway. Robert waved and said, "See y'all when you get back."

When they were alone, Robert turned to Kelvin and asked, "What's up your sleeve for today? You got a hot date?" They were in the backyard looking at the potato beds. Kelvin was drinking coffee and smoking while Robert was drinking coffee and dodging Kelvin's smoke.

"I'm going to hang out here till about noon and head into town to catch a movie, I reckon. You wanna go?"

"Nah. I've got to ride around and check the fields. Theodore said he was almost finished hipping. Won't be long till we'll start planting. This weather is perfect, I tell you. You should skip wasting money on a picture show and ride with me."

Kelvin declined and asked, "Is it still okay that I use the old GMC?"

"Help yourself to her."

Kelvin watched Robert's Bronco disappear in a cloud of dust. He moved to the mulberry shade and sat in a metal swing that time and weather had rusted to a flaky orange that peppered the backside of anyone who dared sit down. Kelvin smoked and waited, making sure Robert didn't come back.

Twenty minutes and almost three cigarettes later, Robert hadn't returned. Kelvin crushed out his cigarette and walked in the house.

Kelvin stood there alone—alone not just in the house, but on the Lancaster property—and felt like a conqueror. Since he'd arrived they had treated him suspect. He deserved it, but what pissed Kelvin off was that they didn't *know* he deserved it. He let the thought roll away. They'd get theirs, and the conqueror would have his day. It was only a matter of time.

Barbara's pot-roast was slow-cooking for Sunday dinner and the beefy aroma filled the house with a savory weight almost too heavy to pass. He wasn't there for the roast, so he walked to the hallway. Karen and Rosalyn's door was closed. Not good. It was never closed unless one of the girls was in there, an impossibility since he'd watched the Fury cart them away.

Kelvin grabbed the doorknob and gave it a twist. It was a no-go. Rosalyn had locked it. It was a futile attempt at keeping him out and only slowed him down.

But slowing him down was all Rosalyn wanted to do.

The lock was easy to pick, even Sherman's fumbling fingers could manage it, but Kelvin's time was limited. If she could slow Kelvin enough, he might get caught doing something he shouldn't be doing. They would be home around noon because Methodists didn't spend all day in church like some other denominations. It wasn't a lack of interest on their part, of course. The Methodists were just better, more efficient worshippers than say, the Baptists or the Pentecostals, the least efficient worshippers because it took them all day to accomplish what the Methodists could do in ninety minutes.

Rosalyn was certain Kelvin would do something when they left. She didn't know what it might be. Whatever it was, it was sure to be despicable, sure to be something of which Barbara wouldn't approve. If they caught him red-handed, he couldn't deny it. Lying wouldn't save him. It wasn't much of a plan, but what else did she have?

Kelvin dropped to one knee in front of the lock and inserted his pocketknife's smallest blade into the doorknob's center hole. He turned it half a turn, and like a magician's *Abracadabra*, the door popped open. Kelvin walked in and surveyed his newly conquered kingdom.

The first field Robert checked was ready to plant. Theodore's rows were perfectly straight. Robert couldn't find a single row out of sync with the others. Robert faced the truth: Theodore was better at most every job than Robert had ever been. Theodore could easily run his own farm and probably would, in another season or two. The daddy in Robert smiled at the thought while the man in him was jealous. Still, there was pride in knowing his son was so good, at least partly, because Robert taught him so well.

Robert got out of the Bronco and grabbed a handful of the rich, black soil. The field was on the Chickasaw/Calhoun county line and was rumored to be the sight of a major battle in the *War of Northern Aggression*. Popular opinion held the dirt owed its richness to all the blood spilled there and while there was nobody to confirm or deny the truth, locals believed that most of the blood came from the Yankees.

There were more fields to check before dinner, so Robert hopped in the Bronco and cranked the eight-track's volume to ten.

Kelvin opened each drawer in the girls' chests and dressers slowly, like he was unearthing fragile artifacts. Before he touched anything, he snapped mental pictures of the contents. He memorized the way each *unmentionable* was folded and positioned. When he was finished snooping, he refolded each item exactly as it had been and put it back precisely where he'd found it.

Details mattered, he reminded himself. *The devil lived there.*

Panties went to his nose first, but he also sniffed the crotches of shorts and nylons on the thought that maybe, if he were really lucky, one of them might've been returned to the drawer after a quick wear. And, if his luck was there and the Gods of Perversion smiled on their disciple, the brief wearing might've left behind a trace of the feminine musk he was hard for. He needed something; anything.

Since Rosalyn started washing laundry nightly, Kelvin was desperate for an ounce of depravity. Some say necessity is the mother of invention, but men's passions are best driven by desperation. Kelvin was ashamed he didn't think of the *treasures* sooner, but after watching Rosalyn ride her fingers to Heaven last night a thought occurred to him, an incredibly *feminine* thought. He bet the clever Rosalyn hadn't thought of these *treasures* yet. As soon as he finished in their bedroom, Kelvin was ducking in the bathroom to test his theory.

Kelvin completed his sweep through the drawers, and everything smelled of Cheer detergent and nothing held his attention. He got undressed and slid inside their sheets. The pillows smelled of lotions and shampoos. He closed his eyes and inhaled the delicate female scents. He laid on one pillow and put the other between his legs. This escapade would have to do him for at least another week, so to get the biggest thrill possible, he dry-humped each pillow. Kelvin flipped the pillows to fuck both sides and thought *Now, you bitches'll sleep on my cock.*

It wasn't enough, would never be enough, but time was getting away from him. He didn't want to get caught where he was, doing what he was doing. He remade their bed as tightly as he found it and closed the door behind him, kissing it as it snicked shut.

Before he walked outside, he made a pit-stop in the bathroom but there were no *treasures* waiting for him. He was disappointed, but not deterred. There were three more weeks in the month.

His *treasures* would eventually be there. Nature would see to it.

Robert finished his survey and decided he'd start planting tomorrow morning. They'd start with the soybeans and knock them out in a few daylight-to-dark days. The sweet potatoes would take longer, but if the weather held out, he was only looking at a few weeks of hard labor. As soon as the potatoes were in the ground, he'd head to Alabama for the digger part. When the digger was fixed, he could return to the clearing and resume training with his sword. Robert pointed the Bronco in the direction of Barbara's pot roast and floored it.

His plan was perfect, but it fell apart immediately.

Barbara's rattle-trap Fury clanked into the driveway five minutes after noon. The church-going Lancasters rolled out like circus clowns.

"Get your hands off me," Rosalyn yelled at Sherman who was trying to steal her Sunday school book. "You've got your own." She whacked his grimy hands hard enough to get their mama's attention. Barbara saw what was going on and said nothing.

Sherman didn't care about his book. He wanted hers, and he didn't care about hers either. He wanted it because she didn't want him to have it. It was reason enough. Little brothers need little in the way of reason to aggravate older sisters.

Albert didn't speak to anyone. He was the first to exit the Fury and the first to the front door. He held open the screen so Karen or his mama could unlock the wooden door and let him in. Impatiently, he tapped the toes of his black, *biscuit shoes* thinking, *hurry up, hurry up, hurry the hell up.*

Sunday afternoon was the only time he had to play, and he intended to soak up every second of it. His mama would make him eat. She always did. He would eat like a snake, swallowing without chewing, and pray to not choke to death—he didn't know if snakes did that last part given their checkered past with God.

"Thank you, sonny boy," Barbara said. She unlocked the door and held it open for him.

"Thank you, mama." Albert didn't look back.

Karen was her usual quiet self. She set her Bible and Sunday school book on her bedside table. The room looked exactly the way she'd left it. Sniffing her pillow to see if it smelled like cock never crossed her mind, not that she'd recognized the smell even if it had. Life was all work, all the time for the eldest sister. It always had been, and she suspected it always would be. There was no time to think about cocks and pillows and who might've been in her room. She changed out of her Sunday dress and went to put dinner on the table.

Rosalyn was the last to come in because she'd been busy fighting off Sherman. She saw her bedroom door open after she made sure to close and lock it. Her pulse quickened, her face flushed, and she knew Kelvin had been in there. Then she remembered Karen, and the red dropped out of her face and her pulse rate returned to normal.

Maybe Karen unlocked the door and Kelvin hadn't been in there after all. "Was the door locked when you came in?" Rosalyn asked.

"I don't remember...no...it was closed, but I don't think it was locked. Why?"

"Never mind. It don't matter." Rosalyn was flush again with clammy hands and sweat beads on her forehead. Her heart shifted gears and beat faster than ever. She sat on the edge of the bed to keep from passing out. Kelvin had been in here. She slowly came around and changed out of her good clothes and joined her family for dinner.

Eating her roast, Rosalyn asked herself, *what's next*? Mother nature answered when Karen excused herself and went to the bathroom.

Nature called, and Kelvin's first *treasure* arrived.

Chapter Thirty-Four

A drop of water is nothing to a drowning man, but to a man dying of thirst, it's everything. Susan was happier than she should've been because she'd been sad for so long. Clark hadn't cured cancer or sacrificed himself for *the greater good*, he'd stopped beating and berating her and stopped yelling at Piper and Sebastian. He'd done nothing to merit the glossy coating Susan painted him in. Still, she pulled out of Sherman's drive singing along with the song in her head and truly loving Clark for the first time since Piper was born.

Susan dreamed she'd marry a sweet man, the kind of man mamas and daddies want for their daughters. In her mind, Clark was that kind of man this morning. And last night. And yesterday. That's a streak, and suddenly Susan was proud to be Clark's wife. With her final paycheck in her purse and while still knowing she needed to save the money, she wanted to do something special for Clark.

In front of the Piggly Wiggly, Susan popped open her compact. She checked her make-up in the tiny round mirror and intentionally failed to recall why she couldn't use her rearview mirror for the job. Ditto for the larger, lighted mirror Toyota saw fit to put on her sun visor.

She pushed a wobbly-wheeled cart down narrow aisles and selected Clark's favorites: T-bone steak, pork chops, Nilla Wafers, bananas, and assorted Little Debbie snacks cakes. These now filled the cart. Susan kept a running total in her mind, and when she chinged a hundred bucks, she checked out and headed home.

Clark knew she should've been back already and paced in front of the living room's double windows, increasing speed with each pass. The inevitable was upon him, and when he saw her pull into the drive, he headed out the door to *talk* to her. She had to learn.

Susan saw his face and wasn't afraid *of* him but was afraid *for* him. "Are you okay, honey? Did you hurt yourself?" Leave it to a *beatfreak* to worry if her abuser hurt himself. Two days ago, her ingrained response would've been fear, but today, she expressed concern.

"*Where have you been?*" he screamed, forgetting his loving-husband facade.

She was diluted enough to mistake his anger for concern. "I stopped by *The Pig* so you'd have something to eat this weekend. I got your favorites. Does *Clarky-Warky* want a T-bone?" She retrieved the grocery bags from the passenger seat as Clark closed the distance between them in giant, angry strides.

In his mind, Clark saw his fist slamming into her lying nose, but he saw the plastic bags before he swung. The outline of the T-bone pushed through the thin plastic, a raised-relief map that led directly to his stomach. With the right hand he'd intended to clock her with, he took the bags from her hands and folded his left arm around her waist.

"I was so worried about you! I thought you'd had a wreck or something."

Susan kissed his check. He was so thoughtful. "My hero," she said, and walked inside in front of him.

She unpacked the bags and displayed each item like game show host for Clark's approval. He regretted he wouldn't be home to eat any of it, and a small part of him appreciated her effort at pleasing him. If she'd tried to please him more often, maybe things would've been different between them.

Maybe they still could be after he talked this Jackson nonsense out of her.

They got undressed and retired to the bedroom where they spent the morning swapping from napping sessions to making love. Around noon, Clark got in the shower, and two minutes later, Susan pulled the curtain back and joined him.

"Wash my hair," she told him. Clark didn't want to play beauty-shop but went along with her to ride the peace-train until it derailed.

Susan dropped to her knees in front of him and looked up into his eyes. "I don't have any money, sir. How will I pay you?" She put him in her mouth, and instantly, being a beautician wasn't so bad.

When her hair was clean and he finished, they grabbed some Little Debbie snacks and snuggled on the couch. She fed him bite-sized pieces of Nutty Bars while some reporter warned them that the current administration's policies were, "Extremely dangerous to our democracy."

Clark killed the television and swallowed his Nutty Bar with a gulp of beer, his first one in two-days. Susan saw the can, smelled the sour, urine-colored drink, but didn't consider its implications. She continued feeding Clark, continued resting in his arms, and continued loving him.

What was the implication? Would alcohol cause him to lose control? If Susan ever thought it or if she'd ever thought he beat her because he drank too much, she was dead wrong. If it were true, correcting his behavior was as simple as not drinking. Nothing is ever so simple, and drinking wasn't the cause of Clark's behavior. It was an effect of a darker, deeper sickness too restless to lie dormant, no matter how *lovey-dovey* they were.

Susan broke off another chunk of Nutty Bar and Clark snapped it up, almost getting the tip of Susan's fingers in the bite. She caught his stare, returned it, and for the last time, Susan said, "I love you, Clark."

Chapter Thirty-Five

Over Sunday dinner, Robert told everyone his plan. "In the morning, me and Theodore are going to start planting soybeans. Y'all can get ready to start pulling potato plants in about a week." Robert wasn't giddy, because real men didn't get giddy, but he was as close to giddy as a man could get.

He ate breakfast Monday morning and went outside. Kelvin had the John Deere 4040 already fueled and hooked to the soybean planters. Robert went to the seed barn and loaded the flatbed GMC with heavy bags. The truck's dual maypops groaned under the weight and Robert prayed to get through the season without a blowout. Theodore arrived just after Robert loaded the last bag.

Theodore led with the tractor and Robert followed to keep speeders from tailgating the planters. The GMC's headlights landed on the rear of the planters and Robert honked his horn, stuck his head out the window, and screamed, "HOLD IT!" His perfect plan hit its first snag.

Three of the hoppers were hanging loosely to the side and two more looked ready to fall off. The planters were in such bad shape they probably wouldn't survive the trip to the field, so Robert told Kelvin, "I need them in the field as soon as possible."

Kelvin cursed the planters but went to work on them immediately. Robert's bad luck turned out to be a blessing for Kelvin.

Robert drove to his brother's house and asked to borrow his planters. His brother was behind schedule and wouldn't need his for a few weeks. Of course, Robert could use his planters. "Just bring 'em back when you're done with 'em." Robert was grateful, but there was a problem.

Robert was counting on using his eight-row planters, but his brothers only sowed four rows. It would take twice as long to plant the fields and would burn twice as much fuel doing it. Even worse, Robert wouldn't start setting potatoes as early as he'd hoped. Everything was going to be a week, maybe two weeks behind. It was unfortunate because it gave Mother Nature more time to screw with the perfect weather. It also meant Robert would have to continue putting off his trips to the clearing.

Sorry, sword. Little Robert can't come out to play, he thought.

To make up the time they were losing with the four-row planters, Robert and Theodore went to the fields earlier and stayed later, often working by the John Deere's headlights. Robert was in the field all day and part of the night, and most of the time, Kelvin was the only man at the house. While Robert was away, Kelvin took liberties he would've never tried had his cousin been there. It started with him sitting in Robert's chair at the kitchen table.

"There ain't no good reason for Robert's chair to be empty while I'm crowding the girls," Kelvin said. He slid his plate into Robert's position. Barbara didn't like the move, but Kelvin's argument made sense. Rosalyn was happy—overjoyed really—to have him farther away from her. The invasion of Robert's chair went so well Kelvin dug in a little deeper.

Kelvin showered, but instead of going to his room in the shed he sat in Robert's recliner. He knew to be gone before Robert came home so he monitored his watch closely. Barbara and the kids finished their chores and shuffled into the living room. It was odd seeing Kelvin in Robert's recliner, but Kelvin didn't speak, so neither did they.

This happened a few nights in a row without anyone raising complaints. Since Robert never mentioned it to him, Kelvin knew no one told Robert about the new *status quo*. If he'd known, Robert would've said plenty. After a few days, Kelvin tried to root deeper.

The things we know are important, but sometimes, it's the things we don't know that are the most important. What Kelvin didn't know was Albert overheard him moaning Barbara, Karen, and Rosalyn's names. If Kelvin had known it, he would've stayed the hell away from Albert.

Kelvin finished his shower, watched TV, and waited for Barbara to tell Albert and Sherman it was their bedtime. They left the living room and a few moments later, Kelvin slowly got up and walked to their room. Standing inside the doorway, Kelvin asked, "Y'all want me to tell y'all a bedtime story?"

"Yes, Cousin Kelvin. Make it a scary one," Sherman said. "Make it about the *ghoulie monster*."

"Mama! Cousin Kelvin is bothering us," Albert screamed and sat in his bed like a stone gargoyle, a dead stare fixed on the intruder.

Kelvin eased out of their room, thinking, *Loud-mouthed, pudgy bastard.*

"Kelvin, what on earth are you doing in here?" Barbara's left hand was on her hip and her right one was pointing a finger in his face.

"Barb," he said, getting too familiar for her taste, "I know that Robert is staying in the field a little later and y'all have done so much to help me. I want to pay y'all back any way I can. I really loved a good bedtime story when I was a kid, so I was going to tell the boys one."

"No harm done this time, but from now on, you need to go back to your room after supper. It don't look right, a man being in here while Robert is gone, cousin or not. I'm sure you understand."

He understood perfectly, but he had no intention of going back to the way things were. The next night, he sat in Robert's chair and said nothing to no one. Barbara let it pass.

A week went by without incident, so Kelvin started *talking-up* Barbara and the girls. He was mildly flirty at first but got spicier when no one objected. Barbara and Karen tolerated him, but Rosalyn would have nothing to do with him.

While Barbara and Karen were preparing supper, Kelvin came into the kitchen. They looked at him but stayed focused on their jobs. He said, "My, my, you two are the picture of beauty tonight."

Karen continued working without acknowledging him, but Barbara said, "Thank you."

"Did y'all have a good day? Shoot, I don't even know why I asked. God wouldn't let his two prettiest angels have bad days, would he?"

This time they both ignored him.

"I've been underneath that tractor all day, craning my neck till I can barely move it." Kelvin demonstrated his shortened range of motion and ended the exaggerated rotations with terrible scowls. "Do either of you angels want to lay hands on me and heal me? I bet a massage would make me a new man."

When neither of them replied, he added, "Now, don't y'all be shy. There's enough of old Kelvin for both of you. Y'all can work on me together. I bet that'll get my stiff..." he cleared his throat and left that last word hanging in the air, "...neck loosened right up."

Barbara had *had it up to here* with Kelvin's suggestive behavior, and Kelvin saw anger in her flaring eyes. He loved it and wasn't worried at all. Why would he be? He wanted to piss her off and anticipated her reaction. He was surprised it didn't come sooner.

Before she could speak her mind, Kelvin said, "Barbara, are y'all going to Wednesday night service? If you do, I'd really like to tag along with y'all...if you think it'd be okay with Robert, of course."

Kelvin's comments and creepy, lingering leers evaporated in a cloud of forgiveness. Barbara's mind turned from his transgressions to his desire to go to the house of the Lord. "Of course we're going, and I think it's marvelous that you want to come with us. Maybe if he sees you go, Robert might want to come too," Barbara said.

Karen, who knew her mama was gullible, couldn't believe her mama was so easily swung she would buy Kelvin's crap. Quickly, to avoid calling her mama out, Karen excused herself.

Was Kelvin creepy? Sure, but Barbara couldn't miss an opportunity to help a hungry soul find the Savior's door.

Kelvin knew the game and played it flawlessly. "Oh, Barb, that would be great. Imagine, all of us going to worship together," Kelvin said, and put his arm around her shoulders. His fingers fell lightly on her breast, but she pretended to not notice. Barbara's joy increased exponentially when Kelvin volunteered to say *grace* before their meal.

Kelvin was on top of the world, master of his domain and of Robert's. He joked around with Sherman—by then Sherman was the only Lancaster kid that would have anything to do with him. To the other kids' dismay, Kelvin and Barbara talked Bible, swapped their favorite verses and giggled like school chums.

To Kelvin, he was getting closer to Barbara, coming together the way a man and woman should before they *came together*. To Barbara, they were sharing testimonies of their faith and celebrating Christ Jesus, and the kids didn't know what the hell was happening.

Kelvin thanked them for the delicious meal, took his shower, and went into the living room, *his* living room. He flicked on the console television, thrilled everything was going so well. It was so simple to rile her up, then manipulating her to accept him again was even easier. It was too much fun. He couldn't wait to do it again. Kelvin reclined and crossed his ankles on the worn footrest.

His intentions were to watch TV and to flirt with the girls when they finished in the kitchen, but they took longer than usual. Maybe there were more things to put up. Maybe they were exceptionally tired and moving slower. Whatever the cause, they were behind schedule.

Kelvin worked harder and made sure Robert and Theodore had everything they needed. That way, they would stay in the fields and out of his way. Because of his honest work, Kelvin was tired, and on top of being tired, he was well fed and gloating.

Pleased with himself and smiling at his good fortune, Kelvin fell fast asleep.

Rosalyn hushed her siblings, and said, "Don't wake him. Let daddy find him like that. See if he's smiling then."

Chapter Thirty-Six

N othing had gone right that day. First, their tractor sprang a hydraulic leak in a rear-lift hose. The planter's weight jetted the hydraulic fluid through the hole like a torn jugular and emptied the hydraulic reservoir before Theodore knew what was happening. "Fuck me, Freddy," Robert cursed as the planter's plummet to the dusty field.

"Do you want me to take it to Kelvin?" Theodore asked.

"No, we'll fix it out here," Robert said, and spit out a string of the four-letter-words he favored in stressful situations.

Running to town and back and replacing the ruined hose cost two hours of daylight. After Robert tightened the final brass fitting securing the new hose in place, he and Theodore worked fast and furious until they emptied the seed hoppers. Disaster struck again when they tried to refill the hoppers.

The top layer of bags was okay, but Robert looked at the next layer of bags. "Dammit!" He threw his hat on the ground and kicked it under the truck. Theodore climbed onto the truck and saw the problem.

Rats or coons or some other shitty critter had gnawed its way into the rest of the bags. Half of the remaining bags were only partially eaten, but the other half was gone. There wasn't enough seed to fill the planters, so Robert told Theodore to use what they had while he ran to the Co-op for more seed.

At the Co-op, things went from bad to worse. The parking lot was full, so Robert parked on the curb. He knew the owners of every truck and was absolutely certain he didn't want to know why they were all at the Co-op instead of in their fields.

"What's going on, Joe?" Robert asked Joseph Parker, who was standing outside the Co-op with several other guys.

"Robert, I hope you ain't after soybean seeds," Joe said, and spit thick brown tobacco to the side. Wiping a string drool from his chin, he said, "They're slap out, and we're all waiting on the seed truck to get here. They said it should be here in about two hours. They've been saying that for the last four hours, so I wouldn't put much stock into it if I were you."

Robert waited three hours for the seed to arrive and waited another hour while the guys ahead of him bought most of the seed. When it was his turn, he bought the few remaining bags and raced back to the field to find Theodore napping.

"Wake up, boy. We got seed," Robert said.

Theodore inspected the short stack of bags. "Is that all you got?"

"It's all they had. The head cock-rocker said they got two trucks delivering tonight. I'll go over first thing in the morning and load up what we need."

They worked till they ran out of seeds, which wasn't long, and Robert went home early.

And in a bad mood.

Robert walked in, looked at the plate of leftovers Barbara left him, and walked past it. He wasn't hungry. He was mad, tired, and wanted one thing—to collapse in his recliner.

"What the hell? Get your sorry ass out of my chair," Robert said. He kicked the footrest and jarred Kelvin from his psychotic dreams, dreams that would've gotten him killed on the spot if Robert had known their content.

"Hey, Robert, what's going on? Looks like I drifted off," Kelvin said in a groggy tone. It pissed Robert off even further than he already was.

"You getting out of my chair is what's going on, if you know what's good for you." Robert clenched his hand into a fist. In his closet, the sword vibrated in its deerskin scabbard.

"Okay, okay, I'm moving." Kelvin was more embarrassed than ever in his life but was angrier than he was ashamed.

When he looked into the hallway Kelvin saw Rosalyn, Karen, and Albert snickering at him. Their smiles and pointing fingers pushed Kelvin from embarrassed to a flaming, red-faced ashamed. Tears filled his eyes as Robert continued chewing into him. The evil man was reduced to a spiteful, teary-eyed little boy. His face itched and burned like it was on fire. He would've taken death right then if it had been offered.

"Why are you even in my house this late at night? I told you that you could stay here and work till you found something better. I didn't say one damned word about you shacking up in my house with my wife and kids while I was out working." Robert still had fists at the end of both arms.

His sword vibrated furiously and fell over.

Kelvin got out of the recliner and walked to the sofa. As soon as his butt hit the cushion, Robert bit again.

"Don't sit your ass on my couch. Ain't you been listening? Get your ass out to your room. If it ain't good enough for you, pack your shit and leave this hill. I'm as serious as a damn heart attack. Don't be back in this house after dark if I ain't here."

"Can I still take my meals in the kitchen?" Kelvin whimpered, almost whispering too low to be heard.

Robert told him to get a plate and eat outside.

Barbara stepped in and said, "Daddy, won't it be okay if he leaves as soon as he finishes his plate? I don't want my dishes drug all over tarnation. They're bound to get broke."

Certainly, Barbara didn't want her dishes broken, but she spoke up because she was worried about Kelvin. Not letting him eat at the table was too much, too hard. It wasn't Christian. Kelvin was going to go to church with them, and if he went, Robert might go. It was a long shot, but Barbara would do almost anything to get Robert in a pew.

"Eat in here if she says so, but when you're done you get your ass back where you belong. If I hear of you being in here after dark again, you're packing your shit and like Hank Snow, you're *Movin' On.*"

"Thanks, Robert." Kelvin left the house with his tail between his legs, holding back tears. He pulled his bedroom door shut, killed the lights, and sobbed into his pillow.

You'll pay for that. I'll get you all. Kelvin cried himself to sleep.

Chapter Thirty-Seven

T he day could've gone better, Susan thought as she pulled on her heavy coat. She and Clark had spent the day *vegged-out*. That part was nice, but he'd been drinking again. Not as heavy as before, but steadily enough to arouse concerns. He hadn't been violent and his comments, while not the sugar-coated sweet-nothings of the last two days, weren't as stinging as his remarks used to be.

Susan jokingly remarked about a CNN reporter's outfit, saying it would've looked more at home on the corner of *MLK* Boulevard and Jackson Street than behind the news desk. Clark snapped back, "You're the one who'd know about whores and their clothes."

She considered telling him, *'That wasn't very nice,'* but decided it was only the beer talking. She pulled on her snow boots, put a hand on the doorknob and turned to say, "I love you, honey," when Clark shouted, "Don't take all damn night!"

Susan quietly left.

She fastened her seatbelt and reached for the radio dial. She pulled her hand back and drove to Sherman's in silence. *Hope* refused to step aside for *reason*, and Susan refused to throw in the towel.

Clark's behavior was suspicious and indicative that the new-leaf he'd turned over was only shiny on one side. Susan knew the signs, but what kind of wife gives up on her husband at the first sign of trouble? He wasn't backslidden, he was only backsliding.

There was still hope.

"Mama," Piper shouted when Susan's car door slammed. He hopped off the sofa and met Susan at the door. Sebastian was two steps behind, but Sherman was slower getting there. The inside of his skull itched and an unquenchable thirst rumbled in his gut.

Susan hid her concerns behind a toothy smile and the boys, still riding high from the wonderful night they'd spent with their parents, bought her act. Sherman saw through her and gave her an opportunity to ask for help. "Did you and Clark have another good day together?"

She didn't exactly lie when she told him yes. The day started off great, slumped in the early morning, but was back up to great around noon. Things didn't go south until late afternoon.

"Are you're still okay keeping my angels this weekend?" Susan asked.

"Of course. Looking forward to it."

Sebastian asked if they were having pizza again tonight and Susan said he and Piper could share the leftovers. Right then, Sebastian decided being an only child had a distinct attraction.

Piper, a pizza lover, didn't care about the pizza. For the first time in years he was genuinely excited to see his daddy. Piper was the first to hug Sherman and say, "See you in the morning." Piper took their bags and stood by the door, waiting for the others to take a hint.

In the car Susan warned, "Boys, your daddy has been a little down this afternoon. I think all this cold weather is getting to him, so y'all be on your best behavior. Okay?"

Piper and Sebastian agreed, but they were young boys and their best behavior wasn't very good. They both intended to make their daddy happy. Neither wanted things to go back to the way they were. Susan parked the car and noticed Clark didn't greet them this time. She grabbed for Sebastian's bags, but he pulled them back. "Mama, you get the door. I'll carry my bags."

"Okay but remember to carry them to your room. Your daddy doesn't like stuff lying around."

The next morning, Susan limped into the kitchen and tripped over Sebastian's bags.

Sherman walked to the spare bedroom and pulled the covers from the bunk beds. He remade them with clean linen and was draping the comforter on the second twin when Ursa spoke to him.

"Are you all right?"

Sherman looked at her like *what the hell are you talking about*, but said, "Yes."

"Don't look at me like that and don't 'yes' me. You know why I'm asking."

"I'm fine, Ursa. I guess it went away again. No claws. No fangs. I'm one-hundred percent great-grandpa." To prove his lie, his stomach growled. The early thirst had grown from his gut and chest and occupied his brain as well. "Maybe not a hundred percent, but I'm fine."

"I can't do what you asked me to do if I'm worrying about you and what you might do to those boys. Call it off."

"Not happening. This is Susan's big chance and I'll see she gets it. I can hold the *change* off if I have to. Thanks for your concern, but there's no way I'd hurt those boys. We're going to have a great time. You just do what I asked you to." He said all this with convincing false conviction but Ursa knew better. Sherman had never held the *change* off. They both knew he wouldn't hold it off now.

Piper walked in the house first and went straight to his bedroom. He set his bags by the door and that's when he noticed they were wet from where he dropped them in the snow. He cringed when he saw a wet trail from the front door, through the kitchen, down the hallway, and into his bedroom. He ran to the bathroom for a towel, but he was too late.

Sebastian made it halfway across the kitchen before Clark stormed out of the living room into the hallway. Clark was already upset and that was before he saw the drip-drop trail running down the middle of the hallway like a watery spine. "What's this fucking shit?" Clark hollered.

"Oh gosh," Susan said, and scurried to the drawer where they kept their dishtowels. "I'll wipe that right up." She saw his dull look, eyes unable to focus through the alcohol curtain, and knew a quick change of conversation was needed. "Do you want me to cook your steak tonight? How about gravy to go with it?"

Sebastian heard panic in his mama's voice and dropped his bags to help. Clark didn't mean to do it. He swung his arm back, getting ready to say *Look at this mess, just look at this mess! They haven't been here a minute and LOOK at this mess*, but in doing so, he backhanded Sebastian.

The hit landed on Sebastian's shoulder and might've stung a little but didn't hurt. Regardless, it startled Sebastian and scared tears flooded from his baby-blues. Sebastian grabbed his shoulder and each of his tears burned Susan's soul like acid. Her heart pumped crazy rage through her veins, and she charged Clark. He saw her expression...and welcomed it.

Piper came out of the bathroom and saw the mayhem. Clark's left hand was around Susan's neck while he threw short jabs with his right. Piper counted six blows. He ran socked-footed down the hallway, dragging the towel with him like Linus van Pelt from *Peanuts*. "I'm sorry, daddy! I'll clean it up. I swear."

Clark turned to Piper. "Damn right you'll clean it up. Do it and get your brother to your room. I don't want to hear a peep from either of you. Is that clear?"

"Don't hurt *mommie*," Piper said, and felt like a little baby when he heard the words come out of his mouth.

"Do what I said!" Clark shouted and took his hand from Susan's neck. She fell to the floor in a heap, like a bag with no bones.

Piper and Sebastian thought she was dead. They went to their room, holding hands and crying. They climbed under the covers of Piper's bed and hours later, all cried out, they fell asleep.

Clark didn't say anything as Susan struggled to get off the floor, instead just watched in sick humor. She held her side and paused for a long minute after straightening her back. She couldn't remember doing it, but she made her way to their bedroom and closed the door behind her.

Clark followed her to the bedroom looking for a fight, but Susan was undressed and in bed when he stomped in. Clark undressed and joined her under the covers. Lying there, pillow rolled under his neck, his thoughts were disjointed. Each time he tried to formulate a string of thoughts into a coherent whole he was jarred out of sync by Susan's incessant sniffling. What was wrong with her? Sure, he'd *talked* to her, but only a little, and it was for her own good.

Of course, he had to straighten her out if she got a little too mouthy or forgot her place. It was a man's job to keep his wife in line. It was tiresome being in charge all the time, but it was his lot to keep his family together. He would do it, too. No matter what.

He knew Susan's plans. He could smell them reeking off her as fishy as her cunt. She planned to leave him, and he didn't blame her, couldn't blame her. It was her sex's lack of constitution and general wishy-washiness that made them the way they were. It wasn't right to blame them for it any more than it was right to blame a dog for biting. It's just their nature and it wasn't just Susan. It was all women.

Occasionally, his daddy had to keep his mama in line with a little boot-to-ass loving. That Clark had to keep Susan in line came as no earth-shattering surprise to him. It was her nature, and it was the reason he'd never cheated.

A new cunt would be cut from the same cunt-cloth as his wife, his mother, and every other cunt. So why bother? He'd concentrate on keeping his own cunt in line.

He watched her all night. At some point, she fell asleep and he believed the noisy bitch snored just to piss him off. When the alarm sounded, he woke her with a stinging slap across her cheek.

"Rise and shine, bitch. It's the first day of the rest of your life."

Chapter Thirty-Eight

S usan stared into the bathroom mirror, and a horribly aged hag stared back. She couldn't hide her two-tone face from the condemning harshness of the bathroom's incandescent bulbs. Her cheeks were haggard and droopy like old saddlebags. One was flesh-toned, maybe olive, maybe beige, but thanks to Clark's *wake-up call*, the other was bright, lively pink.

For a minute, Susan saw herself smashing the five bulbs from the vanity mirror's light bar and tip-toeing back into her bedroom. Clark would be asleep. Susan watched this surreal version of herself open Clark's jugular with a jagged shard of light bulb glass. If she didn't have Piper and Sebastian, she might have tried it.

Only one thing could save her and her kids and that was a 'Good Job.' Getting it was all that mattered. She ignored her stinging cheek, shallow breaths, and throbbing hip and stepped into the shower. Once done, she wiped the fog from mirror and applied her face. With Hollywood-perfect care, Susan hid Clark's handiwork with magic wands available at your neighborhood Walmart. She stared into the mirror. The aged hag had retreated, and a youthful woman smiled back.

Last night, Clark landed a jab squarely on Susan's sore hip and woke the pain troll lying dormant in the swollen joint. This morning, the pain troll was screaming with well-rested fury. Susan opened the medicine cabinet and took two ibuprofens. She pretended the drug worked, and while the pills did nothing, at least the pretense made her feel better.

Susan limped down the hallway and into the kitchen. She wasn't moving carelessly fast, but like anyone in a familiar place she wasn't paying close attention to where she was going either. Entering the kitchen, Susan' good foot ran into Sebastian's day bag and with nothing but her lousy leg to catch her, she fell. Of course, she landed on her sore hip.

Excruciating pain grabbed the reins and she screamed. Clark, who wasn't asleep, jerked open their bedroom door and sprinted into the kitchen. When he saw Susan sprawled on the floor clutching her hip and crying her makeup off, he laughed so hard he had to brace himself against falling.

Piper and Sebastian were getting dressed and heard their mother's cry. Piper reached for the door but heard his parents' door open and withdrew his hand. Clark's laughter infuriated the nine-year-old, but Piper's own fear infuriated him more.

Susan heard Clark's laughter and for some reason she kicked in his direction. Was she trying to kick him? Probably not. He was too far away, and her leg was in too much pain. She kicked out of pain and frustration, not at Clark, but Clark didn't see it that way.

He kicked back.

Clark stepped forward and slammed his barefoot against her hip. Rockets of pain launched in all directions and exploded into a giant fireworks' display in her brain.

"Why do you make me do that?" he asked her, and walked to their bedroom, confused.

Piper and Sebastian helped Susan to her feet. They were ready to go, and in a complete reversal from yesterday, ready to get away from Clark. "We'll leave in a minute, boys," Susan said. She returned to the bathroom, looked in the mirror, and the hag stared back. Susan grabbed her magic wands, but magic or no magic, this time the hag held her ground.

Sherman met them at the door. Piper and Sebastian carried their own bags. Susan's limp was worse than ever. "Boys, put your stuff in the extra bedroom. Susan, are you excited about your trip?" Sherman asked, ignoring the obvious.

"I'm more nervous than anything. I really need this job. Are you sure you'll be okay with the boys?" she asked, with no idea what she'd do if he'd answered, *No, I won't be okay. Take them back.*

"I'll be better than okay, so don't worry about me. Be careful and let us know when you get there. If you have any trouble, call, and I'll load up the young posse and we'll ride to the rescue."

"Thank you, grandpa. I love you so much." She forgot her situation and threw her arms around him. He hugged her back, and the pain was unbearable, impossible to hide. She grabbed her side, gasped for breath, and forced a mouthful of vomit back down her throat.

Two of Clark's jabs hit below her right breast and cracked several ribs. She knew she was bruised, but forgot about the breaks beneath the yellow, blue, and purple rainbow skin. Sherman's hug was light, but even the lightest touch hurts broken ribs.

"You want to tell me about it now or after I *talk* to Clark. We both know what this is and what it means," Sherman said.

"Grandpa, we'll talk about it, I promise. Don't do anything to him...yet. Please. I can't think about it right now. I probably don't have any chance of getting hired, but if I could, it might be just what me and the boys need to get away from Clark. I don't want to screw up my chance by worrying about him. Please...not today, grandpa."

Sherman didn't want to, it was against every grain of his being, but he gave in. "Okay, don't worry about it for now. Just be careful. Keep your mind on driving and getting that job. I don't want you having a wreck because your mind is on—wait a minute. Clark's not going with you, is he?"

"Absolutely not. He said he's going camping with his buddies. With any luck he'll get lost." She had to get out of there before Sherman changed his mind, so Susan said a hurried round of goodbyes and limped back to her car.

Sherman watched from the front door and saw that Susan's ribs weren't the only things bothering her. Her left leg wasn't keeping up with the right. She tried to walk normally, but her heel drew a deep furrow in his driveway's loose gravel.

I'm going to kill you, Clark, thought Sherman. His stomach growled and his gums itched.

Four pairs of eyes watched Susan leave. Sherman watched from the kitchen door. He waved, and she waved back. Piper and Sebastian kept watch from the living room windows. They also waved. She waved and blew kisses. Clark watched from across the road. He didn't wave.

Clark's position faced east and the rising sun bounced rays off his binoculars' objectives. Sherman's old eyes didn't miss the glints. It wasn't difficult to guess who was responsible for those long-distance reflections. Sherman wanted to go after Clark right then and there, but he'd given Susan his word. Besides, the boys were with him. They didn't like their daddy, of that Sherman was sure, but he didn't think they were prepared to see what their great-grandpa was going to do to him.

The reflections disappeared moments after Susan's departure. Sherman had to warn her but didn't want to alarm the boys. "Boys,

I've gotta go to the bathroom. I got a super-sized lunker, and it wants out." Nobody enjoys bowel movements as much as old men and young boys, and all three fell into crazy laughter.

"Great-grandpa has to make number two. *Yuuuuck*," Sebastian said. "Doo-doo butt, doo-doo butt!"

"Be sure to wipe good," Piper said, and demonstrated his wiping technique. He bent forward and reached between his legs and wiped back-to-front.

"Turd, if you wipe like that you'll end up with shitty balls," Sherman said as he closed the bathroom door. He sat on the toilet, took out his phone, and made the call.

When Susan answered, Sherman bypassed etiquette and blurted out, "Someone was spying on you." He told her about the two shimmering, glints he saw across the road. "When you left, so did they. I bet Clark is following you right now. Please tell me you have the gun I gave you."

"I do, grandpa. It's right here beside me, loaded, and ready for action just like you taught me." She prayed Clark wasn't following her but twisted her neck like Hooty the owl to see if he was. She regretted selling the gun, but it'd been pawned for rent a few months ago. She hated lying to her grandpa, but what good would the truth do?

"Okay. Remember to let us know when you get down there. And if you see Clark, get around lots of people and call me immediately." Clark was dangerous, but Susan was safer than she knew.

Sherman hung up and thought: *That bastard is beating her again.* That was bad, but what was worse was Susan had lied about it.

She's not ready to put a stop to it. Maybe Clark following her to Jackson was the best thing that could happen. If Susan wanted Clark to beat her to death, to maybe kick her a little too enthusiastically around her head area, it would be better for Piper and Sebastian to be far away when it went down.

Too many kids get killed when mama gets fed up and goes after daddy, or when daddy gets carried away and kills everybody in the damn house. Susan was *making her bed*, but the boys didn't have to lie—and die—in it with her. If Susan died, it was her own fault, but she wasn't taking the boys with her.

Sherman opened the bathroom door and almost stepped on Piper and Sebastian. They were sitting on the floor just outside the bathroom door, not playing or eavesdropping, just waiting. They jumped up and took his hands, and Sherman asked, "Are y'all ready to find out what happened after daddy kicked Kelvin out of the house?"

Sebastian didn't have much zeal for story time. It wasn't the story or storyteller's fault. The kid was tired. Tired of watching his parents fight, tired of seeing his mama cry, and tired of being tired. He wore his best smile and nestled in next to his great-grandpa in the old recliner.

Piper was on his great-grandpa's other side, grinning like a shit-eating-opossum, but poop wasn't on his menu. When he came into the house, he saw pizza coupons on the kitchen counter. If one plus one still equaled two, pizza was on the menu. His life was hard. Storytime was a great escape, but pizza... Well, pizza was pizza and made everything better. Piper listened as Kelvin's evil surfaced, but the only thing he really thought about was round, cheesy, and went by the name of pizza.

When she'd left the house that morning Clark had stood in the doorway and watched Susan wrestle the boys and their luggage into the car. She didn't cook his breakfast this morning, didn't tell him goodbye, didn't even wave as she slid behind the steering wheel and shut the door. Obviously, she was a slow learner, and a lesser man might've given up on her. Not Clark. He would do his duty and get her straight. Hers was a sickness, and he knew the cure.

As soon as her car was out of sight, he grabbed his *go-bag* and followed her. The contents of the bag were all necessities. Guns and ammo. He had a .357 revolver and a .45 semi-auto with a hundred rounds of jacketed hollow points for each. He stocked a first aid kit to treat common ailments: aspirin, ibuprofen, antibiotics, Benadryl, and several concoctions to treat everything from acid reflux to herpes, and of course, a bottle of potassium iodide tablets because, you just never know.

A separate medical kit contained enough gauze and surgical tape for a small field hospital. Bleeding out from gunshot wounds wouldn't be an issue. He had a water filtration system, a WWII-era gas mask that probably didn't work, and a lightweight, NASA-approved thermal blanket. Behind his seat, he stowed a one-man pup-tent and all the MREs he could get his hands on. If he wasn't prepared for his trip to Sin City, he never would be.

When Susan pulled up to Sherman's front door, Clark parked across the road in a neighboring field. He didn't need to be close because he had a pair of field-glasses he'd won off a buddy in a poker game. They were genuine military issue and brought his targets close enough to smell. He watched his wayward wife hug her grandpa, and Clark said to no one, "You wrinkled old fuck, one of these days you'll get yours."

Ten minutes later, she came out, limping. *I told you to not drag your leg like that. You do it to piss me off. You won't listen to reason, so I'm gonna have to get rough with you to prove I'm serious.* He animated his mental conversation with exaggerated hand movements, and the binoculars bounced up and down as he worked himself into a stupid fury. The huge objectives returned the sun's majesty, but he was too angry to worry about it.

When Susan drove away, Clark lingered a second and watched Sherman through the screen door. He wasn't sure, but thought Sherman looked his way an awfully long time. He dismissed the idea, deciding it didn't matter one way or the other.

It took fifteen minutes to catch Susan but once he caught up, Clark fell back three-quarters of a mile. He had a cooler full of beer, and in his digital library, about every country song ever recorded. He had a two-hour drive ahead, so he popped the top on a cold beer and let the randomizer pick a song. The selection was "Fightin' Side of Me" by the Hag. Clark couldn't have been more pleased.

Chapter Thirty-Nine

Susan drove without stopping for two hours, but when she hit Ridgeland's city limits, she pulled into a Shell gas station to fill up her car's tank and to empty her bladder. In Jackson, her GPS spent forty-five minutes guiding her to the wrong building four times.

Through trial and error, GPS finally delivered her to Allied Health's glass-paneled, multistory office building. Susan marveled at the mirrored skyscraper. It was breathtaking, but the thought of going in made her nauseous.

Susan stopped at the guardhouse and an overweight man in a stretched uniform said, "ID please."

Susan fumbled in her purse for her driver's license and when she handed it to the guard, he looked at the hag in the car and the beauty on the license and thought that this lady has been through the shit since the highway patrol snapped that picture.

Convinced the hag and the beauty were the same unfortunate soul, he found her name on his computer and touched the square box next to it. A check mark appeared, and upstairs, they knew the last prospect was on the premises.

"Good luck," he said. "Follow the signs to the workshop parking." He pushed a flashing button and the red and white striped barricade lifted, allowing Susan access.

"Thank you, sir. I'm gonna need it."

Inside the garage, she saw the signs. They read: Prospective Employees' Workshop. The words were written in yellow on black block letters so big and bright she had to look away to read them. There was an equally big and bright arrow pointing the right way. It blinked on and off in rapid succession and its many lights had to have strained the city's power grid.

Susan followed the signs to a cordoned-off area. A woman with an iPad stood waiting. "Good morning, Susan," the woman said. "Thank you for coming."

Susan held up a finger indicating that she needed a moment. She placed a quick call to her grandpa to let him know she made it safely. She said she couldn't talk because there was a funny-looking redhead waiting on her. Sherman wished her the best of luck with *Ginger*, and said, "Go get 'em." She assured Sherman she would and hung up.

"Good morning," Susan now said to the woman.

"Welcome to AH. Park here and we'll join the others." The redhead pointed to an empty parking spot between a BMW and a Jaguar. They made Susan's car look like an out-of-place jalopy, perfectly describing how she felt.

Ginger's name was Holly, and she said, "It's a pleasure to meet you. I'll be your chaperone today. I'm happy to assist you in any way I can."

Susan and Holly walked to the elevator where they were joined by two other prospects and their chaperones. The prospects exchanged pleasantries. The others were as nervous as Susan and for some evil reason their discomfort put her at ease. The elevator went all the way to the roof and when the doors opened, Susan felt like Dorothy staring at the Emerald City.

Half of the roof was a large atrium with emerald tinted glass walls and ceiling. The other half was like a cruise ship's deck with shuffleboard, a putting green, cushioned loungers, and an Olympic-sized swimming pool. Giant palm trees stood in line around the raised edge of the roof like sentries. It was an oasis in the midst of downtown Jackson. Susan vowed to never leave.

On the roof, she was given a name tag and several forms to fill out. Holly showed her to the convention area inside the atrium. "I'll be just outside if you have any questions."

The forms were a waste of time. Susan put all the same information on her Job Service application. *Guess I filled those fifteen pages out for nothing*, she thought, but filled in the blanks anyway. She gave the completed forms to Holly and was ushered to a folding chair in front of a small stage.

She counted thirty-seven applicants, far less than the hundreds Susan feared. Everyone appeared nervous, and again, Susan was devilishly comforted.

A short, balding man stepped on stage, cleared his throat, and tapped the microphone. "Hello everyone, and welcome to Allied Health. My name is Winston Morehouse and I'm the president of human resources. It's a pleasure to see you all. Regrettably, we only have three positions to fill at this time, so we can't extend job invitations to everyone. Even though we can't hire everyone, we sincerely believe our workshop will benefit you in your career search."

Winston spoke for twenty minutes on the company's history, and Susan questioned her sanity for driving two hours for a job she knew she wasn't going to get. "Well," Winston said, enthusiastically raising both hands high in the air and bringing them down fast and hard. "Let the fun begin."

The fun wasn't fun at all. The fun was a bunch of tests. There were written tests, typing tests, flexibility and agility tests, problem-solving tests, tests of her computer knowledge, and personal interviews with four department heads. At noon, the prospects were treated to a delicious lunch that Susan hardly touched. She moved her food around her plate with her fork, waiting to get the bad news so she could go home.

After lunch, there were more tests. Tests she worked alone and tests in a group setting. At five o'clock, when she thought she'd take a flying leap over the ledge if somebody handed her another test, Winston called everyone inside the atrium. He thanked them for their hard work and promised that his HR department would go over all their applications and test results as quickly and fairly as possible.

"Congratulations, people. You made it through the testing without a single dropout. That's the first time that's happened," Winston said, and actually applauded. The chaperones joined him, and most of the prospects were obliged to join as well.

There was a *"whoop whoop!"* cheer from some of the more enthusiastic Type A's, but everyone else clapped and kept their mouths shut.

When the noise died, Winston said, "For those interested, you are all invited to join us for dinner tonight at Jackson's finest eating establishment, *Le Bistro*. We'll begin at eight, but please come early if you like. Our reservation starts at six. I hope to see you all there."

Holly walked Susan back to her car. "It has been a privilege to work with you today. I hope to see you tonight." Holly extended her hand and Susan shook it with foolish excitement.

Holly walked back to the elevator bank and Susan thanked God for seeing her through all the tests. She wanted to find a motel and crash, sleep for eight or nine hours, but she had a dinner to attend. Susan would've skipped the snotty restaurant but was afraid she'd lose points for being a no-show.

Susan convinced herself it wouldn't be too bad. There were worse things than a free dinner, Susan thought while she waited for the guard to raise the barricade. With a deeply thankful smile, Susan told the guard, "I'll see you tomorrow."

The guard never saw Susan again.

Chapter Forty

Two weeks after being ejected from Robert's recliner, Kelvin got the news he was waiting for. At breakfast, Robert announced he was going to Alabama for parts. Robert didn't give a definite date but when Barbara asked when he was going, Robert replied, "In a couple of days."

Kelvin's black soul danced a jig. He lifted a forkful of greasy fried egg to his smiling lips just as Barbara asked him to say grace. Kelvin put his fork down and happily complied.

Kelvin hadn't missed church since the night he asked Barbara if he could start going with them. While the rest of the family grew to distrust Kelvin, Barbara became his unlikely ally. She enjoyed their biblical discussions because Kelvin knew the Scriptures like he'd personally penned them. Barbara was impressed by his biblical knowledge and dedication and now jumped to his defense.

For the first time in two weeks, Kelvin whistled as he worked. "This is W-*KRM*," a DJ said inside Kelvin's brain. "And this hit goes out to Rosalyn, Karen, and even you, Barb. It's called, *Soon, You'll Be Mine.*

Kelvin grinned as the *K*idnap, *R*ape, and *M*urder disc jockey kept the psychotic records spinning in his muddled mind.

Kelvin ate his lunch in the shade of two giant pecan trees. After he swallowed the last bite of the ham sandwich an abdominal cramp took him low and hard. The shower was running in the first bathroom, so he trotted to the half-bath, dropped trousers, and stained the toilet with a dark stream of liquid shit.

Kelvin wiped his ass and over his own stench, a sweet, pleasing aroma escaped the trashcan. He instantly knew what it was, a *treasure!* He opened the trashcan slowly like he was defusing a bomb and fearing tripwires.

Wrapped in scarlet-stained toilet paper and engulfed in a divine light only Kelvin could see, was the *treasure* he craved. Kelvin left the bathroom, his front pocket swollen with his prize and his pants swollen with a crazy erection. He passed the girls' bedroom and couldn't resist a quick tour, so he went inside.

When Kelvin walked in her room, Rosalyn walked out of the other bathroom. She was going to town with Barbara and had showered early. "Excuse me, what are you doing in here?" Before he could answer and because she didn't care what his answer was, she said, "Get out, now!"

"I saw the record collection and wanted to check it out," Kelvin said as innocently as a guilty man could. "I like checking out things that look good to me." He eyed the young girl, checking her out and not hiding it.

Rosalyn just came from the shower and wore nothing but two towels. One was spun around her long, curly hair like a turban, the other wrapped around her naked thirteen-year-old body. Her breasts were new and were hardly more than fat nipples. Kelvin didn't mind. *More than a mouthful is a waste.*

"You must feel better now that you're all clean. You smell good, too. I bet you taste even better." He licked his lips, held the first two fingers of his right hand in a *Y*, and ran his tongue between them. "Want me to find out?"

He tapped his swollen pocket. "I found a *treasure* in the bathroom. I bet you can't guess what it is. I'll give you a hint. It's a fruit—red and delicious, and ripened to perfection. It's not an apple, but it's oh so juicy. Are you the tree it *fell* from?" Kelvin leaned forward and sniffed her like he was a dog and she was a stranger's crotch. "No, I don't think so. Must've come from your mama or sister."

Treasure? Fruit? In the bathroom?

Rosalyn turned the riddle over in her mind but came up with nothing.

"Umm *leeave*," she said.

Treasure? Fruit? Bathroom?

What would a sicko treasure? She was a tree. Barbara and Karen were trees, too? What fruit could she, her mother, or her sister have grown? She couldn't figure it out, and then she did. Understanding came with a wave of disgust. Shock painted her face red and revulsion escaped her mouth in an uncontrollable *eww*.

A woman's red fruit left in the bathroom. There was only one thing it could be. She envisioned Kelvin digging through the trash and shouting, "Eureka!" as he retrieved his *treasure* and held it above his head.

When they got their periods each month, the Lancaster ladies wrapped their used maxi pads in toilet paper and because flushing them would clog the septic tank, they tossed them in the trash. Enlightened to Kelvin's sickness, Rosalyn envisioned him licking his *treasure*, and she knew it was true. Rosalyn stepped back from his craziness, afraid it was contagious.

He watched her closely and knew she understood. "Let me know when it's your time. I can't wait to sample that fruit." He formed a pistol with his fingers and pointed at her groin.

"Get out," she said, her voice wavering. For the first time, she realized just how crazy he was, and she was truly afraid.

"Are you sure you want me to leave? Everybody else is outside. We've got time to play." A curly lock of her hair fell out of the turban-towel. It twisted and bounced in and out of her eye like a slinky. Kelvin straightened it with the pinch of his fingers, pulling down the full length of the long lock. Water dripped off the end onto her naked shoulder, dammed up behind her clavicle, and then spilled over and rushed down her chest. He leaned in to kiss her.

Repulsed, she jerked backward so fast the turban fell off her head. Rosalyn backed farther away, not knowing what would happen next. There was no one in the house to help her and if she screamed, would anybody hear her? Even if they did, how long would it take them to get to her and what could Kelvin do to her in that time? Those were mysteries she didn't want solved.

There it was, finally. Fear. She wasn't smug now. Kelvin had a feeling she would never be smug to him again. He hated leaving, but the others would be inside soon. No need to push his luck this close to the finish line.

"I'll catch you later," he told her, fully meaning to do exactly that.

Rosalyn slammed her door and locked it, checked to be sure it was locked and checked it again to be sure she was sure. Kelvin had his eyeful and wasn't getting another one. All the strength ran out of her legs and she fell to her bed trembling from head to toe. It felt like the temperature in her room dropped sixty degrees.

She'd taken away their dirty clothes so Kelvin couldn't get off sniffing them, but she hadn't thought about their feminine products. That was too disgusting. Why would anybody think about it?

Not disgusting for a sicko. That's what makes a sicko a sicko, honeychild.

She'd been waiting for the right time to tell her parents about the things Albert heard coming from Kelvin's shed. She'd almost spilled her guts the night her daddy kicked Kelvin out of the house. Robert was mad at Kelvin, so it seemed like the perfect time, but only to an outsider. When Robert was mad, his family knew to leave him alone.

Now, the question wasn't *if* she would tell but *when* and *how*. She also had to decide whether to involve Albert. He had a story to tell, an important one, because it directly involved their mother and that was the surest way to get Robert's attention. In light of that, it seemed like a no-brainer, but Albert had a credibility problem.

Albert Lancaster was eight-years-old and had developed a reputation as a sleepwalker. He looked forward to turning nine in September. He would practically be a grownup then, and grownups don't take midnight strolls in their underwear and wake up wondering where in the hell they were. In the meantime, he prayed feverishly to stop walking in his sleep, and God had granted him a reprieve. It had been a month since his last sleepwalking incident and his mother knew it; his father didn't care.

Maybe they would believe her. She didn't sleepwalk, she didn't lie, but those things didn't guarantee belief. It was bad that Kelvin was Barbara's church-buddy. Barbara refused to see the truth about anybody if they were holding a Bible. What was worse was that Rosalyn was a kid and Kelvin was an adult, always a shitty situation for a kid.

Rosalyn knew Kelvin had been snooping through her room, but she couldn't prove it. She knew for a fact Kelvin just stared at her, played with hair, and tried to kiss her. He'd *Y'ed* his fingers and ran his gross, white tongue between them, spreading them wider as he told her how good she smelled—

I bet you taste even better.

Surely, her parents wouldn't think she made that up. She could say all those things to both parents, but could she tell her daddy about Kelvin's *treasures*? She didn't know.

Things had gone too far so Rosalyn decided to do what she had to do. She knew what Kelvin wanted, and she damn sure wasn't giving it to him. What she didn't know was whether he would take it or not, and she worried he would. "Daddy'll take care of you, sicko. Just you wait and see." She sounded confident as she said it to nobody, but inside, she was doubtful.

When Albert came in from the field, Rosalyn said, "After supper, I'm going to tell mama and daddy what the perv has been doing. Hopefully they'll believe me, but you have to be ready to back me up." Albert looked at his shoes. "I mean it," she tapped his head like Little Rabbit Foo-Foo bopping a field mouse. "This is important."

"You know they won't believe me. Daddy won't, anyway," Albert whined. After enduring a minute of Rosalyn's pursed lips and unblinking eyes, he said, "Okay." He prayed she didn't need his testimony, because if she did hers was a lost cause.

A nervous Rosalyn kept busy the rest of the afternoon but when the time came, she was ready.

Rosalyn had a tiny window of opportunity to snatch her daddy's attention. Each night after supper, Robert passed through his bedroom to his half-bath where he brushed his teeth. When Rosalyn heard him shut the door, she grabbed her mama's wrist. "Mama, come here, please." She tugged, but her mama resisted.

"Wait just a minute, rushy-britches. I've got to help put the food away."

"Go on, mama. Rosalyn needs you," Karen said, and took a bowl of peas from Barbara's hands.

Rosalyn led the way to her parents' bedroom. "You sit there," Rosalyn pointed to the old bed with squeaky springs. In the half-bath, the toilet flushed, and the faucet came on. Robert washed his hands, and Rosalyn visualized him drying them on the red and black plaid towel.

One wipe, two wipes, and his hands are dry.

Rosalyn eyed the door. It would open in *three, two, one*. The knob turned and Robert walked out.

"Daddy, I really need to talk to you for a minute. Will you sit down by mama?" Barbara reached for his hand, and Robert sat down.

Chapter Forty-One

"Bout fucking time," Clark said when he saw the city limit sign. He'd been driving for two hours but it felt more like two days. He was nine beers in and hated Susan more with each gulp. He followed her through downtown Jackson at three-miles-per-fucking-hour, and because they were crawling through traffic, he couldn't pop the top on number ten.

If a commie fag in the vehicle next to him saw a white man tilt a beer, he'd be surrounded by nigger cops by the time he reached the next intersection. Then, a Jew judge would sentence him to prison—life without parole, no doubt—for being white and not apologizing for it. Clark kept both hands on the wheel and avoided eye-contact.

"Where in the hell are we going?" he asked Susan's taillights. She was four cars ahead and he was certain they'd passed the same wino three times.

She's got GPS in that Jap-trap and she's fucking lost. What a loser! And to think I was scared she was leaving me.

Clark considered the implications. Hadn't he married a loser? "Maybe I'm the loser," he thought aloud.

Left…left…left…left, and they were right back at the passed-out wino. Clark beat his fists against the dash and screamed at his wife. "*Give me a break!*" Susan made the same block after block, retracing her path, looking for a building that wasn't there the first or second, or fiftieth pass. *Bitch, do you think they're going to build the damn thing while you circle?*

After all the left turns, Susan's right-turn light blinked on. "*Holy shit, a right turn!*" Clark screamed so loud a woman in the next car gave him an impertinent look. "Fuck off, dyke." Her facial expression said she either heard him or read his lips. Susan stopped at a guardhouse. Clark, not believing she'd finally reached her destination, turned on his flashers and pulled to the curb.

A few minutes later the guard raised the red and white barricade and Susan drove into a concrete parking structure. Following Susan was no longer his chief concern; now he had to find a place to wait without attracting attention. He needed to be far enough away Susan wouldn't spot him when she came out, but he also needed to be close enough to watch the building without binoculars.

A white man in a pickup truck in this area was suspicious… Press genuine, military-issue field glasses to the white face and he was a honky begging for the fags to report him to the niggers so the Jews could lock him away for life. No thanks.

Clark rounded the block and pulled into a four-pump gas station. The small station was across the street from the mirrored building where Susan parked and there was a vacant spot waiting for Clark's truck.

The fueling station didn't allow customers inside. They conducted their business through a sliding drawer that accepted money and returned change when appropriate. The few items available for purchase: condoms, cigarettes, potato chips, and headache and indigestion relief, fit in the sliding drawer. The pimply attendant looked to be twelve years old and at first didn't notice the dirt-brown truck wedged between the electric bubble that *Pimples* called a car and the office building to its right.

Clark smoked and watched Allied Health's exit. He occasionally listened to music but was careful to keep the volume low. He suspected this wasn't an area packed with David Allan Coe and Johnny Cash fans. To his credit, Clark was uncharacteristically well-behaved.

Two guys walked by, holding hands. They stopped in front of the mirrored office building and kissed. One guy went inside, and the other blew his husband a kiss. Clark was nauseous. He saw niggers in suits and ties and shook his head at a joke only he knew. Jews, Japs, and a parade of colorfully dressed Spics walked in front of his truck. Clark gagged at the diversity in this once great Southern city.

There should be more white people down here, Clark thought, but he'd soon question that sentiment.

Pimples finally noticed the truck. It wasn't the dirt that caught his attention, Clark's big stump-jumper tires meant nothing to him, even the Confederate battle flag in his rear glass was irrelevant to him. One word and one word only flashed before *Pimples'* bespectacled eyes, and that word was *loiterer*.

Loiterers weren't as bad as robbers. They were worse. At least robbers had balls and took what they wanted. Loiterers were pussies without cojones. They robbed by occupying 'space' in an area with precious little and exactly zero to spare. They prevented paying customers access to the tiny, sliding drawer.

The scene *Pimples* saw each time he scanned his small concrete kingdom never changed. It was like looking at a postcard over and over. His car was always parked in his "Reserved" spot, that was normal, but everything else was supposed to change every few minutes. When that didn't happen, *Pimples* suspected a loiterer had invaded his kingdom.

As his training—a fifteen-minute video he watched the day he was hired—taught him, he first observed the suspect. After concluding the man in the dirty truck with big stump-jumper tires and Rebel flag was indeed loitering, as defined in the video, he called the police. Two uniformed cops were a mere block away and were there in less than five minutes.

Clark saw the approaching cops, but thought he'd done nothing to arouse suspicion. He couldn't believe it when they stopped outside his window. "Sir, could you lower your window please?" the cop in the shiniest blue Clark had ever seen asked.

"What's the problem, officer?"

The officers explained the situation. Clark hadn't done anything wrong other than sit still in a hustle-and-bustle world. The gas station's owner, a damn *A-Rab*, no doubt, or an authentic dot-on-the-fucking-head Indian, needed him to move on if he'd conducted his business at The Mini-Mart in full.

Clark quickly said that yes, indeedy-do his business was conducted in full. He thanked the officers and invited them to have a great day. He started his engine and got the merry-fuck out of there before they changed their minds. Down the street, he parked at a parking meter and deposited his change. He waited for Susan but dedicated one eye to making sure the cops didn't sneak up on him.

After all the diverse people he had seen who hadn't paid any attention to him, he was reported by a pimply white boy. The icing on the cake were the two cops who politely told him to make like a bee and buzz the fuck off. They were both middle-aged white guys. Clark lit another cigarette, waited for Susan, and reconsidered his racist inclinations.

Allied Health loved testing people. This was a fact Susan knew for sure by the day's end. She'd spent the whole day learning it and thought the dinner party might be another test. Maybe it was used to gauge a prospect's desire to be a team-player or be more company-oriented. It could be a pass-fail assessment that she would pass merely by showing up. She'd come this far, so she wasn't backing down from a snotty, little dinner party.

If she had to go, so be it, but Susan would be damned if she was driving. She didn't know her way around Jackson and she wasn't going to learn tonight. She was mentally exhausted around one or two in the afternoon and was dead-dog tired at five-fifteen. Given her GPS's track record for screw-ups, she figured if she drove she'd be lost in gang-town by six-thirty and raped and killed by eight o'clock. They made cabs for many reasons, and Susan Vance was one of those reasons.

Susan examined herself in the hotel's full-length mirror. The hag was back, but the hag was a *butterface*, below the hag-face was a knockout body. *Whose kidding who, kiddo?* Susan thought.

The dress looked both out of place and strangely at home on her shapely frame. It was a black strapless number with a hemline that rested between the bottom of her bottom and the top of her knee but honestly, much closer to her ass. It had a sweetheart neckline showing off her sizable breasts, and with the right lighting and at the right angle, its sheerness almost gave way to transparency.

This is inappropriate, she thought as she looked from her front to her back. *Mothers aren't supposed to dress like this*. If she'd had another five minutes to mull it over, she would've changed. She didn't though. The phone buzzed.

"Your cab is out front," the voice said.

"Thank you."

Too late. She was going to Allied's dinner party dressed like a whore. Susan supposed she was a whore. Was there any difference between what she was doing and what the streetwalkers did?

They were all trying to find the right dress to make them stand apart from everybody else. Streetwalkers vied to be the lucky girl picked from the crowd so they could have sex for money. Susan wouldn't be putting out, but whoredom was whoredom. She was playing the same game and convinced herself she was dressed like a whore, because she was a whore. It didn't matter because Susan didn't get to show off her whore's uniform.

The cab ride was the fifteen most panic-ridden, anxious minutes of her life. She went over a thousand things that could go wrong but not one that might go right. Other women wore dresses like hers, and other women got jobs at places like Allied Health, fancy women. Women like Susan wore jeans or pants and worked in Mississippi's fields and factories. They waited tables at truck stops where overweight and dirty men told dirtier jokes, slapped their bottoms, and knew how to come on to them but knew nothing about tipping. Women like Susan Vance worked for a living, and she was wasting time and money when she had neither to spare.

Susan would never know it, but the job was hers. She aced all the tests and blew away her competition during her personal interviews. Mr. Morehouse selected her himself, a thing he rarely did. All she needed was the confidence to exit the cab and walk inside the restaurant. There were no more tests. One of the three jobs was hers.

Susan managed the first part fine. She paid the fare and exited the cab in front of *Le Bistro*.

Step one, complete.

Susan started toward the entrance but stopped and turned back to the street. *You can do it*, her inner optimist urged. Again, Susan headed to the door, stopped, and went back to the curb.

Step two, incomplete.

Susan's walking amused the doorman. He opened the door each time she approached and enjoyed the way her dress lifted and showed off her lacy black panties when she spun away. He admired the rise, curve, and fall of the bubble beneath the dress. Three times she approached, and three times she withdrew. Three times the doorman smiled.

You must do this for Piper and Sebastian. She turned away from the street and headed toward the door. Susan was going in this time. Her mind was filled with counterfeit confidence.

Her confidence evaporated in an instant when Clark's hand closed around her wrist. "Well, don't you make a purty slut."

Chapter Forty-Two

H e scares me," Rosalyn said. Albert stood in the doorway as quiet as a mouse, hoping to go unneeded and unobserved. This was Rosalyn's deal. She wanted to talk, so he let her talk.

"When I got out of the shower today Kelvin was in my room. I wasn't wearing nothing but a towel. The creep just stood there looking me up and down. Then, he told me how good I looked."

Rosalyn remembered Kelvin's *Y'ed* fingers and his frothy, white tongue between them, but she couldn't tell her parents about that. Shame already burned her stomach like a kiln, and if she demonstrated Kelvin's perverted sign language, she would be a likely candidate for spontaneous combustion.

Rosalyn's tears broke her mother's heart and pulled tears into Robert's eyes. But Robert knew having a wife and four daughters made him a bit of an expert in this area, that girls cried. Tears, no matter how painful, meant little. Rosalyn's story wasn't enough to sway Robert totally against Kelvin.

"You're making too much out of it," Robert said. "Did he touch you?"

"Yes, he touched my hair." Rosalyn demonstrated how Kelvin tugged on her hair.

"Now, that's not really touching *you*, is it." It wasn't a question. "Did he touch *you*?"

Rosalyn understood that unless Kelvin fondled her breasts or grabbed her ass it wouldn't count as *touching her*. "No, he didn't, but he made it plain that he wanted to."

"But he didn't."

Rosalyn thought her daddy didn't believe her, but she was wrong. Robert believed she was giving an accurate account of the facts, but he didn't believe her interpretation of those facts. She was a young girl, barely dressed, alone and in her bedroom with a strange man. She misread the situation, got nervous, and blew everything out of proportion. That was the full matter right there, close the case file, and stamp it SOLVED.

It wasn't her fault. It wasn't Kelvin's fault. It was nature; like a tornado, nobody's fault.

"Baby," Robert hugged her before continuing, "you just misunderstood is all. There's nothing to worry about. He'd never hurt you. Honey, he's one of us. He's family."

"No, he ain't daddy. He just ain't. Ask Albert. Albert knows." She motioned for Albert to step forward, and reluctantly he did.

Their parents refused to believe Rosalyn and Albert couldn't figure out why she called on him. They'd never believe him, *the sleepwalker*, when they loved Rosalyn more and didn't believe her. This talk was a waste of his time and energy and a drain on his already drained self-respect.

Albert shuffled forward with his head down and his eyes on his feet. He told his parents what he'd heard outside Kelvin's room.

"Kelvin grunted and groaned something awful, like he was dying. I thought at first that's what it was, you know...that he was in trouble. But he started calling out Karen's name, then Rosalyn's, and then yours, mama." Red-faced shame hit him like a ton of bricks. He fought for each breath and had to bend over to keep from passing out. Albert's tongue felt foreign, like some extra-terrestrial worm wiggling between his teeth. He said, "The way Kelvin said it, it was like y'all were married."

Robert and Barbara knew what Albert meant: *married meant sex*.

Robert discounted Albert's entire testimony. "You were just sleepwalking, boy."

Albert was three steps beyond furious. He stomped off crying without saying another word. Talking to them was, as he knew it would be just wasted time.

"Albert, honey," Barbara called after him, but he didn't stop. She wanted to console him, but Rosalyn wasn't finished. "We love you," she called after him. He didn't reply.

"You should've listened to him," Barbara said. She didn't believe the things Albert said about Kelvin, her church-buddy, but she knew Albert wasn't a liar. She was confident this whole thing was a misunderstanding that Kelvin could easily explain.

Robert defended his hasty judgment the only way he could. "He walks in his sleep. He does it all the time."

"No, Robert Earl Lancaster. He used to do it. He hasn't done it in a long time. You owe him an apology." Barbara told Robert he needed to spend more time with his kids and less time playing around with that silly sword.

Ashamed like a boy caught masturbating, Robert thought, *But I haven't touched it in weeks*.

Things weren't going her way. She considered giving up but giving up didn't come easy to Rosalyn. "Me and Karen are both missing panties, and I bet you are too, mama. Plus, I've caught him in my room before. Just ask Karen. She knows what's been going on. Please. You have to believe me."

There was the big gun. Rosalyn knew her parents never questioned Karen's word. Karen's word wasn't scripture, but it was close. Chewing on a mouthful of defeat and swallowing bit by bitter bit, Rosalyn searched their eyes and saw the truth. Her parents would not question Karen about the matter. Their minds were set.

Should I mention Kelvin's treasures? Rosalyn wanted to but couldn't.

"I'll ask him about it, okay?" Robert said. "Let me think it over." Robert's way of saying *no* without saying no was saying, "I'll think it over."

"I want him gone, daddy. He scares me. He's going to hurt me if you give him enough time." She reconsidered mentioning the *treasures*, but the reality was, she wasn't telling her daddy she believed Kelvin was searching through the trash for used maxi pads then licking them like a lollipop and jerking-off the whole while. It was too embarrassing, and besides, he wouldn't believe her anyway and would probably think she needed her head examined for making something like that up. She'd kill Kelvin herself if she had to, but say those things to her daddy—that, she wouldn't do.

Barbara held Rosalyn tightly as they walked to her bedroom. "Just lock the door and you'll be fine." The mother in her wanted to protect her baby girl but there was no way Kelvin was as bad as Rosalyn made him out to be. He led their congregation in the benediction. You didn't lead the benediction then go home to molest a child. It was unheard of, not even possible. A square-circle.

Maybe you'll believe me when you find my bug-riddled corpse down by the pool, Rosalyn thought bitterly.

Barbara carefully locked the bedroom door and snicked it shut behind her. *Lot of good that did, mama. Might as well put out a welcome mat.*

Barbara brushed her teeth and climbed into bed without saying a word. Robert knew she was upset by the way she slid in between the sheets, all hard and spastic. They'd been married too many years for him to miss her subtle cues, and this one wasn't subtle at all. She was royally pissed and wanted him to know, yet she wasn't going to say it.

Two options stared him in the face. He could go to sleep and ignore the giant gorilla in the room, or he could speak up and try to smooth things over and make peace. Out of the blue, a third option appeared: sex.

Option three would make her feel better, and he'd get sex. That breed of dog is called a *win-win*. Robert pulled the cover tight against Barbara's chest. Her breasts protruded, and he rolled to face them.

"What do you think you're doing, Robert Earl Lancaster? How dare you try fooling around with me after you so much as said my opinions and feelings don't make a hill of beans to you?"

Robert had said no such thing, but he'd lost this argument enough to know it wasn't worth starting. "Barb, I'm going to check into their story first thing after breakfast. When I get Kelvin alone, I'll get to the bottom of it." With sex still on his mind, he added, "Your feelings are all that matter to me." He crossed over no-man's land into enemy territory and bravely cupped her left breast.

She lifted his hand off her and rolled to face the wall. "We'll see how I feel tomorrow night, *after* you tell me all about your talk with Kelvin. Goodnight, Robert. I love you."

He kissed the back of her neck and waited on the Sandman. Sandy was a long time coming, and by the time Sandy showed, Robert hated his cousin.

Chapter Forty-Three

The alarm clock sounded, and Robert felt Barbara get out of bed. She didn't jerk out of bed the way she jerked into bed. He took that as a good sign but didn't break the silence just in case he was wrong.

"Daddy, can I go with y'all to Alabama?" Sherman asked as soon as Robert sat down.

"No." Robert thought the worst thing about having seven children was that one or another was always talking to him.

"But please. Mama said she didn't care." Sherman knew the only way to get what he wanted was to keep on. *Keep on keeping on* had to work because it was a saying. They didn't make something a saying unless it worked.

"No. It ain't okay with me. We're leaving too early in the morning." Robert was reminded that the second worst thing about having seven children was that he was always talking to them, as well.

"But I want to go with…" Sherman was *keeping on keeping on*. It was a saying, after all.

"Shut up. You ain't going. Not another word about it." Robert put up with a lot from his baby boy, the dried-up fart who would always be remembered for being too stubborn to be born on time, but not this morning. This morning Robert was preoccupied with confronting Kelvin and worrying over whether he should apologize to Albert.

Sherman pouted. *Keeping on keeping on* failed again. He would try it again later to be sure but for right now he was convinced *Keep on keeping on* should be struck from the Book of Sayings.

Affirming Robert's least favorite thing about having seven children, Albert started talking as soon as Sherman stopped. "Daddy, mama said I could work at the house today if you didn't need me in the field?" Albert's anger hadn't cooled even a degree and didn't want to sit at the table with his daddy, much less spend the whole day trapped in a field with the *unbeliever*.

"Yeah, go ahead and stay here. Help your mama and do what she says."

Kelvin came in, sat down, and told everyone good morning. He caught Robert's eye and asked, "So, you're going to Alabama tomorrow?"

Robert nodded a yep.

"You sure you don't want me to tag along with you and Theo? I might come in handy." Kelvin had to ask but wouldn't go even if Robert wanted him to. Asking made it seem like he wasn't dying to stay behind.

Robert confirmed the trip and declined Kelvin's assistance. Kelvin checked item number one off his worry list. Kelvin planned to knock off work a little early and let Barbara know he wasn't feeling tip-top. If it came up at the last minute that Robert needed Kelvin to go, the seed of his excuse was already planted.

Kelvin finished his breakfast, thanked Barbara for another delicious meal, and headed out to work. *A few more hours, a day…oh happy*

happy joy joy. A few more hours and he'd make Robert—his dear better-than-thou cousin—pay for the way he treated him. *Run me out of the house, make me sleep in the shed, treat me like a child...oh, I'll show you.*

"Are you going to talk to him?" Barbara asked. Normally, she wouldn't say such a thing in front of the kids, but they were all in on the conversation anyway.

Robert nodded in her direction. Barbara stood with a hand on her hip, looking at him in *that way*. A nod wasn't going to cut it with her.

"Yes, mama. I'm going to find out first thing this morning."

Talk, talk, talk...them to me or me to them. There's no peace for a man with a wife and seven kids. Robert marched to the shed, aggravated to the extreme.

"Kelvin, why are you messing around with Rosalyn? She said you've been in her bedroom, nosing around." Robert Lancaster wasn't a small-talker and was ready to be on the finished side of this conversation. Kelvin didn't immediately respond, so Robert pushed, "Say something for yourself, dammit."

Guilt flashed across Kelvin's face and he thanked God, the same one he pretended to worship, he was facing away from his cousin. "Hold on just a minute, Robert." Kelvin dropped his wrench, put his hands up between him and his advancing cousin and backpedaled towards the center of the shed. "I don't know what she told you, but there ain't nothing untoward happening around here."

"You calling her a liar?"

"Robert, I bet I know what this is about. I was in her room the other day thumbing through the records when your baby girl came in with just a couple of towels on. I guess she'd just got out of the shower. We talked for maybe a minute, and I was out of there. It didn't look right, you know...us talking with her having so little on and all."

"You're so full of shit your eyes are brown and your breath stinks. You stay out of the girls' room from now on. You ain't got no call to talk to them so steer clear. You hear me? Stay away. Are we clear?"

I'm going to do a lot more than talk to them, you country-fried moron.

"Whatever you say, of course, but on my name, there weren't no crooked stuff going on," Kelvin said.

"You just keep clear of my girls so they'll stop bothering me. I'm keeping my eyes on you, so you best walk the line around here from now on."

You do that, buddy-boy. Keep your eyes on me when your ass is in Alabama. Kelvin wanted to laugh, but he nodded that he understood and moved the conversation toward lighter topics. "You ever tell Barbara about us catting around with her older sisters? I bet you didn't, you old dog." Kelvin hinted he might tell Barbara how she was Robert's second or third choice.

"I didn't tell her, but her sisters did just as soon as me and Barb started courtin' heavy. It was one reason why her daddy never liked me. Of course, you got your story backwards. Barbara was my first choice. I could've had any of her sisters, but I picked the baby girl. That's what she is you know...my *Baby Girl.* Always was, and always will be."

Robert remembered Albert's testimony, one part especially well: *Kelvin sounded like he was married to them.* Married to Barbara and married meant sex. Already upset, Robert got everything out in the open.

"Albert said he heard you moaning something fierce one night, said you were calling out the girls' names and Barbara's, too. Me and you know what you were doing, even if the boy is too young to know. Do I need to tell you what I'll do to you over my kids? That goes double for my wife."

"Hold on, Robert. A man can't help what he dreams or what he says out loud while he's dreaming. You know that's the gospel truth. I ain't saying I did or didn't say something, but if'n I did, I ain't to blame. Dreams are just dreams."

Then and there, Robert knew he'd been wrong to doubt Albert, and he'd apologize to his son. Since Albert was telling the truth, Rosalyn probably was too. Robert finally believed Kelvin was a liar and almost certainly a pervert. Believing those things was one thing. Believing his cousin was dangerous was something else, and Robert couldn't go that far.

Family don't hurt family. It was a simple idea.

Simple and utterly wrong.

"Well if you're done accusing me of... I'm not even sure what the heck you're accusing me of, but if you're finished with it, I've got work to do." Kelvin turned and went to work, but Robert's callused hand gripped his cousin's shoulder like a vise. Kelvin spun on his heels and pinwheeled his arms to maintain balance.

"Make for sure you heard me. Stay away from my girls. I mean it. And Barbara too."

"Yes, sir. I don't want no trouble, Robert. I aim to get along." It hurt to grovel, but Kelvin took satisfaction knowing this was the last day he'd have to do it. *It'll all be worth it in the morning*.

"I'm heading into town. You need anything?" Robert asked, as if they were best friends again.

"Naw, I'm good but thanks." Kelvin imagined the look on Robert's face when he came home from Alabama and saw what happened to his family. Kelvin chocked down a laugh but couldn't hide his smile. His shiny teeth reflected off the disc's glossy green and yellow paint. Robert saw it but had too much on his mind to give Kelvin's lunatic smile the attention it deserved.

When he returned from Alabama and Barbara told him the news, Robert remembered Kelvin's toothy grin and thought, *I should've killed you right then*.

Chapter Forty-Four

Clark was sober and suffering a bitch of a PM hangover when Susan exited the parking garage. He followed her to the hotel and while she got a room, he parked in the back row. From his vantage point he had an unobstructed view of the hotel's front doors. Susan came out ten minutes later, unloaded her luggage onto a brass trolley and then parked near the entrance. She wheeled the trolley inside and Clark expected her to be in for the night. He was no longer in the public-eye, so Clark popped the top on a lukewarm beer. His hangover receded with the first gulp and was forgotten by the time he pulled the tab on number three.

An hour later a yellow cab entered the parking lot, passed Clark's truck, and parked under the hotel's *porte cochere*. Exactly five minutes later, a fine bitch in a slinky black dress sashayed out to the cab.

The cab driver had once picked up a recently divorced woman who called him into the backseat and boffed his brains out. He took one look at this woman and damn near broke his neck getting out and opening the door for her. Maybe he would get lucky again.

I'd open the bitch's door to get a piece of that turd-cutter myself, Clark thought, and didn't fault the cabby for his pussy-whipped behavior.

Clark never imagined the sexy blonde with the fine ass was his own Susan, not until the cab passed him and he gazed into the backseat. He had to know if black dress's face looked as good as her ass. Susan was too anxious to notice Clark or his truck, but he recognized her in an instant.

"Kiss my fucking ass," Clark whispered. There was only one reason a woman dressed like that—Susan was dressed to get laid, to do the horizontal boogie. He chugged his beer, tossed the can in the floor, and followed the cab to *Le Bistro*.

The cab stopped at a swanky restaurant Susan couldn't afford to even drink water at and Clark knew somebody else was paying the bill. Obviously, it was the same somebody who intended to fuck her. Why else would he buy her dinner at an uppity joint like *Le Bistro*?

The cabby decided he wasn't getting lucky, so he let Susan open her own door. Clark parked down the street and even though he wasn't staying long, he loaded the parking meter's wheel and gave it a twist. All he needed was a pestering meter-maid to stick her nose in at the wrong time and ruin his plans.

Susan walked toward the restaurant and back to the street again and again, making Clark laugh. Finally, he walked up to her and grabbed her wrist. "Well, don't you make a purty slut? Is your date in there, waiting on you? If he is, he can just keep on waiting."

He tugged her toward his truck, but she resisted until Clark showed her the .357 revolver tucked in his waistband. "If I have to kill you here, you'll die knowing that Piper and Sebastian and that old man are next." Susan stopped struggling and went with him.

If she'd had the confidence to go in, she would've had a new job and made a new life for her and her sons.

But if she'd had possessed that much confidence, she'd never been with Clark in the first place.

"What do you want, Clark? I'm trying to get a job for us. They're waiting for me inside!"

"Yeah, that's what it looked like you were doing. No, I think you just met some fancy-pants guy at the office today and y'all decided to get it on."

He dragged her to his truck. The strap broke on her right shoe and she never saw it again. He opened the driver's door and shoved her into the cab. He pointed the pistol at her face and said, "Right there. Sit right there. We're getting your crap and getting our asses home." He drove them to her hotel.

Ursa landed in an alley across from the hotel. Her wings folded behind her and disappeared into her back with a dull snap. Ursa knew Susan was in danger but unfortunately, she also knew it wasn't life-threatening. Sherman's instructions were clear. The favor he'd asked was to keep her angelic eyes trained on Clark, to go where he went. Ursa was to watch and only intervene if she had to save Susan's life. Having her way Ursa would've killed Clark and been done with it.

Like a good *Warrior*, Ursa followed the *Handler's* orders. If Clark didn't try to kill Susan, Ursa's sword was stayed, but the angel prayed Clark would go a step too far. She prayed without ceasing.

Tired of clopping around like a crooked nursery rhyme character with one shoe off and one shoe on, Susan removed her left shoe and threw it in the trash. Of course, they were her favorite pair. Barefooted, she scampered around her hotel room, gathering belongings and cramming them carelessly into suitcases.

Clark said, "Give me your phone. I don't want you to get it in that stupid head of yours to call anybody, like say the cops or maybe that meddling grandpa of yours. I'm going to see that he gets just what his old ass deserves. That's a fact, princess. You're going to have to find a new babysitter, for sure."

She slammed the phone into his palm so hard she cracked the corner of its blue and gray *chevron* cover. "You'll get to pay for that temper-tantrum soon, baby,"

He slipped the phone into his pocket and stared hard at her. "I'll follow you. Drive legal, and don't try nothing funny, neither. I promise the boys will pay for it if you do."

"I won't, you bastard."

Her comment earned her a busted bottom lip and a solemn promise of more to come. "Anything else?" He dared her to smart-off so he could hit her again. "No? You sure? Okay cracker, let's get cracking."

They got in their separate vehicles and headed north. He followed closely but legally, and Susan drove legally for the first time since her driver's exam. Driving legally felt out of place for her, almost like she *was* breaking the law. She drove for two hours and cried the whole time. She cried because she didn't know what they'd do for money, but mostly she cried for Piper and Sebastian.

When she pulled into their driveway, Susan thanked God her boys were safe with Sherman. Nothing would happen to them there. She believed they were as safe as they could be.

But this night, they would've been safer with Clark.

Susan walked through the front door with Clark on her heels. The door snapped shut and the first kidney punch landed. A fusion bomb exploded in her lower back and the blast wave swept through her entire body. She fell to her knees and hot piss soaked her sexy panties. She got sick right there in the kitchen.

This was what he'd waited for, and Clark didn't waste any time. He *talked* to her all night, and right and proper.

Susan was on her knees with the wet heat of her urine running down both legs. If she'd only confided in Sherman she wouldn't be kneeling in her own bloody urine. If asking was too much for her, if her hubris was so great it refused to allow her to show weakness and ask for help, she could've kept her mouth shut. Sherman would've happily dealt with Clark on his own.

Susan knelt in familiar agony with urine cooling on her thighs and vomit drying on her sweetheart neckline. She knew she had no one to blame but herself. Her own stubborn, prideful self.

Well, that wasn't exactly true. Clark bore a great deal of responsibility as well.

Clark was behind her. She could hear him breathing heavy in's and out's, the sound likened to a wheezy mechanical ventilator on its last leg. "You think you're smart, don't you?" He laced his fingers together in the mat of her hair and twisted.

She grabbed his wrist with both hands and tried lifting herself. It was no use. When he pulled, her head felt like a million wasps set down side-by-side and were given the go-ahead to sting at the same time. The pain was nearly orgasmic—nearly.

"Going all the way to Jackson to get a job. What did you think? That I was just going to sit back and let you leave? Let you steal my boys?" Clark drug her down their hallway. Susan kicked her legs, a crazy attempt at swimming backwards. He dropped her on their bedroom floor. "I'm going to make sure you never cross me again."

He wrapped his hands around her neck and lifted her to his level. Her feet dangled, toes barely scraping the carpet. Her tears gave him an immediate erection.

The *stiffies* came regularly now that he was *the man of the house* again. When he'd been too scared of her grandpa to run his own house, Clark's erections had been few, and the few he had were half flaccid, puny things. Since last night, he could chisel diamonds with it.

He stared into her teary eyes—they were bulging slightly from strangulation and accented with jagged, red lines—and remembered that fine woman who walked out of the hotel in Jackson. Things were looking up in Clark's world. He was going to get a piece of that hot ass, after all.

Susan tried to speak but couldn't breathe. Lack of blood was a serious issue, but as serious as it was, it was secondary. Air was what she needed, and she didn't have any more of it. Her own name passed from her knowledge. *Thank God*, she thought as darkness welcomed her home. She went willingly. Briefly, she thought of Piper and Sebastian and wondered if they would be okay, but the blackness soothed her worries away.

"Your grandfather will take care of them," a soothing voice whispered. Susan believed the velvety, thick voice... and let go. Behind the blackness was a beautiful white light. It beckoned, and she went to it. Susan had one foot in the light when she was jerked away.

He sensed she was finally leaving him, getting free, and Clark let go of her neck. Instinctively, her lungs fought for air, gasped faster and faster. Each gasp chased the beautiful white light farther and farther from her reach. She cursed her lungs and commanded them: "STOP!" Nature wouldn't yield to her executive directives. Oxygen flooded her lungs and the familiar agony returned.

Susan was only half conscious as Clark ripped her clothes off. Hours later, she lost that half and slipped into nothingness. Clark pounded away on her for hours, until the sky lightened in the east. It was his best sexual exhibition ever, and luckily, Susan missed most of it.

Chapter Forty-Five

After their showers, Sherman picked up the phone and ordered Piper's favorite food in the whole, wide world. Pizza. Sherman was hungry too, craving something he'd not had in a long, long time, and it wasn't pizza. Rather than look forward to the indulgence, he prayed for strength to resist the *change* he knew was coming.

"What do you boys want to do tonight? We can watch movies, play games, or read. We can even have a party if y'all want to." Sherman pitched his voice extravagantly high, folded his arms against his chest and clapped his hands like a sea lion begging for a fishy treat. "*Party, party, party,*" he said as he clapped.

"Really? A party?" Piper asked. He'd been to birthday parties and was well-pleased with how those turned out. Cake and ice cream were always in abundant supply and nobody fussed when he got seconds. Piper voiced one vote for the party.

"Yeah, boy. We can party big time. We can have a house-cleaning party! Y'all do the bathrooms, and I'll wash clothes. Y'all can do the floors, and I'll dust. Waddaya think, boys? Are y'all up for a party?"

"I think we should skip the party," Piper said now, sensing the rouse. "Maybe we can watch scary movies."

"Are scary movies good with you, Sebastian?" Sherman asked.

"Daddy made us clean our room last night and I didn't like it. And great-grandpa, your house is way bigger than our room," Sebastian said. He voted against any more cleaning and signed onto the movie idea without any reservations.

"Scary movies it shall be. Sebastian, are you gonna be able to hold your water if you get scared?" Sherman asked.

"Hold my water? I want tea if it's okay, great-grandpa." The unsweetened tea was bad enough, but at least it had some flavor. Water was just, so...water.

"Bub, hold your water means to not piss yourself. Can you watch a scary movie without pee-peeing your PJs?"

"I ain't peeing in my pajamas," Sebastian said while in a full run towards his great-grandpa. He punched the old man in his gut and Sherman bent over, *ouching* in fake pain.

"Enough, enough. I take it back. I surrender."

They waited for the pizza and when it came, Sherman tipped the delivery guy twenty bucks. "Boys we're watching *Cujo* tonight." Piper and Sebastian squatted in front of the TV with the pizza between them and Sherman sat behind them, never once looking up at the movie.

Ominously, he eyed them in a new way and thought, *Blood*.

The movie was a hit but that was no surprise. Seeing *Cujo* for the first time was...well, it was seeing *Cujo* for the first time. Nobody ever looked at dogs the same way after they watched it. Knowing that dogs, too, go a little mad sometimes, altered one's perspective of man's best friend.

Leftover pizza? Forget about it. Without his mama's moderating efforts and after unsuccessfully begging Sherman to eat a slice, Piper ate three-quarters of a large pan pizza by himself.

Sebastian held his water just fine. He wasn't frightened at all. When the credits rolled, he asked, "What's next?"

"Who's ready for dessert?" Sherman asked.

Both boys raised both hands. "Me. Me. Me." Their voices were indistinguishable.

"We have chocolate-chip cookies and ice cream. Who wants what?"

Still hungry after the pizza, Piper opted for cookies and milk.

"I'll take a bowl of ice cream and a cookie," Sebastian said.

Sebastian wanted to watch another scary movie, but Sherman thought it best to let them go to sleep on a lighter note. He gave the kids their dessert and switched to a cartoon channel specializing in century-old *Looney Tunes'* reruns.

The cartoons played, Sherman laughing more than either boy, and the desserts disappeared. With full bellies, the boys fell asleep on Sherman's sectional sofa. Sherman sniffed the air. *Blood*. He saw the empty cookie tray and ice cream bowl.

Sugar.

Pointed fangs pushed his dentures out of his mouth and onto his lap and Sherman's thoughts betrayed him. *Blood is best when it's sweetened.*

Chapter Forty-Six

Sebastian and Piper were asleep on the sectional when Sherman retired to his bedroom for another sleepless night. His misfiring circadian rhythm wasn't responsible for his sleeplessness on this night. Tonight, Sherman couldn't sleep because he was *changing*. He wanted to stop it and knew he ought to stop it.

Stop beating yourself up, old man, Satan whispered. *Ought implies can, and we both know you can do nothing to stop it. Embrace it. It's who you are, what you are.*

The Great Tempter fell silent and waited for the fireworks.

Sherman closed his eyes and prayed, "God, please watch over *them.*"

No, no, no. Sherman shook his head like a child refusing a spoonful of medicine. The *change* wasn't coming. It was already there.

Sherman climbed out of bed light as a feather. Almost stepping into the spongy air instead of onto the hard floor. He ran to the bathroom and closed the door behind him. He flicked on the light and the bathroom mirror told the tale.

Sherman's reflection was there, but it was awfully dim; a smoky shadow both transparent and fading fast. The Ten Commandments plaque was there as well. It was hung on the opposite wall, and his body should've blocked it. But it was there, as plain as day, and it was getting clearer as he was getting dimmer. Without warning, like smoke in a surprise gust, his reflection wafted away.

He dropped to his knees and fangs, white, sharp and long, grew out over his bottom lip. He desperately tried to hang onto humanity by whispering a mantra that almost worked in the past.

Suppress...suppress...suppress.

His ribs cracked and realigned around a heart that was now withered, gray, and still. His arms and legs extended and stretched him into a nightmarish *Skydancer*. Sherman's fingernails grew pointy and yellowed, then pushed over his fingertips in bony daggers.

Suppress, suppress, suppress.

His wrinkled, old skin tightened, his age-spots disappeared, but the tight, clear skin grayed and lost all signs of life. He stood, a pale, lifeless creature with a thirst that was terrible at the onset and now undeniable.

With all the resolve he could summon, he tried one last time.

Suppress. The mantra *almost* worked again.

A new mantra rose in his tormented mind. It was freer, not inherently repressive like the puritanical *suppress, suppress, suppress.* He stood in front of the mirror, saw the Ten Commandments where his reflection should've been, laughed at the ones he was about to break, and recited his devilish new mantra.

Blood...blood...blood.

Sherman didn't know what he looked like. He could see his bony, misshapen limbs had knotty, spider's joints at the elbows, knees, and knuckles. His hands were animal claws and were freakishly large with dagger nails that had only one use, and it wasn't playing the banjo. He had paper-thin wings that were lacy and black like funeral veils. His wings were outlined by more of those knotty, spider-joints and in a word, he was hideous. His body was hideous, but what his face looked like, Sherman had no clue.

He could never view his reflection. Not that vanity plagued him. All his thoughts purposed one thing, *feeding*. And he only ate one thing.

Blood.

Sherman was never able to resist it and wasn't able to now. The thirst was too strong, and there wasn't enough of Sherman left to even try. The vampire floated through the closed door, vapored down the hallway, and hovered over the sleeping boys.

Piper and Sebastian opened their eyes on a world of green, the kind of green that one only sees in the middle of spring when winter's brown has been forgotten and summer's heat hasn't had time to spoil the lush rebirth. Birds chirped, butterflies floated on a gentle, warm breeze, and everything said, "Good morning," to everything else. Piper and Sebastian were in the *Clearing*.

Something was different and Piper recognized it straight away. Piper was nine-years-old, a boy, and while he was large for his age he looked like a child, but his younger brother wasn't. Sebastian was eight-years-old, forever younger and always smaller than Piper. That's how it was supposed to be, but not how it was.

Sebastian looked like an adult, a full six-feet tall, muscular, and wide-shouldered. Despite Sebastian's altered state, Piper recognized him without question as, *my little brother*.

"What's going on? Why are you so big?" Piper asked.

Sebastian explained things he didn't even know he knew. "This is how I look without age. This is my *real* body."

"Why am I still small, or young, or whatever? Where is *my* real body?" Piper wasn't exactly jealous, but he gotten used to being the older brother, the bigger brother, and wanted his position back.

Sebastian enjoyed a good chuckle at his smaller, older brother. As if he could read Piper's thoughts, Sebastian said, "Ahhh, don't worry. You'll always be my big bro, bro."

Sebastian seemed to have all the answers, so Piper asked, "Where are we and what are we doing here?"

"We're in the *Clearing*, and here is safer for us right now. Great-grandpa has...umm...company, and we mustn't wake up and disturb them. Don't worry, everything will be okay."

Piper sensed trouble. He didn't know how or why, but he felt the weight of hungry eyes moving up his legs, over his abdomen and chest, and resting on his neck.

The brothers walked mostly in silence and admired the unnatural natural beauty of their surroundings. They held hands. Piper found it both embarrassing and degrading that he had to reach up to take his little brother's hand. It was fine if they stayed in this magical place forever, but Piper wasn't looking up to Sebastian, not literally anyway, for much longer. As he thought this, Piper grew a little. Not much, just a fraction of an inch, but he felt it.

Okay, this is better, Piper thought, and grew a fraction more. He was thinking himself taller.

As they slept, the boys dreamed. As they dreamed, they walked the *Clearing*. And as they walked the *Clearing*, the vampire licked their necks. Which should he take first? How could he decide? Alternately tapping each boy on the forehead with a pointy nail, he whispered in song.

"Eeny, meeny, miney, moe..."

Chapter Forty-Seven

Outside Clark and Susan's bedroom window, Ursa perched in a maple and watched the unhappy couple. Clark stared hatefully at the unconscious woman bleeding beside him. Ursa's sword was drawn, ready to strike. All this watching was killing her.

Guardian angels watched. They lived for watching, but she wasn't a Guardian. Ursa was a *Warrior*. Were they both angels? Yes, but aren't poodles and pit bulls both dogs? She wanted to kill Clark, slice him from skull to groin and watch his organs spill out as he separated like two halves of a chopped watermelon. She watched the Vances but was distracted.

She was also keeping a divine eye on Piper and Sebastian and saw the vampire hovering over them as they slept. Sherman would never consciously hurt them, but Sherman wasn't Sherman right now.

Should she follow the *Handler's* command and protect Susan, or should she rescue the boys? There was really no debate.

Before she left them, Ursa looked back at Clark and Susan. *Maybe you'll kill each other*, she thought. *Would serve you both right if you did.*

Piper and Sebastian were awakened by fluttering wings and a loud THUMP. They grabbed onto each for safety. Taking the mental position that if they couldn't see it, it wasn't real, they squeezed their eyes shut as hard as they could. They heard, "Bitch," in a voice that was simultaneously familiar and foreign, not to mention creepy as horned-shit.

Summoning bravery neither wanted, they opened their eyes and saw what appeared to be an angel bear-hugging what appeared to be a vampire. The worst thing was the vampire looked an awfully lot like their great-grandpa. They promptly closed their eyes and reopened them, hoping for a different result.

No such luck. The angel and vampire were still there. The angel held the *Great-Grampire* in a headlock and cocooned him inside her wings, but it was clear he'd soon break free.

"*Hide!*" the angel screamed. Clearly not a suggestion, the boys hauled ass.

Where do you hide from a nightmare? The vampire wouldn't fail to look under beds or in closets for its meal. It was cold and dark, but they decided to hide outside. Before they reached the backdoor, they heard Ursa scream, "*Run!*"

The vampire was loose.

Startled and having nowhere else to go they ducked into the bathroom, turned on the light, and locked the door. It wasn't even a hiding place. The light made a rectangular outline around the door, a dead giveaway reading—*We're in here.*

Ursa screamed when the vampire burst from her headlock and ripped off her left wing, leaving a short, bloody stump. Using the right wing as a handle, the *vamp* slung Ursa behind his back and then over his head, scrapping her against the ceiling each time. He slammed Ursa into the floor over and over, working her like John Henry laying railroad steel with his famous sledgehammer.

When she stopped screaming and laid still, he turned his nose up and inhaled deeply. *Blood.* He didn't need his nose to tell him the boys were hiding in the bathroom. The tattletale light gave away their location. The bathroom door was a common interior door: two pieces of thin wood and a hollow middle, and that's all that separated him from his first drink in a decade.

From the bathroom, the boys listened. When the screaming and hammering abruptly stopped, they each pressed an ear to the door, listening for anything and hearing nothing. The silence was somehow worse than the noise. They didn't know if they were safe or still in jeopardy, and there was no way in hell they were opening the door to find out.

Piper and Sebastian stood against the door, as if they could hold it shut if either creature decided to come in. Piper's head was nine inches above his brother's. A good bit higher than usual, but now wasn't the time to contemplate growth-spurts. "Do you hear anything?" Piper whispered.

"No. Do you think it's over?" Sebastian asked.

Piper didn't have time to answer. The vampire turned to vapor and slid its head through the door and stared them in the face.

As a vampire, Sherman was Satan's creation, born of the spiritual world but existing in the physical. Neither alive nor actually dead, he was *light* and *dim* and could float, fly, and pass through solid objects at will. Impossibly, the vampire looked Piper and Sebastian in the eyes at the same time.

"Hey, boys. Wanna bite?" He snapped his mouth shut.

Piper backed away fast, but Sebastian was too slow. The vampire latched its long, pointy fingers in the boy's moppy hair and dragged him through the door. The thin wood splintered and peeled patches of bloody skin off Sebastian's cheeks and forehead. The vampire tilted his head and leaned forward like a man preparing to neck his lover. Sebastian was too terrified to cry. He closed his eyes and waited for the bite.

It didn't come.

In the living room, Ursa shook away her pain. "Oh no, you didn't." She stood, straightened her right wing, and regenerate a new left one. In a brilliant flash, she beamed from the living room and into the hallway. The vampire was on one knee in the hallway and a dazed Sebastian lay across its raised leg.

Ursa hit the vampire hard and fast. Sebastian was knocked off the vampire's leg and spun in the air like a whirligig before falling to the floor. Together, she and the vampire crashed into the cabinets at the end of the hallway. Ursa had the upper hand for seventy-five seconds.

Ursa walloped the vampire repeatedly. He was down, his head resting on the hard floor. Her lefts and rights broke bones with each strike, but the shattered fragments fused almost immediately. He was a vampire, a werewolf, and a *Handler*, and his super-regenerative powers were unequaled; even the angel didn't heal as fast. After the shock of Ursa's surprise attack wore off, the vampire smiled. Staring into that toothy grin, Ursa tried harder than ever to knock all those fangs down his baby-killing throat.

Sherman tried to sit up but Ursa's punches bounced his head off the tile flooring. He raised his head just in time for her to land another punch. His head bounced each time. She speed-bagged him that way enough times to crack floor tiles under his head. Tired of her abuse and ready to feed, he raised his head to meet her. It was the vamp's turn.

Ursa's fist fell again, but this time Sherman opened his mouth impossibly wide and took her whole fist into his mouth. He chomped his jaws shut and trapped her as surely as a bear caught in a spring trap. With her hand in his mouth, Sherman grinned and began hitting her.

His lefts and rights were powerful blurs that rocked her backwards. She was saved from falling over only because her hand was trapped in his saw-toothed mouth. She tried to fight back, but one-handed, she couldn't match his speed or strength. Her seventy-five seconds were over.

He stood with her hand still in his mouth, still landing his bone-crushing punches on her face and ribs. She didn't heal as fast as he did, and the damage was taking a toll. Suddenly, his jaws relaxed, and he fell to his knees. When the vampire went down, Ursa saw Sebastian standing behind him, holding *DeeDee's* jeweled handle. Her blade pierced the vampire's heart, staking him not with wood but with blessed steel.

"He was hurting you," the boy said. "It wasn't right."

"Get back," Ursa commanded. Taking Sebastian's lead, Ursa pulled her sword and held it to the vampire's neck.

"Move and I'll cut your head off. When it grows back, I'll cut it off again and again. In Jesus's name, I command you, leave him now!"

The vampire's eyes glowed red. Its double-jointed, spidery arms reached back to remove *DeeDee,* but when it gripped the handle, the blade flamed. The vampire shrieked as the fiery sword burned through its rotten heart. Not even he could regenerate quickly enough to repair the damage. He released the sword, stopped shrieking, and closed his eyes.

Sebastian stepped forward, but Ursa stopped him. "Wait."

The vampire made one last grab for the sword, but *DeeDee* turned up the heat. He shrieked louder and thrashed in the hallway, spearing itself deeper by slamming *DeeDee* against the wall. Finally, he was still.

With Piper, Sebastian, and Ursa watching, the vampire *changed* back into Sherman.

DeeDee removed herself from the *Handler* and flew to the closet. She nestled in her scabbard and waited.

Piper and Sebastian held each other, looked at their great-grandpa, marveling that he'd just been a vampire. *Angels, vampires, and flying swords, oh my.* They thought it was a night they'd never forget. Ursa knew better. She wouldn't let them remember anything they'd witnessed.

"Good to have you back," Ursa said, and helped Sherman to his feet.

Sherman composed himself and contemplated the best way to explain things to his great-grandchildren. Dr. Spock's book didn't address such issues. Before he could address them, Ursa wiped their memories.

"That wasn't necessary," he said, as Ursa put the boys in their bunk beds. To her, Piper seemed excessively heavy for such a young boy.

"Like you're a trusted source of what is and is not necessary," Ursa bit back. She hated that she loved Sherman so much. "Let me help, you monster." She put his arm over her shoulder and carried him to his recliner. He healed while they talked.

"How'd things go with Susan?" Sherman asked.

Chapter Forty-Eight

U rsa told Sherman that Clark followed Susan to Jackson. He watched, he waited, and just when it looked like the woman might escape, he pounced on her.

"I was watching them when I had to come save you, save the boys I mean...*from* you. I thought you were stronger than this. What happened?"

"Ursa, I know it's hard for you to stay on topic, but before we discuss my shortcomings and weak, pathetic constitution, tell me how Susan is? *Is* she okay?"

"She *was* fine. I don't know if she *is* fine or not. She could be dead now for all I know. If she's not dead, she's not leaving him. That's for sure."

He waited for her to elucidate, but she said nothing else. He raised both hands and shrugged his shoulders. His body language said, *What the hell, Ursa*?

"You want details? Fine, I'll give you details. He hit her, beat her, and then raped her, rested, beat her some more... Is that what you want to hear?

"No, I don't want to hear it. Like you, I want to kill him. Clark has to be dealt with, but Susan has to be the one to decide to pull the plug."

"You're giving him too much time. He's dangerous," she warned Sherman, "and getting more so each day. I know what you're trying to do, and why you're doing it. You want her to learn, to see the truth, but it's gone on too long. She isn't learning, and she's blind to the truth. He is going to permanently damage her, maybe one of those boys...maybe both. Stop this, stop him now."

She was right. Sherman felt the danger building like a storm cloud gaining momentum but there was distance between him and the danger. He thought he had more time and made the same mistake he'd made when he was six-years-old. Like then, the distance he felt wasn't temporal. Again, it was aimed at someone else. Sherman was foolishly prideful and thought he had ample time to stop Clark and teach Susan a valuable lesson at the same time.

Sherman was wrong, again.

Wherever she was, she was happy to be there. Her last conscious sensation was of throbbing pain, but now, in this place, she was happy. If not happy, she was at least at peace. Somewhere in the back of her mind she knew Clark was on her, in her. What difference did that make when she couldn't feel it? She was thankful to have escaped to this place, whatever and wherever it was, and had no desire to find her way home.

It was an unusual place, to be sure. The grass was unlike any she'd ever walked though. It was green enough and damp with morning dew, but the way it moved just before her steps fell made Susan think it was dodging her feet. She was having crazy thoughts, like maybe the grass was alive, or something. Lunatic thoughts like those would get you locked up in a room with soft walls where friendly people in white coats give you fat, blunt crayons to color pretty pictures.

The sun was the brightest she had ever seen, but it wasn't coming from the sky. As far as she could see—and there weren't any clouds blocking her view—there was no sunup there.

Maybe it's not sunny. Maybe it's Sonny.

As she considered that, she saw two familiar faces.

Across a gulf—at first, it seemed like a small pond because she could easily see the other side, but when she yelled, her voice faltered over the water—was her sons walking, hand in hand. Each time she took a step toward them, the gulf retreated a step. She considered swimming but knew it would widen with each stroke. She was meant to see—not be seen. Their mouths moved up and down and every now and then, one of them would chuckle. She wanted to touch them, to share their experiences in this special place, but just seeing their joy thrilled her.

She wondered why Sebastian was so big while Piper was so small. It'd always been the other way around. Sebastian looked like a grown man and Piper was still a kid. Like Piper, Susan had no trouble recognizing Sebastian. Big or small, they both seemed happy and that was all that mattered to their mother.

She didn't know how long she watched them. It seemed like days, but that couldn't be right. Being unable to talk with them hurt her, but Susan was content to watch them laugh, even at a distance. Lost in love, she smiled at her boys and as soon as the smile cracked her face—like smiling was the forbidden wherever she was—she was yanked from the clearing and cast into her bedroom.

When she opened her eyes, Clark was staring crazily into her eyes. "Where have you been?" he asked. "You were smiling. You like it, huh? Well, there's plenty more where that came from." He went to work, proving he was right. For Susan, Sunday began with a fresh dose of pain.

Chapter Forty-Nine

S herman slept fitfully, fighting unseen demons. The sun peeked over the tree-lined horizon, and Sherman's eyes popped open, startling Ursa. Sherman knew she wasn't watching over him but was watching out for him.

"Watching me sleep, huh?"

"Watching you, anyway. Don't pretend you don't know why," she said.

He was grateful for her watchful eyes. No doubt, she'd saved his great-grandsons last night.

Sherman crept to the boys' room and peeked in. There were two bunk beds, but the brothers were sleeping in the same one. Last night Ursa mentioned Piper being awfully heavy, but in his damaged state Sherman wasn't able to receive the information. Now seeing Piper lying next to Sebastian Sherman received the information loud and clear.

Piper's head was crooked against the headboard, his feet almost touching the bright red, fire-engine foot-rail. Sebastian looked tinier than ever, no more than a doll against his older brother's chest. Boys have growth-spurts, but boys don't have growth-spurts as extreme as this.

He's doubled, at least, thought Sherman. One more spurt like that and Piper would be wearing his daddy's clothes.

No problem there. Sherman believed Clark's clothes wearing days were nearing an end.

Sherman closed the bedroom door, turned, and Ursa was there. "You see what I was talking about? He's *gigantic*."

Gigantic, thought Sherman, and almost remembered a line from some book. Was it important? He didn't see how it could be, so he pushed the word from his mind.

The word would soon be back.

Ursa said. "I've got work to. I could use your help."

"Aren't you going back to watch over Susan? She's still in danger."

"Handler, that's your fault, and she's your worry. Evil doesn't stop just because Sherman Lancaster decides to play house. If you want me to take care of Clark, it'll be my pleasure to kill him, but you don't want that, do you? You want me to just watch and tell you what I see. I don't *observe and report*. I'm not a security guard. I'm a War*rior*, and I have war to do. Summon me if you need me. Otherwise, leave me to my business." Ursa got the last word by vanishing before Sherman could argue.

Clark's not my worry until Susan makes him my worry, Sherman thought. Thinking he was doing the right thing, he woke the boys for breakfast and let Susan fend for herself.

Breakfast was eggs, some fried and some scrambled, pig pieces that had been sliced up, seasoned, and fried, one toast, a small glass of orange juice, and as much coffee as they wanted. The boys didn't talk much over breakfast. They were groggy, almost seemingly sedated. When they spoke, they mentioned a crazy dream they'd shared, a horrible dream. Neither boy could remember the details clearly, but they agreed it wasn't something they wanted to repeat.

Sebastian remembered being bigger than Piper in their dream. That wasn't the case at the breakfast table. Things were back to normal, and Piper was the bigger brother again. Sebastian was okay with that, but he wasn't okay with how much bigger Piper was.

"Why are you so big?" Sebastian asked.

Piper looked at himself, seemingly for the first time that morning, and blushed. "I'm not much bigger. What are you talking about?"

Sherman noticed Piper's pink cheeks and jumped to the boy's rescue. "Sebastian, eat your breakfast and leave your brother alone. Boys his age grow in the night. If you're lucky, maybe you'll grow a little, too." Sherman wanted an answer to the question as badly as Sebastian, but doubted Piper had a suitable explanation. It was a matter to take up later.

After breakfast, in which Piper ate everything on his plate and Sebastian's leftovers too, and was still hungry, they went in the living room. Sherman sat in his recliner. Instead of sitting with him like they often did, the boys sat side-by-side on the sectional. Sherman subconsciously registered that Piper and Sebastian held hands, but it wasn't important enough to rise to the conscious level. They were brothers, after all.

Sherman's apprentice would be revealed soon, today or tomorrow, for sure, and as all life's pleasures do his time with his great-grandsons would end. Kelvin's story had an ending and it had to be told. That evil man's end was, in many ways, Sherman's beginning. Because it was the day his daddy became a Handler.

"Boys, I'm going to tell you about the day Kelvin died. It was the same day my daddy's sword came to life."

Chapter Fifty

When Robert walked away from the shed, Kelvin was shaking in his boots, literally. He was both scared shitless and excited as hell. He needed whiskey to take the edge off, so as soon as Robert's truck pulled out of the drive Kelvin grabbed his Wild Turkey and took what he needed. Kelvin finally stopped shaking and thought, *that was close*.

Robert's little talk changed Kelvin's mind. Kelvin decided to pack his bags and haul ass before he was either arrested or sealed in a fifty-five-gallon oil drum and tossed in a quicksand pit in the Pyland Bottoms. He chewed a thumbnail to the quick while he decided this.

Kelvin's conscience was scarred and barely there after Betty Jo, but it urged him toward righteousness. *Do the right thing*, it whispered, and to Kelvin's surprise, he listened.

Kelvin's gnawing teeth hit tender skin, and he changed fingers. Because Robert talked to him the way he did, Kelvin knew Barbara was backing her husband. That meant Kelvin had officially lost his last supporter. There was nothing in his future but death or imprisonment. Kelvin made the smart decision and swallowed his pride.

Do the right thing, his conscience whispered again. Kelvin gave in.

Kelvin speedily packed his suitcase trying to stay ahead of his devilish desires. He kneed the canvas top three times to close it and headed to the GMC. If he stole it, they'd look for him, so he planned to leave it at the bus station. He rounded the corner of the shed and Rosalyn stepped out the backdoor. Where she was going, he didn't know. Her intended chore, he supposed but didn't bother guessing. Her walk, her sway, undid all his nervousness and careful considerations.

She was wearing cutoff, Daisy Dukes and a tank top that was two sizes too small. If his future was starving to death in the slick interior of an oil drum, he'd die after he tasted *her*. To hell with Robert and his threats. The plan was back on. Rosalyn was worth the risk.

Kelvin's conscience lost again, and Satan moved closer to total control.

Kelvin walked back to his room, not knowing he'd committed suicide by doing it and slung open his suitcase. He rehung a few pictures and carelessly threw a couple FFA trophies on the rick-rack shelves Robert built for him. It wouldn't do for his room to look like he was moving out. Everything was business as usual in *Casa de Kelvin*.

He oiled and loaded his revolver and tucked it under his mattress. He was raring and ready, but willing to wait. Half of him wanted to shoot Robert in the face, take the girls, and be done with it. If he hadn't hated his cousin so much, he would've done it. He wanted Robert to traipse off to Alabama and come home to an empty house.

Well, not empty, *per se*, but empty of life, anyway.

"I want you to suffer as much as possible," Kelvin whispered.

Thinking settled his nerves, and for the first time since Robert ambushed him in the shed, Kelvin grinned. There were things to do before Robert returned, so Kelvin wiped the devilish grin from his face and made his preparations.

While Robert was doing precisely the same thing to his truck at the Texaco station, Kelvin topped off the GMC's fuel tank with farm fuel. Kelvin checked the oil level, found it to be a quart low and added what was needed. He did a walk-around, kicking tires and making sure all six of them were round, not flat at the bottom. When nobody was looking, he discreetly carried his suitcase to the truck. Kelvin pulled the tarnished, chrome handle and the seat-back leaned forward like an oversized taco. He crammed his suitcase in the narrow storage area behind the seat and had to shoulder the seat-back like an NFL linebacker to get it back into its upright position.

Robert returned ten minutes later. He threw a look toward the shed and waved at Kelvin, who was sitting in a lawn chair smoking a cigarette before supper. Kelvin waved back, and the friendly exchanged brought Robert's mind back to the task at hand. After supper, he had to tell Barbara about his talk with their guest.

Robert devoured the crispy, brown chicken like he hadn't eaten in a week, but he was so anxious over what he had to do after supper the world's worst case of indigestion hit him before he touched the banana pudding. Barbara and Rosalyn were excited and nervous and could hardly swallow their food.

Kelvin sat quietly, chewing his nails between bites of chicken and creamed potatoes. All the nails were gone from his left hand and three fingers bled badly enough to need bandages. He was gnawing on his right thumb and just brought blood. He moved to the index finger. He wasn't thinking about food or how badly his leg was jumping under the table.

Since most of them were thinking things they couldn't say aloud, conversation was light and all about Robert's trip, the only thing they could talk about openly.

"What time are you leaving?" Karen asked.

"Supposed to meet Theodore in Houston at three in the morning."

"How long will it take to get there?" Barbara asked.

"Don't know. Never been."

"How long will you be over there, you reckon?" Rosalyn asked.

"Don't know. Never been. Long as it takes, I reckon."

"Are you driving or is Theodore going to man the wheel?" Kelvin asked. Karen's question was the only one Kelvin cared about, but he wanted to take part in the conversation.

"I'm guessing I will. Not that it makes any difference." Robert wanted to grab Kelvin's throat and threaten his life. *You touch my family and I'll...I'll....* Maybe the reason he didn't do it was because he didn't know how to finish the threat. What would he do? The truth was he didn't know, but he suspected it would involve a sword.

There were many mysteries Robert Lancaster didn't solve during his lifetime. What he would do to someone for hurting his family wasn't one of them.

They finished supper in an uneasy silence. Kelvin wished Robert a safe trip and stepped out the backdoor. Alone in his room, Kelvin didn't even try to sleep. He killed his lights and watched the back door. When it finally opened and Robert stepped out, Kelvin fully surrendered, and Satan happily took the reins.

Chapter Fifty-One

Clark Vance gave up on sleep at four o'clock, immediately after Susan vomited on him. He wanted to fault her and act accordingly, but Susan was unconscious. If he hadn't been there Clark supposed she would've drowned on the chunky, partially digested slop. Ever the loving husband, Clark rolled her onto her side. Susan coughed her way to ragged but vomit-free breaths, and Clark went to the bathroom to clean himself.

Clark flipped on the light, squinted against the harsh whiteness until his eyes adjusted to their environment. He turned on the hot faucet and got a washcloth from under the sink while he waited for the water to show up as advertised. He soaked the washcloth, squeezed out the excess water and had to juggle it from hand-to-hand until it cooled.

When it was cool enough to use, he swiped the warm washcloth across his chest. Answering some unexplainable and morbid curiosity,

Clark's eyes darted downward as his hand rotated and revealed the cloth's contents, and what Clark saw worried him. *Is she okay?*

Clark wasn't worried about Susan the way he'd worried about his dad when the MRI showed tumors in Thomas Vance's brain and lungs. When that happened, Clark worried about his daddy suffering, and more importantly, whether his dad could whip the 'Big C.' That was a different kind of worry.

Clark worried about Susan like he'd worried when the Braves traded their ace pitcher. He'd lost a wad of cash that year betting on his team. Clark worried about Susan the same way.

How's this going to affect me?

He wasn't concerned about the blood in her vomit. Susan had vomited blood many times after she forced Clark to *talk* to her. What worried him was *the* amount of blood. Susan had never vomited as much blood no matter how hard he'd *talked* to her. It looked like the bitch was dying, and that made Clark extremely nervous.

"Only cowards hit women," many people said.

Clark had listened to that bullshit his whole life and knew it for the lie that it was. His father told him it was lie, so Clark knew it was a lie. The lie was started by some bull-dyke somewhere where the population of real men was zero. The lie was perpetuated by pussy-whipped men only a step away from being full-blown fags. Keeping a woman in line, in fact teaching her *how* to behave like a proper woman, was a full-time job. And *talking* to them was a job requirement.

"And you don't hit 'em, anyway," Clark told the bathroom mirror as the narrative played out in his mind. "They're not men. If you hit 'em, you break 'em, and then you have to start over with a new one."

Had he broken Susan? He thought maybe he had, and that was what worried him.

If he did, he'd have to replace her, he knew that much. Clark wasn't the type to live alone and replacing her would be a major pain in his ass. Not to mention the shit he'd catch from the sheriff. In normal affairs, the sheriff was a fair man and stayed out of people's personal business. The sheriff understood and respected the sanctity of marriage. What happens between a man and his wife was their business. But the sheriff's respect and understanding ended when bodies dropped. Dead wives made for a difficult election campaign because even good folks who signed on to, *'what happens between a man and his wife was their business,'* didn't routinely sign up for dead wives.

Clark flipped the light off and returned to bed. Thankfully, most of the vomit had either soaked into the mattress or congealed to a cranberry Jell-O he wasn't tempted to taste. Instead, he scraped it out of his way and slung it to the floor. Susan would either be alive to clean it later, or she'd be dead. Either way, Clark was done with it.

Susan's back was to him, so Clark spooned her. He lightly pressed her carotid artery, and he thanked whatever gods were looking out for the Clark Vances of the world. Susan's pulse was steady and strong. He saw no reason she wouldn't pull through this like she had every time before.

Breathing easier, Clark left the bed and fetched a beer from the fridge. He wanted to wake Susan, to *talk* to her some more, to continue her education, but her blood loss worried him enough to let her sleep.

Clark drank beer and waited for Susan to wake up on her own.

Chapter Fifty-Two

"Sherman, it's me and you again on the dishes," Karen said.

"Why do I always have to do the stinking dishes?" Sherman shouted, but one look at his daddy's disapproving face sent him backpedaling with "I'm sorry," before his daddy could speak.

Albert was as unhappy about going to his parents' bedroom for another round of *Let's Not Believe the Sleepwalker* as Sherman was about washing dishes. But unhappy or not, Sherman and Albert went where they were supposed to go.

Outside his bedroom, Robert waited for the others and closed the door behind his middle son. Albert prayed his daddy would suddenly slam the door in his face and tell him to get lost, but it didn't happen. Robert waited patiently as Albert shuffled in. Albert took a position against the wall. His eyes were on his socked feet.

A big toe protruded from the end of his right sock. His toe made a dingy turtle head Albert couldn't pull his eyes from. They were his favorite socks.

Figures, he thought.

Barbara sat on the bed beside Rosalyn. They both were jittery and had an arm around each other. Albert was against the wall with his arms around himself, staring at the turtle head. Robert shut the door and approached Albert.

"Albert, I'm sorry for the way I acted last night. It was wrong to wave you off like I did. I mean... *I* was wrong, son."

Albert was speechless. He blushed blood-red same as he did when his shorts fell down in gym class. Yes, the whole damned school was in the gym for the Spring Fling and yes, it was his life's most embarrassing moment. There were more embarrassing moments coming, but thanks to youthful ignorance he successfully denied that possibility. Albert wrapped his arms around his daddy's legs and said, "Thank you, daddy. I love you so much."

Robert put his arms around Albert. "I love you too, son. And Rosalyn, I'm sorry for not believing you," Robert finished with tears in his eyes.

Carried by emotional overload, Rosalyn said, "I love you, Daddy." She bounded off the bed and wrapped her arms around Robert, pushing Albert aside as she did.

"And I love you, baby girl."

Rosalyn returned to Barbara's side and Robert told them, "I talked to Kelvin like I said I would. He claimed everything was on the up-and-up, but he didn't deny saying the things Albert overheard. He said he was dreaming. Told me I couldn't blame him for anything he said while he was dreaming. Said a man ain't responsible for what he dreams or what he might say in his sleep. Thing is, I don't think he was asleep. I believe he's lying as sure as I'm dying, and if he's lying about that, I suspect he's lying about the rest of it."

"Did you tell him to leave?" Rosalyn's asked. Her eyes brimmed with bright, foolish hope. Robert had never looked as good in her eyes as he did right then, but it wouldn't last.

Robert's shining coat dulled when he told her, "I don't think that's necessary. I told him to keep away from y'all except when we're eating. No more coming in the house and no more riding to church with y'all, neither. If he wants to go, he can take the GMC and sit in his own pew. I saw the difference in him tonight at supper. He wouldn't even look at y'all. Things are going to be different around here from now on."

Robert didn't know how right he was.

"Daddy, that's just because you were there. He's only ever creepy when you're not around. Please make him leave." She wrapped both arms around her mama and cried like she hadn't in years.

Albert smiled through it all. *Daddy believes me!*

"He was just doing those things because he thought y'all wouldn't tell me. He knows better now, so he'll be straightening up. If he does anything like that again, he's out."

Barbara thought carefully before speaking. She wanted to support her husband and comfort her daughter, but at the same time she had to be sure they treated Kelvin fairly. "Your daddy's right. Kelvin was getting his thrills because they were cheap. They aren't so cheap anymore and I believe he'll leave us alone."

It sounded right in her mind, but it didn't ring true coming from her mouth. Barbara half-believed Kelvin was a creepo, but the other half knew him as her church-buddy. He knew as many Bible verses as Barbara did, maybe more. Rosalyn wanted Kelvin gone but Barbara didn't feel Christian turning her back on a 'brother' who was so obviously struggling. To Barbara, Robert's plan was perfect. Kelvin had one more chance, and that was all any sinner could ask for.

"He's going to kill me," Rosalyn said matter-of-factly, wiping her eyes to pull off the defiance. She resolved to say nothing else on the subject. "Are we done?"

They hugged, said goodnight, and Robert assured her everything would be fine. Rosalyn thought her daddy was mistaken and when she woke up with Kelvin's hand over her mouth, she knew she was right.

Robert set his alarm for two o'clock. He planned to cook a quick breakfast and meet Theodore in Houston by three. Setting the alarm was routine, a failsafe, but it was unneeded because he never went to sleep. He tossed and turned, dreading the trip and ignoring a small whispering voice telling him to call it off and stay home.

At one-thirty he eased out of bed, got dressed, and made a pot of coffee. By two-fifteen, he'd downed all twelve cups. *I'll have to stop and piss every fifteen minutes*, he cussed himself. At two-twenty, he turned the lights off and went outside.

The creaking truck door pierced the night like a screaming banshee hellbent on carnage. A swarm of pissed-off bats swooped in to investigate the disturbance. Robert grabbed the door hard with both hands as if squeezing it would help. His old truck cranked easily. He said a quick prayer and slid the gearshift into drive.

Robert threw a look at Kelvin's shed. He didn't expect to see anything, but his eyes were pulled there anyway. Kelvin wasn't there holding his prick and dancing naked in the moonlight, but Robert wasn't insane for thinking Kelvin might be dancing like that. Robert wasn't ashamed for looking but did feel a little foolish when there was nothing to see.

Call off the trip, the voice whispered again, but Robert didn't know to listen. He was *becoming* but wasn't a *Handler* yet. Robert went to Alabama and left his family to fend for themselves.

Kelvin—his prick wasn't out, and he was fully dressed—didn't think Robert was foolish for looking. In fact, Kelvin was terrified he'd been seen when Robert started the truck but didn't immediately drive away. From where he was hiding Kelvin saw the moonlight reflecting in Robert's eyes and those eyes were trained on Kelvin's room. Kelvin was frightened and nervous and had to will himself to breathe.

Robert fiddled around in his truck for five minutes...the longest five minutes of Kelvin's life. Kelvin lost his last two fingernails to his relentless gnawing. Finally, Robert's truck started moving and disappeared down the driveway. Kelvin spat a shiver of fingernail on the ground and walked toward the house.

It was time.

Kelvin stayed in the shadows and waited until he was sure Robert wasn't coming back. He worked his way around the house, stuck to the shadows, and peeked through the windows to make sure everyone was in bed. He saw covered lumps in every one and believing all those lumps to be soundly asleep, went to the laundry room for the spare house key.

Two years ago, Robert lost his key when he fell from his boat. Since then he insisted they keep a spare key hidden in the laundry room. He tucked it under the outside freezer, easy to get to but impossible to find if you didn't know it was there. Two months ago, Kelvin 'borrowed' the spare key and took it to the hardware store where he had two copies made just in case Rosalyn made this one disappear.

He ran his bloody, nail-less fingers under the freezer's edge, dancing them through cobwebs and rolling mouse turds out of the way. There it was! Rosalyn hadn't moved it—probably hadn't considered it. When the detectives told Robert how Kelvin gained entrance and killed his family, Robert would know he'd personally supplied Kelvin's way in.

Kelvin couldn't be more pleased. Things were working out better than he'd hoped.

Inside the house, he didn't waste time. He tip-toed silently to Barbara's room. She was sleeping a working woman's slumber, hard and fast and snoring softly, but still somehow sexy. He considered taking Barbara, too, but she'd been okay to him. Better than okay, actually. Letting her live meant he couldn't shoot Albert and Sherman, but the most regrettable aspect of letting Barbara live was not being able to leave her corpse alongside Robert's two son's bullet-ridden bodies. Robert coming home to that bloody mess would've been priceless, but Barbara had been good to Kelvin, so he spared her and her sons.

Besides, he had Karen and Rosalyn for fun. Youth was no substitute for experience, so being honest taking Barbara simply wasn't worth the hassle.

Kelvin put a hand on the girls' door. It wasn't, but he swore it was hot to his touch. He gripped their doorknob and twisted. *Locked*, of course it was. It took two minutes to unlock and he pushed it open. Only a crack at first, then wide enough to walk through. He eased the door shut behind him walked to Rosalyn's side of the bed.

He laid his gun on Rosalyn's pillow and with a slick fluid motion, he pressed one hand tightly over her mouth, flipped the bedside lamp on and grabbed his pistol. He shoved the muzzle into Karen's cheek hard enough to make her gums bleed and broke a tooth off at the gum line.

"Wake up, girls," Kelvin whispered.

Chapter Fifty-Three

K aren choked awake on thick blood and searing pain. She was dizzy and wanted to vomit. When her nausea passed, she stared into Kelvin's lunatic grin. In a low and menacing whisper, he told her, "If you do what I tell you not to do, I'll kill her." He nodded to Rosalyn who was too scared to struggle under his hand. "If you don't do what I tell you to do, I'll kill her. If you do anything I think you should've known not to do, I'll kill her. You get how this works?" Karen nodded.

He switched the gun to Rosalyn and grinned wider. "And the same goes for you, baby. If you mess up, your sister pays for your sins. We're going to be very quiet when we get up. We're going to walk out the backdoor in a single-file line, just like when we were little kids in school. Pretend it's a fire drill. I left the door open so you don't even have to touch it. We're little mice, little church mice, and what are little church mice?"

Together, the sisters whispered the answer. "Quiet."

"That's right. They're quiet, and we're going to be quiet, too. If you wake the others, their blood is on your hands, not mine."

He jerked the bedspread off them expecting to find them wearing long, thick cotton gowns, even bundling bags wouldn't have surprised him. He was shocked and happy to be wrong. The Lancasters were modest, as Christians should be, but modesty walks hand-in-hand with necessity. It was summer in Mississippi and even though they had an air conditioner, their parents rarely turned it on. It was sweltering, even at night, and the girls were dressed accordingly.

Karen wore her summer gown. There wasn't much to it. It had a low neck, not so low that she had to worry about exposing herself but low enough to tease. The hemline touched just above her knee when she stood but when she slid from the bed, the gown pulled up and exposed her leg all the way up her thigh. Kelvin touched her naked, inner thigh with the gun's long slender barrel, and pushed her gown higher. Her skin broke out in gooseflesh and Kelvin came in his pants.

Rosalyn was younger and not as modest as Karen. Instead of a summer gown, Rosalyn wore a stomach bearing tank and lacy panties. Barbara didn't allow whore panties in her house. They were a gift from her rebellious sister, Jill, who loved to cause trouble and they survived only because Rosalyn made sure Barbara never laid eyes on them.

Barbara knew there was only one reason a woman wore lacy *whore panties*, red *whore panties*, and that was to please Satan. And nobody was pleasing Satan on Barbara's watch.

Rosalyn's shirt began life as a regular tank, but one particularly hot night Rosalyn cut the neckline lower and scissored four inches off the bottom. It hung just below her breasts and looked like a bra more than a shirt. Rosalyn got off the bed, scared of the gun and the creepo holding it, not thinking about her clothes.

The cutoff shirt rode up and flashed the bottom of her breasts. Instinctively, she pulled the shirt down, but doing so exposed her breasts in the low cropped neckline. Kelvin drooled at the perky breasts with nipples drawn as tight as pinky fingers and even though he'd just blown his load, like Old Faithful, he was ready to blow again.

The girls were quiet and did as told. Neither wanted to be responsible for hurting their loved ones. Kelvin's used their love against them, unabashedly and with wicked enthusiasm. Karen led the way with Rosalyn's clammy hand gripping too tightly to her shoulder. Kelvin tried to pay attention to where they were going but Rosalyn's lace-wrapped ass was right there in his face, close enough to touch. Her tight little ass-cheeks tightened and relaxed with each step, rose and fell, rose and fell. Hypnotized, Kelvin reached for her, stumbled, knocked a vase from the top shelf and miraculously caught it before it shattered on the floor and woke everyone else in the house.

With renewed focus, he pointed and told Karen to walk around the south end of the house, away from Barbara and the boys' open bedroom windows. He'd parked the truck fifty yards from the house, what he'd thought was a safe distance. He quickly bound the girls' wrists and ankles with duct tape, gagged them with oily rags he pulled from under the GMC's bench seat and tossed them in the cab like feed sacks. He turned the key and the straight-six rumbled to life.

In that instant, he was undone.

Sherman, as his family would eagerly agree, had many flaws. One being that he was a poor sleeper. That was the unofficial diagnosis according to every piece of information Barbara uncovered at Houston's Carnegie Library. A few hours every other night or even every third night was all the sleep the boy ever got. The remaining hours were spent tossing and turning and thinking and fantasizing about magnificent places and strange beings. This night was no different. Sherman was wide awake when Kelvin cranked the GMC and Sherman knew the sound intimately.

The black GMC was the only thing other than tractors Robert trusted Sherman to drive. Robert said GM made the old truck like a tank, a prerequisite for anything Sherman drove. The GMC rumbled and rattled each time it started and was music to Sherman's ears. Those rumbles and rattles were as unique as DNA. Instantly, Sherman knew someone was stealing his only ride.

Sherman sat straight-up in bed, totally forgetting about the top bunk and raked his head across the cross-wired underside of his brother's top bunk. His eyes flashed to the corner where the wooden crate he used as a booster seat was, thankfully, undisturbed. He was afraid the truck thief might've tried to make off with it too.

The crate was still there, so Sherman ran to his daddy's gun closet. He skidded on a loose rug and almost crashed out of his parent's bedroom window. He didn't have to look. His hands knew where to go. He reached into the dark closet and came out with his .410 shotgun. He loaded the shotgun and ran out the wide-opened backdoor. He spied the truck. It was seventy-five yards away when Sherman raised his gun and fired.

The slug traveled in an arc just like Robert explained it would. With a hunter's mind, Sherman saw the arc perfectly. At thirty yards he hit the bullseye dead on, zeroed it. At seventy-five yards, he was dead on again.

Kelvin's fuel tank was seventy-five yards away when Sherman aimed at it. The slug arced slowly toward the sky, passed through zero at thirty yards, peaked at forty-nine yards, and at seventy-five yards collided with the fuel tank. It *plunked* an entry hole on the tank's left side and an exit hole in the bottom of the tank. Gas gushed out in two thumb-wide streams.

Kelvin thought he had enough gas to make it to Arkansas, but he would travel only seven miles in Sherman's GMC.

The black *Jimmy* wasn't Kelvin's first choice for an escape vehicle. It wouldn't have been his second or third choice. He didn't pick the loudest, oldest, and slowest vehicle the Lancasters owned because he wanted to disadvantage himself.

Robert's Bronco was an automatic no-go because Robert was the only one with keys to it.

The green Chevy pickup was out because Robert and Theodore took it to Alabama.

The rusted Fury was out because Karen was gone shopping in it when Kelvin loaded his go-bag.

The *Jimmy* was his only choice, so it wasn't a choice at all.

The GMC had a muffler, but it was lacier than Rosalyn's panties. It had more holes than metal, and in another year, it'd rust off completely. The truck's interior was a fucking noise factory. Everything rattled and most everything squeaked, too. Kelvin didn't hear Sherman's shotgun blast or the slug's plunking the gas tank, so he drove off thinking he was the cleverest man alive.

Kelvin turned onto County Line Road. There were no lights behind him and nothing but open road ahead of him, so he slowed to a quieter speed. The rattling and squeaking diminished but was nowhere near absent. However, without the high-speed wind pushing the fumes backwards, and because GM's ridiculous designers placed the fuel tank just behind the cab, so close it might as well have been inside the cab, the interior quickly filled with gas fumes.

Kelvin's eyes filled with tears and he gagged and choked like an eighty-five-year old lifelong smoker. He couldn't drive straight for hacking phlegmy coughs. He fought to stay conscious.

He grabbed the window handle and cranked it madly. The handle was bent and each revolution skinned a little more hide off his knuckles. He cussed the piece of shit handle but kept lowering the window because oxygen was more important than skin.

He reached across the cab to open the passenger window. Karen lay in the floorboard of the truck, and Rosalyn was across the seat, her feet resting against Kelvin's thigh. He hit the Grand Canyon of washouts while he was cranking down the passenger window. The truck fishtailed across the road and his hand slipped off the window crank and fell naturally—and innocently since Kelvin's focus was on staying out of the ditch—to the small rise at the bottom of Rosalyn's abdomen.

He straightened the truck with one hand and jerked Rosalyn's panties to her knees with the other. She tried to move away but to where? She was trapped with his hand between her knees, moving higher. She inched away from his probing fingers. Her head hit the door panel and could go no farther. Her neck bent suicidally, and she escaped another two inches. After that, there was nowhere to go. She pinched her thighs together, but his determination to get in was too great.

Rosalyn cried out when he rammed his fingers into her. He thought it was foreplay, nothing compared to what was to come, but this was the only time he'd touch her.

The stop sign was straight ahead, not a half a mile away. Freedom was within his grasp, and he smelled it. As soon as he reached the pavement and turned right, nobody would find him. He pulled his fingers out of Rosalyn and put them under his nose. He inhaled deeply and held it until he almost blacked out. He moved his fingers to his mouth. They were still moist, and he came in his pants again as Rosalyn's fluids touched off a flavor explosion on his tongue.

It was all he could do not to stop the truck and fuck Rosalyn right there while her sister listened to the muffled screams. *No time*, he thought, but there was time to get his fingers sticky again. He reached over Rosalyn's red lace panties, about to enter her again, when the

GMC sputtered, sputtered, and rolled to a stop. The engine died. Kelvin twisted the key, stomped the pedal, but it refused to crank.

The fuel gauge read a big fat *E*, but it always read *E*. The gauge busted years ago and everybody on the farm knew to use the two-by-two behind the seat to the check the gas. Kelvin knew it too, but he didn't need to check it. He'd filled it yesterday.

But when he got out of the cab, he kicked the tank anyway. The echo answered as well as the two-by-two would've. The tank was empty. Not low, but bone-dry.

Kelvin had a damn big problem, and it wasn't just being out of gas with two hostages. He was stranded less than a quarter of a mile from one of the busiest highways in the state, a state known for its hospitality. In fact, he was in the Hospitality State. It wasn't a question of whether somebody would pull off the highway to help—it would happen—the question was how long until it did.

A Good Samaritan was exactly what he didn't need, but when a pair of headlights turned off the highway and headed towards him, a Good Samaritan was exactly what Kelvin got.

Chapter Fifty-Four

The Good Samaritan was Melvin Parker, and he'd lived in Vardaman, Mississippi all his seventy-six years. He worked for fifty-three years in the wood mill at Pyland. Seven years ago, his boss and long-time friend let him go. Melvin joked when he told the story, "That's a funny way of saying he fired my old ass," but inside, Melvin wasn't laughing.

Melvin Parker planned to die in the wood mill and didn't want to go anywhere, so he wasn't being let go of anything. He was forced out, fired, kicked out, and just plain shit-canned.

He didn't blame his boss for firing him. Melvin was man enough to admit that his eyesight was dimming, hearing was fading, and he was generally wearing out in every way a man could wear out. It was a tough pill to swallow, a jagged little bitch, but he swallowed it. But just because he couldn't work at the mill didn't mean he couldn't visit his old friends. Melvin Parker never missed a morning's coffee with his former co-workers until the day he met Kelvin Smith.

Melvin drove east at his usual forty-five miles-per-hour. Off to his left he saw a set of headlights swerving on the county line. You never know when somebody'll need help, so he slowed to thirty to scrutinize the situation more closely. Finally, the driver regained control of the fishtailing vehicle, so Melvin figured God didn't need his help this morning. Melvin brought his truck back to forty-five and headed to his coffee date.

Then the headlights went out.

The turn for the county line was on his left, and he had to make the call. *Stop or keep going?* There was no one coming and no one trying to pass, so Melvin hit the brake and cut the wheel. If the guy didn't need help, Melvin thought he would be back on the road in plenty of time to enjoy coffee with his buddies.

Melvin was all smiles as he pulled alongside Kelvin's GMC and stopped. "Good morning, young fellow. You having awe-toe-mo-bill issues, are you?"

"Yes sir, I'm having some issues with my old girl this morning. My gas tank sprung a leak. Name's Kelvin Smith. Please to meet you, and many thanks for helping out a stranger." Kelvin stuck his hand out.

"Hahaha that's a good one, sonny," the Good Samaritan said. "Kelvin Smith, my name is Melvin Parker. Kelvin and Melvin, that's a helluva of a *coinkydink*. It's a right pleasure to meet you, young man. Now, what can an old fellow do to hep you out? I ain't much of a mechanic, but I can give you a lift some place." He shook Kelvin's hand and smiled.

Melvin didn't look it, but he was ready for what came next.

"I'm gonna need your truck, Old Timer, and I guess I'm gonna' take your life, too." Kelvin gripped Melvin's hand in a G.I. Joe Kung-Fu Grip and wrapped his other hand around the old man's wiry wrist.

Melvin was thin as a whip and light as a feather, and Kelvin yanked him out the window. Melvin thudded face-down on the gravel road, busting his nose and opening gashes on both lips. The dust blinded him, and he dropped his knife reaching for his stinging eyes. When he could see again, Melvin Parker smiled.

His knife was covered in Kelvin's blood with dust forming a macabre bloody mud-glaze on the blade. *I got the sumbitch,* Melvin thought. Melvin rolled onto his back, supported himself on his elbows, and said, "Didn't expect that, did ya', you little pipsqueak?"

Kelvin was stunned speechless.

He expected to jerk the skinny old man from the truck without issue and drag him into the wood and cut his throat. Kelvin didn't expect the three-inch-long gash that began on his chin and followed his lower jawbone toward his ear. Melvin was old and weak, but he was mean as a snake and plenty spry to make Kelvin wish he had just shot the old bastard in the truck.

"You old bastard!" Kelvin screamed and stomped Melvin's head. One stomp did the job, but Kelvin kept stomping until what remained looked nothing like a human skull. It was flattened and cracked and looked like a turtle that lost a bet and couldn't get out of the road fast enough to avoid being ran over.

Kelvin walked towards the GMC and something yellow and runny oozed off his left boot. With a jerky kick, he flung it to the side of the road. On the right boot, something yellow and not so runny clung to several of its gunmetal lace hooks. He made a note to clean them later.

Kelvin put his hand on the knife wound and hot blood squirted between his fingers. The wound was gushing blood and needed tending, but the sun wasn't waiting on him to play nurse. He'd found the bullet holes in the tank, and that told him that somebody caught him stealing the truck.

By now, they knew the truck wasn't the only thing he'd stolen. They were certainly looking for him and if they hadn't done it yet, they'd soon have the cops in on the search. He'd have to tend to his wounds and clean his boots when he had more time.

He quickly moved his bags to the bed of the stolen truck. One at a time, he dragged the girls from one truck and threw them in the other. He took no care with them. Karen's head struck the inside of the door and knocked her unconscious. He wrestled Rosalyn in the truck next. With her wrists and ankles tied, she fought like a psychotic worm. Kelvin swatted her face openhanded but hit the gag protruding from her mouth and didn't hurt her at all.

Kelvin slid behind the wheel, cranked it, and gunned the engine. He cut the wheel hard and spun around in the road. He made it to the highway, turned right, and floored it.

He made it to Vardaman in record time and lost any chance he had of escaping.

Chapter Fifty-Five

Kelvin didn't know Melvin Parker was arguably the most loved man in Vardaman. Everybody knew Melvin, and they all loved him. If five thousand people showed up for the annual Sweet Potato Festival, five thousand people shook hands with Melvin Parker. It was bad for Kelvin that everybody in town loved Melvin; it was bad for Kelvin that everybody in town knew Melvin's truck, but it was exponentially worse for Kelvin that everybody in town knew Melvin's habits.

When Melvin's truck came back through town an hour early, everybody who saw it paid close attention to it. When they saw it clipping along at speedy fifty-five miles-per-hour, they knew Melvin wasn't behind the wheel. Kelvin thought he was driving slowly to avoid drawing attention. He couldn't know Melvin rarely got above second gear, but everybody else knew it. When Melvin's truck roared by the local breakfast joint, several good ol' boys lit out after it.

The *good ol' boys* were all burly, farming types, and they all loved Melvin Parker.

Also, the good ol' boys were all armed.

Somebody called the cops, but the sheriff and his deputies were out answering calls. The dispatcher made it sound like matters of life and death, but the caller suspected the deputies were running down water-tower-painters and settling fence-line disputes. Trying to sound professional after a boring night behind the desk, the dispatcher assured the caller the sheriff would get right on it.

The caller wasn't confident that he and the dispatcher shared a common understanding of the phrase, *get right on it*. The caller hung up and rather than wait for the sheriff, went to the air waves, sealing Kelvin's fate with a quick CB call.

"Break One-Nine: Break."

"Go breaker," one of the guys said.

"This is Bubba. Jimmy-Ray, you got your ears on? Come back."

Jimmy-Ray was driving the brand-new Chevy chewing up Kelvin's tailpipe. "Yeah, Bubba, go for Jimmy-Ray."

"Dispatcher said the sheriff and his boys are out of pocket, so don't y'all lose that bastard."

"That's a big ten-four," Jimmy-Ray said. "We're going to shut 'em down." Jimmy-Ray and Company proceeded to shut Kelvin down.

They tailed Kelvin, slow at first, just staying with him not really knowing what to do. Most were hoping the sheriff would catch up and take the lead. When that didn't happen soon enough, Jimmy-Ray sped alongside Melvin's Ford. He saw a head that didn't belong to Melvin and radioed that information to the other trucks. Then, they hemmed Kelvin in.

With Jimmy-Ray's truck in front of him, one truck in the lane beside him, and three trucks behind him, Kelvin had no escape. Simultaneously, the trucks slowed and forced Kelvin to slow along with them. They thought they had him, but they didn't know how crazy Kelvin was. They also didn't know there were two bound and gagged girls in the truck with him. If they'd known those two things, Jimmy-Ray & Co. would've behaved differently.

The parade was almost stopped when Kelvin pulled out his revolver. He aimed it at the lopsided head of the man driving the truck in the other lane and without hesitation, pulled the trigger. The man's brains flew out the window and washed back onto the windshield of the truck behind him. The driver of that truck got sick on his dashboard and ran off the road. He wasn't wearing his seatbelt and was crushed when he came halfway out the window as the truck rolled down the embankment.

Kelvin sideswiped lopsided's truck and pushed it out of his way. With a clear left lane, he hammered on the throttle and the old Ford launched forward. Kelvin pointed the Ford's nose into the left lane and blew passed Jimmy-Ray. Jimmy-Ray saw Kelvin laughing like a maniac as he passed. He radioed to the other trucks. "Boys, this sucker is as crazy as a shit-house rat."

You ain't taking me alive, thought Kelvin. His heart was racing, and his vision blurred from the increased blood flow. Kelvin kept the pedal to the floor, but the pursuers were gaining on him. Mr. Parker's old truck was no match for the pursuers' newer vehicles. They would catch him. It was just a matter of time.

Ain't got no choice. I gotta kill 'em. He slowed Melvin's truck and brought his pursuers closer.

Kelvin fired first. His shot went wide and missed everybody. He was looking over his shoulder, shooting with his left hand and driving with his right. The only way he would have hit anyone was if they'd driven into the bullet. Missing so widely only encouraged his pursuers.

After he'd spent his six rounds, their bullets rained in on him and it didn't take long for one of them to find its mark. With bullets hitting the truck like hailstones in a Texas-tornado, it was nothing short of a God-sent miracle Karen and Rosalyn weren't riddled like Bonnie and Clyde.

The passenger of a brand new, red Chevy with over-sized mudders fired a .45 long Colt at Melvin's truck. The shooter had never killed anybody and was pretty damn sure he didn't want to start this morning, so he hardly aimed at all. The heavy lead smashed out the truck's rear glass and hit Kelvin's right shoulder, dislocating it instantly and setting off a chain reaction that ended with Melvin's truck upside down in a ditch.

Kelvin had enough adrenaline in him to handle the pain, but there wasn't a damn thing he could do about the physical results associated with a dislocated shoulder. He held his gun in his left hand and the steering wheel with his right, and the bullet interrupted the connection between Kelvin's brain and his right hand. His brain sent the message: "*DRIVE BASTARD! HOLD STEADY!*" Unfortunately, Kelvin's hand never received it.

Kelvin's dislocated shoulder dropped, his arm dropped, and his hand dropped one inch each. Just one inch. The steering wheel cut to the right, one inch. Melvin Parker had nothing else to do and was serious about maintaining his old truck, and there was no play in his steering.

An inch of right turn took the truck from a straight path towards guaranteed freedom in the West and put it on a forty-five-degree path directly to *Ol' Sparky* down at Parchman prison. The truck ran off the pavement, the driver's side front tire skidding sideways into a pile of loose gravel.

The flip was on.

Kelvin dropped his gun and grabbed the steering wheel with his left hand. He steered into the slide, but nothing happened. There was no resistance at the other end. The truck was already in the air. Kelvin's steering did nothing but reinforce his illusion of control for a few seconds longer. Foolishly and despite all evidence to the contrary, Kelvin believed he would escape.

He steered some more, working the steering wheel one way and then the other with no results. The truck maintained its course. Faced with the unchanging reality Kelvin finally got the message. *The fucking truck is upside down*.

It was a good plan, a damn fine effort, but thanks to a bunch of *good ol' boys* Kelvin's run was over. One short finger-fuck was all he got for his trouble. Kelvin let go of the wheel.

Inside the flipping Ford, Kelvin thought, *there's gotta be more. It can't end like this.*

Eyewitness reports varied greatly. Some said the truck rotated once in the air, landed on its tires and then flipped end-over-end a few times. Others insisted the truck only made a half rotation, landed upside down and then flipped end-over-end a few times. But by all reports and judging by the condition of the truck, it was a bad-ass wreck and a fucking miracle no one was killed or seriously injured.

The last flip ended slowly. The Ford stood upright on its grill for few seconds—those seconds felt like hours to the people inside the cab—and like a felled tree, timbered to the ground upside down. The radiator exploded hot green liquid everywhere, and all four tires spun mindlessly looking for ground that was no longer there.

Jimmy-Ray & Co. jerked the passenger door open expecting to find one dead truck thief and nearly shit themselves when they saw the girls. Gingerly, but quickly in case the truck caught fire, Karen and Rosalyn were snatched from the upside-down truck and whisked away to the medical clinic. The doctor checked them over, head-to-toe, and finding nothing broken or leaking too bad, treated their cuts and scrapes and let them go.

They were interviewed by the authorities but could offer little insight. They'd heard Kelvin talking to someone, but they didn't see him kill Melvin. It didn't matter. Melvin's brain matter—Melvin ended up with a gruesome ending after all and would've loved to hear his buddies tell the story—still clung to Kelvin's boot. The ooey-gooey brain and the fact Kelvin was driving Melvin's Ford was more than enough to earn the death penalty, not that anybody thought he'd live to ride *Ol' Sparky*. Vardaman had always taken care of its own.

After a night neither would forget Karen and Rosalyn were driven home by a deputy who kept apologizing like he'd personally wronged them. Barbara was waiting with open arms, but both girls ran to their bratty, little brother first. When Kelvin discovered the holes in the gas tank, he'd cussed Sherman, and the girls overheard him. They knew who to thank.

"You saved us," they told Sherman.

Sherman was happy to see them and wept for joy. He hardly wondered about his precious GMC at all.

Until, after his sisters stopped crying.

"So, where's my truck?" he asked.

Kelvin wasn't afforded a trip to the clinic. He was breathing and bleeding. Both meant he was alive which was too good for him. He was carted back to Vardaman and locked in the town's only cell which up until now only housed the occasional drunkard. Once when two farmers got into a land dispute, it held the hotter tempered one until he cooled down, otherwise, it was just additional storage space for the police department.

When the county's only doctor, Dr. Wester, finished with the girls, he slowly drove to the jail hoping Kelvin would be dead by the time he got there. Finding Kelvin still alive, Dr. Wester tended to Kelvin's injuries. Denied pain medication and left alone to ponder his certain fate, Kelvin did what no one expected him to do.

He planned his revenge.

Chapter Fifty-Six

Still, Clark waited for Susan to wake up.

Was the bitch dead? Susan never slept this long. She had to be dead.

Clark had polished off a twelve pack watching westerns and pretending he wasn't worried about the woman in the other room. He didn't know what time it was but guessed it had to be noon. Fully convinced Susan was dead, Clark kicked his recliner closed and was slowly standing when Susan rounded the corner.

"You let me sleep in." She sounded genuinely appreciative and freakishly upbeat.

Picking up on her thankful tone and sounding like a returning war hero, Clark said, "You looked like you needed rest." He didn't let on to how worried he'd been because showing emotion was how a bitch gained the upper-hand.

A sick vibration, the sound of a horsefly in a spider's web, broke their conversation. Clark and Susan followed the vibration to its source, and instead of horsefly, they saw the remains of Susan's phone. Clark *spiked* it during an outburst last night, and its shattered plastic lay in three pieces, still tethered by hair-thin wires far more durable than they appeared. If one of the pieces hadn't been touching the coffee table's leg, they'd never heard it.

"I guess that's your nosy-ass grandpa."

"I hope nothing's wrong," Susan said, still somehow managing to sound as cheerful as a grand-prize lottery winner.

Clark gathered the three pieces, broke the tethers holding the pieces together, and threw it all in the trash. "I want eggs and sausage for breakfast and don't burn my sausage. I hate that crispy shit."

Clark's phone rang next, and thanks to Caller Id, they didn't have to guess who it was. "See, I told you it was him." Clark swiped the red *Ignore* and waited for his unburnt breakfast.

Twenty seconds later, Clark phone rang again. This time it was his voicemail notification. Apparently, what Sherman had to say wouldn't wait. Clark dialed *1* and entered *0000* after the robot voice told him to enter his passcode. Clark's eyes were saucers and his face burned danger-red as he listened to Sherman's message. Clark glared at Susan, lifted his Timex from the end table, and checked the time. He hung the phone up and said, "That old fucker is crazy. You better talk some sense into him before I drive over there and shoot him in his dried-up old ass."

Susan didn't know what to expect, but she took Clark's phone and called her grandpa. Sherman answered on the second ring, and Clark mouthed *put it on speaker*. Susan obliged and held the phone flat, halfway between her and Clark so they could both hear. She tried reasoning with Sherman, but in the end, Sherman hung up.

"Well, I guess I better get over there," Susan said, but Clark had other plans.

Sherman lost track of time and had talked for hours. He could hardly believe Sunday morning had inched perilously close to Sunday afternoon. Susan promised to contact them each day but so far they'd not heard from her. He knew she and Clark were at home. Ursa's report told him that much. He could only pray she was still alive. Rather than wait for her call, he called Susan.

The phone rang twice. Nothing. No answer, but still, he waited. Two more rings. More nothing. "Pick up," he told nobody. It was obvious Susan wasn't answering for him, so Sherman called from Sebastian's phone and then used Piper's. He zeroed with them. Pissed off and tired of being ignored, Sherman called a different number.

"This is Clark," the man's voice said. "I'm too busy being busy to mess with the likes of you. If you've got huge knockers, leave a tit-pic and I'll get back to you. Otherwise, you know what to do."

Sherman cleared his throat. He didn't have to think of something to say. He'd rehearsed it a million times in his mind and spoke with conviction. "Susan has exactly two hours to get here. It's eleven-thirty, and the timer starts now. Clark, if she isn't here by one-thirty, your life is forfeit, and I promise that Susan won't be able to cry or beg your way out of the grave this time." Sherman hung up.

Sherman turned to the boys. "In a couple of hours, y'all may have to stay with a friend of mine for a little while. Her name is Ursa, and if y'all are lucky, she'll tell you some of her stories. Believe it or not, she's older than I am. Her stories are much better than mine, too."

"What? I didn't know anybody was that old," Piper joked and poked his ancient great-grandpa in the ribs.

Sherman grabbed Piper's rib-poking finger and bent it painfully backwards. "Don't poke me, turd." Sherman prepared to retaliate, but his phone vibrated in his pocket.

It was Susan.

"Hey Sus—"

"Grandpa, listen to me. Please don't interrupt. I'm with Clark. I'm okay, we're just talking. You know...trying to work some things out. I'll be by this afternoon to pick up the boys, okay? I'm sorry I didn't call earlier. I know I said I would, but time just got away from me."

"Okay, Susan. It's good to hear your voice. We were worried about you. So, you're with Clark. You're not still in Jackson?" He knew the answer, but she couldn't lie if he didn't ask.

"I'm home. I finished up early last night and just came home to save money." That was true.

"That's smart. Glad you made it home safely. What time do you think you'll be by for the boys? Oh, I almost forgot to ask. Did you get the job?"

"No. That job wasn't for me. I'm sure I'll find something better, closer to home. I'll come by for the boys before dark for sure. Probably around four. Is that okay with you?"

"Four o'clock, you say? I have an errand to run, but I should be back by then."

"Oh, where do you have to go? Are you taking the boys with you?" Susan asked, not caring but acting concerned.

"No, I don't think it's a good idea if they come with me, and you know where I'm going. If you're not here by one-thirty, I'll be there by two o'clock killing your bastard-husband like I said I would." Sherman hung up. When he turned around, Piper and Sebastian were staring at him with shiny, full eyes.

"You're going to kill daddy, aren't you?" Sebastian asked. The answer was in the old man's eyes. "Good." Not knowing where the words came from but certain they were true, Sebastian said, "*The guilty must pay.*"

Sherman was speechless after hearing the phrase he'd said so many times. He could only stare at the deep nothingness in Sebastian's gaze. There was nothing there, but at the same time, his little eyes brimmed with ancient truth. Piper joined his brother and together, they told Sherman how their daddy had made their mama suffer.

After Sherman and Susan's father threatened to kill him, Clark curtailed his physical abuse but upped the psychological abuse. To Clark's great surprise, and his even greater joy, he discovered he enjoyed fucking with Susan's mind almost as much as he did the physical stuff. Piper said Clark brought home other women and made Susan watch as they "did it." When Susan protested, Clark beat her, carefully though so he'd only bruise the *hidden* places. When Susan toughened to the abuse, Clark raised the ante and threaten to hurt the kids if she said anything to anyone.

For the most part, Clark's other women laughed at the physical and psychological abuse he heaped on his terrorized wife. Piper said one woman hit Susan while his daddy watched. In words his nine-year-old brain didn't fully appreciate, Piper repeated a phrase he'd learned from his daddy. "She *got off* on it."

Fortunately for that woman, Piper didn't know her name, or there would've been another name added to the list.

I'll kill Clark even if she does get here on time, Sherman vowed to himself.

"Come, boys." Sherman sat in his recliner, and the boys resumed huddling on the sofa. "You boys know that in a couple of hours your lives are going to change, right? You know that?"

They nodded their heads. They knew.

One would be Sherman's apprentice; to take over and fight the good fight. The other? The other wouldn't. That was all Sherman knew. One would, one wouldn't, and what was to become of the one who didn't, Sherman could only guess. His guesses all ended the same way, so he decided it was best to not think about it. It was best to leave such things in God's hands and instead of worrying about things he didn't know, he told them something he knew.

Sherman told them how Kelvin died.

Chapter Fifty-Seven

There was no way to reach Robert directly, so the sheriff suggested Barbara call the New Holland dealer and get them to have Robert call home.

"Sheriff, they ain't nothing he can do from Alabama. He'd just come racing home and kill himself or somebody else. Everybody's okay here, so we'll let him finish his business there and come on home safely." The sheriff figured he'd do the same in Robert's shoes, so with that he tipped his hat and said he'd be back out tomorrow.

That evening, Robert pulled into the driveway with a brand-new blade for his potato digger and several other miscellaneous parts. He needed help unloading the heavy items, so he called Kelvin. Obviously, Kelvin didn't come.

Barbara leaned out the backdoor. "He ain't here."

Before she could say more, Robert asked, "Where the hell is he?"

"You need to sit down," she said, expecting an argument.

Instead of arguing, Robert sat on the tailgate, covered his face with his hands, and as his eyes filled and overflowed with tears, he remembered Rosalyn's words, *He's going to kill me.*

"Oh, dear God. Is Rosalyn alright?" Robert asked.

First, Barbara answered his question and said that Rosalyn—and everyone else—were healthy, happy, and alive. Rosalyn kept the *fingering* incident to herself. This she did out of shame and because she wanted to spare her parents the visualization. If she'd told what Kelvin did to her, how he'd touched her, things would've ended differently.

Barbara relayed as many details as she had, which weren't many. It appeared Kelvin used the spare key to come in through the backdoor; he'd taken the girls quietly by threatening to harm the other if either of them made a peep, that he'd killed poor old Melvin Parker, a man Robert knew and loved and stolen his truck, and the last thing Barbara said was, "He's locked up in the Vardaman jail."

Robert's first emotion was shame. How could he have been so foolishly blind? Robert was happy for his shame to take a hike as rage quickly took its place. Robert wanted nothing but to get in his Bronco, race to the jail, and blast Kelvin into the next life.

After the rage died off, a new, cold emotion, familiar but in an unknown way, crept up his spine. Rough, pimply gooseflesh covered him like a plucked bird and the coldness nested in Robert's brain.

Emptiness, isolation, loneliness.

Robert's hands clenched then opened, clenched then opened. They'd never felt so...

Empty.

In the closet, the sword rattled against the wall and called to him. It—*she*—fully awakened for the first time since coming to Robert.

It's nearly time, *she* said, and he heard her.

She said one more thing. He wasn't sure, but he thought *she* said, *"The guilty must pay."*

Robert liked the sound of that.

Vardaman's Police Department was shorthanded. It was harvesting season and every deputy was also a farmer. They split shifts and covered each other's asses so everybody could harvest their crops. During his second week as the solitary guest of the police department, Kelvin was watched by just one deputy, Deputy Scott Langerhand.

Dr. Wester stopped by the jail each afternoon to change Kelvin's bandage. The deputies thought it was a waste of the good doctor's time since everybody thought they knew Kelvin's future. The doctor waved off their comments about wasted time by saying if he didn't do his job, justice couldn't be done. Justice would come by a short rope with a noose tied to one end and a tall tree tied to the other.

The only reason Kelvin hadn't been lynched already was the sheriff found out about Betty Jo. The detectives investigating Betty Jo and her mother's murders were on their way to interrogate Kelvin. They were confident Kelvin was their guy but with a confession they could close the case. The short rope was in the sheriff's armory-cabinet, the tall tree was where it'd been since time out of mind, and Kelvin wasn't going anywhere. As good Christians, everybody patiently waited.

That was bad because Kelvin was patient, too. He was also an extremely talented pretender, and his wounds were far less serious than he let on. To keep Dr. Wester coming around, Kelvin smeared feces on his stitches and caused a raging infection that quickly spread throughout his bloodstream. He looked sick but felt fine and was waiting for his opportunity. The jail's phone rang as Deputy Langerhand let Dr. Wester into Kelvin's cell, thus Kelvin's opportunity arrived.

Protocol was simple and effective. Doc came, the deputy on duty let him in Kelvin's cell, and then the deputy locked the cell and stood watch until Dr. Wester was finished. Protocol would've seen Kelvin to the town's hanging tree in another day or two, but the phone call broke protocol.

"Go ahead and answer that thing before it deafens us all," Dr. Wester said. "I can handle him."

The phone rang in the office the way phones were supposed to, but it clanged in the jail by way of a refurbished firehouse bell that hug over the door between the two halves of the building. The deputy didn't feel right leaving the doctor alone with a criminal, but the noise was horrendous. "If you're sure," the deputy said and backed away from the cell door.

Deputy Langerhand was in hurry to get to the phone and forgot the most important part of being a jailer: locking the cell.

With nobody watching, Kelvin snapped Dr. Wester's wrinkled old neck. Like a bum through a trash can, Kelvin quickly rummaged through the doctor's black bag, slinging needles and tongue suppressors to the side until he found what he was looking for. Since the cell door was unlocked, Kelvin quietly eased toward the office's opened door and slipped inside without being seen or heard.

Mrs. Langerhand was on the phone giving Scott shit because her sister saw him talking to a woman who looked like a girl he'd dated in high school. The deputy said he didn't know if it was true or not because high school was so many years ago he couldn't remember who he dated, and if it wasn't too much trouble, could she please shut the hell up and let him get back to his job.

Kelvin heard the deputy beg his wife to settle down, and Kelvin knew he'd made the right decision staying single. Scott often told his buddies he wished he didn't have to listen to his wife's jealous nagging all the time. Scott Langerhand got his wish when Kelvin slit the deputy's neck with the scalpel he lifted from Dr. Wester satchel of surgical goodies.

Kelvin took the deputy's revolver and ransacked the office. In the top desk drawer, he found the key to the armory-cabinet and removed three shotguns, two scoped-rifles, an assortment of handguns, and ammunition for the lot. He saw the noosed rope lying coiled in the corner like a snake ready to strike. For the devil of it,

Kelvin wasted time he didn't have stringing up Dr. Wester in the sheriff's office as an early Halloween decoration.

In the locker room, Kelvin found a uniform his size and put it on. He admired himself in the streaked mirror and weighed his options. Escape or revenge? But there was no choice. Hubris made the decision.

Kelvin made a homemade gunnysack by stripping the sheet from his bed, rolling it together, and tying one end. He crammed his stolen munitions into the sack and threw them into the back seat of the doc's Buick. He drove nine miles to the Thorn community marker and proceeded to the Lancasters' house.

Kelvin parked the Buick at the end of the dead-end road with the car's grill facing outward ready to escape. Kelvin threw the gunnysack over his shoulder and backtracked to the Lancasters' driveway.

In the front yard, he crept through the pecan orchard as silent as a ninja, hugging trees and sticking to shadows and got close enough to the house to hear the television through the open windows. They were laughing.

Not for much longer, thought Kelvin. He couldn't stop grinning.

Chapter Fifty-Eight

Sherman was sent to bed early. He didn't know what he'd done wrong but since he was always doing something wrong, he figured he deserved it. He heard the TV and all the stupid laughter from the other room, and he was ready to pout when a startling white light appeared at the bottom of Albert's bed.

At first, it was a pinhead of light surrounded by the wire grid that kept Albert's box-springs from sagging down and suffocating Sherman. Sherman studied the pinhead, found nothing in it worth postponing a good pout, and was preparing to jut his bottom lip out when the pinhead suddenly became a blinding spotlight.

Before Sherman went blind, the spotlight dimmed, and Albert's bed vanished completely. Where it had been there was now blue sky with cotton-ball clouds. The puffy, white clouds parted and a terrible winged figured hovered above Sherman.

He couldn't remember meeting the Warrior angel, but he knew her on sight. Ursa didn't waste time introducing herself or explaining anything. "Kelvin is coming. Warn your family."

Remembering more than he cared to, Sherman didn't question her. He sprang from the bed and bolted down the hallway and burst into the living room. "Daddy! Daddy! He's coming!"

"Who's coming?" Barbara asked.

"Kelvin. He's already out there somewhere."

"How do you know? You can't know that," Barbara said. "You just can't."

"He broke Doc Wester's neck and slit Deputy Langerhand's throat," Sherman said, and made a throat-slitting gestures across his own neck. "He stole a car and parked at the end of the *Big Road*."

Robert had neither questions nor doubts. As soon as Sherman spoke, *DeeDee* whispered in Robert's mind. "*Your Apprentice is right. Come to me.*" Robert ran to his closet and closed his hand on her jeweled handle and was immediately knocked to his knees. In a brilliant flash, he was filled with fantasies he could never have dreamed—fantasies too strange to be fiction.

"My name is *DeeDee*," she introduced herself. "You will be my Handler."

She answered questions he didn't ask and told him things he didn't want to know. They were things he had to know, and Robert listened. He was stronger than ever before. The sword, which was always heavy enough to be burdensome, was weightless in his hand. Power surged through his body and Robert ran outside.

He became a shadow among shadows and continued to *change*.

Inside, Sherman got everyone going. "Mama, you gotta get up. We have to get ready."

Barbara took over. "Do whatever Sherman says. I don't know how, but he knows what's going on."

Sherman handed guns to Karen, Rosalyn, and Albert. He kept his shotgun—his front pockets bulged with extra slugs—pointed towards the floor as he gave orders. He sent Karen and Albert to his bedroom. It had two windows, one for each of them. He sent Rosalyn to her room to watch out her single window. Barbara took position in the master bedroom. There were two windows in there, so she watched the north for a bit then moved to check the east. Sherman took the living room and the kitchen, running from room to room watching as best as he could.

Kelvin was out there, and he wanted inside. Barbara and her children monitored three directions, but there were no windows facing south. Every two or three minutes, Sherman stepped onto the carport and looked into the southern yard. Kelvin was there, somewhere, but it would take a miracle to find him in the sea of darkness.

From the ethereal fog between the worlds, Ursa watched. She wanted to snatch Kelvin's life, but she wasn't allowed to intervene. It wasn't her mission. It was Robert's test; the end of his trial.

He'd resisted evil by sparing Burt's life, but sparing life was only half of a Handler's duty. The other half, the toughest half, was taking lives. Handlers were killers, and Robert would either rise to the occasion, or he wouldn't. Ursa waited to see which it would be.

Kelvin saw Robert dash from the house and disappear into the night. *How'd he know?* Kelvin hadn't made a sound, and they didn't have a phone, so no one could've alerted them. Kelvin had been in the dark for thirty minutes and his eyes were adjusted to the low light like a nocturnal predator. He should've been able to see Robert, to track his movements, but each time Kelvin scanned the yard he came up with nothing. There was blackness and blackness, but no Robert. Kelvin gave up on finding Robert and went back to finding a way in the house.

Robert moved from one shadow to the next. He knew he was being sneaky, moving fast to avoid detection, but he didn't know how fast he was moving. Nothing could've convinced him of the truth because he wasn't running from tree to tree like he thought he was. He was *blinking* in and out of the shadows as if he was made of equal parts darkness and speed...just a blur.

DeeDee spoke to him, instructed him, and Robert tried accepting his new constant-companion. In time, *DeeDee's* voice would comfort and reassure him but right now, sharing the space between his ears was insanely distracting. *DeeDee* gave Robert Kelvin's precise location, even opened Robert's mind so that he could see—not with human eyes, but with the *mind's eye*—for himself, and Robert could've ended it all right there. But his constant-companion wasn't his only distraction.

Robert was busily *becoming*, and all his senses were super-sensitive and on high-alert. He heard crickets crawling up trees and somehow knew the difference between their ultra-soft *tip-taps* and the ones made by the tiny ladybug feet crawling next to them. He heard birds inhale and exhale and heard their tiny hearts beating fast enough to beat the devil. It was nearly impossible to concentrate with the rapid-fire *"thumpthumpthumpthump"* in his ears.

All at once, the world's sights, feels, smells, and sounds surged in through his skin, eyes, ears, brain, and nose. He knew it was impossible. The body isn't wired to see smells and taste sounds and *bizarro world* shit like that. Still, he could taste the pecans he held in his hand, *tasted* them right through his skin.

Robert placed a hand to the ground and like someone implanted a seismograph in his mind, he detected tremors all around him. Faint vibrations came in from somewhere to his right, and Robert knew two dogs were chasing three cats. Somehow, he just knew. A stronger tremor shook his hand, vibrated his arm all the way to his elbow. This one came from his left, and Robert cut his head towards the front of the house. He saw Sherman walk to the edge of the carport holding his shotgun, and Robert attributed the hard tremor to his son. Robert should've known better.

The epicenter was farther out, and the vibrations were moving toward the house, getting stronger the closer they came. Robert couldn't be faulted for the mistake. He was learning to cope with his heightened senses and there was too much to take in. Overlooking something was inevitable, and unfortunately, it was Kelvin that went unnoticed.

DeeDee spoke to Robert again, not in a whisper or soothing tone but an ear-piercing scream. *"He's at the house! GO!"*

That voice wasn't real. Robert was sure of it, and he wouldn't be tricked again. It was his silly paranoia screaming at him because he'd failed his family by going to Alabama. *I let that bastard take my girls*.

He wouldn't give in and drop his guard and go running off to the house with that maniac on the loose somewhere in the yard. There was no way in hell or on earth Kelvin had made it to the house already. It wasn't possible, so Robert refused to believe *DeeDee*.

Robert stayed on guard, kept hunting. *I'm not letting them down again*, he thought.

Robert ignored *DeeDee* and let Kelvin take his family a second time.

Chapter Fifty-Nine

elvin looked at the house and saw a Lancaster staring out
every window. Sherman's face popped in one, disappeared,
and a few seconds later, appeared in another. The little
bastard was like a Whack-A-Mole. Here. There. Everywhere. They
were on guard, but Kelvin had to see what was going on inside. Going
in guns a-blazing was fine for westerns and war flicks but in real life,
it was an excellent way to end up toes-up.

Kelvin made two trips around the house, staying in the shadows so
the window-watchers couldn't get a fix on him. When he eased from
the south to the east, Sherman's head turned...and they locked eyes.
Only Sherman didn't scream or start shooting.

*He can't see me. He's looking in my direction, but he's not looking
at me*, thought Kelvin.

It was a helluva coincidence how Sherman looked his way at the
right moment and Kelvin knew something wasn't right. Should he
retreat? "It's just a coincidence," he whispered to himself. *It's damn*

peculiar, though. But if it wasn't singularly peculiar, it wouldn't be a coincidence, so Kelvin decided to continue his course. Kelvin stood still as a statue until Sherman moved to the next window. Then, Kelvin continued searching for his in.

Ursa whispered in Sherman's ear. She told him where to look, actually put a hand on either side of the boy's pin-head and turned his head herself. "There he is. Use your mind and see him."

Sherman looked where she pointed but like his father, he was only awakening to his powers. Having a power and knowing how to use it aren't the same things, so Sherman gazed where the angel pointed but only darkness gazed back.

Kelvin found his in. It came from nature's calling.

"I've got to run to the bathroom," Barbara yelled to Karen, who was staring out a window across the hall. Having seven children left Barbara's bladder in such condition that when she had to go, she *had* to go. "Watch my windows, will ya?"

Barbara quickly danced into the master bath and dropped her blue jeans and panties. She left the door cracked to hear what was going on but from her position on the throne, all she could see was the bathroom's pink tile walls. Ever the homemaker, Barbara thought, *I've got to bleach the grout again.*

Karen's post was the west window in the boys' bedroom. So far, she'd seen nothing, and nothing was what she wanted to continue seeing. If not for the serious look on Sherman's face, Karen would've thought he made the whole thing up, maybe as revenge for being sent to bed early. Sherman's expression, which was too somber for his six-year-old face, was too unlike him. Too determined, vacant in many ways, but equally present. Her little brother knew something, so she did as he said.

"Okay, please hurry mama." It was impossible to monitor three yards through three windows facing three different directions. Karen did the best she could running from window to window, glancing out each and racing to the next.

Kelvin heard Barbara through the open window and waited for her to drop trouser and squat. With impatience building, he watched Karen enter her parents' bedroom, look through both its windows, and sprint to the boys' room. When she exited, he quickly slashed the window screen with Dr. Wester's scalpel, and unobserved, he climbed into the master bedroom.

Standing outside the bathroom door, Kelvin heard Barbara's urine splash in the toilet water like she was dumping it out of a bucket. Quickly, before Karen returned, Kelvin thrust his arm through the crack Barbara left open. He grabbed her hair and jerked her off the toilet, a stream of urine splashed off his boots. "Hey, Barb. Happy to see me?" He shoved his pistol in her mouth and pulled her into the master bedroom.

"Hi-ho, Lancasters!" Kelvin screamed. "Put your guns down or I'll blow your mama's brains out." He listened carefully and counted guns as they clanged against the hard floor. "Sherman, I ain't kidding. I want to hear that shotgun drop."

"I put down already, butthole." It was serious now. Sherman used *B.H.* in front of his mama.

"Everybody, get in here, or I'm going to see if there's anything in your mama's head other than hot air." Barbara gagged as Kelvin rammed the gun to the back of her throat.

The kids came in and saw Barbara kneeling at Kelvin's side. His revolver was halfway in her mouth and her jeans and panties were bunched around her ankles. They were embarrassed for her, but Barbara was more concerned with the gun in her mouth than her ass in the air.

Karen was first in. "You, over by the bed." Kelvin pointed to the bed as though she couldn't see it. "Peel them clothes off. I want to see what's on the menu tonight." When she didn't immediately strip, Kelvin cocked the hammer on his gun and the metallic clicks echoed in Barbara's head like chomping teeth. Karen started crying and began undressing.

Albert was next. "You, on your knees in front of the closet." Again pointing, although there was only one closet in the room.

Rosalyn was third. She was red-faced mad and so scared she could hardly walk without tripping over her own feet. "Get your fine little ass over there by your sister and get naked. You know what this feels like." Kelvin held up the fingers he'd had inside her. "You're fixing to find out what this feels like." He grabbed his crotch. "Where's your little brother?" No one answered because no one knew.

"Sherman, get your little ass in here!" Kelvin screamed as loud as he could. It was a huge mistake.

It was a muggy night and silent except for the bugs tip-toeing through Robert's head. Kelvin's scream rode the heated air and hit Robert in shock waves. *DeeDee, you were right! Kelvin's in the house.*

Sherman strolled in the room. He was dead calm when he said, "You hurt her, and I'll personally carry your soul to hell." Kelvin wanted to shoot Sherman on the spot but left the gun in Barbara's mouth.

"Stand next to your brother," Kelvin said.

But Sherman didn't move. Defiantly, Sherman crossed his arms over his chest. "What are you going to do now, big man? Whatever it is, you better do it fast. You can bet daddy heard your scream. He'll be here in a minute to talk to you, and you ain't long for this world.

It was hard to think with a madman's gun tickling her tonsils, knocking her uvula around like a piñata and triggering her gag reflex into convulsive dry heaves, but think was exactly what Barbara did. Her thoughts were high-pitched jumbles no one else could've understood if she'd been able to voice them, but they amounted to this: *That's not my baby boy.*

Barbara wasn't right. It was Sherman, but she wasn't wrong, either. It was *Sherman 2.0*. He'd *changed* into a Sherman she'd never seen.

Robert changed slowly. The sword chose him. He trained for six years, was tested for the first time with Burt, and was now in the final stages of becoming a Handler. It was a process for him. Sherman was something new, and his change was different. It had happened immediately, but it had been hidden until now.

Sherman *changed* the day after his third birthday. The repairs Robert made on Sherman's hand-me-down charity crib gave way, and Sherman fell headfirst—literally—into his destiny.

Chapter Sixty

On the night of March8, 1975, his family was asleep, but Sherman was wide awake. He didn't scream or cry the way restless kids often did. He quietly studied his crib's gate with his thumbs tucked into his big boy underwear. Sherman didn't know if he wanted to explore previously explored but forgotten places or sit in a corner playing pattycakes with imaginary friends, but he knew he wanted out of his crib.

The crib's gate was held in place by two small latches and dropped in its tracks when the latches were disengaged. He'd witnessed the operation many times. His mother and father and all his siblings could pull the latches and lower the gate. Sherman knew how the latches worked but lacked the dexterity to perform the task. It was like he had two left hands, or his wires crossed and short circuited somewhere between his brain and his bony fingers.

During one escape attempts, using both hands, he managed to pull back one latch. The bolt didn't travel far enough to completely unlatch, but it was enough progress to trick Sherman into thinking he had a chance at freedom. With failing patience, he worked for hours. Defeated, he kicked the gate in disgust and mumbled his first cuss word. He leaned over the railing, utterly disappointed, sighed and accepted the fact he wasn't lowering the damned gate.

He didn't need to.

Sherman didn't try to shake the gate loose. He shook it out of frustration because shaking it was all he could think to do. After a ten-minute shaking session, Sherman retired to the opposite side of the crib to catch his breath. Backing to the other side reminded him of his toy cars.

The cars had a *gadget* inside. Robert explained it in those terms and Sherman envisioned *gadgets* as tiny trolls sitting astride miniature tricycles and when Sherman pulled the car backward and let go, the *gadget* pedaled like crazy. Driven by the unseen *gadget*, the car took off on its own, extremely fast, and sometimes they hit the wall. Sometimes they hit hard. Sometimes they really *smacked* the wall.

Sometimes they broke.

The idea blossomed so fast he didn't have time to think about consequences, but he probably wasn't smart enough to anyway. He put a bare foot against the back of the crib, kicked off, and ran across the small mattress as fast as he could.

He hit the gate and ricocheted to his ass.

Nothing happened to the gate, so he backed up for another charge.

The gate held firm, but he rammed the gate three more times just to be sure it wasn't going to work. He collapsed over the edge of the gate and let his arms dangle like dead snakes. It was official. He was spending another sleepless, boring night locked inside his crib. If he'd known he was having his life's last thought, he might've tried to come up with something witty.

Knock, knock.

Who's there?

Dumbass.

Dumbass who?

Me.

As Sherman experienced his last thought, three things happened. A *creak*, a *crack*, and a *whack*.

Sherman's last charge did nothing to the gate's latches. Their metallic grip didn't slip a bit, but because Sherman was slamming the gate and backing up and slamming the gate again and again, the entire crib began to sway. Sherman was thin and lightweight, so it was only a slight sway. A slight sway is still a sway, and it was more than enough because the crib *wanted* to fall.

It was bought new by a husband and wife who made their fortune in real estate and were rumored to own half of Houston's courthouse square. They placed the new crib beside their own king-size and laid their baby down to sleep. The infant died two nights later, and the crib passed to the husband's brother whose wife had just given birth to twin boys.

The brother and his wife put the crib next to their bed, so they could lovingly watch over the twins. A week later, the man woke up around three in the morning to check on his pride and joy. He stumbled to the crib, and at first didn't believe what he saw. Both babies had sprouted an arm from the middle of their faces.

Somehow and for some reason, they'd swallowed each other fists and suffocated in the night. The babies' cold, blue, and extremely dead faces robbed his strength, and the grieving father gripped the crib and fell to his knees. He broke the crib's front legs as he collapsed. The noise woke his wife, and she found him unconsciousness with their dead sons lying arms-to-mouths on his chest. She screamed and promptly fainted.

The grieved parents moved in with her parents in Arkansas, never again setting foot in the house. Six months later, they sold the furnished house to a young couple from Tupelo. The young couple wanted to decorate to their tastes, so they donated all the furnishings to local churches. The crib, with two broken legs, found a new home in the Methodists' charity bin. And a few years later, Robert Earl Lancaster found it.

Looking to save a penny, Robert carried it home, mended its broken legs with duct tape, and three years later, it killed his youngest son.

After Sherman's last charge, the crib *creaked* ominously the way a tall pine will in a strong wind. Sherman heard it but wasn't worried.

Robert was a consummate *duct-taper*, and he'd wound the *gray miracle* around the broken legs...and wound and wound...until they looked like knobby, arthritic knees. The swaying was too much for the knees, and both front legs cracked at the fissures beneath Robert's tape. The legs' upper halves went forward, and their bottom halves jutted backwards.

When the crib fell, Sherman, who was leaning with his dead-snake arms thrown over the gate—*whacked* headfirst onto the unforgiving, bare floor.

The next morning, and after a serious tongue-lashing from Barbara, Robert loaded the crib into his truck and carried it to the Atlanta community's roadside dump. He sailed the broken thing down the kudzu lined hill and watched it tumble. Two tails of duct tape fluttered behind it like kite streamers, and the crib, that jinxed piece of wood and metal, falls out of our story for now.

Later that day, it was picked up by Charlie Goodyear, and we're sure to see it again.

It was such a small thing, hardly bigger than twig, and certainly no stronger, and it broke. It had to break.

Sherman contacted the floor ear first and the way the rest of his body continued downward something was bound to break. The something was his pencil-neck. It wasn't something he remembered.

The fall, yes. He remembered falling, but the neck breaking, no. One second, he was alive, and the next second, he was something else.

Sherman was dead. Not dead like when somebody's heart stops beating and somebody brings them back. Not dead like that at all, but dead like when somebody breaks their neck and their soul leaves their body. Sherman stared at the floor as it got closer and just before his face smashed into the tile, he turned. He saw the baseboard. It was his last living sight.

A blink later, he was standing in a white light beyond any white he'd ever imagined. It wasn't just wholly white. It was *Holy White*. He wasn't three-years-old anymore. At the moment he died, his spirit left the fleshy three-year-old body and moved to its eternal, spirit body. Sherman's *Guardian* took his hand and walked him to the throne.

Since he'd died a three-year-old with no conception of sin, his judgment was more a formality than anything else, but still a requirement for entry.

Enter, my good and faithful servant.

Sherman entered and bowed before the Father. He'd only lived three years, but he'd lived them away from God. In God's presence for the first time, Sherman saw with perfect clarity, felt the warmth of unconditional love, and knew he was home. He would never leave. Or so he thought.

God the Father told Sherman what to do. "My son, you must return to Earth."

Sherman said, "No thanks."

Chapter Sixty-One

It may seem strange he told God no to His face, but it happens every day, and in his defense, Sherman didn't tell God: "No, I won't do what You require." It was more like, "No, I don't want to. Please don't make me."

Sherman hated leaving the Father's presence but when the shock wore off, he was willing to do whatever God commanded.

Being in Heaven and seeing with eternal eyes, Sherman knew answers to mysteries his three-year-old self never considered. With God's command, Sherman was told that when he went back to Earth he would return to life as a three-year-old with no recollection of the eternal knowledge. He would lose it all.

"What? Lord, why did you give me all this just to take it away?"

The only consolation was God's assurance. *You'll remember everything when you need to remember.*

Sherman was six-years-old when he needed to remember. The bottom of Albert's bed opened into a blue sky, and Ursa presented herself. Sherman's memories flooded in, and he remembered his death, his God—

And his mission.

Having already died, Sherman didn't have a Guardian any longer. He left heaven alone and descended into his body, and exactly one minute after the fall killed him, Sherman opened his blue eyes again. He was a scared three-year-old with a bad-ass headache and an aching neck. He opened his mouth, drew a deep breath, and just before he let fly a night-shattering scream sure to wake the house, another angel—*ex-angel* actually—appeared and placed his mouth over Sherman's.

Satan inhaled Sherman's scream and exhaled a burst of dragon's breath into the boy's lungs. It would've killed a human, but Sherman was dead already. Satan's fiery breath was Sherman's passport to the netherworld and with his unwilling traveling companion in tow, Satan *poofed* away. A sprinkling of sulfuric dust settled on Sherman's small corpse, now just a soulless bag of bones again.

In the house, Sherman the boy was dwarfed by Satan, but in Hell, Sherman's spirit body was as big as Satan's. He stood eye-to-eye with the Prince of Evil and looked around at a world of torment where every pleasure was pain on high. Scorching heat burned from all sides and even dead, Sherman feared he'd burn to ash.

He didn't melt but got hotter and hotter with no end to the rising mercury. Agonizing screams bombarded his eardrums, offending them. Back in his spirit body, Sherman remembered his mission to defeat the enemies of God, and God's biggest enemy was standing not three feet away.

Unwisely, Sherman charged, and as easily as a man swats a fly Satan knocked Sherman to his ass.

They were the same size, but they were equal in no other way. Sherman needed years of training to take on Lucifer. Lying on fire-blasted ground and bleeding from both corners of his mouth, Sherman was acutely aware he was outmatched and as legions of demons formed a schoolyard circle around them like two boys about to fight, Sherman discovered he was outnumbered, as well.

Summoning courage from where he didn't know, Sherman stood and faced Satan. Bubbling lava flowed around them. It came from nowhere, and it had no end. Each bubble was the twisted face of a departed. The souls of the damned screamed, *Save Us!*

They recognized Sherman's righteousness, his sinlessness, and they cried for mercy. Coldly, he stared at the spirit-flow and for the first time and uttered the phrase that would mark his destiny: *"The guilty must pay."*

Like a whirlwind, Satan grabbed Sherman in a python's embrace. Sherman struggled, but like handcuffs, Satan squeezed harder. "Stop fighting. It's useless. I am The Prince of the Earth, The Prince of the Air, and only I have stood against The Creator. You are nothing...no more worthy than the dirt from which you were formed."

"Stand against the Father? Ha! Don't make me laugh, Luci. Only you are fool enough to think you can stand against the Father. You've done nothing but rebel against the One who loved you. That doesn't make you mighty. It makes you stupid. Return me! NOW!"

Sherman's voice didn't exactly waver, but Satan sensed fear. Considering all Sherman had seen, he should've been stronger, but he wasn't, and Satan had his way.

"Even after seeing God face to face, fear fills your heart. It's your kind's greatest weakness." Sherman's fear weakened him and robbed him of his divine protection. Able to do as he willed to the fearful man, Satan bent Sherman backward.

"You have paid the price so I cannot take your soul, but you can still serve me. Bend to my will and I will return you to your home. The earth is mine, and I will grant your every wish."

Sherman didn't agree but was such a prize Satan couldn't give up. "You've been welcomed in the *Gates*. Your soul is safe and welcome there at any time. Together, we can move *Upstairs*! Serve me."

Sherman didn't care what happened to him. He'd been to his eternal home and was ready to go back. Sherman said, "You're wasting your time, demon, and you don't have much left. I've seen the Father, and I know you for what you are. You have nothing He didn't give you. Release me!"

"So, that is your choice. I can't have your soul and you won't serve me, but I can pollute your flesh." Long, hollow, and razor-fangs grew from Satan's mouth. The bite was quick, and Sherman's scream joined in chorus with the damned. Nowhere but hell could Satan bite the righteous. Anywhere else righteous blood was torment to his wasted spirit, but there wasn't supposed to be any righteousness in hell. And in hell, Satan did what he wanted.

Satan drank Sherman's blood and like a demonic mosquito, Satan spewed his poisoned blood back in.

Sherman's *change* was slow. His skeletal structure reshaped into a nightmare whose origins could only be hell. Sherman yellowed, dried to ashy gray, and sprouted fangs of his own.

"Now, you'll know rage," Satan said. He had one more curse for the new immortal.

Satan *changed* painlessly and fast. In the time it took to think it, Satan shifted between his army of shapes.

Demon...thought...Man...thought...Vamp...thought...Wolf.

From the *Vamp*, Satan's lycanthropy took Sherman by complete surprise. When the wolf chomped into his neck, Sherman prayed for death.

Satan's heavy venom burned in Sherman's veins like a double injection of superacid, and again, Sherman begged for death. Through his pain, he remembered, *I'm already dead.* There was no escaping the unimaginable pain.

Sherman gave in and screamed for eons.

After an eternity of pain in a place where time didn't exist, Sherman opened his eyes. He was a three-year-old on the floor by a collapsed crib with no memory of how he'd gotten there. The pain, unimaginable a second ago, was wholly forgotten. Scared and hurt, Sherman finished what he'd started before Satan took him to Hell and cursed him.

Sherman screamed the whole house awake.

Robert and Barbara raced to check on their baby boy. Barbara saw the collapsed crib and punched Robert in the shoulder. She'd wanted a new crib, but he'd assured her he could repair the freebie. Sherman had two scratches on the side of his head, but other than those, he seemed unhurt. Understandably, his parents attributed the scratches to the fall, not Satan's claws.

Barbara leaned down to kiss them better, but the scratches were gone. She was grateful her baby boy wasn't seriously injured and with that, she didn't give the Mysterious Vanishing Scratches another thought. After a week of busy farm life, the accident was forgotten.

Now with Kelvin's gun in her mouth and with Sherman staring Kelvin down like an Old West sheriff ready for a high-noon shootout, Barbara remembered the accident and the Mysterious Vanishing Scratches, and she wondered if it were possible.

Would Kelvin's bullet even hurt him?

Chapter Sixty-Two

Kelvin stared into Sherman's eyes, expecting to see a boy, but it wasn't a little boy staring back.

"What are you going to do? Shoot me? Go ahead." Sherman raised his arms then bumped his chest. Sherman remembered everything from three years ago. "I'm not afraid of you. I've paid my debt. Are you ready to pay yours?"

"Shut up, boy," Kelvin snarled, and backhanded Sherman. Sherman sailed backwards, hit the doorknob, and opened a bloody gash on his cheek like a painted-on smile. Kelvin was momentarily satisfied with the blood flow but stared in disbelief as Sherman's wound sealed itself.

"Anything else?" Sherman asked, cocky but with reason. He stood and straightened his clothes, pressing them with hands. "Is that all you got?"

In a state of mass confusion, an utterly terrified Kelvin removed the gun from Barbara's mouth and aimed the gaping black-eye at Sherman's nose.

Sherman taunted Kelvin. "You better either shoot me or let my mama go, and you better do it in a hurry or I'm going to dislocate your soul."

It took all the courage he had, but Kelvin managed to stop shaking. He braced for the .357's recoil and pulled the trigger.

The magnum's report was deafening in the bedroom.

DeeDee flashed in front of Sherman and Kelvin's bullet collided with her sacred blade. It clanged and fell harmlessly to the floor. Everyone stared in disbelief. Robert flashed into the room at lightspeed. Sherman was the only one who saw him come in.

Robert put his hand on Sherman's back and guided him out of harm's way. "Let me take it from here."

DeeDee flamed in Robert's hand. "Do what the boy said. Take your filthy hands off my wife and maybe you'll live to hang. Otherwise, you die tonight." Robert brought his arms backed and cocked the sword over his left shoulder. His knuckles cracked when he tightened his grip. Like a tightly coiled snake, Robert was poised to strike.

"Seriously? You brought a knife to a gunfight? You're a walking joke. You don't deserve this woman. I'm taking her. I'm taking them, too." Kelvin nodded to Karen and Rosalyn. "They're all mine."

"Actually, you brought a gun to a sword fight, but it wouldn't matter if you'd brought a tank," Robert said. "I encourage you to make peace with God, for in two minutes you will be in His presence."

Enough words. Kelvin had everybody in one place, and he was the only one with a gun. "This is for treating me like a nigger!" Kelvin shouted and pulled the trigger twice, as fast as he could. Blue and orange fire leapt from the barrel as two bullets streaked toward Robert's heart.

"No!" Barbara screamed. She wanted to help and tried pushing Kelvin, but her legs were asleep. She couldn't gain leverage over the standing man and was forced to watch events unfold as they would.

Robert moved too fast, appearing to be stationary the whole time. All anybody saw were glints, little reflections as Robert flashed *DeeDee* to intercept the first bullet, then changed positions to intercept the second bullet. Both bullets fell to floor. Kelvin stared at them, waiting for them to get up and finished their damn job.

"You were saying something about knives and gunfights," Robert said. "Care to revise your statement?"

"What the hell? That's impossible!" Kelvin fired the revolver three more times to prove his point.

Robert flashed *DeeDee* and intercept them all, proving Kelvin wrong three more times. Kelvin's mouth gaped. Obviously, it *was* possible. But how?

"You have been found guilty. Your sentence is death." Robert passed judgment and successfully completed his test.

"The guilty must pay."

DeeDee flashed one last time, and Kelvin's head toppled from its usual resting spot. It rolled unevenly on Kelvin's outstretched tongue, thumping as it made its way across the room where it bumped Rosalyn's foot. She kicked it away without blinking an eye, and Kelvin Smith was no more.

"Are you okay?" Robert ran to Barbara and planted a volley of kisses on her face. He closed the show with a grand finale: a lips-to-lips, tongue-to-tongue, Rated-R, open-mouth kiss.

"Is this the best time for that?" Sherman asked.

"Son, it's always the best time for this," Robert instructed his apprentice, and kissed Barbara again to prove the point. Robert stroked her hair, tucked a few errant strands behind her ear. "Are you okay?"

"We're all just fine thanks to you. I can't beli—" Barbara was interrupted by a bright orange glow. It filled the room like the sun had taken up residence. Robert and Sherman were the only two who could watch as Kelvin's body—both parts of it—burst into flames. The flames grew brighter and brighter until they turned in on themselves and disappeared, leaving no sign of Kelvin. Even the deputy's gun and bullets vanished in the cleansing fire.

Sherman stared into the space between the worlds, and a *fogway* opened. Out of the blanket of gray fog, Ursa stepped into the bedroom. Robert acknowledged her, but Ursa went to Sherman first.

Ursa had watched Sherman since he was three-years-old, never able to touch him, never able to talk to him, before tonight. She hugged him and held onto him for what the boy considered an uncomfortably long time. Turning to Robert, Ursa bowed, tapped her forehead three times and said, "Handler, my name is Ursa."

Robert pried Barbara's arms from his waist. He tapped his throat three times and said, "Of course you are." Robert extended his hand, and Ursa accepted. With the shake, they became partners and worked together until *DeeDee* passed to Sherman.

The questions came fast and furious. Barbara, Karen, and Rosalyn were unrelenting. How is this possible? Where did Kelvin's body go? How did Sherman heal so quickly? Is she an angel? Are those really wings?

Albert was silent. He didn't want the miracles explained to him. He wanted to forget them all. Farm life was no fun, and he hated it, passionately. He dreamed of graduating high school and going off to college, but as bad as farm life was, it was damn sight better than flaming swords that stopped bullets and psychotic cousins who were so damn crazy they vanished into thin air.

His mother and sisters wished to know it all. Albert wished to forget it all.

For once, things went Albert's way.

Ursa waved her hand and the room fell silent. Barbara, Karen, Rosalyn, and Albert stopped where they were, as if Ursa had paused time itself. Ursa knelt in front of Sherman. "You know who you are and what you are, but you must grow into a man as any child grows into adulthood. You will be like no Handler before you. Your debt is paid, so your potential is limitless."

Inside the privacy of her mind, Ursa wondered about Satan's curses. How would Sherman deal with those? She supposed his divine nature would protect him from them, but she supposed wrong.

Sherman was thirteen-years-old when the *Wolf* showed up for the first time, and he thought nothing could be worse. The *Vamp* arrived a year later and made the *Wolf* look like a furry puppy with milk-breath.

"Robert, your test is over, and we'll start work as soon as things settle down. The guilty are waiting. If you need me before then, I'm only a thought away." She and Robert shook hands again, and after hugging Sherman, Ursa stepped back through the *fogway*. Before disappearing, she waved her hand and woke up the frozen Lancasters.

Barbara, Karen, Rosalyn, and Albert had no memory of the night's events and carried on with life as if life was just...

Life.

Chapter Sixty-Three

*A*fter she hung up with Sherman, Clark socked Susan in the stomach, and she rewarded him by projectile-vomiting on him again...right in his wife-beating face. He punched her again on his way to the bathroom.

"Get your ass in here," a showered Clark yelled from their bedroom.

As obedient as ever, Susan came, surprisingly upbeat for someone bleeding internally and mortally wounded.

"Before you go pick up those little brats, I want to knock another shot-off," Clark said.

The rape warnings on TV say, "No means no," but sometimes, yes means no, too. It's all in how that *yes* is solicited. Susan dropped her robe and crawled onto the bed. Her doing so was a *yes*, but what Clark did next was rape.

He raped her, but it was the last time.

Susan showered and dressed to go out into the cold. Her winter clothes covered most of her bruises, but she dabbed make-up on her cheeks and around her eyes to hide the visible bruises. She checked herself in the mirror and thought, *you don't look too bad, not for the shape you're in*.

Clark met her at the front door. "Get your ass back here as fast as you can. You know I'm not fucking around." He had no faith she'd return and no intention of waiting around to find out.

Susan hugged him and surprised even him with her gentleness. "I'll be right back." She kissed his cheek.

She might be learning, Clark thought. He heard his daddy's voice, "Nah, they never do."

As soon as her car left the driveway, Clark was in his truck. He waited until she disappeared in the distance. For the second day in a row, he followed her to Sherman's house. For the second day in a row, he parked across from Sherman's house. Clark got out and pulled a long black bag from behind his seat. He placed a throw pillow on his hood and stared across the field to Sherman's house. It was nothing but a red-brick speck on the horizon.

He unzipped the bag and pulled out his Browning rifle and laid it on the pillow. Clark knew the gun was loaded but checked the chamber anyway. He uncapped his scope and with a thousand yards between them, Clark got up close and personal. If he saw anything he didn't like, things were going to get extremely personal, extremely fast.

Clark put his crosshairs on Susan's back as she limped toward Sherman's front door. Sherman met her at the door and Clark moved the crosshairs to Sherman's chest. It was the perfect shot, and Clark almost took it. Susan disappeared into the house so like a good sniper, Clark waited.

Susan missed Sherman's deadline by nine minutes. Since Sherman was going to kill Clark whether Susan met the deadline or not, her tardiness was irrelevant. The deadline's purpose was getting Susan away from Clark and out of harm's way before the killing began.

Susan opened her door, grabbed it with both hands, and pried herself from the car like pulling a scab from a throbbing wound, grimacing with every inch gained. Sherman stood at the front door and watched her slow progress.

Susan's dark sunglasses were five times too big for her head. She looked like a bug of an unknown species. They screamed, "Black Eyes! We have Black Eyes here, folks!"

Sherman opened the door for her. "Well, I see you're looking your best, Susie."

"Don't start with me. Just get the boys out here, and we'll be on our way." Susan jerked her glasses off and stuck them on her head like a tiara and revealed two black eyes her make-up didn't come close to hiding. "Don't bother worrying about seeing them again. I'll get a new babysitter. One that minds his business." She tried to push passed him, but he was immovable.

"Boys get your bags. Don't make me wait on you," Susan called down the hall. "I don't have time to wait around on you two. You never do anything to help me. You're both worthless."

Piper and Sebastian burst from their room and raced to Susan, but Sherman intercepted them. "Piper, you and Sebastian go to your room and play. Me and your momma are going to have a chat."

Piper tugged his brother's sleeve and turned the smaller boy in his tracks. They returned to their room and placed their ears against the thin door.

Susan started off by giving her grandpa a piece of her mind, and she wanted to continue. She caught his icy stare and couldn't find any words brave enough to leave her mouth. Clark scared her a billion times over the years, but she'd never been as afraid of him as she was of her grandpa at that moment. The look in the old man's eyes said he'd just as soon kill her as say another word to her, maybe rather kill her. He scarcely looked human. He was a monster wearing a man-suit. Susan backed up.

She should've backed up a few more steps.

He heard the boys' bedroom door snick shut, and Sherman turned to Susan. "So, you like getting hit, huh?"

Susan's attitude flared, and just as her reply reached her lips, Sherman Lancaster *whacked* his granddaughter.

Sherman's palm connected with Susan's cheek hard enough to knock her Jackie-O glasses off her head. They flew across the room and landed in the sink. Susan staggered backwards drunkenly, arms pinwheeling in their sockets to maintain balance. Shocked speechless, Susan's knees buckled, and she fell to the floor. Blood trickled from her lips. Susan didn't see the strike coming. With all Clark's practice, he never punched as fast as Sherman had.

Kneeling, she begged, "Please don't hit me again."

"Why the hell not? This is what you like, isn't it?" He raised his hand again. Susan shied away from the coming blow. "Can you tell I love you? Did I get it right, or do I need to try again?"

"You think you're so smart, don't you?" she cried out now, tormented. "Sherman the Magnificent, the self-appointed moral police." She stood, smeared blood across her lips, and shoved him. "You think I like that bastard hitting me? You think I think he *loves* me? You think I don't want to kill him...or let you exercise your mighty moral right and kill him for me? You're a bigger fool than he is. Clark will kill me if I leave him. He'll kill the boys, too. I have to do what's best for my boys, so I stay."

"If you want out, you're out. Right now, you are completely out. Say the word and he'll never hurt you again." *God, please let her say yes*, thought Sherman.

"Why do you want to kill him so bad? WHY?"

In a moment of contemplation that was so unusual for him it caused a round of confusion about why he was even contemplating, Sherman wondered if there was an ulterior motive lurking behind his murderous desire. Sherman's inner beasts had a history of killing people who weren't, strictly speaking, on his kill list. She waited for an answer, as surprised by his contemplation as he was. Without really meaning to speak aloud, he told her, *"The guilty must pay."*

Oh, and just who is innocent? Susan thought, and considered asking but was afraid to see which side of the scale she landed on. The statement, the warning, rang true in her ears. Her next thought sent shivers sledding down her spine.

If the guilty must pay, we all carry the bill.

Susan fell forward onto Sherman chest and wept uncontrollably. Thinking he'd made progress, Sherman scooped her up and carried her to the sofa. He laid her down gently and as she cried, he stroked her hair, petting her as one might a beloved dog.

With nothing but silence coming from the other room, Piper and Sebastian tip-toed down the hall and peered in the living room. "You boys can come in. Just sit down and keep quiet," Sherman said. Sebastian sat in the recliner. Piper lifted his mother's feet, sat down under them, and held them in his lap. They stayed that way until Susan cried herself out.

The only sound was Susan's sniffling. It was rhythmic, soothing in its repetition, and Sherman's eyelids got heavy. He stared straight ahead, looking as if he was staring into the future. He was. Piper and Sebastian caught each other's eyes, and they saw the same future. After her crying session and as if Sherman had said nothing, Susan's first action was to check her watch. Sherman knew his efforts were wasted when Susan said, "Oh my, look what time it is. Clark said to hurry back." She sprang from the sofa and accidentally kicked Piper in the process.

Sherman's first impulse was to hit her again. "Susan, if you walk into a room and a dog bites you, that's not your fault. If you walk into the same room ten more times and the same dog bites you ten more times, the eleventh time *is your fucking fault!*"

Susan's wide-eyed, doe-in-the-headlight stare said he'd wasted his breath.

"We've got to go," she repeated.

"There's no logical reason for you to go back over there. It's stupid, and you're a dumbass for going."

In a leveling tone only mothers can generate, Susan said, "Grandpa, I have to get some of mama's things before he destroys them. If I don't go back, he'll destroy everything that means anything to me."

It was an excuse to crawl back, and Sherman was angry beyond measure. If anything was worth her care it was her sons, but she was willing to walk them through hell to please Clark. Sherman decided to let Susan ride her train to its inevitable conclusion. An inevitable *collision* was more like it. Before he gave up, he tried one more time. "Susan, a trained monkey always plays the drum."

"What?"

"You're going back because going back is what you've always done. You don't have to. Stay here. Let me handle Clark. Let me help you."

Not one word made it through to her information processing center. She began gathering Piper and Sebastian's toys and clothes and putting them in their suitcases. Sherman put his hands on his hips and said, "I don't know what the hell you think you're doing, but those boys aren't going anywhere."

Piper and Sebastian thanked God for Sherman's protection. They begged Susan to stay. She patted their heads and said, "We have to go back, babies. Daddy's waiting on us." She hugged them tightly, kissed their foreheads, and told them to get their things.

Susan turned back to Sherman. "Grandpa, they're mine. I have to take them home. Clark told me to not come home without them. We'll go pack a few things and be back before you have a chance to miss us." Pleasing Clark was ingrained in her behavior. She never considered doing anything other than exactly what he'd commanded.

"You're out of damn mind, woman. You have no business going back there for some worthless trinkets. You go if you want to, but you're not taking those boys into that lion's den."

Afraid of the consequences of showing up without the boys but more afraid of not returning in a timely fashion, Susan opened the carport door and began the laborious trip to her car. She cranked the car, put it in reverse, and spun her head around so she could see what was behind her. She took her foot off the brake and was just starting to move when she saw an orange flash in the distance.

A second later, she heard the shot.

Chapter Sixty-Four

Sherman followed Susan outside into the cold. He went as far as the edge of the carport and like a chilly statue, stood watching her get in the car, hoping she'd change her mind and wondering if he should force her to stay if she didn't.

Sherman also saw the orange flash and ninety-nine times out of a hundred he'd have dodged, but this was that one time he didn't.

The bullet's ballistic tip entered Sherman's chest at just the right spot and punched through muscle and bone on its collision course with his heart. *Bullseye*, he thought dimly. Sherman's heart exploded. On its way out of his body, the bullet took a three-inch section of Sherman's spine along for the ride. He dropped instantly and twitched involuntarily.

Through his high-powered scope, Clark watched the old man's chest explode into a red *poof* instead of a red *mist*. *I'm either seeing things or he was so old his fucking blood had turned to dust*, thought Clark.

Clark retrieved his casing, put it and his rifle in the truck, grabbed his shotgun from the secret compartment behind his seat, and went to get his wife and sons.

"Great-grandpa!" Sebastian screamed, and raced to the downed man and knelt at his side. Piper knelt on Sherman's other side, took his hand and tried to shake him awake.

Susan threw her car into park and gimped to their huddle. Sherman was down, by all appearances was dead, and it wasn't that she didn't care about that, but her boys were still alive. Keeping them that way was priority one. "Come on boys." She grabbed their collars but couldn't pry them from their great-grandpa's side.

Susan played a losing game of tug-of-war as Clark sped into the driveway. His truck slid sideways and stopped two-inches from slamming into the trunk of her car. Clark jumped from the truck with his shotgun and headed straight for them in a trot.

"Boys get in the truck," Clark said.

The boys didn't move.

Clark pumped the shotgun, and in doing so, ejected a shell onto the ground. He forgot he already chambered a shell and was at first embarrassed by the rookie goof, then furious.

Still, there was no movement from either boy.

"Your mother gets it next if you don't get your little asses in the truck," he said coldly.

Piper's concern for personal safety and the concern for the safety of his mother and brother were lost in the emotional hurricane whirling in his soul. Waves of grief, hatred, love, anger, and fear bashed him in escalating waves. A storm surge was imminent.

The most frequent wave washing over him was grief. The pain of losing his beloved great-grandpa was staggering. *He can't die*. Grief was the most frequent wave, but the most powerful wave was anger. It had one and only one expression: *Murder*.

Piper put his head down and ran at Clark in a mad charge.

Clark couldn't help noticing how Piper had grown since he'd last seen him. To Clark, Piper appeared to have spent the last twenty-four hours injecting steroids and pumping iron. Piper wasn't big enough to tackle his father, but Clark wasn't taking chances. Clark's fist jabbed out lightning fast and caught Piper dead-on his cheek bone. The punch came from nowhere, but Piper felt it everywhere and thought maybe he'd been struck by the hand of God.

Piper's head went down as his feet came up. He came to a hard stop four feet away, head to the ground with the rest of his body collapsing over, an unintentional somersault gone horribly wrong.

Susan shielded Sebastian behind her back and turned to Clark. "Are you happy, *Big Man*? You beat me, a woman not even half your size. You knock around a nine-year-old boy, and you were so scared of a hundred-twenty-year-old man you shot him from what…four-hundred, five-hundred yards away? You're a big man, a big brave man."

"How dare she talk to me like that?" Clark thought. She'd regret it. That was for sure, but now wasn't the time to highlight the error of her ways. Neighbors heard the shot, and while rifle blasts are commonplace in this area, a Nosy Nellie might look out a frosty window and wonder why they were crowding together in the front yard. Said Nosy Nellie, might venture over to see what the fuss is about, and that wouldn't do. Susan would pay for her bold, mouthiness, but she'd pay later.

"Honey, the boy had it coming. He charged me. What could I do? And your grandpa, well, he wasn't one-twenty yet. And there's you, my dear, loving wife. You may be a lightweight woman, but you're a heavyweight bitch." Clark leveled the shotgun to Sebastian's head. "I won't kill you here, but I will blow his little pea-head off his shoulders if you don't get them in the truck."

"We'll go, but the boys are riding with me," she stated matter-of-factly.

"They are riding with me, or they are staying here dead on the ground like the old man. You pick, but pick fast, or I'll do it for you."

He wasn't clever enough to bluff, so she had to buy some time. The only way to do that was to go along with him until she could escape. The fact that Sherman offered her an out just moments earlier didn't escape her, and she deeply regretted not accepting his assistance. She told Piper and Sebastian to get in the truck and do whatever Clark told them to.

"Mama is going to be right behind y'all."

"Good decision, first one you've made in a long time, baby." Clark helped Sebastian into the cab. Piper was dazed and confused but refused Clark's help.

Piper slowly pulled himself up and got in the truck. He sat as far away from Clark as he could and fantasized about killing his father. They'd all be happy with Clark dead, such a small thing to make everybody happy. There just couldn't be anything wrong with that math. Piper worked through his moral quagmire but before he reached a decision, the matter was out of his hands.

Chapter Sixty-Five

They made it home without incident, but once they got there, it didn't take long for the situation to go from incredibly-bad to utterly-fucked. Surprisingly, the first blow came from Susan and caught Clark completely off guard. Why wouldn't it catch him off guard? In all the years she'd suffered his abuse, Susan never struck back, but their last fight was her best.

Clark himself paved the way for her attack by insisting she drive ahead of him. Susan protested at first, because she didn't want him behind her where he could suddenly stop following and disappear forever with Piper and Sebastian. Rather than argue with her, Clark choked her until she tapped out and gave in.

Nervous as a sweaty whore in church, she drove ahead of them. At first, she was careful to not get so far ahead she lost sight of them, but then the idea hit her. She didn't race ahead, but slowly put distance between them. Susan pulled in the driveway three minutes before

Clark. She slammed her shifter into park before the car came to a complete stop.

Susan was inside the house when Clark pulled into the driveway and killed his engine. To throw his mind off the real danger, she stood just outside the door with their pearly, cordless phone in her hand. She held it high above her head like the Olympic torch, so he was sure to see it.

"Give me my boys and get out of here, or I'm calling the cops," Susan screamed, her finger was on the call button like it was a trigger.

They were home, and all Clark wanted was to get them in the house. Inside, he could take his time with them, so threat or no threat, he was happy to let them go to her. Susan knew this but made the threat to keep Clark's mind fixed on the telephone and the possibility of police involvement.

Susan thought again about the gun Sherman gave her, and she regretted selling it even more now than she had on her way to Jackson. She thought about getting one of Clark's guns, but he kept all his firearms locked in a gun safe, away from her and the boys. He said the safe was for their safety, but actually it was for his safety, not theirs. With Clark's behavior, the last thing he wanted was for one of them to get their hands on mankind's great *equalizer*.

"Calm down, Susie. The kids are fine. They're coming to you."

The boys jumped from the truck and ran behind their mother. "Go to your room and don't come out," she said without taking her eyes off Clark.

"Go ahead and put the phone down so we can talk." Clark was once again holding the shotgun. He lifted it Susan's way so she could stare into its huge, black eye.

When Clark got mad, he couldn't think clearly, so she rolled on with her disobedience. "You're out of your crazy head, Clark. You want me to put down this deadly telephone while you're swinging around that innocent lil' ole shotgun like it's your pathetic little dick."

But Clark was in control and knew it, and he wasn't even mad at her. He was perhaps a little impressed she was showing some backbone for the first time, a thing he credited to his loving instructions. He put the shotgun in the truck and closed the door. "There. Abracadabra. It's gone. Now, it's your turn. Put the phone down."

Clark had a .357 Python tucked into the back of jeans. He raised his empty hands above his head. "See? Nothing. I'm coming to you. Okay?" He walked towards Susan with his hands up like an unarmed man.

"I had to do it," Clark said. "Your grandfather was always interfering in our lives. I know you cared about him, but surely you know we were never going to be happy with him meddling all the time. I did what I had to do to keep our family together."

"You killed him, and you didn't even have the guts to do it to his face. You're a chicken, a coward. You're nothing but a little baby who can't control his temper." Clark's face broke open, and he almost yelled at her. Finally, she was getting to him. He'd come for her soon. "You better get out of here. I'm serious. I'll call the cops."

"Call 'em. If they come, you're my alibis. We were here all morning. Remember?"

"Are you really that delusional? You killed my grandpa, you bastard. I'm not lying for you."

"Of course, you will. You'll lie and make it believable, or I'll cut your sons' throats before the cops gun me down. You can watch all three of us die."

His boots hit their porch. He was almost close enough, and she was ready to strike.

The skillet wasn't her weapon of choice. The gun she sold to pay rent was her weapon of choice, and her second choice was the trusty, old *Louisville Slugger* that rested at her bedside. When she played high school softball, she was a badass and had the most homeruns in the district. But neither the gun nor the bat was sitting on the stovetop just inside the front door.

The skillet was there; therefore, the skillet was her weapon, and it was a damn good weapon.

Granny Abigail would've burned her kitchen down and let everybody starve before she cooked with non-stick cookware. "It'll kill you as surely as a bullet," the health-conscious Abby said whenever somebody touted the benefits of non-stick pots or pans. "That mess is toxic."

Susan followed in Abby's footsteps and only cooked in cast iron pots and pans of which she owned in various sizes. Saturday morning, Sebastian begged her into frying him bologna for breakfast. She cooked the meat in her smallest skillet, perfectly sized for the round, red-ringed bologna. While he ate, she cleaned up the mess, and the freshly seasoned skillet waited on the stovetop like a gift from above.

It took a pissed-off Clark two strides to cross the narrow porch and enter the kitchen. Susan was already into her swing when his head passed through the open doorway. Channeling her softball years, Susan swung for the fences and dinged Clark's head with the bottom of her skillet.

Clark's eyes rolled up. He stared at her with unknowing, foggy eyes, and both knees unhinged, and he collapsed. Susan wasn't a Hollywood dumb-blonde and wasn't about to walk away from him without making sure the wife-beating bastard was dead. She moved in for the kill. She wasn't a dumb-blond, but she was an unlucky one.

Susan struck Clark and he twisted at the waist as he fell. His Python fell from his pants as he spasmed on the smooth floor and somehow Susan failed to notice the stainless-steel revolver skittering away.

Susan straddled him. Her intention was clear. She was going to bash Clark's head in until she saw the floor through it. She stepped over the twitching Clark and accidentally placed an already shaky foot on the side on the revolver. The gun skirted across the slick floor, and Susan rode it like a one-legged skateboard.

She went down hard, fast, and backwards, dropping into the best split she'd performed since she was a high school cheerleader. She landed on her back and her head walloped Clark between the legs. Fire exploded in his testicles, but the pain brought him around. Susan bounced off Clark's balls and the muscles in her hand forgot their mission and let go of the heavy skillet. Gravity did its job and the only thing that could've happened, happened.

The heavy iron cookware smashed her face like a wrecking ball. It demolished her nose, fractured both cheek bones and knocked out most of her teeth. Gushing blood from her nose and gums filled her mouth and for the second time, Susan would've drowned if Clark hadn't rolled her onto her side.

Despite the pain in his groin and face, Clark managed to shove Susan onto her side. She coughed and gurgled blood in a horrific eruption. He wanted her to die and die she would, but she wasn't dying like this. She was going-out by his hand, by God. He'd been deprived many things, but he wasn't being deprived of that joy.

Piper and Sebastian cracked their bedroom door and peeked down the hallway. They didn't like what they saw. Both mama and daddy were down. Clark moaned and pulled himself up. Sebastian wanted to call the cops, but Clark took their phones so they couldn't do exactly what they were contemplating.

Their cellphones were still in Clark's truck and the home phone was on the floor next to their parents' bodies. Sebastian wasn't ready to go in there just yet, so he hoped Piper had a better idea.

Piper's idea was to race into the kitchen, knock Clark back down, grab his shiny revolver, and end all this nonsense once and for all. It was a good thought, a mature thought, and later, after everything that happened was over, he wished he had followed through with it.

Clark used his pain as a stimulate to coax his aching body off the floor. His heart pounded in his ears and something strange was going on with his eyes. Even though he was standing level, the world was tilted on its axis. He sensed he was walking up a steep incline. The kitchen seemed to bend upwards in the middle. He used the countertop to stabilize himself while he waited for the horizon to level.

When Clark was able to stand without the countertop's assistance, he stooped over and stuck one hand into Susan's sweaty hair and drug her toward the living room. He snagged a chair from the dining table as he passed it and drug it, too. Susan was soon to suffer a magnitude of pain her feeble, feminine mind couldn't presently appreciate.

In preparation of her thrashing around like someone condemned to die in the electric chair, Clark strapped a belt around Susan's chest and secured her to the backrest. He left her strapped to the chair and limped his way to their junk drawer.

This was in the kitchen next to a drawer holding washcloths and drying towels. It was a mystical place where they all went anytime they needed to find anything. It was the Lost and Found of all things miscellaneous.

Clark cast aside screwdrivers, pliers, spark plugs, toenail clippers, a spool of brown thread, and withdrew a roll of duct tape. It was old with threads snaking from the sides like parasitic worms or hungry tentacles, but it worked like new.

Clark duct taped Susan's wrists and ankles to the chair. Not content with one layer or two, he spun the tape thick and heavy and tight enough to cut off circulation to her hands and feet. Spinning the tape around and around gave him a blue-ribbon case of vertigo, and he dropped to his knees and rested his head on Susan's lap.

Enraged at his weakness, when he could stand again, Clark hit Susan in the head with the tape roll and repeatedly punched her in the ribs. He threw a lunatic haymaker that landed with a distinct *crack*, her side caving in around his fist. With that Clark called it quits. The last thing he wanted was to kill her while she was unconscious. He wanted to see her face when she realized she was dying.

Chapter Sixty-Six

Before he sat down, Clark tilted Susan's chair back on its rear legs and dragged her between his recliner and the television. This way he could sit in his favorite spot and watch her at the same time. Susan opened her eyes and saw Clark staring at her.

"Hello, dear," he said, slurring every other word. "I've been waiting for you."

Clark had always been mean, always scary, but his stare was off-center and his head cocked wildly sideways. The overall effect bespoke major brain damage and his confused, eerie voice scared the literal shit out of her. Her stink wafted to Clark's nostrils, proving things had gone terribly bad in her insides. Still, the fetid odor gave him an erection, which he pulled out and stroked in front of her.

Ignoring what he was doing, Susan asked, "Where are the boys? What have you done with them?"

Clark laughed and she didn't know why. Was it because he'd already killed them? He approached her, still stroking his *thing* and occasionally shaking it in her face.

She asked again. "Where are my boys?"

Clark laughed again and came on her chest.

Her fear gave way, disgust and frustration taking its place. "*Where are they, you sick bastard?*" Susan screamed, and finally understood why Clark was laughing.

She knew what she was saying. She'd be a lunatic if she didn't because she was thinking the words before speaking them. Once spoken, her words were nonsense. The sounds coming from her mouth weren't words at all, they were noises not even good enough to pass for tribal clicks and grunts.

Susan's jaw no longer opened and closed at its hinges. Her lower jawbone rested against her throat. When she tried to shut her mouth excruciating pain was the result. One time she trooped through just to see what would happen and nothing happened. Her lower jawbone remained against her throat. Each time she tried speaking, her grunts rode a string of saliva that didn't spray but trickled out.

Clark understood the word *boys* and knew what she asked. He tucked his half-limp prick back into the stall and zippered it closed. "If I were you, I'd concentrate on my own situation right now. You're got some *'splaning* to do, Lucy, and somebody's got to pay for the soft spot on my head. I think you seriously fucked me up."

He knew he was FUBAR and didn't need a doctor to tell him he was in trouble. Susan's skillet cracked his skull and his cranium was filling with blood. There was already a golf ball sized protrusion on the side of his head. To Clark, it felt like a not-so-jolly giant was squeezing his head, but the pressure was from the inside and would soon burst and paint the room in Clark Red.

Susan was FUBAR, too. Besides the obvious damage to her face, she had two broken ribs lodged in her left lung and blood was slowly filling her chest cavity. Breathing was getting difficult, and screaming was already impossible. With as much volume as she could muster, she yelled, BOYS!" It came out as a floating whisper.

"You wanna see them? Alrighty-roo," Clark said. "Just remember, you asked for it."

Clark stormed down the narrow hallway. "Open that fucking door." Clark grabbed the doorknob and gave it an insane twist. It didn't open. "Fine. Have it your way." Clark kicked the doorknob with his size twelve Dr. Martens and when the door exploded inward, the door frame burst into a hundred miniature spears.

Two hit Sebastian under his right eye, and a third one pierced his right ear. He grimaced and pulled them out, and yelled, "Dammit!" He had no idea what it meant. He just knew it was what you were supposed to say when you got hurt. Piper was spared the splinter wounds but still caught the worst end of the deal.

Piper was standing by the doorknob when Clark's boot made contact. Piper had thought to minimize whatever badness his daddy had in mind by being a good little boy. Piper reached for the door. He did what his daddy told him to do. Without warning, the door suddenly reached for Piper.

The door hit Piper's head and slammed it into the wall, mashing it there and leaving an indentation in the drywall. Piper shrieked, blacked-out, and fell to the floor with pieces of drywall sprinkling him like salt. Sebastian thought Piper was dead and screamed, "HELP!" Clark returned to the living room, shoving a bound Sebastian in front of him and dragging a bloody, unconscious Piper behind him.

Judging by the thick stream of blood flowing from the boy's nose, Clark figured Piper was either dead or dying, so he slung Piper onto the sofa and forgot about him. Clark pushed Sebastian to the floor in front of Susan. "I told you they would pay if you crossed me. Didn't I tell you that?"

"No, Clark. Don't," Susan said, but what came out was, "Awg, Ark. Ont." She reached for her baby boy, but her veiny, purple hands didn't move. They'd swollen around the duct tape the way a tree will grow around a tight piece of wire. She couldn't feel them at all.

"How many times did I warn you? Don't answer. I know you can't count that high, and I couldn't understand you if you could. But you can't say I didn't warn you. Say goodbye."

Clark reached to the dark side of his recliner and brought his Python into the light. "You asked for this."

Chapter Sixty-Seven

In his battles against Satan and his hellions, Sherman had been bitten, speared, shot, stabbed, had lost limbs, and the devious bastards had poisoned the Handler several times, but Sherman had never been this slow to recover from his wounds. But, sure as always, Sherman opened his eyes and raised his head. He rolled onto his right side and used his good arm to push himself into a sitting position. He opened his blood-stained shirt. The bullet wound had healed, but he was weak, the weakest he'd ever been.

Sherman smiled.

His fleshy shell was nearing its expiration date and a more appealing prospect, Sherman couldn't imagine. Whether it would be Sebastian or Piper, he didn't know, but one of them would soon take his place. The apprentice emerges, and in the order of great-power politics, the master declines to make room for his pupil. He was finally going home—for good this time, he hoped—but before he walked into the *Clearing* for the last time, he was settling-up with a wife-beating *POS* named Clark Vance.

Sherman put his hand into his pocket and retrieved *DeeDee*. He held the pocketknife-sized sword at his arm's length above his head and spoke to the heavens.

"*Dextera Dei*!" Sherman's voice thundered, and *DeeDee* grew to full size.

Lightning bolts streaked from the four corners of the Earth and met in an apocalyptic collision above his head. Fire rained over him but neither burned his skin nor singed his hair. The ground around him vibrated furiously as small pebbles and dirt rose in the air and spun around him in a slow-moving vortex. He'd never had to call for a recharge, but he spoke the words he knew to speak.

"I wield Your Right Hand. *In nomine Patris et Filii et Spiritus Sancti*, fill me, My Lord!"

The dancing rocks and dirt circled him, speeding and rising with each revolution until a dusty brown funnel reached the sky. Shielded from outside eyes, the center turned into a dripping red eye. With no pomp, the eye opened, and blood filled the axis-line and cascaded slowly from heaven. The bright, red blood hit *DeeDee's* tip, and instantly, red blood became a blinding white radiance known as *Holy White*.

Holy White was brighter than a thousand suns, a power transfusion from heaven. The *Holy White* flowed down *DeeDee's* blade, into Sherman's hand, down his arm, and filled him to over-flowing. Fully charged, he transfigured into his spirit body. He was stronger than ever, and even without experimenting with them, he knew he now controlled his inner beasts. Satan's curse was finally broken.

Sherman flipped to his feet like a master in a martial arts movie as he vortex around him closed. The *Holy White* faded from *DeeDee's* blade, and she burst into flames. Blue fire took inch after inch of her mirrored steel. She was *Dextera Dei*, the Right Hand of God, and he was her *Handler*. He stepped into the air.

Moving faster than the speed of sight, he flew to Clark and Susan's.

"Open your mouth," Clark told Sebastian.

In a last great act of defiance, Sebastian asked, "What do you think I am, stupid?" He wasn't afraid at all, and that infuriated Clark.

"Open your mouth, or I'll make it hurt!"

Susan said something that might've been, "I'm sorry," but after speaking, her head lolled over to one side. Her apoplexy so complete she stared at nothing, thought nothing, was nothing.

"I love you, mama. It's not your fault." Sebastian's smile treated Susan to her life's second to last joy.

"It ain't got to be in your mouth to do its job," Clark said. He stuck the Python to Sebastian's temple and pulled the trigger.

Sebastian stared at his mom until his eyes and most of his face suddenly exploded and landed on the carpet next to him. Sebastian's body fell onto what was just blown off. He twitched and gargled and spewed blood on Susan's feet. His little legs kicked as if he was swimming in imaginary water. His small arms paddled mindlessly and took him nowhere.

Aroused by grief so intense it had actual weight, Susan's mouth hung open and she bawled as loud as her wounded lungs permitted. With prophetic certainty, she said, "You'll pay for that."

Somehow, Clark understood her perfectly. "We'll see who pays."

Sherman approached the house and his *mind's eye* showed him the interior as if he was looking down on a roofless floor plan. He knew everyone's position and knew their state of health. He swallowed hard at what lie ahead. It would be done. He had always seen to the hard doing, and he would see to it again. And now he knew the identity of his *Apprentice*.

Sherman crashed through the roof and most of the walls disintegrated on impact. Those that didn't disintegrate were blown outward like a cherry-bombed mailbox. The concrete foundation crumbled to gravel when Sherman's feet crashed into it. Windows throughout the house shattered and turned into razor sharp missiles that sliced holes in tires, cut down hedges, and killed two fighting squirrels.

"Oh honey, I'm home!" Sherman called up the hallway.

It can't be, thought Clark. *I killed him.*

"I killed you!" Clark screamed at the impossibility headed his way.

Sherman walked into the living room. *DeeDee* pulsed white hot in his hand. Clark pointed the Python at Sherman's chest and squeezed off five rounds then stood silent when nothing happened. As if supported by invisible strings, the bullets floated in the air. Sherman swatted them to the floor like lead bugs.

Who was the young man with Sherman's voice? Clark was stupefied by the absurdity of everything. Clark kept pulling the trigger on the six-shooter, but the hammer fell on spent rounds. Stuttering and stammering, he said, "Bu...bu...but I sh...sh...shot y...y...you."

"Yes, you did, and you were no better at that than you are at anything else." Echoing Susan's prophecy, Sherman said, "And now you'll pay for it." Sherman pointed *DeeDee* at Sebastian's faceless corpse. "And you'll pay for that, as well."

With astonishing speed, Sherman brought his sword up Clark's right side and down his left and lopped off both arms in one strike. *DeeDee's* superheated blade cauterized the wounds, and deprived Clark of an easy out.

The Python was on the floor. Its hammer continued hitting spent rounds as Clark's trigger finger followed the last command it received.

Clark tried speaking and found it impossible to form words. It took all of five seconds of this senseless yammering to get on Sherman's nerves, so Sherman shut Clark's mouth permanently.

On one of their last nights as a semi-peaceful family, Susan mended Sebastian's Superman pajamas, and the needle was still threaded with bright red thread. Sherman wagged his finger at it and the needle shot across the living room with a tail of red thread fluttering to keep up. The needle zig-zagged through Clark's upper and lower lips, ensuring he'd spoken his last words on this side of the grave.

The pain was astounding, and Clark grabbed at his face with hands that were no longer there. His arms were severed above the elbows and flapped uselessly at his side like a baby chick's wings. Reaching for his mouth with them, Clark looked like a T-Rex and bent his neck to bring his mouth closer to his embarrassingly short arms. Clark screamed through the stitches, but only bloody spurts and muffled moans escaped the seam.

Clark tried to run. His legs were wobbly and weak, but through sheer force of will, he managed to stay upright. He almost escaped.

"Stop," Sherman commanded.

Sherman's psychokinesis froze Clark's gait mid-stride and levitated Clark one foot above the crumbled floor. Clark kicked and ran like a rat on an invisible treadmill. Sherman made a *come here* gesture, and Clark floated to the center of the room.

Clark cried uncontrollably for the rest of his life. A total of six minutes and fourteen seconds.

Chapter Sixty-Eight

"Grandpa Sherman, what's going on?" Susan asked. Through her broken, toothless mouth and swollen, blood crusted lips her words were a linkage of hisses, slurs, and spits.

"Silence, fool," Sherman barked. The cutting was done, so he returned *DeeDee* to her scabbard.

He knelt by Sebastian's bloody body, patted his lifeless chest, kissed his hand and stood. Sherman walked to the sofa where Piper's body still lay as it had landed, half on the back and half over it. He looked draped intentionally, a horror-house decoration. Sherman picked his Apprentice up tenderly and laid him on the plushy sofa cushions. Sherman placed a glowing right hand on the boy's head and immediately, Piper's eyes opened.

"Are you okay?" Sherman asked.

The boy nodded, *yes*. In truth, he was pretty far from okay. "I think Sebastian is dead."

"Yes, your brother has passed into the next world. His job here is done. Yours, however, is just beginning. What does your conscience tell you must be done now?"

"I don't know, great-grandpa."

"Pray for guidance. The course will be lighted, the way made straight." Sherman kneeled, bowed his head, and prayed in silent reverence.

Piper did the same.

Two minutes passed, and they opened their eyes at the same time.

Holy White fell from heaven and engulfed Piper's bowed head. It filled his body and spilled out his eyes, nose, mouth, and ears, turning them into life-lights. Piper stood and answered the Handler's question.

Piper said, *"The guilty must pay."*

"Correct. The guilty must pay; must always pay." Sherman turned toward Clark, raised his hands skyward, and for the first time, called the *change* and transformed into the *Wolf* at will. No longer under Satan's curse, Sherman grinned and howled in Clark's face, spraying the frightened man with gluey strings of saliva Clark's cascading tears couldn't rinse away.

"Great-grandpa...you're a werewolf!" Piper's eyes were saucers.

Sherman willed the *change* again. This time he called the *Vamp*, and with him in control, there was no pain and the *change* was instantaneous. Piper's saucers were full-size plates now. There were to be no secrets between *Handlers* and *Apprentices*, and Piper saw the Handler as he truly was.

Sherman grabbed Clark and pulled him close. Clark's hair went white, like someone or something sucked all the life out of it. Sherman bent Clark's head to the side and sank his needle fangs in the weeping man's jugular. As the hot coppery liquid filled Sherman's stomach, Clark's tears soaked the floor. He tried to scream, but the red thread held firm.

Susan never enjoyed horror movies, finding them too violent to be enjoyable, but watching this was her life's last great joy. Despite her physical and emotional agony, she laughed when Clark's bladder let go and *The Big Man* pissed his pants the way he'd made her piss herself so many times.

Sherman drank till there was nothing left, and Clark's veins collapsed in on themselves. He released his grip and let Clark's light gray corpse fall to the floor, and in burning flashes, Clark's body and severed arms vaporized Sherman sighed and *changed* back into the Handler. The fun part was behind him.

The hard part lay ahead.

Chapter Sixty-Nine

"Grandpa, untie me please. I have to check on Sebastian," Susan said. Her voice was crackly like footsteps on dried leaves. Her words were gibberish, but Sherman and Piper understood her perfectly because they heard with their hearts, not their ears. Sherman's warning never entered her mind, so she didn't suffer the anticipation of what was coming.

"You needn't worry about Sebastian. He is waiting for you in the *Clearing*. Don't worry about Piper either. I will train him well, and he will serve with honor, loyalty, and humble love." Sherman prepared to move, but Piper moved fast enough to surprise even the Handler.

"*The guilty must pay,*" Piper said, as he moved behind his mother.

He didn't fly, run, or walk. He vanished from where he was and materialized there. Even Sherman couldn't do that. Parts of Susan's face were alive with sparkling pain and other parts were numb, so she didn't feel her son's hand on her chin. Remorseless, Piper snapped her neck and sent her painlessly to the *Clearing*.

Sebastian was, as Sherman said he'd be, waiting for her, and hand-in-hand, mother and son entered paradise together.

Sherman was stunned. He expected to use Susan's punishment as a teaching tool, but Piper seemed to understand things already. *The guilty must pay*, no matter the person, but there was something in the way Piper almost joyfully broke his mother's neck that cautioned Sherman about his Apprentice.

And there was the size thing again. As soon as Piper executed Susan, he grew even more. Now, he was physically bigger than Sherman, and Sherman once again tried to remember the line about giants. Suddenly, he remembered.

That wasn't just a line from some book he'd read. It was from, *The Book*, from the *The Good Book*, the *Bible*. Genesis 6:4. Was that possible? Something was possible, because the truth of giants was staring at him through nine-year-old, crystal blue eyes.

I've got to find his father, thought Sherman, and kept the first secret from his Apprentice.

Clark wasn't Piper's father.

"Why did you kill her?" Sherman asked.

"I didn't kill her. She killed herself. You warned her and offered the help she needed. Daddy pulled the trigger, but mom put Sebastian in front of the gun. You told her what would happen, and *the guilty always pay*."

"Very good. She was warned, and we do not lie."

"We? Am I like you, great-grandpa?"

"No, not like me." Sherman considered the truth of this and didn't know exactly where to go next. "But you will be a Handler. I will train you, and when the time is right, *DeeDee* will pass to you. The future is not set, Piper. I cannot tell you what lies ahead. I'll teach you what has happened and prepare you as best I can. The future is yours, not mine.

As my father did before me, and as I have done, so you, too, will do whatever you must."

Piper nodded and accepted the task.

"The memory of this day will be returned to you, but for now, I must erase it from your mind. The police will ask too many questions, and you mustn't know the answers. Kneel."

Obediently, Piper knelt and Sherman laid his hand on Piper's head. Carefully, Sherman constructed mental walls around Piper's memories of the last week, but he didn't erase any of them. They would return, some a little at a time, others all at once...when the time was right. As the memories faded, Piper returned to his normal size, which was big for his age, but not gigantic.

Piper fell into a deep sleep and Sherman positioned him by his brother.

The investigation was ongoing and would stay that way forever.

The house looked like a tornado hit it, but a tornado didn't explain the dead bodies. It was suspected that Clark Vance killed his wife and youngest son, but what happened to Clark? An exhaustive search revealed nothing, but the BOLO order remained active. The authorities were hopeful they would find him. Sherman was certain they would not.

Piper, the only survivor was traumatized and could offer no insight. The poor boy suffered from PTSD and had no recollection of the events of the previous week.

With no other family and with Sherman's unblemished reputation, it was an easy matter of course gaining custody of Piper. It was temporary to begin with, but the social worker assured them in time it would become permanent.

Sherman would never have permanent custody of Piper, but they didn't know it. They all thought time would continue ticking by, measured in lives born and lives lost, one giving way to the other, but they were wrong.

Time was short, and nobody would have custody of Piper for long.

Chapter Seventy

T he cookout was over. All the cousins and aunts and uncles were gone back to whatever rock they'd crawled out from under. The house was clean, and the maids and caterers were gone. The mother was passed out on the sofa and the son sat outside with his dad. They drank thousand-dollar scotch and smoked hundred-dollar cigars. The firepot crackled and warmed their outsides while the scotch warmed their innards.

"Whose brilliant idea was it to have a family reunion in January?" the son asked. He blew a perfect smoke ring above his head.

"Aunt Harriet is on her deathbed, so we had to have it before she kicked. It would've suited me to just let the old bag die," the father said. It probably wasn't nice to talk about his sister that way, but she'd been a bitch to him when he was a kid, and he hadn't forgotten it.

The father turned his head toward the East. "Did you hear that?" he asked. His son heard nothing.

"Listen," the father said, and the boy turned his ear to the wind.

"Sounds like a dog to me," the boy said, and puffed another ring into the air.

"That's no dog, you idiot. It's a wolf."

The howl wasn't far away. Father and son looked toward the howl, and then to each other. They shrugged, almost able to ignore the intrusion.

The next howl was closer, much closer, and ignoring this one was out of the question. Father and son sat straighter in their chairs. Wolves weren't common in their area, but they weren't unicorns. They thought about getting their guns, but neither man moved. They waited to see if it would howl again.

Wolf jumped the hedges and howled in their faces. The monster's breath was dragon's fire and scorched the hair from their heads. It's lungy volume deafened them both. Neither Preston Wilcott nor his son Chris dared move. *Wolf* stood in front of them and *eeny meeny miney moed* them with a front paw. *Wolf* ended its count with Preston and tore the man's heart out.

Chris Wilcott watched the beast shred his father with detached amusement and truly believe he'd be spared. His death was unimaginable. Men like Chris Wilcott didn't die, not like this. He was God's gift to the world and was sure he would survive to tell the story of his father's death. He'd tell it over and over. He believed that until the beast turned a murderous gaze his way.

Wolf leapt to Chris's lounger, straddled the man. Preston's blood dripped off *Wolf's* hairy snout and fell into Chris's wide-opened mouth. The metallic sting woke him from his shocked stupor and filled him with one terrible certainty. *I'm about to die.*

That look, that terror, was the reason Preston died first. *Wolf* made sure Chris suffered the terror of what was to come. Satisfied Chris's dread reached its apex, *Wolf* uttered two words before biting into the man's abdomen.

Susan Vance.

Chris remembered Susan Vance all too well. He saw her beautiful face, smelled her perfume, and even remembered how bad it was wanting to have her and not being able to get her. Chris said, "I'm sorry." Chris Wilcott would've begged, but begging takes time and *Handsy* was all out of time.

Wolf disemboweled him and grinned when it was finished.

Chapter Seventy-One

A pair of yellow eyes more than twelve feet above the ground peeked over the fence and watched the Wilcotts' final moments. *You're lucky my Master dealt with you. I'd have taken my time*, thought Piper.

Piper vanished and reappeared in his bedroom as a nine-year-old boy. He looked at his small hands and bony legs in disgust. In a word, he was *frail*, and he didn't like it one bit. Not when he could be so much more just by thinking it. He didn't need his Master's approval or guidance to use his powers. He proved that tonight.

It was the first time Piper used his powers alone, and it was the first time he'd kept a secret from the Handler.

It wasn't the last time he did either.

About the Author

Max Cherry was born in Thorn, Mississippi on what he believes is a hotbed of psychic activity. His bedroom was the most terrifying place on earth, and his parents had to nightly reassure him that the monsters he swore were in his closet and under his bed were only in his head. He quickly discovered his parents were right, but it was not until he picked up his first pencil and started writing that he fully realized how crowded it was up there. As the pencil worked its gray magic on every piece of scrap paper he could scrounge, Max discovered that writing was the only way to chase the monsters away.

Max currently lives in Yalobusha county with his wife and daughter. He refuses to trust empty boxes and cannot tolerate sitting next to food he cannot pronounce. When his family goes to sleep, Max still passes the time by writing the monsters away.

More from Foundations Book Publishing Company

Reborn
By Jenna Greene

The marks on Lexil's skin state she is a Reborn - someone who has lived before. As such, she must toil in service to those who have only one chance at life. Sold at auction, she is fearful but accepting of her new life. Everything changes when she must save a young child from a fate worse than death.

With the help of a new ally named Finn, she flees to the Wastelands. There she struggles to survive, while discovering more about herself, the world, and what it truly means to be Reborn.

Dark Prisoner: The Kuthros Key
By D. Thomas Jerlo

Imprisoned for over a thousand years by the Diveneans of old, Lord Balthazar covets one thing: his freedom. Using his minion, Isafel, and an evil imp spawn called Ilio, they will search Etharia for the one thing that will set their master free and bring chaos to the lands—the Kruthos Key.